The House of Hidden Secrets

CE Rose is the pen name of Caroline England, the author of psychological suspense novels, *Beneath the Skin*, *My Husband's Lies*, *Betray Her*, *Truth Games* and *The Sinner*.

As CE Rose, Caroline has written gothic-tinged psychological thrillers, *The House of Hidden Secrets*, *The House on the Water's Edge* and *The Shadows of Rutherford House*.

Also by CE Rose

The House of Hidden Secrets

CE Rose

hera

First published in the United Kingdom in 2021 by

Hera Books
Unit 9 (Canelo), 5th Floor
Cargo Works, 1–2 Hatfields
London SE1 9PG
United Kingdom

A CIP catalogue record for this book is available from the British Library.

Print ISBN 978 1 80032 606 4
Ebook ISBN 978 1 912973 58 3

Look for more great books at www.herabooks.com

Printed and bound in Great Britain by Clays Ltd, Elcograf S.p.A.

2

To Charlotte, my perfect breech baby.

Prologue

The minutes have felt like hours, but the time is finally here. I'm coming for you.

I hold my breath and creep into the gloom. I haven't slept. How could I when I've been swamped with thoughts of you? Not just thinking but obsessing, my mind delirious with anticipation. I'm going to do something very bad and I don't care. The need, the compulsion is driving me, consuming my body, my whole aching being.

Hearing your footfall, I hide in the shadows. Though my fingers twitch to reach out, I clench my fists. I have to be careful, soundless, stealthy. I must bide my time and wait for the moment, the perfect instant to catch you.

Oblivious, you pass me by, so I follow. Have you any idea of what you're making me do? Can you hear my thrashing heart as I inch in the darkness towards you?

Now so close I can smell you. Can I do it? Is the impulse still in me? I call your name. When you turn, a surge of adrenaline engulfs me and I reach out my arms. Then you're falling backwards, your shriek piercing the still night as you clatter to the ground.

The silence overwhelming, I close my eyes and suck in gasps of fetid air. When I open them again, you're still there but you're broken. And so much blood surrounds your head. Pooling and glinting and glowing through the dusk like a halo. Then there's your gaze. Staring, accusing.

But undoubtedly dead.

Chapter One

Serena

Surrounded by fields and white-tipped stone walls, the Renault falls silent at the junction. Her pulse racing despite her resolve, Serena squints at the unfamiliar dashboard. Has she stalled? Stalled before she's even started? She lightly touches the foot pedal and it purrs in reply. Ah, that's right; it's a fuel economy car. For a newer, better and cleaner future. Less harmful pollution; a healthier environment. Like her life hereon in? God, she hopes so.

She turns to her silent passenger. 'Lana? Are you OK, love?'

Lost in the front seat, her daughter looks tiny today. But she is only four and apprehension does that. Serena feels fearful and frail too, a dot of insignificance in this expanse of frozen Cheshire greenery and the low, pale sky.

'Turn left. Now turn left.'

She jumps at the voice of the satnav. She's glad it knows the way, but there'll be no more commands. From today she's taking control, going forwards and not looking back.

Lana nods, but doesn't speak. Tense-faced and gazing through the passenger window all the long journey, she's been quiet, too quiet. But that's no surprise; she's been almost mute for weeks.

No, for months.

Turning left, Serena accelerates down a bush-lined, winding road. 'I think we're nearly there, love.' Then, when Lana doesn't reply, 'Did I tell you that the house is actually a farm? Maybe there'll be some animals.'

Her daughter's eyes brighten. 'Like cows and horses? One morning I counted the sheep from my window.' She covers her neat smile with her hand. 'They were a long way away, but I think one was a goat.'

Her chest tight and tingling, Serena tries for a light tone. 'A goat? That was a good spot.' Then going back to Lana's question, 'Cows and horses? Maybe.'

Though she really doesn't know much about the job, her new start. The advertisement was for a private live-in housekeeper at a Grade II-listed farmhouse in Goostrey. A temporary placement to look after a father and son, it said. Or did the owner tell her that? The man she telephoned with fumbling fingers.

Perhaps he mentioned the 'Grade II-listed' too. Wondering exactly how old the property will be, the habitual warning to her daughter not to touch *anything* pops into her head. She turns to say it, but the satnav interrupts.

'*You have reached your destination.*'

Slowing down to a crawl, she peers left and right through the windscreen. The shrubs have turned to dense woods. Like a light turned off, it's suddenly dusky. Gloomy and foreboding too, somehow. She bats the shiver away. The whispering shadows are just trees, that's all, bowed and reaching out their knobbly branch hands to touch their family the other side.

She sighs deeply. *Family*. There's just her and her daughter now.

With a reassuring smile, she glances at Lana. 'Well, we must be very near if the satnav says so; keep a look out for a house...'

Her heart thumping with apprehension, Serena follows the narrow lane around a sharp bend, then hugs a high parapet for half a mile. Daylight finally floods in.

'This must be the entrance.'

Though a stark twisted oak looms with raised arms at one side, an incongruously modern barrier cleaves the wall and thick foliage. She peers at a weathered plaque swinging from a rusted bracket.

'Yes, here we are. That sign says Ramsay Hall, love. I wonder how we...' She scans the pillars for a buzzer or an intercom, but the gateway smoothly slides open.

'Wow,' Lana says. 'It's like magic.'

'Isn't it just,' Serena replies, steering through.

As the gates bump behind her, she blows out the breath she's been holding and feels something shift, deep in her belly. Relief, of course. Or could it be a spark of excitement? A glint of hope piercing the heavy, dull nerves which have rumbled since she picked up her mobile to apply for the job?

Lana sits forward, her cheeks flushing pink. She points to a low building. 'That's pretty. Do the people live in there? Is that where we'll sleep too?'

Pleased to hear her daughter so responsive and talkative, Serena drives at a snail's pace and takes in the single-storey, red-brick construction on the left. Its panelled windows are almost concealed by winter climbing shrubs.

'I don't think so. It looks like an outbuilding,' she replies. 'Maybe it's for tools and machinery. Perhaps farm workers lived there back in the old days.'

A fading purple teasel seems to wave a cheery greeting. She inwardly snorts. Cheery greetings aren't always what they seem.

'It's a really long driveway. I wonder what's around the corner,' Lana says.

What indeed. Literally, metaphorically. Serena has no idea, but Lana is ogling at this rolling, russet, frosted new world, and her eager anticipation is infectious. 'It is lengthy, love, like a storybook...'

Her voice dies as the farmhouse comes into view. The word 'adventure' gets stuck in her throat, but 'storybook' it certainly is.

Lana presses her nose to her window. 'Gosh, it's really big!' she exclaims, her excitement clouding the glass. 'It looks like zigzags mixed with noughts and crosses,' she says, describing the peaked roofs and façade to a tee.

Gaping with astonishment, Serena brakes and stares. Of course she should have known from the word 'Hall' but she'd been too distracted by the description of 'farm-house'. Farms weren't spectacular seventeenth-century mansions with fine black and white detailing to the front elevation; they weren't set behind a charming stone terrace and a huge courtyard. Farms were stuck in the rough, thistly Welsh landscape of her early years, cramped and muddy and half falling down.

Her heart clattering again, she squeezes the Renault between a Range Rover and a huge woodland pine, then she looks at her watch. Six minutes until her appointment, but it would feel odd just to sit in the car while they wait. Slightly early is acceptable, isn't it? Far preferable to late – she learned that good and proper.

Hiding her anxiety with a smile, she turns to her daughter. 'Ready?' she asks brightly. 'A brand new adventure, remember?'

–

Holding Lana's hand, Serena climbs the steps to the timber porch, takes a deep breath and rings the ivy-clad doorbell. There's no reply for several moments. Wondering whether to use it, she peers at the elaborate brass knocker. What is this strange hybrid? A Moses-like man? A horned beast? Either way, it's not the most cosy of welcomes. She almost laughs at her reluctance to touch it – and anyway it would be rude to repeat with the rapper after using the bell – so she waits and inhales the frosty air.

The wind sharp on her neck, she lifts her coat collar and glances around. A farm? Surely no longer if ever it was one; there's a marked absence of the odours she remembers from childhood – manure, slurry and freshly turned soil – smells that used to bring a fond grown-up smile. But that's rose-tinted nostalgia for you.

Deceptive, deceitful and dangerous.

She looks down to her daughter. 'We're a bit early. Maybe we should go back…'

But Lana's tight, pallid face is turned towards the fir tree. Her gaze wide, she points. 'Look,' she whispers. 'Look over there.'

Serena peers too. 'What, love? What have you—'

Her sentence is cut short by the groan of the door. A mix of antiquated aromas leaks out and an imposing man appears on the threshold. Wearing a Paisley housecoat, he stares for a few seconds. Unblinking, observant, proud. An eagle, Serena thinks, though she couldn't say why. Is this Mr Ramsay, the master of the house? A long-haired German Shepherd with a spectacular cream coat quietly appears and sits by his side. No one mentioned a dog but it's fine.

'Hello,' she says. 'I'm Serena Green. We made an appointment.'

The man turns from her to Lana. Appearing satisfied, he speaks. 'Sorry about the wait. Do come in.'

Yes, it is Mr Ramsay. Or at least his eloquent deep voice suggests as much. Despite leaning on crutches, he's tall and broad with striking green eyes. Though his hair is thinning, it's still a pale ginger, lightly sprinkled with grey.

Squeezing Lana's fingers, Serena steps through the oak door. Her brisk, efficient tone emerges, surprising herself. 'Not at all. You said it might take a while when we spoke on the phone.'

He manoeuvres around cautiously, then lifts a large hand. 'Come on through, then.'

Lana's shoes tip-tapping on the parquet floor, they slowly follow the master and his silent dog along a dark, panelled hallway, past an elegant polished staircase and several closed doors. Letting through a shower of un-expected light, the double entrance to a room at the far end is open.

Mr Ramsay turns. 'The drawing room. Sadly no fire today but this is my favourite place.' He gestures to a parlour which would have been cluttered with the glut of antique pieces had it not been so huge. 'As you can see, it has a triple aspect of the grounds, so I can still enjoy the gardens and not let this damned thing bother me too much.' He pats his hip. 'A tumble at the golf club. Did I mention it on the telephone? And not a very elegant mishap, I have to confess.'

His sharp features soften as he grins and Serena knows that she'll like him. He must have been a handsome man in his youth. And with that dash of devilry in his gaze, vibrant and personable too.

He stops at a button-backed armchair, gives her a crutch, then his hand. 'Could you? Trickier to sit down than to stand up. Peculiar really, but it was a rather bad fracture, I'm told. Might take up to four months to fully heal.'

She grips his palm firmly, taking some of his weight as he lowers himself with a wheeze of discomfort. Once settled in the velvet chair, he nods to a spindled seat by an elegant walnut table.

'Was sitting there earlier with my laptop, but now someone's here to haul me out, I can revert to being a feeble old man and devour the newspaper.'

Catching the twinkle in his eye, Serena returns his smile. How old is he? Sixty-five? Certainly no older than seventy. 'Something tells me you're not anyone's *old man*,' she says.

He chuckles. 'Ah, a lady who's nobody's fool. I like that.'

He watches the dog settle on a plush Indian rug, then turns his attention to Lana. Her fingers clasped at the front of her best coat, she's staring open-mouthed through the French doors to the gardens.

'So you must be Lana. Do you play tennis, young Lana?' he asks.

Apparently transfixed and not hearing the question, she doesn't move.

'Lana?' Stepping over, Serena gives her daughter a reassuring squeeze of the shoulder. 'Look, a tennis court. It would be fun to learn, wouldn't it, love?' Wondering about her strange smile and palm lifted in greeting, she follows Lana's gaze. No people nor animals, but a neatly manicured network of hedges and paths.

Thrilled that Lana is animated, even just a little, she turns back to Mr Ramsay. 'I think the maze has caught her attention.'

'Ah, it was ever thus.' A shadow passes across his face before clearing again. 'Yes, our mini labyrinth. Built for my wife when she was your age, little Lana. She told quite a few tales about it. Mostly about getting lost in the middle.' He digs into a pocket, waves his mobile and smiles. 'Not that you need to worry about that, young lady. Didn't have these back then.'

He reverts to Serena with a thoughtful frown. 'Though it's only small, it's a devil to maintain. Some things are worth the effort, though.' Then after a beat, 'You'll be pleased to learn your duties won't cover that. Mainly keeping a check on me and the old hip until I'm back in full swing. Think you're up to the task? Settle in this afternoon and start tomorrow?'

Both relieved and winded by his confirmation that the job is secure, Serena clears her throat. 'Yes of course. So... that's it?' Throughout the long journey she'd been terrified something would go awry once she was here. 'I...' She glances at Lana. 'We've met the requirements?'

'Great believer in first impressions. Besides, it works two ways.' His hooded eyes rest on Lana. 'Have I passed the test, young lady? Would you like to live here for a few weeks? Fetch my newspaper and slippers when I need them?' He leans forward. 'Feed Lexie and the bad-tempered old geese if they come?'

He nods at her shy smile. 'I'll take that as a yes. If you look carefully, you can spot a thatched roof through that window. Our little cottage. You can't see it properly from here but it's like a doll's house. Doubtless it'll need a good clean, but it's yours. Off you go then. There are keys somewhere but it'll be unlocked.' He taps his thigh. 'Would show you around, but not quite up to that yet. Come back when you've had a gander and let me know what you think.'

–

Trepidation vibrating through her daughter's fingers, Serena guides her across the darkening courtyard to the tiny lodge the other side. The black and white façade matches the main building's elevations, but the pattern is broken by a small leaded window housed in worn wood. Her hand stiff from her daughter's grip and the cold sharp wind, she lifts a rusty latch and pushes at the door. A fug of stale aromas breathes back, but when she steps in, the front room is unexpectedly warm, the low sturdy beams reassuring.

Blowing out her trapped breath, she flicks on the light and looks around. A doll's house indeed; it's minuscule inside. The small panes and every surface are powdered with dust, but the emulsion between the timbered wall panels looks cheerful and bright.

She turns to her daughter. 'What do you think, love? Do you like it?'

Though stuck to the spot, Lana's eyes resemble saucers, drinking everything in. She swallows and nods.

Despite her jangling nerves, Serena laughs. 'It's pretty, isn't it? If a little pongy. But that's nothing a bit of fresh air won't cure.' She opens a window, surprisingly not stuck fast, then gestures to the linen-draped furniture. 'I wonder what's hidden. Shall we explore?'

Lana finally speaks, her voice tremulous. 'What's under there?' she asks, pointing to a covered object.

It's clearly the shape of a rocking horse. 'Hmm, I wonder. Do you want to have the first peep?' Serena asks with a smile.

Lana reaches out, but as though it's come to life, the toy's sheet billows from the breeze through the window. Shaking her head, she jumps back. The usual jolt of grief hitting, Serena closes her eyes. It's fine; Lana's just apprehensive, that's all. Why wouldn't she be? And kids are adaptable, mend far sooner than adults.

Yet she knows for a fact that isn't true.

She strokes Lana's soft hair. 'Let's try something else first.' She turns to the settee, but pauses in surprise. As though a phantom is sitting and looking out to the garden, there's an adult-sized dent in the linen. 'Shall I go first?' she asks, shrugging off the icy shiver.

Intending to snatch it away like a magician, she grins at her daughter, but old habits die hard, so instead she lifts the soft cloth, carefully pleating each corner to collect the fine powder.

'Look, Lana. Perfect! A lovely sofa, just for two. Let me shake this outside, then let's start on the rest.'

Her back to the wind, Serena holds out the sheet and watches the dust waft across the courtyard. She begins to turn away, but sensing movement right behind her, she snaps around to look. There's no one nearby, but a thick-set figure is loping up the terrace steps to the main house. A red-headed man, so that must be the son.

She returns to the cottage. 'Next one, love?'

Aping her mother, Lana joins in the heedful folding and between them they expose an armchair and a round dining table with three seats.

They finally return to the item Lana noticed first. She bites her lip. 'It looks like a pony,' she says.

'Do you think so? There's only one way to find out.'

Timid with expectation, Lana gently tugs the dusty cover. 'Wow,' she says, covering her mouth with delight.

Far grander than the shabby furniture, the wooden animal is crafted from rich chestnut, more a work of art than a toy.

Taking a quick, emotional breath, Serena watches Lana stroke its dark flank and long elegant mane. It's as though both daughter and horse have miraculously come to life.

Yes, a new start. A fresh, exciting adventure.

'Do you think I'm allowed to sit on it?' Lana asks.

Though Serena knows she doesn't have to say them, the words emerge all the same. 'If you're very, very careful and don't break it, yes you can.'

Chapter Two

Hugh

Hugh hops up the steps, lets himself in and makes a fuss of Lexie for several minutes at the door. Then taking a deep breath, he strides to the drawing room and greets his father by slapping his back.

The newspaper falls from his dad's knees. 'Hugh,' he says, his voice clearly sleepy.

'How's it going, Dad? Hot drink or something stronger?' He falls back on the sofa and stretches his legs. 'Have I caught you napping, old man?'

'No and less of the old.' His father picks up a crutch and slices it like a sword. 'I'm armed, so be warned. What time is it?'

'Ten past five. Sent you a text to ask if you wanted something picking up for dinner on the way in.'

'Really?' His dad scoops up his mobile and squints.

Hugh guffaws. 'Probably came through when you *weren't* asleep.'

He jumps up, steps to his dad's 'work table' and lobs the reading glasses into his lap. Then he picks up the decanter and pours a measure in two glasses. What does the old man always say? '*A small one won't hurt us so long as it's after five.*'

'Just a dram since you're driving, Hugh,' his father comments, his gaze on his phone. He shakes his head. 'Look at that. The Dow Jones has dropped 1,000 points for the second time this month.' He takes off his spectacles. 'Always the bloody way after showing signs of recovery. Just have to hold steady, but where's the fun in that? Did I tell you about the gamble I made...'

His dad tells a story he's told before. Probably. But Hugh drifts; numbers have never been his thing. Finances and forecasts, graphs, statistics and fractions always merge and melt before his eyes. Words too, for that matter. But it's fine; not everyone's a genius like Jack.

Slipping down onto the carpet, he absently runs his fingers through Lexie's soft fur and hums 'Cigarettes & Alcohol' in his mind after listening to it in the car. Oasis, of course. They played the song at Heaton Park in 2009 before announcing it a free gig and abandoning the stage. He wouldn't have cashed the 'Bank of Burnage' cheque refund anyway, but he's particularly glad he framed it, as that performance turned out to be the end. Well sort of. Not that he acknowledges Liam or Noel's individual music since they split up. Brothers should stick together. More than anything, he wants them to re-form the band.

'Kiss and make up, Hugh? Don't get your hopes up,' Jack says. But what does his brother know? He never gets his *hopes up* about anything these days.

Lexie's whimper interrupts his thoughts. 'You OK, girl?' he asks, carefully examining her thigh. Then he remembers the Renault outside. 'Whose is the car parked under the fir?'

His dad lifts his eyebrows. 'Ah. Seems I've taken on a temporary housekeeper.'

Making a mental note to mention Lexie's injury to Jack, Hugh climbs back on the sofa. 'A housekeeper. That's a joke, right? Very funny.'

'No, not a joke, Hugh. I have, actually. That blasted hip pain last week. Thought I was cursed with it forever, so I posted an advert on a whim and forgot about it until she called. She sounded…'

Speechless from surprise, Hugh gazes at his father's thoughtful expression, wondering what word will emerge to explain such a plain odd decision. OK, so his dad had a bad fall and broke his hip. He was winded and shocked and in a '*great deal of pain*', even after the operation. He '*struggled*' with his crutches. But still.

'Nice. She sounded very pleasant,' his dad finishes. 'Turns out she's agreeable in person too; she doesn't smoke or have any apparent bad habits, so I employed her there and then.' He peers at his watch. 'An hour or so ago. She'll start tomorrow.'

Sitting forward, Hugh stares at his dad's placid face. He's alarmed and confused and wants to shout, but he needs to count to five before saying anything at all. Hell, nothing makes sense.

'You're kidding,' he blurts. 'Another woman in the house? You can't be serious; you need to think this through. I know you've been… struggling, but…' Raking fingers through his hair, he tries to process what his dad is *really* saying. 'I get it, your hip; you need help…'

He eyes the silk dressing gown and slippers: shit, his dad hasn't been dressed all day. 'But hey, I'm here! Tell me what to do and I'll help.'

His father snorts softly.

'Really, Dad. I could take a break from work.' He quickly thinks. He doesn't like it when Bob brings his son to help out, but he can't come up with anything else right this moment. 'And we can get Bob in to do a few chores after he's finished the gardening. Tell this housekeeper person you've made a mistake, that—'

'Enough, Hugh.' His dad cuts in with a dismissive hand. 'She's in the gatekeeper's house. It'll be fine. That's all in the past. You worry too much.'

'Does Jack know—'

A light cough interrupts Hugh's sentence. He turns to the sound. Her hair in a severe bun, a pale-faced woman is standing at the door. Putting her hand to her neck, she smooths the buttoned collar of her blouse and looks at him coolly. 'Hello. I'm Serena Green. I'm sorry to intrude, but the front door was ajar. I knocked but…'

'That was me. Sorry.' He stands and automatically thrusts out his hand. 'Hello, I'm Hugh, Hugh Ramsay. Dad was just telling me about you. Thing is, there might have been a—'

The woman turns and lightly guides a small girl to her side. 'And this is my daughter, Lana.'

Stumped for words, Hugh looks at his father, but his expression is blank which means he must have *known*. He goes back to the housekeeper and her young, pretty child.

'Lana, right. A nice name.' He tries not to stare, but both are eerily still, as though they're not breathing. He needs to change tack, '*turn the problem on its head*', as Jack often says. 'So, yes, the cottage. No one has lived there for quite some time. It might not be… well, it'll need some repairs before you—'

'Yes, that's why I popped over, actually.' Spots of pink abruptly colour the woman's cheeks. 'It's lovely; it's warm and feels like home already, but there's no water, I'm afraid. I couldn't find a tap under the sink, so I thought it

17

would be easier to ask rather than…' Her blush deepens and she laughs. 'Rather than drag up all the floorboards.'

'Right.' Wondering why she'd pull up the flooring, Hugh looks at his feet, but he realises from his father's ready chuckle that she's joking.

His dad finally speaks. 'Not a tap but a small screw in the pipework, as I recall. Tiny little thing.' He smiles and holds up his spectacles. 'I'd be no help even if I was mobile, but Hugh's good with his hands, aren't you, Hugh?'

'Sure. Absolutely.' He gazes a moment longer at his dad's strange, vacant look, then turns to the lady. With her flushed skin, she's prettier than he'd thought. And younger too. Not at all his mental image of a *housekeeper*, whatever the word really means. 'Right, absolutely. Water. You lead the way and I'll be right behind you.'

He takes one last perplexed glance at the old man, but the newspaper is lifted, a sure sign the conversation is over. Trying to dip beneath his worries about what Jack will think about this alarming development, he strides from the room. The girls are already at the front door, Lexie looking on.

His stomach rumbles. 'Hold up,' he calls. 'Dad's hip and all that. Don't suppose he showed you guys around?'

Wide-eyed, they both shake their heads.

'OK, so…' Wondering where to start, he scrunches his face. 'Yeah, so Ramsay land stretches as far as the village, but here we've about ten acres of grazing and woodland. Then there's…' He counts on his fingers. 'The… your cottage – Dad says it was once a gatekeeper's house – the outbuildings on that side, the workshop. The triple garage and hay barn at the top for the goats.' Cringing, he glances at the kid. 'Not that we have them any more. Sorry about that. Tennis court and maze. Then further down the drive there's the games room.'

Feeling bad about the lack of animals, he goes back to the girl. How old must she be? No older than five. 'It has a pool table in there. If you stood on a stool you could…'

Oh God, he's talking without *thinking* again. He squeezes his mind for more things to list. Nope. He shrugs. 'But, I guess the kitchen's pretty much what you'll need.' He opens the door and beckons them in.

Expecting them to follow and have a gander, he makes his way to the fridge. Lord, he's hungry. Selecting a pork pie, he liberally squirts on mayonnaise and pops it in his mouth, but when he turns, they're still hovering at the entrance.

He quickly swallows the food down. 'Oh right, I thought you'd…'

The kid's worried expression rouses a sad but warm feeling in his chest. He tries for a reassuring tone. 'You're allowed to come in.' When they do, he points around the room. 'So there's a table, cupboards, fridge.' Yeah, Hugh, that much is obvious. He strides to the other side, flings open the first two panelled doors and gestures to the girl. 'Come and look, er…'

'Lana,' the woman says.

'Yeah, Lana.'

She shuffles towards him and peers in.

'Can you guess what it's for?' he asks her. 'Boot room – a bit smelly – and this is for laundry.' He unlatches the next one and squints into the darkness. 'This is the cellar for Dad's vino. Steps are a bit steep, so you have to turn on the light and take special care.' He moves along and waves her over. 'This one's the best; you'll like this.'

He opens the pantry, but the kid doesn't move. White as a ghost, she sticks at the basement entrance, staring in with huge eyes.

He inhales theatrically; everything's bought from the supermarket, and in truth there's not even a whiff of home baking, but he wants to cheer her anxious face. 'Yum, cookies and cake. Can you smell them? Come over and try.'

The woman steps forward and takes the girl's hand. She clears her throat as she tugs her away. 'Sounds wonderful, thank you. Lana's a little timid, I'm afraid. She's not keen on the dark.'

Feeling a sharp stab of empathy, Hugh nods. 'I get that, absolutely.' Desperate to finish on something jolly, he clocks the mum's glances at the Aga and grins. 'No idea how to work it either, but don't worry, I just shove whatever I fancy from the freezer in. It's blinking hot, so ten minutes seems to cover everything.'

Her eyes flicker, but she politely smiles. 'Thank you, Hugh. That's all very helpful.'

Helpful, that's good; he likes to be helpful. But a tight band of worry still squeezes his chest. Why on earth has his dad brought a new woman in the house? More to the point, what the hell will his older brother have to say?

Chapter Three

Jack

Jack rests his head on the leather-topped desk. Though he's almost asleep, he knows she's there, curled up in the green Chesterfield chair, her slender hands like a prayer beneath her pale cheek.

A breeze from the doorway alerts him moments before he hears his visitor's voice. 'Mr Ramsay? Sorry to disturb you. I knocked but…'

He turns to the sound. A woman is watching him, her eyes interested and appraising as though she can read his soul. 'Are you coming upstairs?' she asks. 'It's gone seven o'clock. Mr Cranston is waiting for you. He wants to say a few words.'

He hauls himself from his stupor. 'Right; yes of course…' Though he can't summon a name, she's the chambers' new manager. In her early thirties, probably, her black skin and black hair glowing with vitality, health.

His gaze slides back to the green seat and he swallows. Empty, thank God. But it's fine; this woman doesn't know; she does not know. How could she or anyone else? The dark, dirty truth is all his alone.

He returns to her chestnut gaze. 'Thanks for the reminder.' Then rubbing his face, 'I'll just be a moment.'

She doesn't move. 'Is there anything I can get you? A glass of water?'

'That bad, eh?' He smiles thinly and snorts. 'Long week, not helped by the trains. There's nothing more soul-destroying than arriving at Euston station with seconds to spare, manically searching the departures board, then seeing that flashing delay sign. Forty-five long minutes. When it finally arrived, an old lady took my seat so I had to stand like a sardine.'

He's speaking too much, which isn't like him. Talking doesn't help; it simply results in more questions. But she's nice, this woman. She has those inviting, dark eyes that say, 'Tell me, tell me, you can tell me.'

But he can't, he never will.

'Then there was the coffee,' he continues. He lifts his stained cuff. 'A hefty shove by a man the size of a house. So, maybe a new shirt if you've got one spare?'

She smiles a perfect white flash. Kiva is her name, he remembers.

'A shirt? We probably do. I'm still unearthing the stationery cupboard and finding all sorts of treasures, a pink thong and a packet of condoms included. Might not be an improvement on the one you're wearing though.'

'My pink thong or my shirt?' He stands. 'Maybe I won't bother changing, then.'

'Yes, that would be wise.' She steps away. 'See you in a minute. Don't keep the boss waiting.'

When the door clicks to, he looks around the dusky, wood-panelled room. Though it's effectively in the Victorian building's basement, it does have a window of sorts. Perhaps it's the tiny space or the dull shaft of evening lamplight, but the room feels claustrophobic today. As ever it's dense with documents – the law tomes and lever arch files lining the walls, the heaps of paper and cerise ribbon covering every inch of his desk, the unopened legal briefs piled on the small table.

Clutter everywhere, save for the empty Chesterfield.

He shakes himself back to the mission at hand. Today's a happy day, isn't it? Wanting to feel it, he stares at the new court robe, still wrapped in cellophane on its hanger. A specially designed silk gown to show the world his enhanced lawyer status. That of Queen's Counsel, no less! Appointed by the monarch to be one of 'Her Majesty's Counsel learned in the law.' A mark of outstanding ability; one of a small pool of barristers and advocates reserved for serious or complex cases; a likely future judge.

A silk cloak for the honour of 'taking silk'.

Glancing at the vacant chair, he sharply inhales. Nothing; it means nothing. And he's so busy, too busy. Only God knows why he applied.

But that isn't true. Dad, of course Dad; even now at thirty-nine, he wants his father to be proud.

—

Straightening his tie, Jack takes a deep breath at the conference room door, then he steps in to immediate applause.

'Finally!' his rotund Head of Chambers booms over the clapping. 'Fashionably late, but the bride has finally arrived. Get the man a drink.'

Kiva hands him a flute of champagne and Cranston steps forward. 'So now our newly wed is here, a few words of congratulation.' He loudly clears his throat, a sure sign of a long speech. 'The days involving secret meetings and taps on the shoulder for the selection of Queen's Counsel are long gone…'

Jack hears a loud whisper behind him. His old mate, Phil Meadows, of course. 'Lucky for the old bugger he got in early.'

Trying not to smile, Jack focuses on Cranston's resonating tones. 'Applicants are carefully considered for their competency, not just in understanding and using the law, written and oral advocacy, but in their respect for diversity and working with others. And above all, in the case of this young man – for their integrity. Ladies, gents and our esteemed clerk, I'd like you to make a toast to our young pretender, Jack Ramsay. Still in his thirties and granted silk on his very first application.' He pats Jack's back and looks around the cluster of suits. 'I think that says it all, but you're not getting off that lightly...'

The forty or so people in the room laugh and Cranston goes on to say the usual about 'first class representation' and 'taking Jack under his wing' and 'expert in his field', but despite his usual angst about the word 'integrity', Jack finds himself zoning out as he tries to stifle the yawn. He's so astonishingly tired; he could sleep on the spot. When he's alerted by more whooping, he catches that inviting dark gaze.

Phil Meadows grabs his shoulders. 'Speech! Come on, Jackie boy, speech.'

He rouses himself to the task. 'I'm not sure I can follow that wonderful accolade. Thank you for your kind words, Cranston. And to everyone else who's stayed beyond the call of duty, thank you for raising a glass with me.' He lifts his flute. 'To my colleagues, the clerks and support staff.' Then with a grin to his fellow QCs, 'And to the er... more senior members of chambers... watch out, it's time to hold on to your briefs!'

Perked up by the bubbles and canapés, Jack moves around the room and chats. Eventually the numbers thin and it's a reasonable time to escape. Taking a step towards the door, he feels a gentle tug on his arm. It's Kiva.

'A few of us are going onto the pub or a bar. Do you fancy it?' she asks with a smile.

There's a jolt of something in his stomach he hasn't felt for some time, yet the excuse is still on the tip of his tongue. 'Thanks for asking but it's been a long week and I'm...'

What? What reason should he give? That he's tired? That he really mustn't drink? That alcohol makes him this other person he doesn't like or even recognise?

But before he can say more, Phil's beefy arm is around his shoulder again. 'Come on Jackie boy. It's not every day you take silk.' He propels him forward. 'Onward to the pub, people! The newly crowned Jack Ramsay QC is a-paying.'

Chapter Four

Serena

It's very late or very early, Serena doesn't know which. She might have slept at some point, but she's been staring at the rafters, trying to steady her anxiety for what feels like hours. She now does it again, breathing in slowly and deeply through her nose, counting from one to four. Then a little longer out through her mouth. 'Tummy breathing', as she used to describe it at work. But it's more than just respiring; it's fighting those dismal, murky night thoughts. How do you visualise a happy place when there aren't any? When only very bad ones fire in? But she has to get a grip and rationalise – this attic room mattress is less than double size, but she's comfortable and sheltered with her daughter, so that's actually more than fine.

Propping her head on her hand, she strokes the wispy hair from Lana's forehead and watches her for a while. Her face is almost translucent in the moonlight; so like the newborn she was, when her skin was paper-thin and the delicate noodle veins transparent through it.

Bitter-sweet tears prick her eyes. Was that the moment things changed, when she put her child to her breast and knew there'd be no greater love than this new perfect being?

She kisses Lana's cheek, then noiselessly sits up and glances around the small bedroom. Her lips twitch at the sight; doll's house furniture too: neat drawers with pearly knobs, a slim wardrobe and an ornate dressing table with an oval mirror. A curtain rail but no drapes to cover the aged panes. Perhaps they'll be in the cupboard downstairs. She found clean bedding but ran out of time to dig deeper as Lana was dog-tired by eight. And the heedlessness of sleep is always a good thing.

The floorboards creak and complain as she stands. Remembering the step, she bends her head at the door. She wouldn't have caught it, surely, but it's a habit of being tall. Like wearing flat shoes and making an effort not to loom by standing a pace away. Occasionally stooping to suit others and make them feel taller. Not that she's *that* lanky.

But this cottage is very dinky. Yes, a doll's house indeed. Is little Lana the marionette or is she? Playing housekeeper in some stranger's home? Whatever a 'personal' housekeeper is supposed to do. Nothing like Fräulein Schwein, the malevolent head *haushälterin* in Gstaad, she hopes. What did she and the other English chalet maids call their terrifying boss back then? That's right; 'The Swine'. Instigated by fearless Rhona, of course.

She chuckles to herself. Perhaps she should reinvent herself in The Swine's mould, intimidating the owners as well as guests and the staff. But Mr Ramsay did seem very nice. He asked if she knew how to make up the open hearth before she left him in the drawing room.

'Yes of course. I can do it now,' she said, even though she'd never done it before in her life. But how difficult could it be? Back in their school days, she and Rhona had watched the boys build fires in the woods often enough.

'You don't start until tomorrow,' he replied. 'A deal's a deal. Besides, you need your water supply. See you for breakfast.'

Hugh was pleasant too. He *did* have to stoop at the cottage door. Having inspected the pipework and checked the steadiness of the kitchen shelves, he seemed pleased to fetch a tool box from an outbuilding, fiddle with the tap, replace a washer when it dripped, then go through the cottage brandishing his screwdriver. As though looking for a purpose, somehow.

His eager handiness seemed at odds with his floppy hair and posh accent. But that was her making assumptions. She knows more than anyone not to judge a book by its cover.

She takes the first step down the stairs from the loft. Her feet are longer than the shallow risers, so she tiptoes with care. At the bottom, she puts her palm to her hot lower neck. 'See you for breakfast,' Mr Ramsay said yesterday. What did that mean? Him coming down to the kitchen or dining room, or her taking it up to him? Feeling the heat rise, she softly rubs the tender skin. Should she ask what he likes for his meals when she sees him in the morning or just look in the fridge and hope for the best? It's a huge leap into the unknown in every way. Like cooking with a flaming Aga.

Hugh seemed to read her mind about that. As soon as he opened the kitchen door, the familiar oily smell from Rhona's place drifted out, so she knew there'd be an Aga, but she has no idea how one works. Ask or not ask? Set out her stall or pretend everything's fine? Or perhaps just go for Hugh's ten minute rule.

28

She smiles. A pleasant man. Disarming charm, like his father. Innocent and trusting, somehow. And so sweet with Lana. Yes, she likes Hugh very much.

She pads to the kitchen, opens the small fridge and stares at the contents. Once Hugh had finished his check-up of the cottage and returned to the big house, she and Lana walked down the winding, dark driveway. 'To explore,' she said to Lana. It was really for provisions. She hadn't thought about that on the journey here; she hadn't focused on anything save driving safely and arriving, but she'd vaguely supposed she'd be living in the main house with the father and son and eating their food. Not with them of course, but polishing off the leftovers, the scraps, whatever was going.

Though Lana didn't complain about hunger, neither of them had eaten since their rushed piece of toast for breakfast, so they donned hats, coats and mittens and walked the quarter mile until they reached the gate. It didn't open this time – apparently big brother wasn't watching – so she pressed the black exit button and hoped for the best. The barrier seemed to hesitate, and for an iota she panicked. What would happen if it didn't open, if she was imprisoned forever? Incarcerated yet again? But eventually it relented and she was released to the shadowy lane. And she knew to turn left. Right was just the silvery countryside from earlier, which seemed like a lifetime ago already.

Now feeling her stomach rumble, she stares at their meagre purchases. Unappetising sliced bread, butter, jam and milk from the dusty corner shop fifteen minutes up the road. Digestive biscuits, orange squash and a tiny packet of tea bags, proudly displayed on the Hugh-straightened shelf. When did she last eat? She must remember to eat. She reaches for a yogurt pot, then puts it back. They are for Lana. Besides, she's not yearning for food. What she really, really wants is a cigarette.

Almost laughing at the sudden desire above all others, she flops down on the sofa and pulls over the throw. By bedtime the slatted iron radiator had become oppressively hot, so she turned it off to help her and Lana sleep. Now the cottage is freezing and she's still only *almost* laughing at her need for a fag. Closing her eyes, an image of Rhona flies in, a memory of them from school, blowing smoke against the orange brick of the sports hall. She throws back the blanket. The Renault! A long shot there'll be a packet there, but still worth braving the icy cold, despite her lack of dressing gown.

She grabs the car keys, drags on her boots and unbolts the cottage door. Gasping at the shock of sharp wind, she looks out at the night. Lit only by the cloud-covered moon, it's astonishingly black, the house ghostly and menacing despite its luminous noughts and crosses.

Gently hugging her chest with her arms, she jogs towards the terrace but almost slips on the icy courtyard, so she slows and walks tentatively to the fir tree silhouette. But when she reaches the car, she knows her mission's in vain; the Renault's fairly new; Rhona gave up smoking years ago.

Her eyes now accustomed to the inkiness, she begins to tromp back, but the echo of footsteps in the still night catches her short. Then a cough and ragged breath. Goosebumps spreading, she turns. A figure is walking unsteadily towards her. A man. Hunched behind his collar, he's dark-haired and slim. What the...? He's tall but he's certainly not Hugh. Aware of her white nightdress almost glowing in the dark, she steps back to the woodland pine and holds her breath in the shadows.

Almost by her side, the stranger stops and looks up at the sky. His breath an icy cloud, he seems to mutter to the heavens before striding away. Then, as though sensing she's there, he snaps his shoulders towards her and stares. After a beat he recoils and sharply inhales. Clearly stunned to see her, he gapes for a moment longer, then he slips his hands to his knees and bends double as though winded.

Serena runs. The need to escape overwhelming, she darts away. Her heart whipping and her feet barely touching the ground, she scampers to the safety of the cottage. Once inside, she slots the top and bottom bolts with fumbling fingers.

Her back to the door, she slides to the floorboards and exhales. Her neck itches and burns. Who the hell was that man? That hollow face, the tenebrous gaze. Oh God. Though only fleeting, there was a darkness in those eyes she recognised all too well.

Chapter Five

Jack

Covered in sweat, Jack wakes with a sharp jolt and sits up. He can't look but she's there, he knows it; even in deep, groggy sleep he heard her breathing.

Waiting for the dizziness to pass, he lowers his head. He *heard* her? Hold on; he's never heard her before. Felt her presence, yes, smelled her soft soapy scent, seen her blue accusing eyes, but she's usually silent and still.

Lifting his chin, he peers at the sofa. Not just breathing but bloody snoring. Huge feet one end, floppy hair the other. His arms hugging a cushion, his mouth lolling open. What the hell is Hugh doing here? And instead of sleeping like a mountain goat on a ledge, why didn't he pull out the bottom mattress?

The usual draught through the floorboards – or from some nook, cranny or other corner of his ancient home – cools Jack's skin. God, he feels rough, his mind slow and sluggish. Alcohol of course; far too much to drink. He slumps back against the pillow, pulls up the sheet and scrunches his eyes. A chestnut gaze flashes in. Oh hell. What did he do? What didn't he do? What *couldn't* he do? His heart racing, he swallows. God, he's parched. He needs water and a pee, but firstly last night, last evening. He needs to piece it together, needs to know what happened, needs to be sure, please God, that he didn't go too far.

Trying to rise above the threatening panic, he focuses his mind. The drinks party at chambers, then the pub. A crowd of ten or so, Phil Meadows holding court. Drinking beer, so that was fine. The 'young pretender', 'teacher's pet', Cranston's 'golden bum-boy'. Everyone taking the piss but in a nice way: 'You did it, mate! You're a fucking Queen's Counsel!' Then on to a nightclub. Kiva's warm gaze and white smile across the table. Inviting, inviting. Oh God, drinking whisky like water. Pounding music, flashing lights…

What then? What then? Oh hell. Her hand, Kiva's slim fingers slipping into his. Her soft breath in his ear: 'My Uber is here, Jack. You live miles away; you can stay at mine if you like.'

Alcohol; oh God. It makes him forget. It prevents him thinking straight, stops him asking *what if she knew?*

So he said through the bass beat, the euphoria, the haze, 'Thank you. That would be nice.' And despite Phil's raised eyebrows, he left with her, pushing through the safety of bodies and noise, climbing into the taxi and watching the bright lights disappear as they headed along the parkway to her South Manchester flat.

What then? What exactly happened then?

He now rolls from the bed and stumbles past his sleeping brother to the en suite bathroom door. Gropes blindly for the handle and strides to the loo. The urine spurts out in concord with his long, relieved breath. That's right; he saw sense when the cab pulled up at her place.

'Sorry, Kiva. Completely forgot about my father. Just me at home. He'll need me first thing. Broke his hip ten days ago and had to have an op…'

Talking too much despite struggling to speak at all, he said goodnight, wished her a great weekend, watched her walk to the front door, then asked the taxi driver if he could take him on to Goostrey.

The usual conversation: 'Sure. Where's that?'

'M6, junction eighteen. You know the Jodrell Bank telescope? Near there.'

Lowering his head at the sink, he breathes away another swell of nausea. The gates. He didn't even attempt to remember the code. Besides, he'd needed to vomit, so he bunged fifty pounds to the driver and tumbled out, willing him gone before he spilt out his guts. Sat on the grassy bank for a good half an hour, vaguely wondering if he'd die of hypothermia, and if he cared anyway, before remembering he had the remote fob in his pocket.

His gloomy face in the mirror sparks another thought. A white nightdress, wild hair and those terrified animal eyes. He pushes the image away. He pushes *her* away. He couldn't cope with *that*. It was only a dream; a stupid flash of memory from a long time ago. He just needs to rest; he'll be fine in the morning.

Opening the bathroom cabinet, he stares at the selection of boxes and bottles. Sleep, pretty sleep. What did Ernest Hemingway say? Something about loving it because his life fell apart when he was awake. Too, too bloody familiar. He pulls out a blister packet, pops out a pill and places it on his tongue. Then he shakes his head and spits it out. Alcohol and pills. Oblivion, even death. Dangerous, and tempting for sure. But he has his dad to worry about. And most of all, Hugh.

–

Jack's attempt to turn over is blocked by a wall of back muscle.

'What the hell, Hugh?'

Hugh turns, his face guileless. 'I waited on the sofa and fell asleep. Woke up bloody freezing.' He yawns and stretches like a contented cat. Then, more hound-like, he leans towards Jack and sniffs. 'You smell rank. Whisky and puke.'

Jack pushes his brother's broad chest. 'Give me space then. You could've pulled out the bottom mattress and grabbed a blanket. You're not five anymore.'

Hugh's expression falls and Jack feels an immediate stab of guilt. He ruffles his hair. 'Much as I love you little bro, you're a bit on the big side for sleepovers these days.' He gazes at his brother's soft face. He has their father's eyes and colouring but their mum's neat nose and apple cheeks. The features he remembers from his infant school years, at least.

'Does Dad know you're home?' he asks.

'Yeah, sort of. I've been coming over after work this week like you said. Texting to see what he needs bringing in.'

'That's good. How's the job going?'

Hugh looks at the ceiling. 'It's OK. Mr Barnes is nice and Jess is at home at the moment, so she makes me lunch.' He rocks his head back to Jack. 'Dad didn't have a job. Well, not for years. He just married Mum.'

Jack sighs. 'Yeah, but it wasn't a good idea to say that to him. Don't just speak what's in your head, Hugh. Give it a few moments, minutes even. Think it through; try and stand in someone else's shoes.'

He almost laughs at Hugh's frown. 'You know what that means. Dad didn't just marry Mum, he took everything on – the house, the grounds, the lettings, the finances.' He shrugs. 'I don't know, like managing an estate. Sorting the maintenance of the land, fences and walls. Selling off parts when necessary. People get paid for that. And he's proud of this place, so he felt offended. Understand?'

He watches Hugh process the information. His brother is generally happy-go-lucky, moving on quickly with a shrug when things that perplex him are explained, but sometimes he gets stuck, bringing up his angst again and again. Their dad and this employment business, particularly. Unfairness, Jack supposes, pecking away in his mind. He inwardly snorts: just like him and his past.

Sitting up, he tests his head. He drank glass after glass of water from the grimy toothbrush cup, but it still feels as though someone has been threshing his brain. He goes back to his bed fellow. 'So, why did I have the honour of your company last night?'

Hugh's eyes dart from side to side. Counting, of course. Whether it'll last for moments or minutes is yet to be seen, so Jack hitches down the bed, wishing he could kip for the rest of the day, the week, the bloody year. It's still only January, but he could do it, for certain.

Hugh's voice splinters the cusp of sleep. 'Dad's got this woman in. You know, until his hip gets better. She's really nice. Thing is—'

'What?'

'A woman to help out. You know, as a housekeeper.'

Wondering if he's in dreamland, Jack pulls himself up.

'A housekeeper? To do what?'

Hugh shrugs. 'I wondered that. Cooking, I suppose. He definitely wants her to make up the fire.'

'You mean another cleaner from the village?'

'No. Well, I don't think so. I mean, she might do the cleaning…' Hugh pulls at an escaped thread of cotton. 'Thing is, she's going to live here. Well, not *here*…'

An icy chill spreads down Jack's spine. He stares at the empty sofa. 'Where?'

'She's at the cottage. Well, where else would she go? Not here in the house. That would be a bit strange.'

His headache forgotten, Jack lets out a long breath. 'Right.'

'I helped.' Hugh beams. 'I had to sort out the water and a few other things that needed attention, so I…'

He continues to speak but Jack zones out. Pictures a fair-haired woman in the shadows, that glimpse of her frantic gaze, then her white nighty billowing behind her as she runs towards the cottage.

A sense of relief pierces his shock – it wasn't a dream, a nightmare, a vision. He goes back to his brother. His face flooded with colour, his eyes now resemble green marbles and he's flattening his hair.

'What is it, Hugh? There's more. What else do you need to tell me?'

But Hugh's already out of the bed and heading to the bathroom. 'If I don't eat breakfast, I'll get hungry. If I'm hungry I'll get grumpy. If I get…'

The rest of his sentence is drowned out by the spurting sound of his pee. Not that Jack needs to hear the ending. It's just one of the little mantras he taught his younger brother many, many moons ago.

Flopping back against the mattress, he covers his face. A woman at Ramsay Hall? A bloody *housekeeper*. Not just poking into their lives, their home, their rooms and their belongings, but living in the cottage. Why would his father do that? What the fuck is going on?

Chapter Six

Serena

All fingers and thumbs, Serena turns on her mobile and stares at the screen. She's overslept, unbelievably overslept for the first time in years.

Her chest fiery, she tries to steady her fast, shallow breath. No messages, so it's fine, really fine. And it's still dusky outside. Late for her, but not that late for most people.

After last night's fright, she returned to the bed, desperate to cuddle her daughter but fearful of waking her. Instead, she listened to Lana's light breathing and her own thrashing heart. Trying to block out the memory of those dark, hollow eyes, she focused on her new job for the first time, forcing herself to be dispassionate and rational. Sure, she hadn't worked for several years, but it wasn't as though she was an incapable woman. That's just how it had felt for too long.

Yet the doubts flooded in. 'Inept', 'clumsy', 'worthless', even 'crazy'. She'd had to give herself a swift, sharp reminder of her new resolve. Forwards, not back; action, steps, drive. Confidence. So she sent Mr Ramsay a text around three am.

'*Please let me know when you wake and what assistance you'll need before breakfast,*' she typed.

That seemed to cover it; she could ask him what he wanted to eat or what tasks she should do in person. Or respond to his message. Or whatever. But it had felt like progress, a plan.

She now sighs. Clearly a sleep-inducing one.

Putting down the phone, she glances at Lana, surprised to find her awake. Her blue gaze is troubled. A reflection of her own, Serena knows, so she tries to replace her anxiety with a perky grin.

'Time to get up, love! Our adventure begins. A quick wash and then we'll…'

Oh God. What about Lana? Things had happened so quickly, Serena hadn't thought ahead. She's here to work. What should she do? Leave her in the cottage? But what about the stranger in the night? Would she be safe?

She inwardly nods. No question; decision made. 'Then we'll go to the big house and ask about the geese.'

-

The wind nipping their cheeks, Serena holds Lana's hand as they negotiate the icy surface of the courtyard. They head for the front porch, but at the bottom of the terrace, Serena thinks again. She's paid staff, so the back door is more appropriate.

Trying to shake off the feeling of being watched, she turns and squints at the white rendered building ahead. Like the two halves of a face struck by paralysis, one side of the roof is dilapidated and sagging, the other half's slates are neatly tiled. Same with the arched double doors – the left are worn and rickety, the right smooth and new. She thinks back to Hugh's summary of the premises yesterday. He mentioned a barn and a triple garage, so this must be it. Nodding to herself, she glances at the Renault. Surely there'll be room for a small one? But that can wait for now.

Their footsteps loud in the frosty silence, neither of them speak. But when they round the rear corner, the dull morning is illuminated by bright lights from the kitchen. A figure's at the table, eating cereal from what looks like a serving bowl.

'It's Hugh,' Lana whispers. 'And there's Lexie the dog.'

As though sensing they're there, Lexie pads to the back door. Hugh lifts his head and waves, then bounds over and flings the door open. A wall of oily heat fires through.

'Morning!' he says, his eyes bright, his face rosy. 'Come on in, guys. Take off your coats.' He pulls out a chair for Lana to sit. 'You look hungry, kiddo. I've just put in four slices of bread. Want some toast?'

Lana looks to Serena. For permission, of course. 'Sounds lovely,' she replies for her. 'Thank you very much.'

'Brill.' Hugh frowns. 'It's white, though.' He nods to the larder. 'Dad likes wholemeal, but I prefer—'

Wholemeal. Serena makes a mental note. 'White bread sounds perfect. Thank you.'

Checking her top button is securely fastened, she sits next to Lana and taps her fingers on the table. She wants to ask Hugh about the stranger in the early hours, but Lana is keenly watching him at his chore. He's busying himself at the fridge and the pippy oak cupboards, extracting a variety of jellies and jams and describing each flavour.

He moves on to another shelf. 'We have honey and lemon curd too.' He opens a lid and sniffs. 'But I'm not sure how long they've been here and I wouldn't want you to get a bad tummy...'

Seeming to understand his uncertainty, Lana finally speaks. 'Strawberry jam, please.'

'Excellent choice, kiddo,' he replies, falling quiet as he replaces the jars, lining each carefully so the labels are equidistant. The toaster pops and he animates again, loading the food on a wooden tray and pinging questions at Lana.

'So strawberry's your favourite jam? What about biscuits?'

She smiles behind her hand. 'Chocolate fingers.'

'Good choice. And cereal?'

'Weetabix.'

Hugh eats a piece of toast in two bites. 'OK, now to the really big question…' he says, licking his thick fingers.

Lana waits with rapt breath.

'Animals,' he says. 'What is your favourite animal, then?'

'All of them,' she replies immediately. Her shiny eyes turn to Lexie, 'But especially dogs.'

So pleased to see her daughter interact and relax, Serena doesn't interrupt the breakfast or chatter, but when Hugh abruptly looks at his watch and says he has to go, she follows him out after a moment or two.

She finds him in the hallway, pulling on a pair of smart boots. 'Do you think it'll be OK for Lana to sit quietly in the kitchen whilst I do my work?' she asks in a low voice.

Instead of answering, he stills as though listening. Then he seems to rally. 'Sure and there's the snug because it used to be…' He pauses and squints. 'Well, it was our cosy place when we were kids.' His cheeks colour. 'Yeah, that should be OK. So, I'll see you later.'

He's clearly in a rush, but she needs to know about the man, so she takes a quick breath. 'Before you go, Hugh. Last night, there was—'

But her question is cut short by conversation on the landing.

Eloquent tones waft down the wide stairway. 'So what's going on, Dad? Some strange woman who replies to an online advert. Without any bloody references? You must realise it's ridiculous to just let her have the run of the house. How do you know she's even trustworthy? She could be a con artist, a thief—'

'Well I like her. She's nice.' Then in a surprisingly petulant tone, 'She'll be company for me when you've gone to your flat or whatever it is you've decided on—'

'For God's sake, give me the crutch and take my arm. I haven't decided anything, Dad. It was just an idea, save me travelling home from chambers during the week. I'd still be here at the weekends…'

The cold breeze blasts Serena's back as Hugh leaves the house. She knows she should move, but finds herself stuck to the parquet, waiting for the inevitable.

Wearing loose slacks and a polo shirt, Mr Ramsay eventually reaches the bottom few stairs. Her efficient mask in place, she holds out her hand and grasps his.

'Morning,' she says briskly. 'Let me help you.'

His irascible companion finally steps out from her new employer's shadow. His face stubbly and stony, it's the man from last night. He fixes that gaze. Alarmed? Wary? *Ashamed?*

Yes, his dark, culpable eyes are exactly as she remembers, but this time they're not staring at her. They're fastened on her daughter, silently there by her side.

Chapter Seven

Jack

His lumbar region tender, Jack drives. Blind to the towering Jodrell telescope, the white-tipped countryside or the speed limit signs, he presses his foot hard on the accelerator of his dad's Range Rover. He's probably still over the limit from last night, but he had to get out of the house. Away from that child. His father doesn't know everything, but still, he knows enough. What the hell was he thinking, inviting her in?

He dares his eyes to the rear view mirror, but it's just his dad looking at him from the back seat. 'Slow down, Jack,' he's saying. 'Thought you'd put your boy racer days behind you. Besides, it's icy. We'll have an accident if you're not careful.'

Jack steadies his speed and tries to release the tension from his jaw. 'Boy racer'. A euphemism, of course, even though there was a time he couldn't get behind the wheel at all. But Hayden Ramsay is right. His reasonable, measured father generally is. He doesn't know if he loves him or loathes him. Not just right now, but forever. That bloody fine line he's always walked. Endlessly wanting to please him, but resenting him too. Needing to escape most days, but feeling rotten when he does. Never sure if he's the controller or the one who's controlled.

He inwardly sighs. And the rest.

Glancing again through the mirror, he spots his father shift position and wince. For God's sake, what sort of son is he? He barely let the poor man's breakfast settle before chivvying him out of the house. 'Come on, Dad, here's your jacket. You need some fresh air. Let's take the zimmer and grab a coffee at the golf club.'

'Reenact my fall,' he replied dryly. 'Hmm, charming, I'm sure.'

But still he hauled himself from his armchair and held out a dry hand. 'Right son, I'm up. Pass me the crutch. I'll say goodbye, then leave Serena to it.'

His attention back on the road, Jack slows down for the bend. Leave Serena to what, exactly? Wearing a uniform-like buttoned dress and her hair in a bun, she bore little resemblance to the wild-looking woman from last night. But he'd been a different person too. At the club he'd been carefree and drunk; laughing, chatting and dancing like a teenager.

What had Phil said at some point? 'Glad to have the old Jack back. Hope he stays.'

The old Jack. Oh God. Why on earth has his dad taken on a woman with a daughter? And what's he contemplating now as he passively gazes through the rear passenger window? There's no point asking, of course. Hayden's realm, his rules. And the injury, the hip, his obvious need for help. What eldest child wouldn't welcome an extra pair of hands around the house? Especially when he's so bloody busy. He should be working in the study now, but he didn't lug his paperwork home on the train as he'd planned. He'd gone to the pub and a club like the 'Old Jack'.

He pictures Kiva. Her curves and glowing skin; her inviting eyes and warm grin. He was tempted, that's for sure, but he can't feel it right now. He has no idea where that past desire came from or why it should appear on a Friday evening when all he really wanted to do was go home, put up his feet and watch some inane television before sleeping a thousand sleeps. Well, it has now gone, thank God. He's back to tetchy self-flagellation and he feels a whole lot more comfortable.

Though he doesn't need to, he checks the rear view mirror again. Not his father's pale green gaze but blue, a child's innocent, yet accusing, blue.

–

The golf club lift is out of order and Hayden struggles with the stairs, stubbornly refusing Jack's offer of help, but they finally reach the bar. Now sitting on the enclosed balcony, they watch a chilly-looking four ball game on the eighteenth hole below.

Easing his aching spine by moving his shoulders, Jack sips his coffee and ruminates on what he has in store for next week. Work, of course. Work, work and more work, both a curse and his saviour. A complex three-party trial in the Leeds High Court. He'd intended to drive across the Pennines each morning and evening to keep an eye on his father, but on reflection, the new bloody woman can see to that.

As though reading his mind, his dad clears his throat. 'What time did you get in last night? Expected you at some point before ten. Had to ask Hugh to help me change the towels and the bedding before he left.'

Jack tries to keep his voice even. 'You didn't ask the new housekeeper, then?'

45

'She didn't start until today. Fair's fair.' He smooths back his thinning hair. 'She needed to settle in first. Thought the old gatekeeper's house would be perfect. Standing there unloved, cold and empty.'

An image of the cottage garden flashes in. Jack shoves it away and stares at his father's equanimous expression, marvelling at his incredible talent for whitewashing the past. *Everyone makes mistakes. What's done is done. No point looking back. You can't change it.* And so on.

Except when it comes to his brother. Poor bloody sod.

'You should give Hugh a break, Dad. Let him come back home. He's around most of the time anyway. What's the point—'

'He needs to stand on his own two feet.'

Jack waits for 'cruel to be kind' and all the other idioms his father's so keen on to sum up momentous decisions in just a few words. Never talking it through or explaining. Just middle-class English repression. Like him. But it seems to suit Hayden. Rarely stressed or angst-ridden, he takes life in his large stride. So long as he's getting precisely what he wants, of course.

Jack studies him. Sharp bone structure, long nose, a Hellenic profile. But 'striding' is out of the question today and for several weeks to come, now he's lamed by his 'damned hip'. It was a shock to see him in the hospital bed two weeks ago. Despite his height, he'd looked small and frail, his whole body strangely cowed; fear and panic had been etched on his face.

Like bonfire night, bloody bonfire night. Explosions in more ways than one.

But no set phrases come from his father's mouth today; his attention is on the putting green. 'See that? What a dolly miss. I suppose you were out celebrating last night?'

'Yes.' Jack looks at his hands. They're still shaking. Too much alcohol, too little sleep. But life's actually OK. He didn't go too far. Not like the last time.

Taking a deep breath, he steadies himself inwardly, outwardly, in every possible respect. 'Yes, I went for a few beers with Phil Meadows and some others from chambers.'

His dad snorts at the mention of Phil's name as always, but he doesn't ask more nor tear his eyes from the view.

'It was good of them to come out and make a fuss of me.' Though appalled at his own neediness, Jack continues to speak doggedly, wanting a little praise, just for once. 'And before that Cranston hosted a champagne get-together in chambers and said a few words.'

His dad makes a 'hum' sound, so he stumbles on. 'It was really heartwarming. Cranston was nice. Said complimentary things. Called me the "young pretender".'

Briefly turning, his dad frowns, so Jack elaborates calmly, even though he wants to stand up and shout very loud.

'You know – with me being the youngest barrister in chambers to take silk. Cranston likes to mention it whenever he gets the opportunity, bless him. I think he's actually quite proud of me.' He grits his teeth. 'I did explain it before, Dad.'

'That's right, you did.' His father drags his gaze from the course and pats Jack's shoulder. 'That one's down to your old man. You were reluctant to apply but it was me who told you that—'

'Hayden!' A voice interrupts. 'How's the old hip?'

'Fogie!'

With a beaming smile, his father greets his golf buddy Gary Fogleman. 'Less of the old. The new hip is settling in by the hour.' He cups his fist in his other palm to demonstrate. 'A perfect fit like a driver in a snug-fitting sock. Marvellous surgeon. You'd better look out; I slipped him a tenner for an even better swing...'

Fogie pretends to hit a shot. 'Ah, but how about your slice?'

The two men continue their golf analogies for several minutes, so Jack zones out. He comes back to the present when he hears his name.

'Jack? Well done on your promotion, lad.' Fogie takes his hand and shakes it firmly. 'Never seen your dad look so pleased as when he told me and the missus. First time applying and youngest QC in chambers, eh?'

He turns to his old friend. '"Badge of excellence with global credibility". Think that's how you put it, eh Hayden?' He reverts to Jack. 'Seriously, though, well done, lad. Dawn's nephew tried several times and even then he was in his fifties. Fabulous achievement. Like your dad says, hard work and dedication pays. No wonder he's so damned proud.'

Jack nods and smiles thinly. Sure; good old Hayden likes to brag about his eldest son's achievements to others, but can't quite manage to say anything to his face. But he really shouldn't moan; look at poor Hugh, always spoken about as though he's not in the room.

'He's thirty-six; he needs to grow up. Just like he needs to stop lazing around the house doing nothing all day. He needs to get a job and for once hold it down.'

A lecturing tone one minute, bangs and fizzles and splutters the next. Not just from the fireworks outside, but from the man's own windpipe.

With a deep sigh, Jack pushes the memory away. Yet the image of Hugh's white-knuckled hands still persists.

Chapter Eight

Serena

Similar to when she was pregnant, the aroma of fresh coffee turns Serena's stomach. Ignoring the unavoidable rush of fear, she breathes deeply from her diaphragm and continues to unload the dishwasher. It's a Monday, day three, but it feels like she's been here for weeks. The back door is open, the breeze and Lana's chatter are fluttering in. Though it's still icy cold, she's pleased her daughter is out in the fresh air, walking the dog around the yard on her lead.

Stilling, she listens to her high, happy voice. 'Shall we play house again today?' she's asking Lexie. 'Do you want to be Mummy or the baby this time?'

A pause as though listening to a reply. 'OK. I'll be a nice mummy, I promise.' Then, 'Yes, mine's a panda bear called Panda.'

Noting the absence of a 'daddy', Serena stands upright and rotates her shoulders to relieve the tension still there from the weekend. Her stiff blouse chafes her chest, but she resists the urge to scratch it. She shakes her head and smiles faintly. So many things to worry about: Daddy, discomfort and stress; safety and alarm. At least the latter is assuaged, well, sort of. The stranger from Friday night wasn't a ghoul, a flashback or child snatcher; it was Jack, the moody older son who lives with Mr Ramsay, when he's not working away, at least. Hugh, it seems, lives somewhere in the village.

From the vantage of the cottage dormer, she saw Jack climb into a taxi at half past six yesterday, apparently going into work on a Sunday. Though he did the same again this morning with a wheeled suitcase, she doesn't know a great deal more about him or the family dynamics. According to Hayden, he's a barrister, and will be working in Leeds all this week. And she's glad about that. He unsettles her, that man. Once they'd manoeuvred his father down the final few stairs on Saturday morning, he dragged that intense gaze from Lana and glowered at her. Though the usual dread hit her belly, she tried for a brisk but pleasant stance, holding out her hand and introducing herself. He took it but barely concealed his hostility.

'I'll get my own later,' he grunted when she asked what he and his father would like for breakfast.

The ill feeling had lifted as soon as he left the kitchen. Hayden settled himself at the table and twitched his lips. 'How are you at bacon and eggs sunny side up?' he asked.

She returned the smile. 'Excellent, as it happens.'

He invited Lana to explore the house, then chatted about the headline news, the inclement weather and other miscellaneous matters until she couldn't bear it any longer. A trial period of a month, then a mutual review of terms thereafter, he'd said on the telephone. It was sketchy, for sure, but the offer of accommodation had nailed it. But now she was here, she needed to know where she stood; she had to pin him down. 'May I ask what my housekeeping duties are, please?' she asked him.

'This fry-up's a good start,' he replied, a hint of northern vowels piercing his eloquent deep tones. Then he looked at her face and seemed to know she required more. 'Carte blanche, Serena. Whatever you feel needs doing.' He gestured to his hip. 'Running the house while this old bugger mends.'

She now looks through the window and sighs. 'Carte blanche' didn't help a great deal, but he and Jack left soon afterwards, so she was able to breathe through the rising panic, find Lana on the bottom rung of the staircase, then stroll down the panelled hall, taking in the musty grandeur of the downstairs, the portraits of pale ancestors and glossy horses, the elaborate light fittings and frames.

Of course she'd already seen the magnificent room at the rear with its 'triple aspect' view, but she also peeped into a book-lined study. Sensing it was Jack's workplace, she didn't step in, but spent a few moments at the door, noting the dusty bookshelves and smeared sash window. Her hand over her mouth to hide her giggle, Lana tugged her into a cloakroom. It housed an antique toilet, complete with a chain and a sink with cabriole legs. Then there was the formal dining room, shuttered and dark. Though undoubtedly handsome with its mahogany period pieces, it felt cold, dank and unused. Glad to escape the goosebumpy feeling, they finally found what Hugh had described as the 'snug', a homely sitting room with a low-beamed ceiling and soft leather sofas, a pretty canopied fireplace and a second door, which was locked.

After their tour, Serena returned to the kitchen table and made a note of the obvious chores, cleaning all the window panes included. Like an oracle, or perhaps the National Trust's *Manual of Housekeeping*, she's been using it for reference since. She now studies it again. Meals, naturally. Laundry and cleaning, bathrooms and toilets. Dusting everywhere, including beneath the fragile antiques.

She sits back. In truth it feels daunting, a million miles away from her training. But that was a lifetime ago. She lifts her chin. Embracing her new role is the thing. Or at least playing the part. Firstly, her employer's lunch. He said half past twelve, but she made it half an hour ago, just in case he rang his little bell earlier. Silly though it is, it feels important to be ready an iota before the jingle demands her.

Reassured by the distant echo of Lana's laughter, she carries her master's tray down the shadowy corridor. The double doors of the drawing room are open, but still she taps on the glass before entering.

'Are you ready for your sandwich, Mr Ramsay?'

Sat in his usual armchair, he closes his laptop and takes off his glasses. 'I am, thank you. Please call me Hayden.' He lifts his pale eyebrows. 'I asked you before.' And though he says it nicely, her stomach clenches.

She places the food on his side table. 'Of course. Anything else I can get you for now?' She smiles and adds, 'Hayden.'

He studies her for a beat. 'Yes, five minutes of your company would be pleasant. I usually read the newspaper with my lunch but…' He gestures to the pile on the floor. 'I'm pretty much up to date, so it would be nice to have a chat.'

'Of course.'

A *chat*. About what? Hoping her alarm doesn't show, Serena perches on the sofa and watches the orange and red ribbons of fire spit and sizzle in the grate. The imagery takes her back in time, so she focuses on her breathing.

Hayden's deep voice breaks the moment. 'How's it going so far?'

'Fine...' Realising she's put a protective hand to her chest, she lowers it to her lap. 'Very well, thank you.'

'Found where everything's hidden in the kitchen cupboards and elsewhere?' His expression seems amused. 'As well as the ancient secrets, rotting bones and stolen gems, of course.'

Unsure how to respond, she nods.

Chuckling, he flexes his fingers. 'Hands all intact, so I can still manage the online shopping myself. Shout if there's anything you need. Delicacies, detergents, toiletries. Or even better, make me a list.' He cocks his head. 'You and Lana might have favourites you particularly like. Our kitchen is yours while you're here.'

Stupidly relieved that food is officially included, she nods again. 'It was the first thing Hugh asked Lana – her favourites. He's so sweet.'

Hayden frowns and speaks, as though to himself. 'Hugh. His mother died when he was eight. I must remember that.' Then shaking himself back to her, 'Probably my fault as much as anyone's as I became both mother and father. Though I had already been that for quite a while. Perhaps I made too many allowances.' He thinly smiles. 'The benefit of hindsight, eh?'

He leans to a slim drawer, pulls out a thick wallet and rifles through a wad of cash and calling cards. 'Ah, here she is,' he says eventually. He unfolds a rectangle of paper, glances at it for a second, then hands it to her. 'Go on, have a peep,' he says, his eyes glistening.

Though blemished by the creases, it's a photograph of three couples. Serena peers at the bride and groom, confused for a moment, but Hayden speaks again. 'That's Lucinda and me on the left at the Fogleman's wedding. A beauty, eh?'

She tries not to show her surprise. Not their wedding, but someone else's... How odd not to keep a memento of his own. But perhaps it's a particularly good snap of his wife? She studies it more closely. Though she can't make out the fair-headed woman that clearly, she smiles. 'Yes, a very handsome couple.'

'Indeed,' he says, replacing it. Then, as though the sudden intermission hasn't happened, he lifts a corner of his bread. 'Wholemeal; excellent. So what have we got here?'

'You said to surprise you, so I have.'

'Excellent.' He throws back his head and laughs. 'Excellent. I'm going to enjoy having you here.' He takes a bite of his sandwich and swallows. 'Tuna and sweetcorn with a hint of onion, if I'm not mistaken. Delicious. Oh, yes, I've just remembered. A chap's going to bob by later for a couple of pieces to renovate. Marvellous craftsman. Only a writing box and a beautiful Queen Anne table that have seen better days.' He nods to his crutches. 'I'm not quite up to lugging them around yet.' He leans forward with a mock conspiratorial expression. 'If I tell you where the treasure is hidden, will you do the honours for me?'

–

Feeling the usual rush of guilt, Serena watches her daughter at the kitchen table. Her head down, she's working bright shades of waxy green into her colouring pad. She's not due to start infant school yet, but most kids her age would be playing, hopping, skipping and dancing at a nursery or playgroup. Not stuck with their mum in a Georgian time warp.

She laughs at the expression. 'Time warp' it is indeed, or at least a hybrid. Part functional, modern and living in the moment; part ghostly, isolated and stuck in the unspoken past. But she understands that more than anyone; in many ways coming here was a marriage made in heaven.

She peeps at Lana's drawing. Two blonde stick people surrounded by hedges.

'Is that us in the maze?' she asks.

So absorbed, Lana doesn't reply, so she lightly pulls her thin ponytail. 'That's a nice pink scrunchie, little miss. Where did you find that?'

Smiling, Lana covers her mouth, then taps at the picture. Sure enough, one stick lady has pink bobbles in her hair.

Leaving Lana engrossed in her artwork, Serena puts her cleaning equipment in a bucket and quietly climbs the stairs. The toilets and bathrooms are on her memo as a daily task from today onwards, but still she feels furtive. Perhaps it's because she hasn't been up here before.

Sensing someone right behind her, she spins around on the landing. 'Lana?' she asks.

No one is there. Stepping back to the stairs, she looks down and listens. Silly Serena. It's just her imagination; she can hear Lana's chatter from the kitchen. Could it be Hayden? Well, that's a stupid thought. Besides being incapacitated by a broken hip, he was napping when she cleared his lunch tray only minutes ago. Why she has the sensation of being watched, she doesn't know. But that isn't strictly true. It's memory, isn't it? Echoes of the past playing tricks.

Shaking the discomfort away, she moves to an open door and pops her head in. The main bathroom. Save for a sprinkling of dust in the four-legged bath and the two matching sinks, it clearly hasn't been used for some time. Hardly surprising; most of the bedrooms will have an en suite in a house of this size. She counts the doors on the oak-panelled corridor. Eight. A lot of space for only two occupants. The master of the house and his adult son. How old must Jack be? She hasn't seen him close enough to really judge, but Hugh told Lana he was thirty-six in that sweet way he has of swapping information 'Which fruit is your favourite, Lana? Mine is banana.' 'What music do you like? I love Oasis.' 'What month is your birthday? Mine's in June.' 'How old are you, Lana? I'm thirty-six.'

She inhales deeply. Thirty-six; same age as *him* the first time they met. Older than her but so handsome, polished and attentive, maintaining just enough eye contact to show he was interested in her and only her. Plucking her from the doldrums of a long term relationship break-up, making her feel special and wanted, attractive and interesting, the absolute centre of his world, exactly when she'd needed it.

Love-bombing, in short.

Snorting to herself, she gazes at the shower. So deeply attracted to him, she couldn't wait to see him naked, to feel his hard body in hers. Yet even that first time of sizzling passion, he'd stopped their embraces to take a shower. Then invited her to do the same. She gently taps her head against the glass cubicle. God, she should have known. She really should have known.

A sudden clunking noise prods her back to the echoey old house. Though she knows it's just a geriatric pipe doing its thing, she still glances over her shoulder. Chuckling out loud, she shakes her head. Living human beings are far more dangerous than ghosts; there's no one here but her and it's time to crack on with her duties.

Buffing up the bathroom doesn't take long, so she makes her way to the room at the far end of the landing. She knocks like she politely rapped all those years ago in Gstaad. She and Rhona had gone there the summer before uni, paying their way by cleaning rich people's chalets. Was it preparation for this? Though a less exotic location, Ramsay Hall also has a wintry setting and clearly wealthy folk.

The grand title of 'housekeeper'. Bloody hell; how her young self would have laughed at the thought.

Having waited long enough for a reply, she finally enters and takes in the huge corner suite. The rafters are painted and four panelled casements are framed by extravagant drapes. She turns to an entire wall of handsome fitted wardrobes. An elegant dressing table centres it. The master bedroom, surely? Yes, Hayden and his wife's, the beauty who died when Hugh was eight. She quickly does the maths. Oh God, poor boys, poor Hayden. They have been motherless and he's been a widower for nearly thirty years.

Picturing the petite blonde in the photograph, she glances around the room. There's no evidence of her here, nor anywhere else in the house, now she thinks of it. How strange that Hayden should keep the one image in his wallet. Next to his heart when he wore a jacket? Feeling a wave of sadness for him, she steps to the bed, plumps up the pillows, shakes out the duvet and smooths it with soft hands. She then turns to the chintz sofa, bashing out the dents in the cushions and lining them diamond-wise down its length.

She pauses at a window, looks out to the frosted maze and overgrown tennis court, then opens a latch to let in fresh air. At the bathroom door she taps again, waiting for a moment before turning the handle. Like the bedroom, the old beams are disguised. But then again, they'd look odd in something so astonishingly modern – a walk-in shower and sunken bath, bright LED spotlights, a mirror taking up a whole side.

Trying not to glimpse her reflection, she applies a glass-cleaning product and rubs it with a leather. Yet of course seeing the *she* she's become is unavoidable, someone she struggles to recognise, even now. She stops and stares for a beat. Prim, proper and efficient, yet still like a rabbit caught in the headlights.

Moving on to the sink, she reaches to close the cabinet above it. But the small bottles, boxes and blister packets catch her eyes. Tramadol and codeine. Zopiclone, zolpidem, nitrazepam, diazepam. She stands back in surprise.

Bloody hell. Not just pain killers, but enough sleeping pills to incapacitate an army.

Chapter Nine

Hugh

The wind grating his cheeks, Hugh pulls the tractor from the shed and heads towards the rimy fields. He likes this part of the job, the freedom, the space, the thrumming sound of the engine, the comforting vibration beneath him. He loves the long hours alone with his thoughts because he doesn't have any. Mostly anyway. But the sudden change at Ramsay Hall has thrown him and it's in his head far too much. He promised Jack, so he's popped in every day after work as normal this week. Serena and the kid are still around, and he likes them well enough, but why are they there? 'Don't over think things, Hugh,' Jack always says. 'Sometimes it's just better to let go of whatever's bugging you. You only end up hurting yourself. Know what I mean?'

He met his brother on Sunday night for a half in The Bull. He'd intended to keep his worries inside, but they popped out as usual.

'Serena and Lana. Why are they here, Jack? Dad says it's to help, but what does he really mean?'

But instead of giving him a firm answer, Jack sighed and said, 'Who bloody knows?', with flickering eyes. Only when he was leaving did he take him by the shoulders, look at him solidly and say, 'It's nothing for you to worry about, so don't. OK, Hugh?'

Trying to shake the angst away, he now turns right up a bumpy track and concentrates on Mr Barnes's instructions for the '*foreseeable*', as the farmer always says. He's known him for years and should call him Stuart, but old childhood habits die hard. What did *Stuart* Barnes say?

That's right. He repeats it under his breath. 'Divide the back pasture into three for rotation; turn the manure pile.'

What else? There was more. What else did he say? That's what nerves do; they make him forgetful. When he first started here in November, he'd whispered Mr Barnes's 'job description' to himself so often that he'd learned it by heart: '*Tractor driving and cleaning, general handiwork, tending to the livestock, ploughing, planting and harvesting crops. Then there's basic maintenance and repair work on vehicles, machinery, fences, gates and walls. Is that all right, lad?*'

He'd liked the word 'lad'. He'd liked the farmer's rough hands and warm eyes.

Sighing with relief, he remembers the rest of this week's tasks and mouths them.

'Spray the cereal crops and if you get time, pick up and haul away the scrap metal from the far yard. I can sell that. No hurry though, lad, and keep an eye on your mobile in case your dad needs you.'

In case his dad needs him. Hmm, no chance of that. The usual 'hopeless', 'lazy' and 'stupid', more like. Still, he's earning 'his keep'. Unlike his father, *he* has a job.

–

Hugh is numb with cold by lunch time, so the warmth of the kitchen hits his hands and face like a sauna.

He sniffs today's delicious food aromas. Goat's milk and puff pastry. Excellent.

Jess is at the oven door, peering in. 'Hiya,' she says, tentatively touching a sausage roll on the tray. 'Two more minutes,' she says, slotting them back in. She turns to him. 'Hugh! You look flipping freezing. Shouldn't you be wearing something warmer? Look at your fingers, they're blue!'

She tugs him to the sink, turns on the tap and tests the water. Her scent reminds him of parma violets as usual. 'Lukewarm is best. Keep them under there until they work again.' She tuts. 'You should be wearing gloves, Hugh. Dad has a thousand spare ones. I'll find you a pair for this afternoon.'

Hugh does as he's told. He has a fond spot for Jess, especially when she takes charge. Others might consider her bossy, he knows, but he likes the way she has no fear of touching him, pulling him this way and that. He loves her caring eyes and easy laugh.

He watches the water splash his skin. It might be 'lukewarm' but his knuckles sharply sting. As though she knows, Jess gently takes his hands into hers and pats them dry with a tea towel from the radiator. Then she unzips his jacket and tuts again.

'You should be wearing layers of clothing, Hugh. Nice though it is, a designer sweatshirt doesn't do it. Light layers trap the warm air. Two pairs of socks too.'

Though she's so much shorter than him, he can smell her sweet toasty breath. 'Teach you this in Agricultural College, do they?' he asks with a grin.

'Cheeky devil,' she replies, pushing him to the table and sitting him down by the shoulders. 'Common sense, more like. Tea's in the pot.'

Itching to turn off the disco rubbish she's listening to on the radio, he pours the strong brew and observes her pick the hot rolls from the baking tray with expert fingers. Yup, he's always liked Jess; though she's still in her twenties, she has 'mothering ways', according to Jack. He gets that. It's how he imagines his own mother might have been. Tactile, fussy, loving. Of course he should remember his mum, but he can't. Sometimes he really tries, but Jack tells him not to bother. 'The memories will come when they're ready,' he says. 'No point in trying to force them.'

Dragging out an old stool, Jess joins him at the table and nibbles the flaky pastry. She's a little overweight but she has small and neat teeth like their old border terrier.

'These are from the new place in the village. Not as nice as Mum's, but not bad,' she comments. She lifts her eyebrows. 'But hers were the best, so... Come on, eat up while they're warm. There's also—'

'Don't you feel sad?' The words are out before he can stop them.

Shit, he didn't *think* before speaking, but Jess doesn't seem to mind. Though her eyes are shiny like wet pebbles, she smiles.

'Course I do. We're all really sorrowful. But it was horrible to see her suffering like that. It was a relief for us all, if I'm honest, Mum in particular, I'm sure. I really miss her, but I try to think about all the happy times we had.'

She plucks a tissue from her sleeve and blows her nose loudly. 'Besides, there's nothing we can do to bring her back and the bakery's stuff isn't too bad, so eat up!'

Hugh nods and pictures the ripple of *something* which passes through Jack's gaze on the rare occasions their mother is mentioned. And the word 'suffering' rings a bell, an uneasy chime he doesn't like. But Jess's still talking, thank God.

'…given up flipping meat. I'm not making separate meals just for him, so he can stick with the veg or feast on bread and soup.' She glances at the sink. 'Or goat's cheese; we've plenty of that.'

'Sorry, what?' He shakes himself back to Jess's look of mild irritation. The word finally lands. 'A vegetarian?'

Hugh shifts in his seat. Really? Mr Barnes has become a *veggie*? Ah, perhaps it's because goat's milk has higher levels of calcium. Yup, he mentioned that the other day, but in all honesty Hugh likes his meat very much, can't imagine meals without it.

He swallows. 'Oh, right. So if your dad's become a veggie, does that mean we all have to…?'

Jess rolls her pretty brown eyes. '*Dad?* As if. No. Didn't you hear the shocking news? After all this time, Robbie's decided to come home.'

Chapter Ten

Jack

Jack leaves the robing room and stifles a yawn. Underlying his tiredness he's hungry, he knows; he worked on documents all through the lunch break, he should really get food. He snorts at the thought of what he constantly tells Hugh about eating regularly, but preachers rarely teach themselves and he just needs to lie down for an hour, close his eyes and think of nothing. Maybe he'll take up the offer of dinner with Jamal later. He knows him from way back at Bar school and he's funny, easy company after another dour day in court number two.

The only problem is Jamal's instructing solicitor, Wanda. Will he invite her too?

The dull pain easing from his lower back, he hops down the court steps and heads towards the traffic lights to cross the chock-a-block road. It's only a nine-minute walk to the Premier Inn. The 'guarantee' of a good night's sleep didn't happen, but the hotel is clean with decent WiFi. In the end he decided not to commute between Leeds and Goostrey; though the inevitable pang of self-reproach was there and still is, it's easier to stay away – his dad, his pill cabinet, his brother, the new bloody woman. Not just her, but that quiet little girl, those innocent and beguiling huge eyes.

Blinking away the stirring image, he abruptly stops and pats his jacket pockets. Oh hell, he's left his mobile in the locker. He could leave it and use his laptop tonight, but it's his lifeline to Hugh. Or more accurately, his brother's lifeline to him. Hugh can message if he needs to, but it takes him too long and by then his current worry will have spiralled, sometimes out of control. Far easier to speak, talk it through on the phone. Like last night and this morning. Like tonight, no doubt.

Turning back to the red-brick building, he stares at the monstrosity. A combined court centre like so many others in large cities. Modern and soulless and scored with graffiti. The artwork takes him back to Hugh's breathless conversation last night. Did Jack know Robbie Barnes had returned from Australia? Everyone seemed to know except him.

Jack shakes his head at the thought. Tagger, tearaway, trouble-maker, bad bloody influence and Hugh's only close childhood friend from *back then*. Closing his eyes, he blows that particular problem away. It'll be fine. Robbie went 'travelling' barely out of his school shorts; he's a grown man now. Memories fade, things change, feelings too.

He sighs. Hugh. Once Robbie had gone, he rekindled some friendships with boys from King's; they'd turn up in their smart cars and hang out in the games room, but by the time he hit eighteen or nineteen, they seemed to vanish from both the house and his life. God knows why. University maybe, but whatever the reason, it left his brother a loner.

Yup, he must keep a careful eye on Hugh, check he stays steady. Get him back living at home for a start.

An angry exchange of car horns reverberating from behind, he heads up the steps two by two. Nearly colliding with a gowned usher coming out, he slips into the revolving entrance a fraction too late and it stops moving. Aware of the flash of annoyance from a person stuck opposite, he lifts his hand to apologise.

'Sorry,' he says through the glass. Then, when he sees who it is, 'Oh hi. Thought I saw you earlier with…'

The door moves again, parting their gaze. For a moment he stands motionless in the foyer. He could just walk on without looking her way, but that would be cowardly. And rude. He steps back to the entry and follows her out.

'Wanda?' he calls.

She turns. Dark-haired, dark-eyed and young. God, she's young. Far too bloody young. What the hell is he doing? He should just have left it. 'Hi. Thought I saw you earlier with Jamal.'

Her expression non-committal, she nods. 'Yes. Our closing submissions finished today, thank God. Judgment tomorrow if we're lucky.' She moves away. 'Nice to see you again, Jack. I'm off to dictate my notes then have a Netflix and crisps fest for the rest of the evening.'

He feels rotten. He should have got in touch; he treated her badly, made her feel she'd done something wrong. An image flashes in of her slim, child-like body, her small and pert breasts. Why the desire was there back then, he can't say. He feels nothing today other than remorse and shame.

He tries for a smile. 'Any particular recommendations?'

'Sweet chilli Sensations.'

'Sounds like a rom-com.' He pictures his dad's old LP and laughs. 'Or maybe a seventies soul band.'

Wanda lifts her palms. 'Seventies? What's that then?'

He grins. 'Touché.' Then taking a quick breath, 'Look, the last time we met… It ended badly and I wanted to say—'

'It's fine,' she says, cutting in quickly. Her eyes cloud. 'It's completely forgotten.' She half smiles. 'Sorry, I'm really, really knackered. Beauty sleep and all that, so… Bye then.'

'Good luck with the judgment tomorrow.'

Trudging back to the robing room, Jack sighs. No atonement there then. He was foolish to try.

—

Jack listens to Jamal's theatrical monologue. He's describing his day in court and taking the piss out of his co-counsel's slight stutter. He should be more careful; they're in a busy Italian restaurant and walls have ears. He pushes the rest of his Cappelletti to the side and puts down his fork. His stomach's so leaden it feels as though he's swallowed his meal without chewing, the beautifully shaped pasta bowl included. Agitation as usual. Why can't he be more like his dad? He'd like to stop picking at the past. Like a boy with a scab, he mithers the crusty flesh, pulling it off before it's healed and making it weep. Pushing the wheel of the bloody vicious circle instead of leaving it alone.

Time heals, as his dad would say. Only it doesn't.

Sipping his sparkling water, he looks around the table. Five barristers tonight, but even he gets fed up with the incessant 'in talking' at times.

The vibration of his mobile makes him jump. He peers at the screen. It's Hugh. 'Excuse me,' he says to no one in particular. 'I need to take this call.'

Half listening to his brother's chatter, he inhales the smell of cigarette smoke and paces beneath the restaurant canopy. Then he stops and stares at the flurry of snow falling from the night sky. It has settled on the ground, a neat white carpet, patterned by footprints.

He feels his heart clench. Snow. How beautiful his boyhood winters were when covered in white. He pictures himself and Hugh in the bedroom, yanking open the curtains. Snowflakes! A glorious fluffy covering everywhere. Fumbling with zips, wellies and mittens, tumbling outside; crunching through the endless virgin fields towards the merging sky before looking back to their home, the pretty Christmas lights in the windows, and their even prettier mother framed like a painting. It's on the tip of his tongue to mention it to Hugh, to say, 'do you remember the last Christmas before Mum became ill? It was magical, wasn't it?'

But there's no point asking and he isn't even sure if the image is real or just his desperate imagination. Telling Hugh he has to go, he sniffs back the emotion. Same as the white sheets covering his sofa in the cottage, it's best to let the heavens smother the past and forget it.

Chapter Eleven

Hugh

Hugh blows on the murky glass and rubs it with his sleeve but the mist doesn't clear. Oh, right. It's just a hazy and cold early morning. He kneads his goosepimpled arms. Freezing, in fact.

Jess invited him into the farmhouse last night. She tapped on the caravan door at midnight.

'Do you want to come into the house?' she asked. 'Robbie won't be home until tomorrow, so you might as well take advantage of a warm bed while you can.' She stepped into the van. 'You really should, Hugh, it's bitter in here.'

He didn't feel the chill right then; he was still warm from the pub and four pints. The usual spirit chasers too, but he knew not mention them.

'Thanks but I'm...'

Jess didn't let him finish. Instead she said, 'You're all the same, bloody stubborn men! Don't go to sleep yet. I'll bring you a hot water bottle.'

It gave him time for another slug of whisky from his flask, time to *think* before he asked the question which had been bubbling and burning and worrying him all day.

'Why is Robbie coming home?' he blurted when she finally returned.

'Only heaven knows,' she replied and pressed her lips like a duck. Whatever that meant, she didn't elaborate further.

He now dresses quickly and opens the door. A cloud of his breath billows out. He barely slept a wink for pondering teenage times with Robbie Barnes. The swigging of *anything* alcoholic going; the petty theft; the graffiti; the two of them hurtling through woods and fields on the quad bike; smoking pot around a bonfire and staring up at the stars which pierced the black sky. The fun, the laughs, the bloody exhilaration of it all.

And his father's astonishing anger.

Carrying his work boots, he hops over the icy grass to the path. The light's on in the kitchen so he takes a quick breath and walks in.

There's a satisfying sizzle from the hob. It's nearly as beautiful a sound as the start to 'Champagne Supernova'. But only nearly. He deeply inhales the pungent smell. Fantastic; it's bacon, the best start to any day.

'Butty?' Jess asks without turning round. Then when she does, 'Hugh! What are you like? Your socks will be wet.'

'Ah.' He looks down. 'Thought it'd save me from having to remove my Dickies at the door...'

His voice comes out too la-di-da as usual. Sure, the Ramsays have been around for generations, benefactors as well as owning much of the village farmland, so he understands that some people think he's stuck up or a class apart. He got used to the 'posh boy' jibes from the locals growing up, but he wishes he didn't sound like that here.

When Jess disappears, he drags his gaze around the rest of the room. No Robbie yet, but Mr Barnes is at the table, slumped over a mug of tea. He's usually friendly of a morning but today he catches Hugh's eye and makes a single grunting sound before going back to his drink. 'Morning', Hugh supposes the mumble must mean, so he says the same back.

'Here you go,' Jess says when she returns. She hands him a pair of woolly socks which look as though they've been knitted by someone's blind grandma. 'Go on then,' she says, holding out her hand for the damp pair. 'Take them off. Someone needs to stop you from getting frost-bite.'

What? Not his favourite pair. Well, one of a set with embroidered designer logos. Wondering if he'll ever see them again, he stalls for a moment, but Jess returns to the frying pan. She stabs several slices of bacon and roughly shoves them into a floury bap. Best do as he's told.

'Here you go then,' she says, handing him a plate. 'Let's do a swap.'

He strips off the socks. 'Cheers.'

He eyes Mr Barnes as he eats. He seems very quiet today. When his dad goes silent it's a sign that he's angry. Jack says to keep schtum and let it pass, but it's usually him, 'stupid Hugh', that's caused it in the first place. Saying or doing something wrong. Or just bloody breathing. But if his dad doesn't *say* why he's annoyed, how's he supposed to know? So sometimes he asks and his dad goes ballistic. Or did.

Jess sits next to him, opens her bread roll and squeezes a huge dollop of HP sauce on her meat. Remembering how Robbie always did exactly that, he can't help today's vital question from popping out: 'When will Robbie be back?'

His chair making a loud screech, Mr Barnes abruptly stands. 'Who knows? Robbie's a law unto himself. He's always done exactly what he wants to do. We don't get a look in.' He stares through Hugh, his grey eyebrows knitting. His focus eventually returns. 'Come on lad, socks and boots on. It's a new day and that muck needs turning.'

–

Trying to space out, Hugh drives the tractor up and down the far field. That's what Jack used to call it. 'Stop spacing out, Hugh and listen'. But now he seems to approve of it. 'Like a mindfulness expert, you are,' he'll say. 'Living in the present, cutting out the noise of the past. I wish I could do it.'

But it's not happening today. It only works if he doesn't try. If he *tries*, he just gets stressed, then he starts thinking too much. Like now. Robbie Barnes, Robbie Barnes. Last time he saw Robbie was in the back of a police van.

Thrown back to the past, he scans the horizon, searching for the dry stone wall they'd crashed into for a lark. On that fateful day, they'd finally finished rebuilding it. Not just the one they'd partly demolished on the quad bike, but all those that needed attention. That was Mr Barnes's punishment. Unpaid work for '*being so bloody daft*'. It had taken them from daybreak to dusk, trudging the fields, carrying and fetching, lifting and chipping away at the heavy stones. Their limbs had ached and their hands were sore but they'd had a good laugh.

'Know what we need now?' Robbie had asked as they hobbled back to the farmhouse.

'A hot bath?' Hugh'd replied, wondering how he'd manage the mile hike to Ramsay Hall.

'Nah, a bender,' Robbie had said. 'We deserve to get pissed, very pissed.'

No money, of course, so they'd 'improvised', as Robbie put it, Hugh distracting Mr Kumar at the convenience store till whilst Robbie helped himself to an armful of crisp packets and a half bottle of vodka, then casually sauntering out. The fiery liquid hadn't lasted long.

'Plenty to drink at my place,' Hugh had said, so they'd ad-libbed again by flagging a taxi, then doing a runner when the cab stopped at Blackden junction.

Finding free booze at home hadn't been a problem. Hugh hadn't even had to look far – his father's 'cooking' brandy was in the larder, ripe for the taking, and there was some expensive gin in the fridge. Still, he knew to keep quiet, so they'd tiptoed from the house down the drive to the games room, played several rounds of pool as they took turns to swig the spirits, then they'd retreated, heavy-limbed, to the barn. That's where his dad had found them, half asleep.

Now feeling the heat rise again, Hugh spins the tractor wheel. His dad, his bloody dad. He can still picture him now, his face white with fury as he'd spat the words: 'Stealing from a village shop. Not paying a local taxi firm. Did you honestly think I wouldn't find out? They are *crimes*, Hugh.' He'd taken a raggedy breath. 'Those crimes are bad enough, but your stupidity is unforgivable. You're a Ramsay; you're known. Bloody unforgivable. And this? I can't bear to look at you. Get out of my sight. Now. Go on, get out of my sight.'

Groggy from the alcohol, he and Robbie had tumbled off the straw and staggered into the yard. A police van was waiting, its rear doors open wide. The shock had felt like a heavy blow to his stomach. He'd been shopped by his dad. By his own fucking father.

Suddenly aware of sharp hunger pangs, Hugh looks at the time. Hell, it's gone two; he'd better get a move on before Jess starts on her cheese at the sink. If she has, he'll grab some bread and squash it together with salad cream. He's already teetering with annoyance; he needs to eat pretty quickly before he gets really grumpy.

It takes far too long to heave off his boots and wash his muddy hands at the outdoor tap, but finally with a big sigh, he hops over to the farmhouse. The old guy, Samuel, comes out of the dairy and grunts a greeting, so he reaches for a cheery 'hello' in reply. When he steps into the kitchen, a man he doesn't recognise is sitting at the table opposite Mr Barnes. Their stony faces towards their drinks, neither of them speak. Jess is at the hob, but even she doesn't turn, so he shuffles to the bread bin and quietly lifts the lid. Without warning the black knob comes away, the cover crashing down with a loud clang and waking the room.

Everyone seems to speak at once.

'Gosh, I'm so sorry. I didn't know it was broken…'

'Hugh! Can I get you something…'

'You're late in. Hungry, lad?'

And a voice he recognises despite the Aussie twang, 'G'day Hugh; long time no see.'

Chapter Twelve

Jack

The need to pee prods Jack half awake. Registering he's back under his own duvet, he drags himself through the slug of gluey slumber and props himself up. Expecting to see her there, he glances at the sofa. It's empty right now but the soft aroma lingers. Soapy, innocent. Pure.

Wondering where she goes to, he pads to the loo. He's still sleepy, thank God. No need for pills. Drugs make him groggy. More dazed than lack of sleep? That one's still up for debate. But he's OK right now, he can feel unconsciousness pulling him in. He just needs to keep under the radar of wakefulness, shuffle back to bed with almost closed eyes, return to emptiness. Then he'll be fine in the morning, alert and ready for a weekend of intense paperwork. He can do it, he can.

When he returns from the bathroom, he almost reaches the divan but sees he's not alone. There's someone in the middle, unmoving, a statue. Her fair hair spread across the pillow, she's wearing a white nightdress. Though it's still dark, her pale, bony face and her fixed button eyes are lit by a fizzle of fireworks from outside.

Holding his breath, he creeps forward and stares. No breathing, no rasping, no noise. Is she dead? Is she really,

really dead? Then she blinks and his heart almost snaps from his chest.

'Hello darling,' she whispers. 'How's my beautiful boy?'

-

'Sorry, darling, I can't take you today. Mummy's not very well…'

'Sorry, darling, I'll come downstairs later. Mummy's not very well…'

'Sorry, darling, could you pass me a glass of water? Mummy's not very well…'

His mother's voice fades as Jack stirs again to the dull night surrounding him. Propping himself up, he stares at the empty sofa and feels the overwhelming clutch of grief he hasn't had for years. Eleven and twelve, fourteen, sixteen, even twenty, the heavy sorrow was still there, fresh every morning. Mummy is dead, Mummy has gone, not just for today, but forever. But at ten years of age, it was too hard to grasp; she'd been absent for so long, it didn't feel real. He'd run to her bed, *this* bloody bed and had just known she'd be here, her hair splayed on the pillow, her voice slurred and sleepy, that peculiar aroma breezing from her breath.

She'd smile with those teeth which seemed to rot more each day. 'Hello darling, my lovely, handsome boy. I'm going to get up later and see what you and Hughie are up to. No, really. I want to dance! Don't shake your head, I'll surprise you, just you see.'

And occasionally she did, appearing silently in the snug and watching them play with eyes far too big for her face.

'Mummy!' they'd say, crowding her. 'Come and see what I've built!' 'Let's colour this farm!' 'Please stay and watch some TV.' 'Can we read my new book?'

But the joy was soon dashed. The effort was too much. Lucinda's trembling fingers couldn't slot a building brick into place, colour to the edges, even turn the page, let alone dance. Her tears would soon come, then she'd touch their faces and stroke their hair with desperate hands, pleading for forgiveness.

'Jackie, darling. Hughie? Hughie, listen. I know I'm a bad mummy right now, but I'm not very well. I'm so sorry, so sorry. I just need to lie down.'

Then their dad would appear and shake his head, not unkindly. 'Come on darling, good try but back to bed,' he'd comment, lifting her like a soft dolly and carrying her away. 'Wish the boys night, night,' he'd say at the door, but all they'd hear was her whining voice echo back. 'I'm so, so unhappy, Hayden. You have no idea. So very unhappy and unwell. Please give me something to make it stop.'

The tears now seeping, Jack covers his face with trembling hands. Is he really back there? Back in that dark, dismal place? Like his mum before him, does he still feel that need to make everything stop?

–

Finally waking to morning, Jack throws back the covers and stalks to the bathroom. So much for a night of deep, peaceful sleep.

He stares at his hollow, weary face in the mirror. Bloody hell, what a sight. His disturbed night was hardly surprising, though. After brokering a decent settlement of his trial in Leeds yesterday, he returned to chambers and worked until midnight. Unbelievably knackered, he eventually arrived home and came straight to his bedroom. He was ready, willing and desperate to sleep, but even before he glanced at the sofa, the lingering smell of cleaning products alerted him. Someone had been in there; that bloody 'housekeeper' had been there. Yes, she'd straightened the cushions and bedding, cleaned the bathroom, neatened his books. Bloody opened the window...

He immediately checked his bottom drawer and it hadn't been disturbed, but he still wasted valuable sleeping time by looking for another, more private, hiding place. Then he went to bed angry, picturing the wretched woman crossing the courtyard in her nightdress, her hair wild like his mum's. Then he visualised her sweet, innocent daughter and felt nothing but cold hopelessness.

Stepping into the shower, he roars loudly. What the hell, what the bloody hell? Guilt should fade; time should heal. But instead of getting better, his life's a bloody fuckup.

–

Hungry despite his agitation, Jack scoots down the stairs and follows the breakfast aromas. The sound of talking filters back, so he stops for a moment. The bloody woman, already. His jaw clenching, he shakes his head. It's his home, his kitchen, his food as much as anyone's, for God's sake. But when he storms in, there's just Hugh, kneeling on the floor and chatting to Lexie. He tells her to sit, then turns to him with a frown.

'See how she's sitting? She seems tender on one side.'

Jack crouches too. 'Here girl, let's see.' He softly smooths her flank and she lets out a whimper. 'It's the same as before. Maybe it's her hips already.' He rubs her soft ears and moves on to her chin and her chest, scratching them just as she likes. 'She's a bit too young yet, I'd have thought. Can you mention it to the vet at the—'

'Yeah, yeah I will.' But Hugh's attention has drifted already. He plods himself down at the table and pours cereal to the brim of his bowl.

Jack sits too and sniffs. There's the smell of fresh coffee, fried eggs and toast. 'Where's the woman?'

'She's called Serena,' Hugh says.

'OK, where's Serena?'

'Must have been and disappeared somewhere. Her Renault's gone.'

Hugh pours milk on his cereal but stirs it without eating.

'What's up, Hugh?' Jack asks.

'Robbie's back.'

'Yeah, you said.'

'Saw him yesterday.'

Stepping to the cafetière, Jack pours a cup. 'How was it?'

Hugh puts down his spoon. 'He's old. He's got this long hair.'

Trying to hide his smile, Jack dips his head level with Hugh's. 'How old? About as old as you? Couple of months younger, even?'

'Yeah, but—'

'He's changed? Course he has. We all have. It's called growing up, Hugh. It just feels odd because you haven't seen him for years. Your mental picture of him is how he looked when he left. How old was he then? Eighteen?'

'Seventeen and eleven months, but…'

His eyes catching the steady flurry of snow through the window, Jack sips his coffee and drifts off. Last night's dreams trickle back. What would their mum look like now? He tries to picture her from the good days when her cheeks were still plump and her teeth pearly white, when she'd laugh and 'big dance' to Whitney or Prince, but he can only see the wild-haired woman who opened his bloody window.

He sighs. God, what's wrong with him? Why this deep resentment for someone he doesn't know from Adam? The highlighting of his clear failure to look after his father for starters. Then the intrusion in their home, their lives. As for the cottage, the child…

But Hugh is still speaking.

'No, he's really changed, Jack. His hair used to be short. He liked it cropped short. And he has an accent—'

'An Aussie one? Come on, Hugh, that's no reason to be upset. He's still the person he was, he's still your friend.'

'Yeah, but that's just it.' Hugh shrugs, but the sadness shows in his eyes. 'He isn't anymore.'

Chapter Thirteen

Serena

Unused to wearing a hat, Serena pulls it off as she and her daughter round the last bend towards their current 'home'. Lana's fingers skim the pale red Cheshire brick of the high wall. A large section has clearly been rebuilt, the new blocks a slightly different colour and uneven in one section.

She tuts to herself. There was a time she wouldn't have noticed the absence of perfection. These days she spots it all the time.

'You've mismatched the creases in this sleeve. Surely even you can manage to press a simple shirt?'

Yes: his perfectionism, superiority, entitlement. But mostly his control.

Lana breaks into a skip along the slushy pavement. As ever, she doesn't say much, but it's great to see her carefree. Her eyes glowed when she carefully selected a rainbow of five pence sweets at the newsagent's with the last of Serena's coins, but she didn't stick in a greedy hand and gobble them as soon as she was outside the shop as Serena would have done as a child. Instead, she twisted the top of the paper bag and slipped it in her pocket like a stash of treasure.

'Aren't you going to have one or two now?' Serena asked.

'I'm saving them,' she replied.

'Oh, yes?'

A shy smile. 'I'm going to share them with my friend.'

'Hugh, I'm guessing? Has he told you his favourite one?'

A nod and those cute pulled-in lips.

Yes, she seems content, even happy. Thank God for that.

Trying to ease her tension from top to toe, Serena now stretches. As usual, her jumper chafes her sore chest. Shrugging that worry off, she reverts to another: Hayden's inquisitive gaze. She prepared his breakfast at seven as usual. He thanked her but tilted his head in that benign, eagle-like way he affects when he's curious.

'It's Saturday, remember? Of course you're very welcome to stay here, but you're free to do as you wish at a weekend. See family or friends, go shopping. Perhaps you have plans?'

The 'housekeeper' arrangement has been casual, but she's sure she would have remembered weekends off if he'd mentioned it. Her salary too. How much and when? Will he ask for bank details or pay her in cash? The latter, she hopes. Though she's been working for a week now, she doesn't want to push it too soon.

Feeling the soft spatter of more snowflakes, she looks up to the pale January sky. So, today's her 'day off'. She and Lana have had their expedition to the local village. What to do with the gaping afternoon ahead? Last night she asked Hayden if she could stow the car in the garage to keep it from freezing, so she's pleased to leave it safely there. And anyway, where would she drive? Her real home is two hundred miles away. Or was.

She pictures the lounge in her flat. Facing leather sofas, a soft silver Chinese rug and a plethora of cushions. Even accounting for the dimensions of outer London property, that room alone was larger than the square area of the cottage. *His* place on the other side of the city was spacious too, his bedroom lined with state-of-the-art sliding wardrobes, his thirty plus shirts lined up neatly and colour-coded from white to striped to shades of blue, his Turnbull & Asser ties given a whole section to themselves. She grits her teeth at the image. In the early days of passion he'd spoken of 'home from home', yet even then she'd been allocated a measly single drawer and two coat hangers for her visits.

She remembers that frown. 'Don't you iron anything? You'd look so much nicer if you took care of your clothes.' And that was before she moved in.

Shaking the memory away, she loosens her scarf and gently fingers the hot and tender skin at the base of her neck. Why she's thinking of him again, she doesn't know. What did she promise herself? Onwards and forwards, no looking back. Besides, she's cured, isn't she? Rehabilitated from that weak and pathetic human being who took ridiculous measures to escape his criticism, or even worse, his silence – rubbing the granite and glass surfaces to erase Lana's fingerprints almost hourly; buying a cheese slicer to ensure a flawless edge; throwing out a perfectly acceptable dish of food and starting again from scratch. Giving up all her hobbies, then eventually the few friends she had left. And begging for sex just to feel loved. That's a woman she doesn't recognise anymore, thank God. And perhaps the lack of physical – and emotional – space in his flat was preparation for *this* – living in a doll's house with dolly-sized wardrobes and drawers. Not that she minds; despite being given no keys, she feels safe here, hidden and protected behind this electronic gate.

–

The barrier closes behind them with a final, solid thud. Blemished only by one set of wheel tracks, the driveway is covered by a new dusting of snow.

Lana watches her own footprints make a pattern. 'They look like black fish,' she says. Then, glancing for permission, she gently propels herself forward to slide along the path, past the outbuildings, the bowed plants and startled-looking trees. As she almost topples several times, her laughter pierces the muffled silence.

Hoping no one is watching, Serena steps over to the games room. Leaning forward as much as the thorny bushes will allow, she peers through the panelled windows. A huge pool table centres the space and the beanbags on its perimeter match the brightly coloured dots in the curtains. But it's too tidy, somehow; the heaped boxes and neatly lined bookcases appear unused and forlorn. A shame; she prefers a little cheery chaos. 'But untidiness is happiness', as she once said to *him* before she lost her confidence completely.

She turns back to the handsome house, then rotates a full circle. Attractive outbuildings and pines; fresh and pure air; no neighbours but acres of white smattered green. Such a wonderful place to bring up kids, it seems a dreadful waste there aren't any here. Just a kindly older man and his offspring rattling around the huge farmhouse. One son affable, sweet. And the other? Well, the jury is still out on him. Jack hasn't yet spoken to her and he's avoided eye contact even when they were standing only metres apart. Perhaps that's just as well; when he gazed at Lana for too long, it sent shivers down her spine.

Her stomach rumbles; Lana must be hungry too. Glad she remembered to make up sandwiches at breakfast, she hurries to catch up with her. Anticipating the usual cottage heat, she unzips her jacket, flings off her scarf and trots down the patchwork path.

Almost colliding with her daughter, she comes to a standstill. What's going on? Lana has stopped at the open door like a statue. Anxiety creeping in, she peers over her head. What the hell? Jack Ramsay is in their front room, sitting on the small sofa. His dark eyes flick from Lana's to hers.

The alarm flies out before she can stop it. 'What are you doing in here?'

His expression faltering, he turns to the window. 'I thought you were out. Your car wasn't there.'

Thrown for a moment, she follows his gaze to the small patch of cottage garden. 'It's parked in the garage. It's been really frosty, so...'

Noticing the small footprints in the otherwise pristine patch of white, she steps closer to the pane. Like black fish. Oh God; Lana must have ventured out alone this morning. Though goodness knows when. While she was still sleeping? Or perhaps having a shower. And this man, this stranger...

Trying not to grip too hard, she puts her hands either side of her daughter's shoulders and leads her to the kitchen, then she takes a deep breath and returns to the sitting room. Jack's still there, but he's leaving. Though she hates confrontation, she just has to say it.

'Even if we were out, this is our home.' She lifts her chin. 'You have no right to be in here.'

He shakes his head and steps out of the door. '*You* have no right,' he mutters under his breath.

Feeling a surge of angry heat, she follows him out. 'What's that supposed to mean?' she calls to his back.

He turns, his face pale and tight. 'Don't ever go into my bedroom again. The bedding, the sofa...' He swallows. 'Opening the window; cleaning the bathroom. Stop interfering with my life.'

'Sorry?'

He takes a step towards her. 'Whatever you're doing here, leave me out of it.' He glares for a moment. 'What *are* you doing here?'

She stares, stuck for words. Then the old professional fire tumbles back. 'I'm employed by your father to help out while he's convalescing, as you know. He offered me this cottage and so long as we're here, my daughter and I have a right to privacy. Please don't come in here again.'

He stares at her exposed neck, then he frowns. 'Your girl. How old is she? Why isn't she at school?'

'My child has nothing to do with you.' She tries to cover the panic in her voice. 'She's just tall for her age. She'll be starting in September, as it happens. Not that it's any of your business.' She puts her hand to her chest. 'Please can I have your assurance you'll stay out of my home. If not, I'll have to ask your father for a—'

Jack snorts. 'Do you know, that's actually funny. You'll report me to my—'

'What's going on?' Hugh's striding across the courtyard towards them. 'I heard shouting. Why are you two arguing?'

He looks from her to his brother, but neither reply. Then he points behind them and they turn. Holding onto the door jamb, Lana's gazing, her panda under an elbow, her thumb in her mouth.

Jack stares into the distance before shaking his head. Apparently replaced by remorse, the anger has drained from his face. 'Sorry,' he says. 'I'm so sorry.'

Her heartbeat finally slowing, Serena watches him walk away. She rubs her goosebumped arms. Who on earth was he apologising to? It certainly wasn't her or her daughter.

Chapter Fourteen

Jack

Jack wakes to the echo of shrill shouting. 'Get out, just get out!' Then the usual teary voice. 'Sorry, my darling, you know I don't mean it. Come on Hughie, don't cry. Mummy's just so tired and you should be asleep in your own bed. You know that and you promised the last time...'

Almost expecting to see his little brother next to him now, he flicks his head to the other side of the mattress. The darkness looks back. A dream, just a dream but so very real. He squeezes his eyes and tries to shake off the old memory. Oh God, how Hugh would sob, his whole body convulsing, his face saturated with tears and snot. Then he'd get angry, pounding the pillow with clenched fists.

'Mums are supposed to love their children. All my friends have nice mums. They wait at the school gates and walk home holding hands. Robbie's mum loves him. If he has a nightmare, she lets him sleep in her bed. He *told* me, Jack. He told me, so it's true! Mummy's just mean. She only thinks about herself.'

'Mum's poorly, Hugh, she doesn't want to be mean, but she can't help it...' he'd reply.

But it was said without conviction because he'd felt exactly the same way. No one kissed or cuddled him anymore. Before she was ill, he and his mum used to dance. If ever he was moody or sad, she'd take his hand and say, 'Come on darling boy, don't look so serious; it's not the end of the world. Let's dance!'

How he yearned for that; her laughter and love. He longed for her soft touch and undivided attention far more than the morsels she doled out.

But it wasn't her fault; she was very, very poorly, a mantra he had to repeat both to Hugh and himself. He never dared ask what the illness was, but he knew it was cancer. He'd watched his father give her pills and medicine for the pain often enough, and besides, he'd seen the invasion for himself. The curse had slowly stolen his pink-faced, plump and smiling mummy, and replaced her with a scared skinny animal he barely recognised. Only her hands and eloquent voice had remained.

Wiping away a stupid tear, he stares at the ceiling. Bloody Ramsay Hall and the blight inside these gates. That transient and elusive, grudging and destructive maternal love. And yet… He pictures a mother's face from yesterday. Serena's. Etched with fierce, unswerving and protective love for her child. He admires her for that. And the conflict in his head isn't her fault. It's his dad and that love-hate dichotomy. And the abhorrent rest. She's just a stranger who's stumbled into this…

How does one begin to describe it? He dryly laughs. Yes, this prison of the past.

-

Relieved to find the kitchen empty, Jack greets Lexie, then clasps his hands behind his back and spends a few moments stretching. The pain is more manageable these days, but it's a positive effort to remember his exercises.

He ruffles Lexie's fur again, grabs a bag of carrots from the pantry and yawns. He prolonged his 'lie-in' until seven, trying to doze, but thoughts of Hugh had prodded.

'*If you can't stay still, Hugh, get out! Go on, get out of my sight.*'

How many times had their dad said that over the years? But he meant out of the lounge or the dining room in those days. Not out of the whole bloody house like now. Sure, Hugh had needed to be taught a lesson back in November, but nearly three months in a freezing and decrepit caravan was more than enough punishment.

And it was a Sunday, a day of supposed rest from chambers and the new instructions crying out to be opened and read. So he decided he'd do the cooking, make a roast with all the trimmings, Yorkshire puddings and a shed load of crispy golden potatoes just as his brother likes. Even try rice pudding with clotted cream, prepared from scratch. His favourite dessert would cheer Hugh up; once upon a time their beautiful mother had made it.

Now stepping to the sink, he searches the cutlery drainer for a peeler, but a shadow outside catches his eye. Oh God, it's the child, peeping in through the window. Stupidly intending to hide, he steps back, but Lexie rises from her basket and trots to the door. With a sigh, he follows and opens it.

'Hello?' he calls. No movement for a moment, then the girl appears at the corner, her blonde hair like a halo in the weak morning light.

'Hello,' he says again, his attention stuck on her slim frame and small hands, her pale serious face punctured by shining blue eyes.

She's looking at Lexie by his side. He drags his gaze to the dog who turns to him as though asking for consent to go to her.

'Have you come to see Lexie?' he asks.

The girl nods.

'Where's your mummy?'

'She's asleep.'

'Oh right,' he replies, staring, still staring, his heart threshing his chest.

A waft of sharp air breaks the moment. There's still snow on the ground and the child isn't wearing a coat; her small teeth are chattering.

'You're cold. You'd better come in.' Then to recover himself, 'There are some dog biscuits in the larder. Do you want to find them? Lexie will show you where.'

The child steps inside, then abruptly she stops, staring with a wide-eyed expression as though she's seen something which frightens her. He follows her gaze and swallows.

'Not that door. That's the cellar. Best not go in there, it's…' He lifts the pantry latch and opens it. 'This is where the food's kept. Lexie's, too. If you see anything you like, you're allowed to help yourself.'

Nodding, she enters the larder. Listening to her quiet prattle, Jack sits at the table, lowers his head and waits for the nausea to recede. He can move on from his mistake; he can make amends and become a better man; he just has to do it.

Busying himself with the potatoes and parsnips for lunch, he tries not to watch the girl – squatting next to Lexie, stroking gentle fingers through her fur, whispering soft endearments – but after the dog has finished several snacks, he takes a deep breath and tries for a smile.

'I bet you're hungry. Have you had any breakfast yet?'
Solemn-faced, the child shakes her head.

'Well, Lexie's had her treat, so it must be your turn.'
He fetches a stripy apron and pulls it over his head. 'I'm
the chief chef for today.' He bows. 'What would madam
like for breakfast? Continental or full English? Your wish
is my command.'

Chapter Fifteen

Hugh

Hugh wakes with a jolt from a dream. Where is he? Where the hell is he and why's it so black? Oh God is he *dead*? Did he die in the night like his mum?

Taking in the aroma of parma violets, he punches out of the darkness. Well, that's a blinking relief! It isn't a coffin but the heavy army blanket which had appeared on his bed when he rolled in from The Bull last night. Jess, of course. She asked for his permission to pop it into the camper yesterday.

'Sure you can, it's your dad's caravan, after all,' he replied. 'And the lock doesn't work, so…'

She looked at him quizzically. 'No, Hugh, it's yours while you're here. It's your temporary home. You're entitled to privacy so long as you live here.'

Temporary bloody home. He wants to ask when he can move back to Ramsay Hall, but his dad barely makes eye contact these days. He's civilised and replies when Hugh speaks to him, but there's something strange in his brief gaze before he looks away. He asked Jack about it, but his brother just said that their dad needed '*space*'. Space for what? He's said sorry. Shouldn't that be the end of it? Wasn't that what his dad always said when he was small?

'If you behaved I wouldn't have had to shout, Hugh, but that's the end of it. Stop sulking and move on.'

Yanking back the mustard-coloured curtains, Hugh peers at the frosty world outside. The hunched dairy guy's shuffling to the cow shed. How old must Samuel be? Too old to be working. Maybe that's why he never speaks.

Working! The word fizzles in his ears. He got a job in November, just like his dad said. He even turned up at home to tell him in person.

'Helping out at the farm is hardly a job, Hugh,' he replied. 'They just took you on because they used to be Ramsay tenants and they're kind. I hope you don't get in their way. They're good people.'

Of course Hugh had needed to shout very loud again that day; he wanted to say he worked bloody hard and that his dad hadn't thought the Barnes family were 'good people' when he was a teenager, but Jack put a hand on his arm, squeezing it in that way he does, a warning to take a deep breath and cool it.

He sighs at the memory. It's really frustrating when his brother does that, but it's sort of comforting too. God knows what he'd do without him, but he tries to give back if he can. Like breaking things up yesterday at the cottage. Something was wrong with Jack's voice; he hadn't heard it like that for a long time and it scared him, if he was honest.

Puffing the worry out, he takes a single stride to the loo and has a long piss. One side of his head thumps badly. Perhaps he shouldn't have had that last whisky nightcap. He was just about to leave his usual spot at the bar when he spied Robbie Barnes at a corner table. So he ordered another drink, a double for courage, determined to casually stroll over and say hi. But every time he stole a glance,

Robbie was on his mobile, deep in conversation. He was about to give up when his old friend pulled back his chair and headed towards the gents'.

He seemed surprised to see Hugh. 'How are you doing, mate?' he asked with that twang that didn't belong. 'Your dad and Jack OK?'

Hugh took a breath to reply, but Robbie pulled his phone from his pocket and frowned. 'Got to take this. See you later.'

Of course Hugh didn't see him later. It's just an expression, he knows that. Bloody '*mate*' too. Clearly they're not.

–

Feeling a little sneaky, Hugh bends his head and enters the farmhouse kitchen. It turned out his black middle-of-the-night awakening was at ten o'clock in the morning. He could go straight home to Jack and Dad for breakfast, but his head hurts so much and he's too hungry to wait.

The warm room is empty. Remembering the broken bread bin, he lifts the lid carefully, tears off a chunk of malty loaf and stuffs it in his mouth. The teapot on the table is half warm and half full, so he pours out a cup, sloshes in the creamy milk top and slugs it down.

'I thought I heard you slam the caravan door past midnight,' Jess says, padding down the stairs in fluffy slippers.

Her hair in a high ponytail, she steps towards him and snatches the cup. 'That's from twenty minutes ago, I'll make you a fresh one.' She eyes him thoughtfully. 'How about a couple of boiled eggs while you're here? It looks as though you need food.'

'Thanks.'

Taking care with his throbbing temples, he sits down.

Jess is still watching. 'And paracetamol, I'm guessing.' She rifles in a cupboard and throws him a box. 'Then just as I'm about to drop off, in comes Robbie. I'd forgotten how he bashes around. Kettle, taps, toilet seat. Not to mention a long argument. He's not in the outback anymore. Paper-thin walls in this place. You don't have a row here and not expect everyone else to hear too.'

Hugh's mind is too sluggish; he tries to catch up. 'So Robbie came in after me and had an argument with your dad?'

Jess's ponytail bobs as she snorts. 'A reasonable assumption. Dad's pretty pissed off with him. Not so much for coming back here, but not seeing things through at home. Course Robbie doesn't see it that way. He's been in Brisbane for half his life, so it's not as though he returned after two minutes.'

'So who was Robbie talking to?'

'His wife, of course.'

'Oh right.'

Half expecting a woman to materialise, Hugh looks to the staircase. Bloody hell, Robbie's married. Robbie Barnes is married! Unbelievable. He tries to absorb the shock, but another immediately follows.

'His kids.' Jess carefully lays an egg in the saucepan and sighs. 'He was probably arguing about them again—'

'Robbie has *children*?'

'Yeah, two, though I don't know why I say probably. I pretty much heard his side of the argument word for word.' Gazing at him, she laughs. 'Oh Hugh, sometimes you're such a numpty. Robbie was on the phone. His wife's in Australia with the kids. That's why Dad thinks he's done—'

'A runner?'

They both turn to the voice. His eyes half closed and his fair hair tousled, Robbie's on the bottom stair. He yawns and shakes himself to his sister.

'Paper-thin walls, remember, Jess? Why not open the door and windows and tell the whole village while you're at it?' He briefly looks at Hugh. 'You look as rough as I feel, but at least I've got an excuse.' Then pulling up a chair, 'Bloody hell, Hugh, you stink. Isn't it time you trolleyed off to your palace for a shower?'

Jess points a wooden ladle at her brother. 'Well it's not as though it'll be a secret for long, not around here, Robbie. You chose to come back; you take the consequences.' She spoons out the eggs and hands them in two stripy cups to Hugh. Her eyes softening, she shakes her head. 'He means his jet lag, Hugh. That's his excuse for feeling rough and being particularly horrible today. Come on, take the painkillers and I'll pop in some toast.'

Chapter Sixteen

Serena

Still groggy with exhaustion, Serena slips from the bed and tiptoes to the tiny bathroom. At the door she has to pause to let the dizziness pass. Leaning her head against the jamb, she thinks about last night. Did she sleep at all? Though her chest felt on fire, she was shivering from the cold, seeking as much heat from her daughter as she could without waking her.

Struggling to peel back her eyelids, she unbuttons her nightdress with shaky hands, then peers at her skin through the mirror. Oh God. The ruddy stain has been raked by her own stupid fingers. She can't remember doing it, so perhaps she did nap after all. She examines the dark tips of her nails. Yes, revolting dried blood. She really must cut them as short as they'll go, but later, much later; now she just needs to rest.

Half asleep, she pees, then returns to the bedroom. Careful not to disturb her sleeping daughter, she nods to Panda teddy propped in between them and closes her eyes.

The sound of a crying baby rouses her. Trying to climb out of the woozy blackness, she listens. Not any sobbing infant, but hers. Oh God, will he wake, his features thunderous and loathing? Will he hiss the usual words? '*I'm tired, woman, shattered in fact. You managed to lose yours but*

I have a job, a very important job. You wanted this baby; you deal with it.'

Paralysed, she stares at his shadowy back. Dare she say, 'Then I'll leave and take Lana; we'll live somewhere else!' But suppose he takes her at her word? Where would she go? She sold her flat and moved in when she found she was pregnant. Her mum and dad adore him; they think he's a saint. Her old work buddies too. She doesn't have a job, and even if she tried to find work, who would employ her after the investigation? And the baby's still bawling. She has to move now before he turns and spits the usual venom in her face. *'See, I knew you wouldn't cope. You're not mother material. Take a look in the mirror. You're a mess. If you can't look after yourself properly, how can you care for a child?'*

She clenches her fists. How she hates him. At the door before work he'll kiss her forehead and smile that reasonable, patient, benign smile. *'Sorry, darling, I was tired last night. I shouldn't have alluded to your mistake. We all make them and I love you despite it. You just need to make a little more effort. With the flat and yourself. Yes?'*

Her mistake, her mistake. God, she abhors him. She punches his shoulders, then smacks the back of his head. The surge of energy's so unexpected, she laughs and hits again, harder and faster until she's almost delirious. But icy consciousness breaks through. She's thrashing thin air.

A nightmare, just a dream.

God, did she wake Lana?

She flips her head to the other pillow, but only Panda stares back. The bed is empty, so is the room. Where's Lana?

Without breathing, she listens. Oh God, oh hell, it wasn't entirely a dream; a child is still crying, her child, *outside*.

With a sudden rush of realisation, she springs from the bed, dives to the dormer window and looks out. It's actually bright morning and Lana is sitting on the wet courtyard, nursing her knee; Jack Ramsay's beside her, holding out his hands. His lips move and Lana smiles, then she raises her arms and he scoops her up. He kisses her hair and she circles his neck.

What the hell? What the hell? What's that man doing with her daughter? And instead of coming here to her mother, he's heading for the house.

Almost tumbling down the stairs, she bolts through the parlour and flings open the door. Her bare feet skim the slithery gravel as she runs. 'Lana!' she tries to call, but her voice is stuck in her throat.

Almost at the corner, Jack stops and suddenly turns. Lana's head is nestled against his shoulder.

Speech finally pelts out. 'What the hell are you doing? What the fuck are you doing with my child?'

Flushing a deep red, he carefully places Lana down and steps in front of her. 'We're getting the first aid kit from the kitchen. Lana was walking Lexie. She slipped on the ice and grazed her knee. She just needs a plaster.'

He says the words evenly, but there's panic in his eyes; she can see it so clearly.

'You kissed her!'

She's shivering and screaming, she knows, but there's nothing she can do to stop either.

'You kissed her; I saw you through the window.' She pats her own hair. 'You kissed my daughter. You don't know her at all. It's not normal.' Then, as her mind starts to focus, 'She was with me in bed, asleep... You've been in the cottage, our bedroom. You've done it again. You can't do that! It's not legal, not normal...'

He takes a step closer and holds out his palms. Integrity and concern flood his face, but she's seen that before, she's fully aware of how superficial *respectability* can be.

'Take a breath, please,' he's saying. 'Everything is fine but I think you're frightening Lana.'

She pushes hard at his chest. 'Don't tell me how to look after my own child.' Then, stepping to one side, 'Lana? Are you all right, love?'

Lana hangs her head and tears drip from her nose. As if in solidarity, the dog leans against her. 'Sorry Mummy,' she whispers. 'You were asleep for ages. I didn't want to wake you, so I put on my clothes and crept out.'

Wildly staring at her daughter, Serena tries to breathe through the overwhelming stench of ground coffee. Though drowned by a huge jumper coming down past her knees, Lana's wearing trainers and woolly tights. Oh God. Not snatched from the bed in her pyjamas but fully dressed.

Wondering what on earth she can say to apologise, she shifts her gaze to Jack but he's moving and blurring and shrinking away. He's frowning; more perplexed than angry, she thinks, as blackness sucks her in.

–

Serena wakes on the velvet sofa to three sets of eyes. Lana's teary blue and two green. One pair deep pools of concern and the other more curious… Oh God, her employer, how bloody embarrassing.

Pulling a soft blanket with her, she carefully manoeuvres herself into a sitting position. That's right, she fainted. More mortification floods back. Oh God; she was shrieking at Jack like a fish wife and making all kinds of insinuations. What the hell is wrong with her?

Her chest, that's what's wrong. And this raging temper-ature. Paracetamol's the thing, as soon as she can. A cool flannel and water and rest. That'll be enough. Surely enough to get her back on her feet.

Because if not… She glances at the dark figure standing by the door. Jack. His arms are folded and he's scowling. Hardly surprising after her outburst. But if she had to trust him, could she?

Hayden Ramsay hobbles forward and pats her shoulder. 'So you're back with us. Morning, Serena. How are you? Jack says you had a fright on the ice and toppled over.' Bird-like, he cocks his head. 'It's a good job a pair of strong arms were there to catch you and carry you in here. Are you all in one piece?'

'Yes…' She looks at her daughter and pats the cushion for her to sit. Lana, poor Lana witnessing that. Taking her hand, she squeezes it reassuringly, then goes back to Hayden.

'Yes, thank you. I am.' She gestures around the room, his blessed drawing room. 'I'm so sorry to have made such a fuss and interrupted your Sunday morning. I can't think what…' She catches Hugh's worried face and knows he needs an explanation. 'It was my own silly fault. It's happened before when I've been rushing around without eating breakfast. You know, low blood sugar?'

Hugh's frown relaxes into a smile. 'Absolutely! Me too.' He glances at Jack, still at the door. 'I don't faint, but I do get grumpy. Had eggs at the farm just now. With bread and a hot drink too.' He comes back to her, his expression earnest. 'Food is important, Serena, breakfast especially. I'll get you something now. I'll put on some toast.' He thinks for a moment, then grins at Lana. 'Marmite's your favourite spread. Lana told me. Am I right? And a huge mug of tea…'

'Thank you, but…'

The aroma of roast beef hits her senses and she swallows. The thought of any food turns her stomach, but she tries for a smile. She's half naked beneath the throw, her nightdress gaping at the neck. She needs to get out of this room, to escape the prying eyes. To carefully examine those scratches. Would it look odd to take the blanket?

'That's a really kind offer, Hugh, but it's your family day. I'll go back to the cottage and have something there.' She looks at Lana meaningfully. 'You'll make your mummy something to eat won't you, love?'

Jack's voice breaks the small silence. 'It's still biting outside. Lend Serena your coat, Hugh.'

'Oh right, sure thing.' Hugh takes off his jacket and strokes the sheepskin collar. 'Yup, this'll keep you warm, you know, just while you—'

'You can fetch it later, Hugh,' Jack adds.

'Yeah, of course…' Still looking a little anxious, he hands it over.

Jack steps out of the room. 'Come on then, little bro. I need help in the kitchen. Dad? Are you coming?'

But Hayden doesn't move. He's rubbing his chin and observing her with those sharp, knowing eyes.

'Lunch,' he says. He glances at Jack. 'Did you say the full Sunday works at two o'clock? My eldest son has hidden talents in the kitchen, Serena. I insist that you join us. We'll eat in the dining room for a change. You can have Melanie's place.'

Chapter Seventeen

Jack

Jack chews but struggles to swallow the sodden pastry. Thank God for Hugh. He's been talking incessantly since they took their places around the huge mahogany dining table. About farming and animals, about seeds and crops. He's surprisingly knowledgeable but he's talking at Lana's level, making it interesting too. How to spot sheep mites, counting rings on a cow's horn to work out its age; finding a goat up a tree, digging up a corn root which was taller than him. The stories are so vibrant and visual, he could be a primary school assistant. He must remember to tell him that.

His stomach still churning with apprehension, he glances at Serena. She's now pale and composed like her name. Nothing like the dishevelled, raving woman from earlier. But in truth, she was right. He shouldn't have kissed the child's hair, shouldn't have allowed her to envelop him in her arms and press her damp face against his neck. Her soapy scent and the feel of soft skin against his had been almost overwhelming. Then he'd heard Serena's voice. No, her howl, a parent's howl. He can't blame her for that. He was weak and he gave into temptation. But what to do now? Apologise to her or brush it under the carpet as usual and pretend it didn't happen?

Least said soonest mended? Yes, the Ramsay bloody motto.

He turns to his father. He's telling Serena a humorous story about fishing in the mere with waders before 'this damned hip'. So charming and charismatic, no one would know he was angry underneath. Is 'angry' the word, though? When he's really livid, he shouts. Tetchy or irritated is probably the better description today, petulant too. It's just a question of working out why. Why breach the unspoken family rule? Why sit in the shuttered old dining room and mention Melanie today?

Inhaling a bouquet of *old*, Jack looks around the dark, panelled room. The usual grimy pelmets, crushed velvet drapes, dated furnishings and furniture are there, but it's not as cluttered with period pieces as he remembers. A thick must of amber and wax seems to hang in the air like the smattering of snow through the stained glass. He snorts wryly to himself. Perhaps they should fling open a window, let the smell, the memories and the haunting guilt seep out.

With a sigh, he pushes a Yorkshire pudding to the side of his plate. Like his mother before him, he served them as a starter with rich gravy from the beef. He's only eaten one but he's stuffed, crammed with nerves, anxiety, work worries. Serena; her child.

His dad mentioning his 'gold-digger' bloody wife.

Don't you dare walk away. Come back. I haven't finished speaking!

If you leave, then I'm following.

Aware of Lana's blue gaze, he lifts his head. Her eyes travel to his plate and the remaining Yorkshires. He briefly looks to her mum who gives a tiny nod of permission. 'Quick,' he says, pushing the dish toward her. 'Before Hugh spots it.' The shy smile of appreciation is there, he knows, but he really can't look; he mustn't.

'Hugh! Starter plates need clearing. Chop chop.'

His father's sharp tone interrupts Jack's thoughts. He quickly stands. 'It's fine, Dad, I'll do it. Hugh's doing a sterling job keeping us all entertained.' He squeezes his brother's shoulder. 'Your stories about work are really interesting, Hugh. I can picture each one. Tell us about the new-born calf who… who wouldn't wake up until you rubbed her with a cloth.' He turns to the child, 'Hugh was only fourteen but he'd seen it on TV and remembered what to do.'

Carrying the crockery to the door, he catches his dad's frown. Hayden's heard the story many times before, so perhaps it's boredom. Or maybe it's yet more annoyance. The reference to Hugh's time at Selwyn Farm as 'work' or letting him off a chore, probably.

Jack smiles a little inwardly. See? Two can play the needling game, Dad.

Melanie. Sweet smiley Melanie. Trying to rise above the prodding memories, he returns to the kitchen, drains the vegetables and tips them into ornate serving dishes once reserved for Sunday lunches. Placing them on a tray, he carries them to the dining room and shoulders the heavy door. The old spasm passes down his spine like a fork of electricity. Perhaps he needs to go back on the painkillers.

He catches his dad's cool gaze. Mentioning Melanie is far more than a 'needle'. It's a brutal stab through the heart. It was a surprise to hear him call her a 'gold-digger' once she'd gone. He'd always thought they'd got on like daughter and indulgent father. Him pandering to her parasitic new life:

'If you want the master bedroom, it's all yours. Do your own thing with it. A complete make-over sounds perfect. You have marvellous style.'

'Gin time, Mel? Bombay Sapphire as you requested.'

'Oh, let her have it, Jack. Don't be such a grump.'

'Join me in a glass of this sublime Châteauneuf-du-Pape, Mel?'

'Oh, go on then. Who says champagne's just for celebrating anyway? A drop of crème de cassis for colour?'

Jack turns to Melanie's 'place' at this table. Hardly hers, really. Not at lunch times, at any rate. She'd still be in the sack, her 'brunch' on a tray and flicking through a magazine with a beauty product smeared on her cheeks. Too like his mother, whose bed it really was. But the difference between them was stark: Lucinda hadn't wanted to be incapacitated past noon every day, and her skeletal white mask was real.

Instead of his wife, Serena gazes back. Realising he's staring, he blinks. 'Sorry,' he says. 'I'm miles away.' Then he takes a second glance. Her face is so pallid, she looks ready to faint again. 'Serena? Are you OK? You don't seem…'

Hugh jumps to his feet and rushes over. 'Serena?' His eyes dart to his father. 'She doesn't look very well.'

'Sorry, I'm fine.' Pulling herself up, she seems to rally. 'Really, I'm OK. Just extraordinarily tired.' Spots of colour appear on each cheek. 'I'm so sorry to ruin the meal, but I think I need to lie down.' She turns to her daughter. 'Nothing to worry about, love, I'm just sleepy today. You stay here and enjoy this delicious lunch. Just a ten-minute lie down and I'll be as right as rain.' She reverts to Hayden. 'Sorry again. I'll be at the cottage if you—'

He covers her hand. 'Don't be ridiculous. We have plenty of bedrooms upstairs. Then you can call out if you need us.' He nods at Hugh. 'Take her up, son. And fetch her a glass of water. Run the tap so it's cold.'

Rising unsteadily, Serena rocks on her heels before straightening her spine. She smiles weakly at Hugh. 'Would you mind staying with Lana?' Then eyeballing Jack, 'Could you show me which room? If you don't mind…'

Jack stands, but says nothing. So there it is; she doesn't trust him with her daughter; his moment of weakness won't be brushed under the carpet. His own bloody fault; perhaps it really is time to come clean and confess. Cupping her elbow, he guides her from the room, down the hallway to the stairs. She stops at the first step and lowers her head. Her whole body is shaking, her breath rapid and short.

'Can you manage?' he asks, slipping his free hand around her waist.

Though she's tall, she feels surprisingly bony and fragile. Afraid she'll collapse, he all but carries her up the staircase to a spare bedroom, yanks back the duvet and helps her down.

Remembering the water, he turns to the bathroom, but her hand catches his.

'Close the door,' she whispers.

Oh God; he has to tell her, somehow apologise, explain.

'Look,' he starts, when he returns to the bed. 'I'm so sorry I—'

'Listen.' Cutting him short, she keenly searches his face. She nods after a few beats. 'I need antibiotics.'

'Sorry?'

'I need antibiotics urgently. Meropenem, imipenem or piperacillin–tazobactam preferably.'

He stands back in surprise, not only at her request but her obvious medical knowledge. 'OK. We can make a doctor's appointment. Ah, it's Sunday… I'll call the emergency number.' He rakes back his hair. She said *urgent*. 'For what, exactly? What should I say? Or we can go to the hospital, if you think that would be—'

'No,' she almost shouts. Then more quietly, 'No. No doctor, no hospital. I know what it is: my chest is infected. I think I have sepsis.'

'A lung infection?'

'No, the scald, the burn. It's fine; I know you've seen it. You were… kind with Hugh and the coat.'

Tears spill from her eyes. 'There was discharge earlier and I have a fever. Sepsis can… It can be dangerous, so I must start on them now.' Her voice cracks. 'I need to be here for my daughter. Do you understand?'

'Right.' Jack reaches for his back pocket. 'Right; I'm calling an ambulance.'

'No, please Jack, no.'

Her body heaving, she doesn't speak for a moment. Then she takes a deep breath, roughly wipes her cheeks and looks at him intently. 'You asked why I was here. Well, here's the answer: I can't be found right now. Hospitals have ears. Everyone knows everybody else. Supposedly respectable people. Do you understand?' She unbuttons her blouse to reveal the livid spread he saw yesterday and again this morning. 'This is a burn from a carafe of boiling coffee. It could have been my face.' She closes her eyes briefly. 'It could have been my child.'

Jack tries not to stare. Good God. At the cottage he assumed it was a port-wine birth mark, but... what the hell had happened?

'Are you saying someone deliberately scalded you?' His head pounds with questions. It must have happened recently. Shortly before she came. 'Who did this to you? When Lana was there? Why haven't you—'

'Don't.' Serena holds out the flat of her hand. 'Look, I have no idea if I can trust you but I need your help and I need it now. Please. I'm taking that risk for my child.'

'OK.' He gathers his thoughts. 'OK; I get it. Someone's hurt you and you're scared. You don't want to be located. I'll go with that for now.' He frowns. 'But what can I do? Why ask me?'

She sighs. 'Because I've seen your bathroom cabinet, Jack.' She rocks her head and smiles weakly. 'Believe me, I know – no one has a hoard of drugs like that without a friendly, no-questions-asked supplier...'

Chapter Eighteen

Hugh

Hearing the front door, Hugh yawns and stretches. It was unbelievably good to be in his own bedroom last night with his perfectly puffed pillows, sweet-smelling bedding and mattress. He has his brother to thank for that.

'For God's sake, Dad, let him stay,' Jack said after dinner. 'I need sleep. Someone has to keep an eye on Serena tonight and tomorrow. You're hardly up to it. I'll spend the morning in chambers, then take over after lunch.'

The man himself now appears in the kitchen. 'It's freezing out there, Hugh. Put on some more layers before going to the farm.' He wearily laughs. 'It's not as though you have a shortage of clothes. How's the patient?'

'Patients,' Hugh replies. 'Dad's been really grumpy. Complaining about aches and the usual. He wouldn't let me help him get up, so he's still in his room.'

Jack has dark circles beneath his eyes. 'Right.' He shakes his head. 'I keep telling him he needs to move around more. And Serena?'

'Asleep on and off. Lana's up there with her now.'

'Thanks, Hugh, you've been a really great help.'

Hugh grins. Like the good old times. 'Yeah, Lana was tearful but I kept her busy. We fixed the old Postman Pat puzzle and she told me about the farm animals she could spot from the window.'

Jack lifts his eyebrows. 'From her home?'

'I guess so. She wanted to see the goat in person but she wasn't allowed out or something.'

Hugh falls quiet. He mentioned their billy goat to the kid before remembering that he shouldn't. 'I told her about Mr Tumnus and the Aslan stories,' he says quickly.

'So you remember Mum reading us the Narnia novels before bed?'

Hugh shakes his head. Jack does this sometimes, sort of peers intently and asks about their mum. 'Nope. You did, though.'

'Yeah, tell me about it. A blinking chapter every night.'

'And we played dominoes in here. Me and the kid.'

Hugh glances at the cellar door. Lana kept turning to it, so he asked if she'd like to look. She pulled in her lips and sort of nodded, so he opened it, flicked on the light and peered down the stone steps.

'It's for Dad's wine,' he explained, but she grabbed onto his jeans and hid her face. Truth be told, he didn't blame her. He'd never been that keen on going down there himself. Jack neither.

He stands. 'I'd better get off to the farm.' Then, remembering how Serena's white skin had made his stomach summersault, 'Do you think Serena's OK? She was so fast asleep, I thought she was—'

'Yeah, I'm sure she's fine.' Jack's eyes flicker. 'Enjoy work. You did let them know you'd be late, didn't you?'

He had such fun playing with Lana that Hugh forgot about the time. When he finally looked at his mobile, Jess had sent him loads of texts. He nods – a fib but it's fine; he doesn't have to tell Jack everything.

Pulling up at Selwyn Farm, Hugh ejects *Definitely Maybe* and slots it carefully in its box. Flakes are tumbling out of nowhere again. They're pretty, of course, but bad news for the farm. Not damage to the crops as he'd imagined – Mr Barnes told him that snow actually protects them from ice. And sheep can cope in temperatures as low as minus twenty, he now knows. It's the *amount* of downfall the farmer worries about. Five years ago, one of his sheds housing cattle collapsed under the weight of it. Some cows were injured and it cost him '*six figures*' to mend.

'A lot of money, Hugh,' Jess explained when her dad mentioned it.

Nice Jess, kind Jess. Not like her bloody brother. The boy he doesn't recognise anymore.

Still feeling jolly from his *helpfulness* all morning, he slams the car door and hops over the wet grass to fetch his work boots. He stops and sniffs. Funny that: the dusting of snow seems to have frozen the decaying potato-type smell which usually greets him. And it's amazing what a difference additional layers make after all.

As though watching from the window, Jess bursts from the farmhouse door.

'Hugh! Are you OK? You didn't come back to the caravan last night. Then there was no sign of you this morning. I was worried. You didn't reply to my messages either.'

He mumbles to his size thirteen feet. 'Sorry, I meant to text…'

He knows Jess is looking at him expectantly, wanting to hear more, but Jack said it'd be less complicated just to keep schtum about Serena's illness. He steps to the side. 'So I'll just grab my boots and get on with mucking out. Unless there's something else Mr Barnes wants doing first…'

'You got lucky. Dad's in town on business today.' She folds her arms and frowns. 'You've not been drinking, I hope. One's too bloody many.'

Hot with indignation, Hugh scrambles to the camper, sits on the step and pulls on his Dickies. What the heck? He didn't even have a single drink last night! He wanted one for sure, but Jack had gone to bed and he was in charge. He shakes his head. Jess isn't the only sensible person with responsibilities.

Picking up the wheelbarrow, he stomps into the barn, but the huge eyes of the pregnant heifer gaze back. He holds out his fingers and she licks them with her long, sandpapery tongue.

'That's a girl,' he says, his angst quickly receding. He strokes the top of her back and she responds by stretching her neck. 'That's my sweetheart. Such a beautiful girl!'

'That's my sweetheart. Such a beautiful girl.'

Hugh spins to the voice mimicking his.

Robbie's crouched in a corner, smoking a roll-up. He repeats it again, making it sound even posher. He guffaws. 'Charming all the females are we, Hugh?' He scrapes back his blond hair, stands and rocks on his heels. 'Hugh, darling Hugh! Are you OK? I was *worried*,' he apes in a high-pitched voice. 'You didn't reply to my messages either…'

Not knowing how to respond, Hugh nods to the cigarette. 'You shouldn't be smoking in here. It's a fire hazard.'

Robbie guffaws. 'Oh right. Wet floor, wet straw, the coldest fucking day of the year.' He makes a show of crushing it in his hand. 'Satisfied? Not that burning this shithole to the ground would be a bad thing.'

Hugh folds his arms. He likes Mr Barnes; he likes Selwyn Farm; it's his '*second home*'. 'Then why did you come back?'

'Good fucking question!' Robbie swings his arms to the rafters. 'Because I'm off my bloody rocker. I return to my beloved family to find my job's been given to a fucking imbecile.' He stares for a moment then laughs harshly. 'That's you, Hugh!'

Hugh pictures Jack's face and counts to five. He can smell the stench of puke on Robbie's breath all the way from here. He looks at his watch. 'It's only half past two and you're drunk.'

Robbie claps his hands. 'Ten out of ten! You should've been a brain surgeon after all, posh boy.' He make a show of burping. 'Just a little tipple or two with my pub grub. That's allowed, isn't it? My dear sister says not, but she's clearly on heat worrying about little you.' He takes a step closer and pokes Hugh's chest. 'You know what *on heat* means, right? They must have taught you that at the posh private school.'

He teeters again. 'Lucky for some, eh? Cos all I was good for was farming.' The spittle flies from his mouth. 'Ten GCSEs and only good for farming. Not here at my *home* but Australia.' He pushes Hugh's shoulder. 'Only on the other side of the world and I hate fucking farming! Farming's for thick boys like you.' His ruddy face curls into a sneer. 'Imbecile, idiot, school bloody dunce. Couldn't do your three times table even when we left primary!' He shoves him again. 'Come on then, Mummy's boy, let's give it a try. Three, six, nine, twelve…' He snorts. 'Come on big man. Or are you a bloody coward?'

Even before Hugh registers what he's done, his old friend is on the ground, doubled up from the hard punch to his stomach. Paralysed by his own reaction, he stares as Robbie coughs, curls up and breathes deeply. After several moments he laughs and hobbles up to his feet. Holding his arms out, he staggers and sways. 'Come on, big man! Let's go again. Give me your best on the chin. Show me what you're made of!'

The blood pulsing in his ears, Hugh stares.

'Knew you were thick, Hugh, but never took you for a sissy.'

Hugh turns on his heels.

'Coward; fucking wimp...'

But Hugh doesn't hear the rest, and even Jess's shocked expression and outstretched arms don't stop him from running.

Chapter Nineteen

Serena

Serena is gaping. Shock, confusion, astonishment. Then she looks down at her camisole. No longer white, it's stuck to her torso, seeping and drowning in brown liquid. What the hell? What the...

The stench of coffee hits, then agony shoots in. Searing heat on her clavicle, deep scorching to her chest. Oh my God, she's been scalded; her skin is on fire. She needs water from the tap. Quickly water, cold water; she must drench her exposed flesh to kill the blistering pain.

But someone is blocking her way.

'Oh dear, an accident. Just a slip of the hand. You do believe me, don't you?'

'Water, for God's sake. Please move. I need water, cold water...'

'It was an accident. Say it first.'

'Yes. Yes, it was an accident, a slip of the hand. Now, please let me—'

'You don't sound as though you mean it. Say it again.'

'I know it was an accident. Just a simple accident. Really.'

'Where are you going?'

'To the sink—'

'No; where do you think you are you going?'

'Nowhere.'

'*Are you sure?*'

'*Yes.*'

'*Promise?*'

'*Nowhere; I promise, nowhere!*'

Bursting from the nightmare, Serena jerks upright and exhales a ragged breath. A dream, just a dream, thank goodness. She claps a hand to her mouth. Oh God, did the screams come out loud? She turns to the other pillow. The bedding is blue and Lana isn't there. Flopping back, she frowns at the ceiling. Where on earth is she? Not the rough joists of the cottage roof but a much more elaborate affair. Darkly stained timbers lit by two sparkling chandeliers. That's right, she's in the main house. Because? Oh God, the green-tinged discharge from her scabs, the nausea and high fever. And the smell of strong coffee; the sour reek that's always there, in her mind, her nostrils, her belly and memory.

Her eyes prick and sting from the bad luck, the bloody injustice of it all. She'd secretly and carefully made a plan to escape. She and little Lana were so nearly free. She could almost taste the liberation from being watched and inspected, from walking on eggshells, from the constant tension and rules and obligations to comply.

Then, '*No; where do you think you are going?*'

So cruel and unfair. She'd needed to wail and shriek from both pain and frustration, but she had to stitch it in to protect her beautiful girl.

Tears tumble out with a will of their own. Like yesterday when everything unravelled spectacularly. Irrational panic, real fear. Screaming at Jack, then all but blackmailing him for drugs.

Trying to calm herself, she breathes deeply from her diaphragm. Everything is fine. She had to take the risk for

Lana. And Jack seemed to take it on the chin. Said he'd see what he could do. Said he'd go with her secret for now.

For now, for now. Whatever that meant.

She rocks her throbbing head to the bedside table. The glass of water and tub of pills are still there, thank God.

'The strongest dose I could access,' Jack said when he woke her up at some point. 'They should be given intravenously. You should be in a hospital.'

'I know,' she replied when she finally unstuck her thick tongue and found her voice. 'But beggars can't be choosers.'

An ironic expression really. She's been a 'beggar' for far, far too long. How and why she'd stumbled so often – turning from a strong, professional woman to that timid, fearful creature – she doesn't understand.

With a huge effort, she pushes away the prodding past. Right now is what matters. Dare she look at today's damage? No, she's tired, too tired. Like pennies on her eyelids, darkness is pulling her down. But she mustn't give in just yet. She has to take her medicine; she has to be strong for her child.

–

A distant knock, then a dark-haired figure saying something from afar.

Dragging herself to the surface, she carefully hitches herself up. Her eyes finally focus. It's Jack, carrying a tray. Yes, Jack Ramsay, her strange ally, her partner in crime. He's peering at her with knitted brows.

'You're awake. How are you feeling?'

In truth, she doesn't know. 'Where's Lana?' she asks.

'She's been in and out of here but she's watching TV and eating her tea in the snug at the moment.' He rubs his weary face. 'Fish fingers and peas. Hope that's OK. With Lexie, of course. I had work to do and Dad's not the best company at the moment. He refused to get up for Hugh this morning.' He snorts faintly. 'I think he's missing your company.' Then after a few seconds, as though speaking to himself, 'I guess I didn't appreciate how lonely Dad would be, rattling around this house on his own. Frustrated, too. No driving, no shooting nor fishing, barely walking. Missing his usual golfing holidays with Fogie. God knows, I'd be.'

He places a four-legged tray on her lap and smiles wryly. 'I thought chicken soup, apparently the cure for all ailments.' Then glancing at the tub of pills, 'I didn't want to wake you, but it's important to take them regularly. And of course you need to eat to… to get your strength back.'

'Thank you.'

His thoughts clearly elsewhere, he gazes through the window.

'Is Hugh not around?' she asks to fill the silence.

He shakes his head. 'No.'

There's a beep and he pulls out his mobile. Staring at the screen, he scans it for a while. 'Sorry, work stuff. Always work.' Then he frowns. 'No, no word from Hugh. I thought he'd be back by now. I guess he's making up time for—'

'I'm sorry, my fault.'

'No, it's not anybody's. It's just one of those things…'

Seeming to change his mind, he clears his throat and his shadowy eyes meet hers. 'It is someone's fault though, isn't it, Serena? I know you need to get well first, but no one can go through life hiding. In a strange way I know that better than anyone, and—'

A thump at the door makes him turn. Wearing his Paisley dressing gown, Hayden struggles through.

He hands a crutch to Jack. 'You're awake, thank God,' he says to Serena. His gaze rests on the pill pot. 'Are you free for some intelligent conversation? Even five minutes will do. My son's been ensconced in the study all afternoon, and as much as I like playing snap with Lana, losing three times on the trot is my limit.'

Jack helps him settle into a Regency-style armchair.

'Soup first, Dad,' Jack says, leaving the room.

Obeying his son's command, Hayden quietly watches her eat. Then, when she's finished and taken her medicine, he lifts his pale eyebrows: 'I thought you might be wondering about Melanie.'

Who? She'd supposed he'd enquire about her 'prescription'. Letting out her trapped breath, she shifts focus. Melanie? She squeezes her memory but no one of that name springs to mind.

Hayden leans forward. 'Slip of the tongue. I shouldn't have mentioned her. Jack doesn't like to talk about her. Too painful.'

Serena nods. That's right, she remembers now. Was it really only yesterday? Something about sitting in Melanie's place for Sunday lunch. But in her agitation, she'd assumed Hayden meant his wife. What was she called?

As though reading her thoughts, he sits back and smooths his hair.

'Losing Lucinda was dreadful for us all. Hugh only eight, Jack not much older.' His eyes shine and he swallows. 'But she'd been ill for some time, more or less bedridden, so it was really just us boys for years even before she finally left us.' He smiles tightly. 'A little too much testosterone at times, if I'm honest. Then Melanie came along, a breath of fresh air. Beautiful, noisy, gregarious; sassy and fun.' He laughs. 'And how many daughters-in-law would be happy to live with their husband's old man? Take over the master bedroom as her own. She did. She brought the house alive.'

Though still groggy, Serena tries not to show her shock. Bloody hell; Jack was married. He's a good-looking man, so it's not surprising on that score, but she's never found any trace of a wife in the house – no photographs nor mementoes, no woman's touch. Yes, except the master bedroom and bathroom.

Not that the old Serena would have approved of the archaic 'master' description.

Hayden tilts his head. 'He cleared everything away. Everything. Too many reminders; too painful. Not just for him, but Hugh and I as well. A massive void in all our lives. But...' He puts his hands to his mouth like prayer. 'But I do miss her very much. Perhaps that's why her name escaped yesterday; maybe that's why I'm talking to you now. Of course I don't tell Jack that. You tell your children what they need to hear sometimes, anything to help them through the grief. You're a parent – you must know what I mean.'

A flash of Lana's white, terrified face hurtles in. Shutting it out, she nods again. Yes she does, she really does understand that.

Another wave of fatigue washes over her. Aware Hayden's still speaking, she tries to grasp what he's saying. Jack had a wife who died. Simply dreadful. How does that make her feel about him? More kindly towards his constant scowl, certainly. Sad, sympathetic too.

Her lids heavy, she lies back and drifts towards sleep. So Jack Ramsay was married. How did Melanie die? She pictures his expression when they met unexpectedly at the fir tree. Not just startled, but frightened. And more than that. There were other emotions too, weren't there? Bad ones, deeply furtive and hidden...

Chapter Twenty

Jack

Jack stares at the TV screen and taps his foot. He's sitting on the sofa with his father, the same couch Hugh used to hide beneath when he was upset or in trouble. Their dad didn't know about the space behind the flap at the back and sometimes he'd stay there like a statue for hours. If he wasn't so huge now, Jack would be tempted to check. Where the hell is he? And why isn't he answering his mobile?

'A little too heightened for my taste,' his dad is saying.

He's been commentating throughout the programme as usual. Hugh used to ask him to shush so he could concentrate on the story, which didn't make father and youngest son the best of television companions.

'I like a good drama but they're squeezing out the emotion for all it's worth,' Hayden adds. 'And the back story is hardly realistic. As though the landed gentry gave two hoops for the proletariat.'

An image of his mum's apple face rushes in. 'The Ramsays did, didn't they? Generous benefactors back in the day?' Jack replies. Times change though, and in fairness he has no idea what the series is about, let alone the 'back story'. He's usually working at this time on a Monday evening, either here in the study or in a generic hotel which could be anywhere from Barnstable to Birmingham or Bognor. Quite frankly, save for checking the venue of the court, he wouldn't know which.

He stands. 'I'm getting a coffee. Do you want a one?'

His dad lifts his crystal tumbler. 'Got a drink, thanks.' He lifts his eyebrows. 'Coffee? You won't sleep.'

Snorting inwardly, Jack leaves the room. If only caffeine was the cause of his insomnia. Usually it's self-reproach, stress and ghosts, but he knows it'll be less nebulous tonight. For fuck's sake, where is Hugh? They had a deal. There's a child in the house, a young girl who needs something Jack Ramsay can't give.

He sits at the kitchen table, puts his head in his arms and sighs. Little Lana, little Lana. She was a very good girl earlier.

'Half past seven, Lana, I think it's your bedtime,' he said. 'Same bedroom as last night? And remember to clean your teeth.'

She padded to her room and got changed by herself, coming out five minutes later in heart-patterned flannel pyjamas and furry slippers, her blonde locks an aureola of static.

'You've given your hair a good brush, I see,' he commented with a smile.

But she didn't return it; holding her panda teddy, she was sucking her thumb, her face scrunched with emotion.

He had to crouch to hear her quavery voice. 'Is Mummy going to be all right?'

'Of course she is. Do you want to kiss her good night?'

Her eyes solemn, she nodded. 'Suppose she doesn't wake up?'

'Then she'll be awake in the morning.'

'No, I mean never.' Her gaze was watery blue. 'Because some people go to sleep forever. They never wake up.'

Too many images flashed in his vision. He had to swallow hard. 'Well, that won't be your mummy. She's just really tired. Come on, let's go in and see her now.'

Serena stirred, thank God, and cuddled up with her daughter. Embarrassed to watch, he began to step back but she held out her hand, pulled him to her and whispered. What did she say? He couldn't be sure. Then she kissed Lana goodnight. 'See you in the morning, bright and early!'

But despite her mother's chipper voice, Lana wept and reached up her arms, not to her but to him. So of course he had to lift her and breathe in her smell.

Soap and toothpaste and child.

He now pulls out his mobile and looks at his contacts. He needs distraction. No, not just diversion, but the feel of skin, warm and willing flesh in his arms. It's been too bloody long. He stares at the screen. Kiva? Or even Wanda. He could call Kiva right now. She flashed her stunning smile at him only this morning. 'Are you free this evening?' he could ask. 'I know it's a school night but we could meet for a quick drink, if you fancy. I'll collect you in half an hour...'

He won't, of course. He's procrastinated long enough. He needs to find Hugh.

Taking a deep breath, he punches the number for Selwyn farm. He doesn't have to wait long as Jess Barnes answers almost immediately.

'Hi Jess, it's Jack Ramsay. I don't suppose Hugh is there?'

As sweet as always, her tone is loaded with concern. 'He's not home either? Oh no. His car's still here but I looked everywhere and couldn't find him.' He hears her heavy sigh. 'Thing is, Robbie was blind drunk at lunch time and… Well, I only caught the end of it. He said something which upset Hugh and he darted off. I'm sorry; I guess I should have phoned you earlier but he's a—'

'A grown man. I know and it's fine. Don't worry; really don't. He'll be in The Bull. Catch up with you soon.'

Hoping his voice didn't betray him, Jack ends the call and tries to focus. Fuck! Bloody Robbie Barnes and trouble. Seems a leopard doesn't change its spots even after a twenty year or so stretch on the other side of the world. What the hell did he say to make Hugh run away?

He stares into space to organise his thoughts. The pub seems unlikely when he's in a state, but where else would his brother go? He can't just turn up at the farm and demand to search every barn and outbuilding. Besides, he's in no doubt Jess has already done that.

Scooping his keys from the hall table, he calls to his dad. 'I'm just popping out for an hour, Dad. Keep an ear out for Serena and Lana.'

A reply duly fires back but the frosty breeze through the door snatches it away. The friendly snow from the weekend has been replaced by bitter ice. Hell, he should have left earlier. He pictures little Hughie beneath the sofa, as still as Aslan the great lion, refusing to come out even for a packet of Toffos or Opal Fruits or his favourite crisps. Suppose he's outdoors somewhere? It was lunch time when he left, Jess said. He could have chilblains or exposure by now.

Pulling up his jacket collar, he carefully hops over the shiny surface to his car. The Bull first and if that doesn't yield results, he'll confront Robbie Barnes. Find out exactly what he said.

Taking in the full moon, he heads the Porsche towards the gate. If he still liked cars as much as he used to, he'd appreciate its defrosting efficiency, its near silent purr and heated seats. But somewhere along the line, material possessions ceased to please him. A lesson from Melanie.

He sighs at the thought. Melanie, Melanie, who could never get enough of anything – clothes, shoes, trinkets, booze. *Don't you have this design in a different colour? Oh, don't be mean, Jack. We can afford it, can't we? Besides, a girl can never have too many handbags.*

Did Serena really whisper, 'Sorry for your loss'?

Breathing away the stab of grief, he waits for the barrier to open, but a delayed observation catches up in his head. A dull light was glowing from the games room windows, wasn't it? Turning the wheel, he circles the car, parks up and strides around the rear of the outbuilding. Like small protective hands, a spread of ivy has almost sealed the door. But on closer inspection, it's broken in places.

He takes a steady breath, lifts the corroded latch and steps in. Like icy falling flakes, the atmosphere's dense. Absorbing the scene, he turns and turns again, blanching at the irony of a pure and white smattering everywhere. On the scattered books, the lamed pool table and the snapped snooker cues. On the pelmets of the spotted curtains and the matching beanbags, now deflated, disembowelled.

It isn't snow, but particles of dust and polystyrene.

His stomach clenching, Jack walks around the chilly room. When was he last in here? Two years ago? More? Shaking the old images away, he drags his mind back to his brother. He's been here, clearly, but there's no sign of him now. He squats down, scoops a handful of 'beans' and tests the texture with his fingers. Who'd have thought they'd be so insubstantial, artificial? He'd stupidly supposed the huge cushions would be filled with natural fillers – real seeds, rice or corn. But it's hardly surprising; he was duped in the past. Yes, tempted by the superficial – by prettiness, sexuality, a tinkling laugh.

As vacuous as these *beans*, as things turned out.

He tosses them away. He needs to concentrate and find Hugh. What next, where to go? Where would his brother hide? Of course, hell, of course! Groaning at his slow-wittedness, he retraces his path, drives back to the house and scans the farm buildings for lights. He leaves the car, trots across the courtyard to the husk of the old barn, rubs his freezing hands and skids to a standstill. The rusty bolts are undone.

He pushes the worn door and steps in. Save for a slice of moonlight through the ramshackle roof, it's almost pitch black inside. The dull smell of ancient smoke wafts by his senses. Whether real or imagined, he's never sure, but the old shiver is there.

'Hugh?'

No reply. He walks further in. 'Hugh, are you here?'

No response again, but the rustle of straw gives his brother away.

A spread of relief weakens Jack's legs. He lets out his caught breath and turns to the sound. 'Come on Hugh, I know you're in here. Where are you?'

His eyes accustoming to the dark, he sees a dark shape move up ahead. 'Come down, Hugh. I'm knackered.' Then checking his impatience, 'Let's go home where it's warm. We can have a drink and talk.'

Hugh doesn't budge.

The smell of dank hay in his nostrils, Jack sighs. 'Fine, I'll come to you but there'll be trouble if I break a blasted leg.'

Using the poly twine for purchase, he climbs several bale stacks and finally slots next to his brother at the rear of the barn. 'What happened?' he asks his shadowy face.

'You said I should find a safe place when I'm cross.'

'I did.'

'Take out my anger on things that don't matter.'

'You're right, Hugh, I did.' Jack takes his brother's hand. It's solid and surprisingly warm. 'But what made you angry?'

Hugh shrugs and falls silent. Then after a few beats, 'Robbie Barnes said I was a coward.'

Jack nods. The perfect trigger. How on earth did Robbie know that?

'And other mean stuff.' He wipes his nose with his sleeve. 'I'm never going back.'

'To the farm?'

Hugh nods. 'He was horrible.'

'Was he drunk?'

'Yeah, but still.'

'People don't always say what they mean or mean what they say, Hugh. Especially when they've had too much to drink. Of course you'll go back, you love it there. You're a strong and reliable worker, so they need you too.' Groaning inwardly, Jack thinks of his frequent advice to himself. 'Put on a brave face and carry on, pretend you don't care what Robbie says.'

'But I took his job.'

'Hardly.' Pulling Hugh towards him, he laughs wearily. 'He left Goostrey, what, eighteen years ago? I think that's a bit long to keep open an employment opportunity, even for family.' Then with a sigh, 'You were due back for dinner. I've been bloody worried about you. Why didn't you answer your phone?'

Lowering his head, Hugh flattens his hair with both hands. 'I trashed the games room,' he mumbles. 'I think the pool table's broken.'

'I know.'

'Dad'll go ballistic.'

'No he won't.'

'He will. Stupid Hugh and the rest. I hate it.'

'I know.' Jack stands and holds out his palm. 'Come on, time for bed.' Balancing himself, he yanks Hugh to his feet. 'How will Dad know? He can't exactly stride down the drive to have a look.' He picks a dry stalk from his brother's red hair. 'Cheer up, Hugh. I'll make sure it's all sorted.'

He pauses at his own sudden insight: his father's not able to 'control' everything as usual. Control, influence, demand and decide. Even manipulate at times. He laughs. 'Besides, right now, our dad is pretty much fucked.'

Chapter Twenty-One

Hugh

Hugh hums 'Live Forever' as he trudges across the top field to the derelict building. The chimney breast is crumbling and there's no glass in the boarded windows, but it still has a sturdy front entrance. Mr Barnes told him it had been a shepherd's cottage '*once upon a time*'.

'Not like those wooden huts they use for luxury glamping these days,' he added. 'They're moveable with wheels, but quite frankly one of those wouldn't last a day in this Russian wind.'

He didn't like to ask what Russia had to do with it, but Mr Barnes went on to explain that the stone building had been useful for lambing in the past, 'a relatively warm livestock shed, of sorts, before we had quad bikes to get around'.

Hugh had actually been there several times and had tested its warmth for himself, but even at twelve or thirteen, he'd known better than to say so.

He now closes the door behind him, takes off his backpack, settles down on his blanket and carefully peels away the tinfoil. Since his 'exchange' with Robbie in the barn, he's made his own lunch. Today it's a salad cream sandwich again, but he's determined to keep away from the farm kitchen, so there's plenty of time to 'ring the changes', as his dad says. Not that his old man or Jack know about the homemade butties.

Taking a huge bite, he smiles in satisfaction. Against all the odds, the week has gone pretty well. He drove his father to his hospital check-up this morning, and though he held his breath the entire length of the driveway, his dad didn't look towards the games room, let alone mention it. Instead he was quiet. Not the deliberate angsty type of silence, but thoughtful, he felt.

'All right, Dad?' he asked, Jack-like.

'I'll feel a lot better after this appointment. But thank you for asking,' he replied.

He nods to himself. Yup, it feels great, really great to be in his dad's good books for once.

Much like he did as a kid, he delves again in the rucksack and lines up his booty. KitKats, Ritz crackers and a packet of McCoy's Hot Mexican Chilli. Two cans of Coke and a single beer. Not a bad grab from the larder during the two minutes Jack wasn't looking at breakfast this morning.

He opens the bread and inserts a few crisps. Would his brother really mind he wasn't having proper meals made by Jess? 'I'm proud you're still going into work today,' he'd said on Tuesday morning. 'What did Mum always say about sticks and stones? They may break your bones but words will never hurt you. Remember that?'

He'd been about to say no, that he couldn't recall anything their mum said, let alone that, but Jack had looked so keen, he hadn't wanted to let him down, so he'd sort of nodded. And of course that meant he couldn't go on to mention his decision about not eating at the farmhouse. Still, it's gone to plan so far. Doing his job as usual but not bumping into Robbie, nor Jess. Not even seeing Mr Barnes. Well, only from a distance.

Stretching out his legs, he pulls up the blanket and closes his eyes. Just five minutes. He's always been able to kip 'on demand'. It makes Jack shake his head and smile wryly, like that mindfulness thing.

–

A crackle and a sputter jerk Hugh awake. The distinctive oaky smell of burning wood soon follows. Pulling in his knees, he quickly covers his ears. After a few seconds he dares himself to peep. Yes flames – flickering, winking, flashing and goading. He slowly lets out his breath. *It's fine, Hugh, it's fine.* It's in the old grate where fire belongs.

For a moment he stares, perplexed. What the hell? Then the door creaks open and Robbie Barnes appears with an armful of kindling.

Robbie briefly glances his way, then nods to the fire-place. 'It's just to warm us up, mate. Like in the old days?'

Hugh doesn't reply. Instead he folds his arms. What's *he* doing here with his ridiculous Aussie accent and his bleached blond shaggy hair? Never mind what came out of his stupid mouth on Monday? But he won't think about that. He can do it if he tries. Like when he blocks out the old shame.

Rubbing his hands, Robbie looks around. 'Thought you might be here,' he says. He gestures to the line of swag. 'Bloody hell, mate, don't tell me you still like those salty crackers. They were revolting twenty years ago, they can't taste any better now.'

He spends a few moments layering the twigs on his fire, then turns to Hugh again. 'Saw you on the tractor yesterday. Told Jess you were fine. Said you weren't coming to the kitchen 'cos you wanted to escape her shit cooking…'

He waits for a moment, then sighs and hunkers down opposite. 'Look, I'm sorry, OK? I was drunk. Paralytic. I can't even remember what I said.'

Hugh loads his goodies back in his bag.

'Come on, mate. Don't be like that. I said sorry. Talk to me!'

Hugh folds the tinfoil until it can't get any smaller. 'You said I took your job.'

'Did I?' Robbie snorts. 'Well that's bloody stupid. I haven't even been here for eighteen years.'

'That's what Jack said.'

'Golden boy at the top of the bloody class?' Then, when Hugh doesn't reply, 'Sorry, out of order; I always liked Jack. How is he? Still living with your dad, Jess said. But working at law courts all over the place. Must be pretty full on.'

'Yeah, but we've got…'

He thinks of mentioning Serena and the kid. After all, he used to tell Robbie everything. But then he'd have to explain about her illness and the nasty crusting scar on her chest. Every time he glimpses it, it freaks him out, if he's honest. 'What are you doing here?' pops out instead.

Robbie shrugs. 'Nothing. Just chatting.'

'No, here in Goostrey, back at the farm. Jess said you have a wife and kids in Australia.'

Robbie stares at the flames and doesn't reply. He rubs his face eventually. 'Everything's gone to shit, Hugh. I was so desperately unhappy there. So miserable for years. I had to leave before I… deflagrated. But I can't *feel* that anymore. Right now I'm just consumed with fucking guilt. I'm a deplorable bastard for leaving them. I've no idea what to do next.'

'Deflagrated?'

'Exploded, I suppose.' Then after a moment, as though speaking to himself, 'No, not that really. Wanting it to stop. Her unhappiness, mine, the kids. The long hours alone at work just thinking about it. Finally getting home each evening, then the nagging, the badgering, the sheer despondency. So tired, too tired to take it. Needing to walk away. Knowing that *I'm* the problem, and there's nothing I can do except… end it, disappear.'

Oh hell, he's crying. Hugh digs in his rucksack and pulls out the drinks. He slides the bottle of lager towards him.

Robbie continues to speak, his voice cracked with emotion. 'So I left them and came here, instead of…' He looks to the old rafters and shakes his head. 'And I'm on the plane knowing I've done the right thing, absolutely the right bloody thing. For thirty-three hours, Hugh!' He taps his temple. 'For fucking thirty-three hours I was free of all the crap in here. Then I arrive home and it all starts again. Pecking my head. Selfish, irresponsible. A bastard, a shit. My wife on the telephone, Jess, my dad. Then there's you…'

Remembering Robbie's ugly words, Hugh feels his knuckles tensing. 'What did I do?'

'Nothing.' Shaking his head, Robbie sighs. 'You did nothing, Hugh.' He stands and steps away. 'Remember to extinguish the fire when you're done.'

His head throbbing with frustration, Hugh counts to five. Then trying to be calm, he follows Robbie out. 'I don't understand. What did you mean by "then there's you"? Just tell me.'

'I didn't expect you to be here, working at the farm. And it's fine that you are, more than fine. But it's a reminder, isn't it?'

Hugh looks at the frosty ground and hops from foot to foot. 'A reminder?'

Robbie's face darkens. 'Of where it all began.' He roughly wipes his nose and stalks away.

After a moment he stops and points a finger back at Hugh. His voice flies up on the *Russian* wind. 'Your bastard dad, Hugh. You know that.'

Chapter Twenty-Two

Serena

Fearful of slipping and smashing the twin handled piece into smithereens, Serena follows the taciturn antique dealer to his van. Quickly saying goodbye, she returns to the house and closes the door. Only then does she look at her trembling hands.

The guy's a ceramic restoration specialist, Hayden told her, so perhaps handing over broken pieces of Staffordshire porcelain wouldn't have been the end of the world, but her whole shaking body is pretty embarrassing. She feels a little dizzy and out of breath too. Perhaps not surprising, considering she had to collect the key from Hayden upstairs, then find the pedestaled vase and a box of period crockery from the room adjacent to the snug. And before that she'd done her Friday chores – loading the washing machine several times, vacuuming the downstairs and cleaning the loos.

She now returns to the kitchen and flops down on a chair next to Lana. She's done enough for now, pushed her limbs as far as they'll go. Not that she'd mention it to the Ramsays. She awoke at seven today, and for the first time since the weekend she felt relatively alert. She wasn't drenched in sweat and the scratch wounds were nicely crusting. As though she was checking a baby's temperature, she gently felt her own lower neck and chest with the back of her hand. It had cooled substantially, thank God. She could stop panicking about sepsis and bloody hospitals. Hayden's daily inquisitions too.

She sighs. Hayden. He didn't actually ask much when he popped in to see her, but his sharp had eyes seemed to. Then there were his comments: 'Spent a lovely hour with your daughter. She's really opening up and getting chattier every day.' 'Good job you're on the mend. Wouldn't have enjoyed calling your next of kin…'

This morning she'd wanted to show him she was perfectly well, so she checked up on Lana, padded downstairs and followed the sound of eloquent voices. All three men ogled in surprise when she entered the room. Feeling herself flush, she tightened her dressing gown belt and went for the usual sardonic brisk tone.

'Morning, all. Thought I'd just let you all know I'm still alive.'

Hugh's grin dropped from his face. 'Gosh, I didn't know you were—'

'It's just an expression, Hugh,' Jack said at the same time as his father's, 'She's being sweetly ironic.'

Hayden held out his hand, his eyes bright with pleasure. 'And may I say how nice it is to see you with colour in your cheeks, Serena. Up and around too. Marvellous!'

She accepted his gesture and sat next to him. 'Breakfast,' he continued. 'What can we get you? Jack was having none of it when I asked for mine in bed.' He nodded at Hugh. 'You'd have brought me something up, wouldn't you, son?'

'Work, Dad.' Jack replied. Groomed and rather hand-some, he adjusted the knot in his tie and pulled a smart jacket from the back of the chair. 'Which is where I'm going now. Good luck at the hospital appointment, Dad. I'm sure there won't be any problems, but call me if you're worried. I'm in chambers all today, so I can come if I'm needed.' Looking at his father, he paused. 'Dad? All right?'

Turning away, Hayden ignored his son's question. 'You drive, don't you Serena? You have a car?' he asked.

Hoping the alarm didn't show, she nodded and smiled. 'I do, though heaven knows where the keys are. I haven't set eyes on them since—'

'Not a problem. You can use mine. It's automatic. Even a child could drive it. Save Hugh from missing work and—'

'There's Lana to think of, Dad.'

Jack's voice came from the door, crisp and impatient. 'It's hardly fair to drag a child to the hospital. Hugh's already arranged the morning off to take you. It's all sorted.'

Serena wanted to turn, look at Jack meaningfully and somehow thank him for saving her, but the door clicked behind her, then the front door slammed.

'You'll have this one day,' Hayden said. 'Ungrateful offspring. Being treated as a child.' He shook his head and smiled thinly. 'The tables turning, eh? It was ever thus. Expect I did the same to my father. How about you? No, don't answer that. You were a sweet child, I can tell. Like little Lana.'

She now looks at her daughter. Blonde hair falling across her eyes, she's ferociously colouring at the table.

'Has that man gone now?' she asks without lifting her head. 'The man who came to the door?'

'Yes, thank goodness.' She didn't think Lana had noticed him. 'Do you want a drink, love?'

'Yes, orange juice please. He smelled funny. A bit like Rhona's house.'

'Ah, then mothballs, I expect.'

Feeling a little winded at how perspicacious a four-year-old can be, Serena makes up the squash, then tries to peep at her daughter's creation.

'What are you doing?' she asks.

'A picture,' she replies, not moving her protective left arm. Then, smiling shyly, 'A picture of Lexie.'

'Oh, that's nice.'

Her cheeks flush a bright pink. 'It's for Jack.'

Shaking an uncomfortable sensation away, Serena studies her child. She's undoubtedly sweet, as Hayden described, but she's timid, far too timid. Her jaw tightens at the thought. Because of *him*, of course; the endless rules, the expectations; the criticism, humiliation and reprimands. Unexpected gifts and confusing generosity from time to time, too.

Would her little girl have been so nervous and shy anyway? She doubts it. And what about her, Serena? Had she been 'sweet' too? Maybe, maybe not; she'd just been a typical kid, playing on the Welsh pavements with her pals at primary, then hanging out with Rhona in secondary, a little naughty and defiant at her new friend's instigation, but nothing too outrageous. Those days had been wild but fun; it had been great to have a daring, if bossy, best mate.

Yes, she'd been normal, doing all the usual things teenagers do – listening to music, dating unsuitable boys, drinking and smoking, occasionally playing truant. But working just hard enough to get the grades needed. Then finding her niche at university, losing her accent and becoming her own person, loving her chosen subject and flying without even trying.

She sighs at the memories. That girl she doesn't recognise at all.

–

It's dark beyond the snug curtains. Her legs curled under her bum, Serena turns the page of the novel Hayden asked her to read. 'So we can discuss it,' he said, 'like a small book group'.

She doesn't mind at all, in fact it's a luxury – having time without her mind consumed with worry, that trying-to-anticipate *everything* cycle she constantly had in her head. Had she cleaned every fingerprint, swept up every crumb? Had she said the right thing, done the right thing, offered the correct opinion? Been duly attentive, appreciative, admiring? It had been exhausting and left room for nothing else.

Spotting a stray piece of pink jigsaw, she uses it to mark her page, then puts the novel down. The mystery has been gripping so far, but right now she's distracted. Hayden and Lana are in their bedrooms and Hugh's gone to the pub. Not making eye contact and his face a little pink, he asked her if she fancied going with him, 'now that you're better. I should've asked you before'.

'That's so kind, Hugh, but Lana might wake, so I'd better say no. Have a small one for me,' she replied.

Of course she won't ever go, but the pang of regret is there – the decisions she made, the life she could have lived. Not that any of the choices were deliberate; she was just caught up, blindsided by what she thought was love and then... Well, it was the way fate had rolled her life out.

She comes back to thoughts of Hugh. What a nice man he is. Perhaps a little on the autistic spectrum? Even Asperger's? But a gentle, sweet giant. Picturing his amiable face, she smiles. So guileless, so childish, so open, showing his heart to the world. The polar opposite of his brother...

She feels herself blush. All day she's been unable to get Jack's image out of her head. His gaze, his steady handsomeness. His unexpected kindness, too. She'd thought his eyes were brown, but they're actually blue. Unfathomable pools of deep blue.

Then there's the way she'd behaved at the weekend. She'd been so sure about the malevolence in his stare and intense focus on Lana. But she can't summon up those feelings anymore. They've evaporated, gone. There's darkness for sure, but it isn't what she'd thought. It's grief. His wife died. So deeply in pain, he'd erased her from his life. That's what she'd do too. It's what she's trying to achieve now – scrubbing out the memories.

Feeling the scabs beneath her fingertips, she gently strokes her chest. Trouble is, the past doesn't want to go away.

The slamming front door breaks her thoughts. She looks at her watch. Ten o'clock, so it's finally Jack, surely? She picks up the drawing of Lexie and studies it. A pretty good likeness of the dog, then a dark-haired man standing beside her with blue eyes and a caring smile. Lana, little Lana. She saw what her mummy had been blind to. And the stick people in the background? Herself and Lana, of course, fair-haired and stuck together like Siamese twins.

She sighs and puts it back on the low table. She tried to persuade Lana to hand it to Jack herself in the morning, but she was insistent: 'No, you give it to him; I don't want to.'

That timidity again. The poor child had been stung by rejection too many times to risk it.

Serena eventually stands. No sound of further movement, nor the creak of the stairs; Jack must be in the kitchen. A little apprehensively, she ambles down the corridor and peers in. His back to the door, he's sitting at the table with a bottle of lager. Though Lexie pads towards her, Jack's as still as an effigy, so she lightly knocks.

'May I come in?'

He spins around, then shakes his startled expression away. 'Sure. I'm just winding down with a beer. Can I get you one? Or a glass of wine? White or red? Or pink? Seems rosé has become the fashion these days.' Almost bashful, he runs fingers through his silky, dark hair. 'Listen to me. "The fashion these days". It makes me sound like I'm eighty.'

'I shouldn't but...' She thinks about Hugh and the pub, that desire to be normal. 'A small glass of red won't hurt.'

'The good stuff is...' He glances at the cellar door, but his eyes seem to falter. 'I think there's a nice malbec in the pantry. Let me check.'

Aware of her increasingly flushed cheeks, Serena takes the opportunity to quickly speak whilst he's turned away. 'I popped in because I wanted to thank you for everything you've done for me, Jack. I'm very grateful. And also to say sorry for putting you in a difficult situation...'

He steps back, his face questioning, but cloudy too.

Oh God, she shouldn't have said anything. She stumbles on. 'You know, the... the medicine. Asking you to do something that's not...' How to put it? 'Not through the usual channels. I know you could get in trouble and I'm sorry to put you in that position.'

He looks at the ground and dryly laughs. 'I'd already put myself there. Not terribly wise of me.' Then, busying himself with the bottle and a corkscrew, 'You're very welcome. It's been good having you in the house, a nice break for us men and our general tetchiness.' He glances at the dog. 'Save for Lexie, of course.'

Serena looks at her too. 'She's so well behaved; I don't think I've heard her bark yet.' Yes, now she thinks of it, Lexie is a strangely silent dog. 'Does she ever woof?'

Jack briefly frowns. 'No, no she doesn't,' he replies.

He doesn't elaborate but pours the glossy wine, hands her the glass and sits down. 'Having Lana here too, of course, she's… a joy.'

Serena slides her daughter's drawing across the table. 'I think the feeling's mutual.'

Lowering his head to the picture, Jack gazes and then nods. 'It's lovely, really lovely,' he says quietly.

The silence stretches out. Finally he speaks, holding out the creation to show Lexie. 'Pretty damn good. What do you think, girl?' he asks, but there's a croak in his voice. And something in his expression she can't quite interpret.

Oh God. His wife, Melanie, of course. Was Lexie her dog? How did she die? What on earth happened?

Before she can stop herself, she reaches for his fingers and finds herself speaking.

'If ever you want to talk, I'm a good—'

'Thank you,' he replies, cutting her short. But he doesn't pull back his hand. Instead, he puts hers in both of his and holds it like a precious pebble, testing its weight and smoothness before carefully putting it down.

He clears his throat. 'It's up to you, of course,' he says. 'But you can't hide away forever.'

Caught by the change of subject, she takes a quick breath. 'I know.'

'Is he Lana's father?'

'Yes.'

'Look, I can…' He seems to change his mind. 'The law can protect you.'

She wants to say no, that nobody can, but the tears are already pooling, preventing her from speech.

Concern etched on his face, he continues to stare. 'Only when you're ready. But when you are, please come to me and I'll help, put the legal wheels in motion…'

Paralysed by anxiety, she can't find an answer, not even a nod.

'Well…' He stands and stifles a yawn. 'I think it's time for bed.'

She stares at the wooden grooves in the table. He's going. Oh God, she wants a hug; just someone to hold her, for once. No, more than that; she needs someone to kiss her and stroke her, make her feel special and loved. Feeling him hover near her arm, she wills him to stay, but he doesn't touch her. Instead, his shoes drum over the tiled floor.

'Stay in the house if you like,' he says at the door. 'Even when you're completely better. You and Lana can each have a bedroom here, more space. Use the cottage too, of course. Whichever you prefer. And when you're ready, just ask me, OK?'

Chapter Twenty-Three

Jack

Jack slides from sleep and turns over. Bloody hell, he has an erection. He hasn't woken up with such a stonker for a very long time. He snaps his head to the other side of the room. It's fine, she's not there. She hasn't been for days, even over a week. And that's a good thing. Isn't it?

He goes back to his dream and feels himself blush. It wasn't just the first erotic fantasy he's had in eons, but one involving Serena, of all people. Feeling a little guilty, he focuses on today. Patterns of morning light are dancing on the ceiling. What time is it, exactly? That's right; he stirred earlier, and twigging it was a Saturday, he allowed himself another hour. God, he must be going soft.

Snorting to himself, he flings back the duvet. He's not that self-indulgent. A brisk run's the thing to set him up for the day; he'll have one right now.

He stretches his back muscles, cleans his teeth and splashes cold water on his face. Padding it dry with a towel, he stares at his reflection. Pretty much the usual physically, but he feels so much better. More energy, enthusiasm and drive. And, dare he say it? Hope.

He opens the cabinet and stares at the pills. He hasn't taken anything since last week. Is he brave enough to flush his hoard down the bog? He closes it again. No, not quite there yet. Besides he's going for a freezing loop around the grounds. That's a start.

Searching through his drawers, he finds shorts and socks, but no hoody or sports top. Hmm, he was using weights at the gym in Leeds; they must've been washed by now. Then he remembers his conversation with the 'housekeeper' when she first arrived. Hardly a conversation; more a hysterical yell. Not to go in his bedroom. Ever.

Bloody hell, what a prick.

Sighing at his own pig-headedness, he makes for Hugh's room but abruptly stops half way down the landing. Followed by a blast of fragranced hot air, Serena is stepping from the bathroom, wrapped in just a towel. He's half naked himself; it's best he turns back. But as though sensing he's there, she abruptly swivels round.

He holds up a hand of apology. 'Sorry, didn't mean to make you jump.'

She stares for a moment before shaking her head. 'No, it's fine. After all, it is your house.'

Remembering her soft kiss in the dream before waking, he flushes again. Bloody hell, he needs to explain why he's standing here like a lemon. 'I was just on my way to Hugh's bedroom. Need to borrow a top.' His lips twitch. 'He'll probably say no. You know what he's like about his designer gear.'

She smiles back, but says nothing. He tries not to gaze at her glowing scrubbed face and her hair, wet and slicked back. Sexy, so sexy. *Just stop!*

'Not that I'm borrowing it in terms of daywear fashion, I hasten to add...' God, he's talking too much. 'I'm just off for a run.'

Her eyes travel down his torso to his shorts. Trying not to think about the erection, he looks too.

She laughs. 'I sort of worked that one out. You know, Lycra pants? Though who knows with the Cheshire set. We might yet see Hugh don them for the farm.' Then, tightening her towel, 'I didn't know you were a runner...'

'Was, rather than am, really.' He puts a hand to his stomach. 'Probably collapse at the first hurdle. Not as fit as I used to be—'

'Oh, not at all. You look very... well.'

The pink of her cheeks deepens and neither of them stir for a moment or two. Then Jack catches her blotchy, sore chest. God, the burn. In the moment he'd forgotten this woman's dreadful trauma, her past and her need to hide from a man who had brutally hurt her.

'Right, I'd better...' he says, moving forward.

Taking in the smell of limes, he carefully pushes past her, then stops at Hugh's door.

'Wish me luck,' he says over his shoulder. 'He won't thank me for waking him, but here goes.'

—

Jack paces past the dense woods. The winter air swamps his lungs. As though plunging in cold water, it's taking some time for his body to acclimatise. Because he was so bloody warm! Hot from embarrassment. Burning with weird bloody desire. Spontaneous self-combustion, like when he was a teenager.

No, not just then. He was like that afterwards too. With Melanie. Pretty, enticing and smiley. Batting her long lashes, poking out her pink tongue. Knowing exactly which buttons to press. A thirty-two year old man and he

149

couldn't get enough. Even before they'd finished making love, he wanted to start again. Holding, kissing, touching, invading. Wanting to possess her.

Well, he *possessed* her all right. Like a chattel. 'I belong to you now, darling,' she had said with a kiss at the altar. She hadn't needed to say, *And you belong to me. All that is yours is mine now.*

He'd already known that.

And now, even now, she has a grip on his windpipe like he had on hers. Though irrevocably gone, she's still bloody there.

Turning up his music, he tries to focus on the pine trees neatly bordering the narrow lane. He really has to stop his mind from wandering. Thinking about her does no good. However much he wants, he can't change the past, can't re-write the tragic ending. Nor blot out the guilt. He needs to park it and move on. And today's a good day. His face is almost frozen, his fingers dropping off, but his body's pumping with life. He had a fucking erection, he felt glorious desire! That's progress, surely? Not that he'll do anything about it. Apart from all the usual reasons not to get involved or be intimate, Serena isn't for him.

Nor is any woman with a child.

–

Jack finally stops at the gate. Bending double, he breathes deeply. He took the old 10K route along 'The Bongs', the wooded valley on the northern side of the village. Before his injury, he used to run it with Hugh and talk about the land which belonged to the Ramsays before it was gradually sold off. They were a pretty good match; what he gained by being slighter, Hugh made up for in stride.

Maybe he'll suggest they do it tomorrow. Give his brother some one-to-one time. Talk about what happened with Robbie and where he's up to at the farm. He must really do that; Hugh's been uncharacteristically quiet since trashing the games room.

The barrier slides open. His back still feeling supple, Jack decides to sprint to the house, see if he has the legs. He sets off at a fast pace, but slows down when the outbuildings come into view. Yup, Hugh's rage; the havoc in there… Their dad walking this far is highly unlikely, but he has to sort it sometime and now's as good as any. What does he require for a quick turn around? Bin liners, a brush and a shovel's a good start. The pool table will have to wait for repair or even removal. How he'll explain that to his father, he doesn't know, but he'll find a way.

Jogging past the house to the garage, he enters at the side and looks around the jumbled annexe for what he needs. Like a straw matting, hay has escaped from the barn, and the shelves are chock-a-block with a lifetime's clutter – from rusty spanners to broken kites, from stiff gardening gloves to punctured footballs. There's Hugh's paint pots and brushes, his aerosols, varnishes and turpentine too, the remnants of a whole summer spent repairing perimeter fences and gates.

Digging deep, he unearths a roll of black bags and what at first glance seems to be a pink boa. Pulling it out gingerly, it turns into a feather duster. Puffing out with relief, he slots it under his arm, picks up the spade and strides to the door. But before leaving, he does another take. There's a car covered by a sheet parked next to his dad's. He squints at the number plate peeping out. A Welsh emblem? Who on earth does it…? Then he twigs. Serena's, of course. If she's Welsh, it isn't obvious. But then again, the few inflexions in her voice when she smiles and speaks freely… Maybe, maybe not. Hardly a surprise, though; he knows nothing about her. But it's fine, really fine; what little he's gleaned is plenty enough for him to like her.

Armed with his equipment, he briskly retraces his steps. The air chilling his damp limbs, he makes his way to the games room, but stops before lifting the latch. A memory is rushing back. He often came here with little Hugh, but his mum was there that day too.

Picturing the moment, he closes his eyes. Hugh not far behind, he's tiptoeing to reach the high catch.

'Me first, me first, Jack! Let me do it!'

Though Jack longs to dive in first, he waits for his baby brother to charge through the bushes, then he circles him by the waist and lifts him up.

'You are a kind boy, Jack.' It's his mother's soft tones behind him. 'That's a real gift, because not everyone is.'

It is said so solemnly and sweetly, he turns to look at her.

Did she really have tears in her eyes?

He tries to push the emotional image away. Too like Serena last night. He should have held her; he should have been kind. Something held him back, just like that day with his mum. She needed a hug too, but he was afraid, fearful she'd break down and say something she couldn't take back. Or perhaps it was his imagination again. One of the million pieces he later coloured in to make up for her absence.

The destruction inside the room is as bad as he recalls, but he puts in his earphones and sets to work, beginning with the feather duster on the pelmets, then moving on to the scattered picture books. Attempting not to dwell on their broken spines, he keeps what he can and piles the rest in black liners. He does the same with the cushions, tying the bin bags tightly and piling them outside. Pushing the furniture to one side, he starts with the brush, cursing each time a puff of polystyrene lands on a patch he's just swept.

Nearly finished, he studies his handiwork. A damaged pool table, but a relatively 'bean' free zone. He bends to flick the final pile in his shovel, but a blast of cold air blows it away.

'What the—' he begins, turning to the door. He stares for a second. It isn't Hugh as he expects, but Serena. Wearing jeans and an open blouse, she looks different.

She shrugs and says something.

'Sorry?' he says, pulling out his earphones.

She gestures to her chest. 'I know it's unsightly, but it'll heal more quickly if I give it some air.'

'Yes, of course.' Then, like a stupid kid, 'I wasn't looking. Well, not intentionally.'

'Sorry, I'm being over sensitive.' She glances around. 'I saw you from the kitchen window looking like Carson.' She cocks her head. 'The butler in *Downton*? What are you up to? I did knock.'

Hoping she hasn't clocked the broken table, Jack looks around too. 'Getting rid of the old beanbags. Maybe go for proper chairs or a sofa. Perhaps a drink's fridge.'

She chuckles, steps towards him and pulls something from his fringe. Her breath soft on his face, she tiptoes and collects more from the top of his head. 'Beans, I assume,' she says, holding out her palm.

Without thinking, he leans forward and kisses her cheek. 'It isn't unsightly at all. Nothing about you is.'

Compelled to say more, he inhales, but she slips her arms around his neck and her lips are touching his. Soft but firm; full, warm and insistent. So exquisite, it's almost painful. Drawing her to him, he kisses her back. He mustn't think about it too deeply. *Go with the moment, Jack. Dance and feel alive, just for once.*

Finally pulling away, she laughs breathlessly. 'That was nice, though it isn't actually what I came in for.' She pulls a mobile from her pocket and hands it to him. 'Yours, I believe. It kept ringing in the kitchen. I thought it might be urgent, maybe work.'

'Oh, OK...'

His whole body aches. From crouching down, from the run, but mostly with desire. Wishing he wasn't wearing damned Lycra, he tries to focus on what this glorious woman is saying. His phone; right. He goes to missed calls and glances at the number. Five attempts on the trot, but no voicemail message.

'You're right, they were persistent.' He shrugs. 'Number not known and no message. PPI's my guess.'

Suddenly feeling bashful, he takes a pace back. 'Sorry, I must reek from sweat and grime,' he says. Then, quickly, before he changes his mind, 'You've had a rough time recently. Let me take you out somewhere nice. A meal or a drink. Or we could even go somewhere for a dance.'

Her gaze flickers. 'I don't really—'

A woman in hiding. And ill. What the hell was he thinking? 'No, of course not. Besides, you're not fully better and...'

Moving to him again, she leans her head on his chest. When she lifts her face, her eyes are glistening and sincere. 'I used to love a good old bop. You have no idea how wonderful that would be, but it's early days since… I still don't feel ready to…'

His jaw clenches. The man who hurt her. The bastard, fucking bastard who did that. 'Sorry, you're right. Absolutely. It's too early in the morning, my brain hasn't engaged yet—'

She cups his face, kisses both his cheeks, then his lips, lingering there in a tender and meaningful way. 'But we could go for a drive sometime if you like?'

Oh God, the heat, the burning bolt of desire. It takes a moment to register what she's saying and when he does, he can't hide the grin. 'Yup, a spin in the car sounds good. Sometime when I'm not clammy and covered in particles, perhaps?'

'Maybe.' She smiles. 'Like tonight?'

He wants to laugh and punch the air. 'Tonight, eh? Sounds good, though I'll have to check my incredibly busy social schedule and see if I'm free…'

Chapter Twenty-Four

Hugh

Hugh catches his reflection in another shop window. He's styled his hair differently today. More quiff-like than usual. He isn't sure if he likes it; he isn't sure about anything.

Chester town centre on a Saturday usually cheers him. 'Retail therapy again?' Jack always teases. 'You're the best dressed Ramsay in Goostrey.'

Sometimes he feels bad that Jack still gives him an allowance. 'Don't even mention it,' Jack says. 'You earned it. When I needed... strong arms, you were there.'

He sighs, opens the glossy shopping bag and peers in. He's been walking aimlessly for two hours and he hasn't bought much; Ralph Lauren socks to replace the ones Jess failed to return and a three-pack of Calvin Klein boxers. He tried on a shirt, but couldn't even be bothered with the buttons. He doesn't feel hungry at all, but perhaps that's the problem. He nods. An Oreo McFlurry usually hits the spot and it's on the way to the carpark, so a 'win-win' as his dad would say.

Feeling a little brighter at having made a decision, he strides along Watergate Street and looks up at the half-timbered galleries. He knows The Rows are unique in the world to Chester and that nobody's quite sure why they were built that way, but what he particularly likes is the name. The Rows are, well, rows, a second row of shops above the ones at street level. Why can't life be like that? Why can't people actually say what's on their mind? Jack might be right about people not meaning what they say or not saying what they mean, but quite frankly it's doing his head in.

'Hugh? Hello?'

He turns to the familiar voice. A small woman in a thick winter coat bobs into view.

'Hello, Hugh, how's it going?'

He automatically touches his hair, but his fingers get caught up in the dense web of styling spray. 'Uh, yeah, fine.'

It's Mrs Amara, her gaze as dark and intense as he remembers. He feels himself flushing. 'I'm very well, thanks.' As though needing proof, he lifts his bag. 'I've been shopping.'

'That's nice.' She leans her head to one side and studies him in that way she always did. It's spooky, like she's reading his mind. 'I was just going for a cappuccino. Do you fancy joining me?'

He hears his dad's voice: *'For God's sake, Hugh, just try! Be more amenable to change.'* But he's on his way to McDonalds; coffee's not in the plan. 'Thanks Mrs Amara, but—'

Though half his size, she slots her arm into his and propels him to The Flower Cup coffee shop. 'It's just Amara, remember? Come on. Just a quick one. I could do with some company.'

-

Even before the drinks arrive, Hugh finds his worries pouring out.

'One minute he was friendly like he used to be, then he just stalked off…'

Struggling out of her coat, Mrs Amara puts her tiny fingers on his wrist. 'Let's just rewind, shall we? So who's Robbie? Take a really deep breath and start at the beginning, same as we used to.'

Like the steam from the next table's teapot, Hugh feels the angst easing out already. He usually talks to Jack, but he's seemed far away and besides… His thoughts pop out as words.

'I haven't told Jack.'

He waits for Mrs Amara's reaction. He tells his brother about most things, but not this. Nor the burn of shame which still hits him from time to time.

Wearing a spectacular red sari, Mrs Amara sits back. She knows Jack, of course. It was he who arranged the counselling sessions way back. 'OK,' she says. 'Let's start there. Why haven't you told him?'

'He doesn't like Robbie.'

'And how do you know this? Has he said so?'

Hugh thinks. No he hasn't. Jack's never said that. But he frowns and rubs his temple whenever Robbie's mentioned. And if he tells Jack, he'll ask more questions than he wants to answer. Mrs Amara does that too, now he thinks of it. But she's a professional, as Jack pointed out: *You know you can always talk to me, Hugh, but no one spills the beans about everything. You can tell her anything you like and you can trust her because she's a professional and it's all confidential.*

He looks at her now, her hands folded patiently as she waits for him to speak.

He takes a big breath. 'So, Robbie was my best friend when we were kids. Then he went to Australia. He came back and I thought we'd be pals again but he's changed, he was horrible, really mean…'

Can he say he punched Robbie? Should he tell her he wanted to beat him to a pulp? Admit to those uncontrollable, angry feelings which brought him to her in the first place? But that's not what's really been bewildering him for the last few days. It's what Robbie was saying. And the way that he said it, with those desperate, hollow eyes.

'Then later he said he'd been really drunk and was sorry. It was like he came back, you know, the old Robbie. Then he was…'

Hugh thinks. Sad? No more than sad. That's why he's been worried. After all, look what happened to Jack when he… But his concern is mixed with anger too. Every time he tries to work it out, he gets hot and cross: you can't just be nice to someone one minute, then nasty the next.

Mrs Amara takes off her glasses and rubs them with a serviette. 'He was what, Hugh?'

'Upset. *Really* upset. He said he'd been so unhappy in Australia that he had to leave. Now he feels guilty because he has a wife and children who're still there. He doesn't know what to do.'

Mrs Amara waits.

'He said everyone was having a go at him, including me. But I didn't say anything. I hadn't said anything before I…'

The waitress interrupts with the drinks and he's glad. He won't mention the heavy blow to Robbie's stomach. She'd be too disappointed to hear that. Instead, he comes back to what really bugs him. 'It just isn't fair. He wasn't being fair.'

Mrs Amara sips the foam from the top of her coffee, then wipes away her milky moustache. After a beat, she speaks slowly. 'Robbie's behaviour. Getting angry and drunk, feeling sad and guilty. Could it be that this has more to do with him than you?'

Hugh pulls his doubtful face, but Mrs Amara continues, her voice going higher at the end of each sentence: 'Do you remember why you first came to see me? You were frustrated and unhappy, so you got angry with Jack? Jack hadn't done anything wrong either, had he? You were taking it out on him because he under-stood? Because he's your brother and you love him? Well, friendship can be like that too. I'm not saying it's right, but sometimes you have to look deeper and search for reasons.'

Spooning sugar in his tea, Hugh mulls her words over. He never hit Jack, but he often shouted until he was blue in the face and then ran away. He knocks the drink back in two gulps.

'OK, so how do I do that?'

'Speak to him, of course. It sounds to me like your friend needs someone to confide in. Ask him how he is, how things are going, then he might talk back, explain his strange behaviour and tell you how he feels. It might not be easy for either of you, but it's worth a try, surely?'

Thankful he ordered tea for two, Hugh refills his cup. Talk to Robbie. Find out how he feels. He likes that idea. Sure, it makes him a little nervous, but it excites him too.

Chapter Twenty-Five

Serena

Sure she's being watched, Serena walks down the icy pathway to Jack's waiting car. Her fingers on the handle, she lifts her head to Hayden's front corner window. The curtains are open but there's no sign of him. Not that it would matter if there was. She's doing nothing wrong. Though she didn't say where she was going, she asked him if he could keep an ear out for Lana while she 'popped out'.

He barely shifted his attention from his laptop. 'Of course, not a problem. She's asleep, I assume?'

'Yes she is,' she replied, still wondering what had become of Lana's panda. She usually wouldn't settle without him, but she'd just giggled behind her hand when Serena asked where he was.

'That's fine, but leave her door open so I can hear,' Hayden said, still looking at the screen. Then he nodded to the empty decanter with smile. 'But if you could do the honours before you go, I'd be most obliged.'

The usual need to please him was there, so she went downstairs to replenish the brandy and cut him a large size of cake. 'Ah coffee and walnut,' he said when she presented it. 'Thought I could smell something delicious going on this afternoon. And it's my favourite. Thank you.'

Taking a last glance, she now climbs into the Porsche. The door closes with a solid thud and Jack sets off smoothly down the driveway.

'OK?' he asks and she nods.

Her heart is actually thrashing and her throat's bone dry. Excitement and nerves. Anxiety, too. It was her who instigated this tryst. If that's what it is. Did she read the signs correctly? What did he make of her forwardness in kissing him first? In truth, she'd surprised herself at the emergence of bold Serena – a woman she hasn't seen for years.

She glances at her 'date'. Does she like him or is she just following her bodily needs because he happens to be here?

God, she has no idea. He's undoubtedly attractive, yet so was *he*. But this man isn't controlling; she's seen him snap and scowl, but it hides vulnerability and kindness. Doesn't it?

At the barrier, he turns to her and smiles. 'I'm afraid I don't have much of a plan. Maybe turn left, then left and then left. Then we'll know to turn right—'

'On the way back. Sounds good to me. It's just nice to get—'

A ringtone interrupts. Jack looks at the dashboard. 'It's Hugh. Sorry, I'd better…'

'Of course, no problem.'

He speaks to his brother briefly, then drives through the gate. 'Left it is…'

Following the moon's silver beam, they fall silent. But Serena's mind is clanging inside. Why is the old breathlessness there, almost clogging her throat? It's been there, if she's honest, since this morning in Hayden's bedroom.

Full of unexpected energy, she'd persuaded him to get up so she could strip and change his bedding. Wafting out the clean sheet, she'd set to work at the edges, then thrown on the blankets he prefers to a duvet.

'Hospital corners, I like that,' he'd said from the chair behind her.

'Sorry?' she'd replied, turning.

He'd lowered his newspaper. 'Hospital corners, the old-fashioned way. Rare these days. Bet my sons don't know what one is, never mind how to do them.'

She'd felt a prickling then but she'd nodded and smiled. He was still in his pyjamas, refusing to be chivvied downstairs, yet again.

As though reading her mind, he'd tilted his head. 'Everything's here in this bedroom, Serena. My laptop for the world wide web and all its dirty, dark secrets. Windows to observe the comings and goings along the drive. Newspaper and breakfast on a tray. My little bell when I need Lana to do an errand or have one of our interesting chats. The television if I fancy. And right now, your company.'

She'd perched on the bed. 'True, but it's important you get around more. Build your muscles. And your confidence. It's vital to do your rehab exercises to get your strength and movement back. Just the stairs will make a big difference. Shall we give it a go later?'

'Yes, nurse.' He'd gone back to his reading. '*Nurse* Serena. Yes, that sounds about right.'

She'd been on the point of leaving when he spoke again. 'Your wages. Online banking makes thing so easy these days. Just jot down your details and I'll sort it out later.' He'd peered for a beat. 'Or perhaps you would prefer cash?'

Now shaking herself back, she turns to Jack, surprised to see he's pulled up the car in a lay-by set back from the road. And he's staring intently. 'Are you OK?' he asks. 'Would you prefer to go back?'

'No, of course not.' Then after a moment. 'No, why?'

He massages his forehead. 'Nothing, ignore me. You just seemed far away, a little… worried, I suppose.'

She gazes at his face, his sculpted handsome features and those beautiful eyes. She's been waiting for this moment all day. A chance to cuddle and chat, to ogle and stare, to take him in and devour him. Not to be the restrained, bunched up person she's become, but the Serena of old, the woman who was liberated, carefree and yes, bloody fun. She so wants her back, but adult life got in the way. Bad relationships, poor decisions, mistakes. From the frying pan and into the fire. Oh, God. But she has Lana, her Lana; she has to focus on that. And this man here and now, who she's desperate to kiss.

Despite herself, she chuckles.

His frown clears and he smiles. 'What?'

'I'm just nervous! I've been excited all afternoon, not daring to look at you in the house. Wondering if we were still meeting. Worrying if this morning's gorgeous… *moment* was just my imagination. You didn't say anything until your text.' She inclines to peck his lips, then affects a sad face. 'That was mean, Jack.'

As though to speak, he inhales, then seems to change his mind. Instead, he pulls back his seat. 'So, this morning,' he says, 'remind me.'

Experimenting with soft lips and tongues, they kiss for some time. She finally breaks away with a small laugh. 'I feel like I've been running,' she says. 'I'm not sure I took a breath.' Then, peering outside, 'Where are we parked? It might be easier to *breathe* in the back.'

Nodding, he leaves the car and walks around to her side. Feeling a little shy, she takes his hand to climb out, but before opening the rear door, he pins her against it and kisses her deeply. Completely lost in the moment, she returns his caresses. It's bloody cold, she knows, but she can't feel it, only his warm, spicy smell, his hard body and her ache to feel loved.

Finally settled in the back, Jack sweeps a lock of hair from her cheek. 'I like your hair down. I like it up too, actually. It's beautiful either way.' He draws a finger from her forehead, down her nose, to her chin. 'Symmetrical, classical and… just perfect.'

Quickly leaning in, she dissolves that word with another kiss. She's far, far from ideal. But she mustn't think about that. No future, no past, just the here and now, the warmth, the intimacy, the desire. Moving to his crotch, she feels for a zip but finds buttons instead. Needing two hands, she sits up.

Jack laces his fingers through hers. 'Let's just chat and cuddle,' he says.

'Are you sure? I'm more than happy to…'

'I'm sure.' He draws her to his shoulder and pecks her forehead. 'Just being with you, holding you is lovely.'

'OK…'

Insecurity floods in but she wills it away. He's pulling back for sure, but it's not about her. He's a man who lost his wife. A man who's clearly still grieving for her. She must remember that. Can she ask about Melanie? Should she?

A sudden squall raps the rooftop. She takes a sharp breath. 'Talk to me, Jack. Is it Melanie?' she asks, sitting forward to study his face.

'No, not at all.' He pauses and looks thoughtful. 'Actually, yes, perhaps it is.'

He seems to drift for a time, then comes back to her. 'I will tell you, I promise. It's still so… so raw. I'm sorry I can't just…' He smiles thinly. 'Besides, you don't need my angst, you have enough on your plate with—'

'Pierre.'

There, his name's out. She isn't sure why she said it. Trust, she supposes. Yes, you need to give it to earn it back.

Enveloping her in his arms, Jack holds her tightly. 'What happened?' he asks into her hair.

The heat is immediate, the anger still there. God, she can feel it right now – that constant bloody tension – her body filled with dense, heavy air, weighing her down.

'Manipulation, control. But so cleverly done. Slowly, stealthily.' She's glad he can't see her face. And though she doesn't know why, she can't quite bring herself to explain it in the first person. 'Everything you need when you're weak. The centre of his world. Making you feel special, cared for and loved.'

She thinks for a moment. 'But keeping you feeble by reminding you about your vulnerability, your frailty, your mistakes. Then when you grow a little stronger, the rules change to keep you submissive. Isolation and criticism, directives and all kinds of gaslighting.'

As the memories hurtle back, she feels her eyes welling. His lack of affection and her desperate need for physical love to replace it, too. So badly that she had begged. But she won't tell Jack that. Instead, she nods to the windscreen and her brisk voice comes out. 'The rain has stopped. It's probably a good time to get going.'

–

Serena breaks the silence when the barrier thuds behind them.

'I'll get out here if you don't mind.' She catches Jack's frown. 'I just fancy a bit of fresh air before going to bed.'

He nods. 'It's late, let me take you a bit closer.'

Clambering out near the games room, she watches the rear lights of the Porsche clear the bend. She wants to stamp with frustration. Pierre, bloody Pierre, still controlling somehow. He clouded a lovely evening as only he could. Her own fault, really; it was she who let him in.

Like Jack that very first meeting, she pulls up her collar and strolls towards the house. Jack, lovely Jack. So troubled, so tender, so intense. Oh God, she wants him to hold her, to kiss her and yes, to invade her willing, wanting body, but she's just pushed him away. Though she tried to rise above it in the car, she'd been stung by his gentle rebuff, his rejection.

She offered him sex; he didn't want it.

She deeply sighs. Jack isn't *him*. She must remember that. And though she occasionally tried to play Pierre at the snubbing, silent game, she never, ever won; she was always the worthless, needy loser in the end.

Desperate to connect before bed, she hurries to the Porsche and peers in the windscreen. Jack isn't waiting. Nor is he at the kitchen table with a beer as she'd hoped. He's gone to bed and why wouldn't he?

Willing him to appear, she spends several minutes in the bathroom, has a shower she doesn't need and cleans her teeth until her gums bleed.

167

Pierre, bloody Pierre. She should not have let him in.

Her jaw clenched, she stares in the mirror until she finds a steely glint in her eyes. The old Serena *is* still in there. She won't let her mistakes rule her; they poisoned her past; they won't kill her future.

Straightening her shoulders, she nods, turns off the landing lights and feels her way in the dark until she finds the final door. She gropes for the ceramic handle and turns it. It gently clicks open, so she pushes inside, makes her way to the bed, drops her damp towel and climbs in.

Chapter Twenty-Six

Jack

Woken by a breezy sigh, Jack turns to the other pillow.

Recall softly spreading, he smiles. Serena, sweet Serena, still asleep. Careful not to disturb her, he peers at the time on his mobile. Nearly five o'clock; four solid hours of blissful sleep. He won't get back off now, but that's more than fine; he's happy, content to gaze at the slim outline of her shoulder.

He rests his head on his arm and settles back down. What a day, what a night. That unexpected kiss in the games room, the buzz of anticipation throughout the morning, then the fear he'd made a humiliating mistake. Wondering and waiting for her to give him a glance or a sign all afternoon, which she didn't. Finally preparing himself for rejection, but too cowardly to just ask, so sending a text: '*Still on for tonight? Eight o'clock?*'

Then the 'date', the drive out. Needing so badly to get it right. Swinging from the low of the halting journey to the heavens in the lay-by, then plummeting straight back to earth with a painful thud. Hard and aroused, he wanted Serena so much, but suppose he went soft? What if he lost his erection? The mortification when he'd been unable to 'perform' with Wanda was bad enough, but he'd been pretty damned pissed that night, and though he hadn't disabused the poor girl of her assumption that she'd done something wrong, it didn't mean anything emotionally. The other women too; the one-night disasters he'd tried to blot out. Erectile dysfunction, oh God. He couldn't even bring himself to type the letters in a search engine, let alone go to a doctor.

But last night was important; it meant something. Better to stop it in the car with his pride almost intact. In mentioning Melanie, Serena had clearly misread his reticence. He was initially surprised, but of course she was right; the two things are connected; everything bad is.

He now stares into space. He's not sure how or why, but he offended Serena in the car somehow. Came to bed thinking it was the final bloody blow and probably just as well. Then he heard the door open, inhaled her sweet scent and felt her soft caresses on his goosebumped, tingling skin.

Feeling his groin stir again, he flips onto his stomach. No he didn't come, but it didn't matter a jot. He stayed hard, bloody hard. His eyes accustoming to the darkness, he watched the intensity in Serena's face until it peaked, then relaxed.

'Thank you,' she whispered with a sigh and a smile. Then moments later, her eyes flicking open, 'You didn't...'

But it was absolutely fine. 'But you did,' he replied with a grin.

Like a gift, a perfect gift he couldn't explain if he tried.

-

Gentle breath and soft lips; warm skin and stroking.

Jack opens his eyes. A crack of light through the curtains… He fell asleep after all and, oh God, what a waking.

Nuzzling down his neck to the base of his throat, then onto his chest, gradually following the line of his hair as it tapers to his belly. A few moments there, then slipping down further.

Oh God.

Slim arms and long limbs, a waist he can almost circle with his fingers. Then rocking, slow swaying, his hands on her bum. Her voice low and sleepy, her lazy, contented smile. Then her face, her perfect features, stilled in concentration. Then a pant, a gasp, then another and another.

Responding in kind. Heart pounding, rapid breath. Vividness, intense pressure, building in force. Oh God, he's exploding, he's fucking bursting apart.

–

Waking to a new morning, Jack tries to snatch the warm childhood recollection back. A nice one for sure, but it's floating away, just out of reach. His mum's loving smile is all that is left.

Surprised to see the pale sunshine, he sits up. The curtains are billowing through the window, but that's absolutely fine. It must have been opened by Serena; unknowingly letting the bad memories and spirits fly out. And last night, when she miraculously slipped into his bed; oh Lord. He flicks to her side but already knows that she's left.

Then the second lovemaking… A dream, an incredible, erotic dream? He laughs and falls against the warm mattress. No, not a fantasy, his body's too knackered for that. Well, not exhausted exactly, but replete and satisfied, yet insubstantial too. He ejaculated, he bloody came and what an incredible blast. One minute his whole body was being sucked out, the next he was unconscious.

He smiles; *la petite mort* indeed.

He turns onto his belly and stretches out. Maybe he should lie here all day like his dad. It's a Sunday; he could do it if he liked. He's his own bloody boss; he doesn't have to head for the study and work. Though in reality he does. With the time off this week, he has an even bigger backlog than usual. Paperwork, instructions and research, not to mention the hearings and trials coming up. But it was worth it, absolutely. It felt so good to be here for Serena when she'd needed him.

He deeply frowns at the thought of what she's been through. The dreadful burn and her illness. As for the man who hurt her… The heat rises, the anger robbing him of breath. Pierre, he's called Pierre. He'd like to track him down and pulp him to pieces. Throwing boiling coffee at a woman; what person does that? The bastard will pay for what he did, but Serena needs legal protection first and he can't help with that until she's ready.

Feeling his stomach rumble, he throws back the duvet and stands up. Shower, then food. Her lovely smile. And little Lana's. But he's OK about that. Isn't he?

–

Smiling at the thought of the beanbag bits caught in it yesterday, Jack lathers his hair. It seems like a lifetime ago already. So much has happened since. *That* has happened since. He feels like he did when he lost his virginity; he wants to punch the air, or possibly belt out a tune. But perhaps that isn't wise: though he wasn't aware of doing it yesterday, Hugh caught him lightly whistling.

'You're humming, Jack,' he said. 'Why are you whistling?'

He laughs at the memory. Like it's a criminal offence! But that's his brother for you; picking up on things that others wouldn't notice, yet ignoring issues that stare him in the face. That's a thought. Will he mind when he finds out about him and Serena? And what about their dad?

He briskly rubs himself dry, then pauses to listen. The peel of his phone again; he heard it earlier in the shower. It might be chambers-related, it's best to grab it. He hops from the en suite to the bedside table, but inevitably it stops the moment he reaches it. He peers at the screen – the same number from yesterday. Perhaps it is work; the case in London next week, or the one in Chester after that. Still, if it's important, they'll leave a message.

Finally shaved and dressed, he stops and inhales at the top of the staircase. The whiff of bacon tells him Serena's up and making breakfast, but he must quell his excitement. Who knows where this fledgling relationship will go from here? He can't look that far forward; he daren't. But he's happy right now, an emotion he hasn't felt for years. *Hold onto that; remember it, bottle it.*

He opens the kitchen door and she's there at the sink.

'Morning, Jack. Did you have a good night's sleep?' she asks.

Letting out his trapped breath, he returns her sunny smile. Everything's OK, it's bloody OK.

He thinks how to reply, but Lana flies from the table and grabs his hand. 'I've taught Lexie to give me her paw. You have to watch!'

Belting to the pantry, she brings out a box, digs in and stands before the dog. Her legs apart, she hides the biscuit behind her back.

'Sit, Lexie,' she says solemnly. Lexie does as she's told.

'Paw,' she commands. Lexie obeys and gets the treat for her troubles.

Jack claps. 'Fantastic. You'll both be on *Britain's Got Talent* before we know it.'

Wiping her hands, Serena steps from her chore. 'And what did you make for Lexie?' she asks Lana. 'Go and get it so you can show Jack.'

He watches her skip from the room. When the door clicks to, slim arms circle his waist from behind.

'I'm glad you slept well,' Serena says. 'So did I, as it happens.'

He turns and pecks her nose, her eyes and her cheeks, then finally those sensual lips. 'Someone woke me up early, though.'

'Too dreadful; poor you. Perhaps you should demand recompense.'

He kisses her again. 'Perhaps I should, and very soon.'

The door fires open and they pull apart. Pink-faced with pleasure, Lana brandishes a piece of cardboard. 'It's made from toilet paper and tissues. It isn't finished yet. I need to cut it out and Mummy's going to find me some ribbon.'

Jack studies her creation. 'Wow, a rosette for our clever dog. You are talented.'

He gives her a quick hug, but she lifts her arms and wraps her legs tightly around him. He wants to kiss her too, but it's emotion, that's all, just pure, intense joy.

Serena breaks the moment. 'I think that's yours again, Jack.'

'Sorry?'

'Your mobile.'

'Oh right.' He puts Lana down and pulls out his phone. 'Same number again. How odd.'

But as gazes at the screen, a message soon follows.

> Don't you ever answer your phone? I need to talk to you. It's urgent. Call me back. Please.

Serena's still gazing, a small frown marring her face. 'You've gone as white as a sheet. Is everything all right?'

'Sure.' He tries to look normal, to breathe through the panic. 'It's just work stuff I need to sort out. In fact...' He smooths Lana's fine hair. 'I'd better go to the study and get stuck in now. I'll grab some breakfast later.'

Wondering if they can hear the clanging of his heart, he heads for his refuge.

'*Don't you ever answer your phone? I need to talk to you. It's urgent. Call me back. Please.*'

No name, of course, and that reluctant 'please'...

Melanie, bloody Melanie. What the hell does *she* want?

Chapter Twenty-Seven

Hugh

Wondering if the smell of butter is real or imagined, Hugh lifts his head.

'Ouch. Shit.'

He lays it back very gently. Like a loose crankshaft bolt, something has obviously come free.

'That bad?' Robbie closes the door and puts a tray on the floor. 'Tea and toast.' He holds out two pills. 'From Jess, of course. Told her you were rat-arsed and that I had to ply you with water last night. She wanted to check you out herself before hitting the sack but I did you a kindness…'

Hugh carefully hitches up the bed and takes the proffered pain killers.

'Because I thought you might have puked again,' Robbie continues in his lilting voice that always sounds like a question. He sniffs and snorts. 'Smell the air, mate, still stinks. Don't you remember?'

Frowning at the 'mate', Hugh accepts the mug of tea in one hand, the food in the other. His head throbs and his bare chest is pimpled from the cold, but his stomach feels surprisingly fine. In fact he's bloody starving. Did he eat dinner yesterday? He has a vague recollection about the take-out in the village. That's right. 'Peas or beans;

vinegar, tartare, curry or gravy on your chips?' the sullen teenager asked. The tartare being a recent option. It had made Jack laugh when he first told him. 'Only in Cheshire,' he'd commented with raised eyebrows.

His belly slightly turns at the memory. 'Bung them all on,' he'd replied. That was after several swigs of cheap whisky. And the beer at the pub.

Taking the second slice, he eyes up his visitor. What's *he* doing here anyway? The last he recalls of bloody Robbie Barnes is seeing him in The Bull.

Trying to concentrate, he scrunches his face. Yup, it's all coming back. Robbie was at a table with two lads from his school. Robbie's state school, of course, not Hugh's '*posh*' one.

He breathes heavily through his nose at the thought. The posh school, the posh school. Well, that's hardly his fault. And he'd hated it, actually. Sitting through endless lessons of double bloody Dutch. The only thing that got him through the week was his excellence at sport. Each parents' consultation evening was the same: 'Strictly speaking, Mr Ramsay, Hugh shouldn't still be with us, but we were delighted with his cricket performance for the school. No one can ask for more than six wickets and a half century...'

The two pub 'mates' had looked familiar, probably the same ones who'd taunted him back in the day. But then again, most of the locals had. His nickname at his private school was 'Huge', but that was OK. 'Posh boy' and 'village idiot' wasn't. Yet Robbie had still been his best friend, the one person, apart from Jack, who *got* him, who'd listen without laughing... So he nodded to himself at the bar: if Mrs Amara said he should encourage Robbie to talk, then he was willing to give it a go. With perfect timing, Robbie stood to go for a piss. That was Hugh's chance to get him alone. What had Mrs Amara said? That it was worth a try. So he followed him in and waited at the sink. Robbie finally came out and caught his eyes in the mirror, but he didn't even acknowledge him. He grabbed a paper towel, lobbed it in the bin and left without a word.

What the fuck? He'd tried to '*search deeper*' and look for '*reasons*' but as usual he couldn't get anything right. That's why he went on a whisky bender and ended up in the caravan instead of his own comfy bed. Suffered from bloody spinning and whirling too.

Hugh now glances at his ex-friend. Yeah, and vomiting. He finally remembers that. At some point there was a blast of cold air, and Robbie appeared holding out a litre bottle of water.

'You ignored me in The Bull. I wanted to talk, look for reasons,' he managed to stutter.

Robbie frowned. 'Then call me, send me a text. Find me here at the farm. Don't follow me into the dunny.'

Double bloody Dutch. Hugh wanted to ask what that meant, but his mouth wouldn't work anymore.

'The bloody toilets, Hugh. If you want a conversation, fine, but don't try it there.' Robbie stared for a moment, then shook his head. 'Come on, Hugh. You're not stupid; you know exactly why.'

Hugh now finishes his last mouthful. Trying to ignore the old stirring – and shameful – sensation, he shrugs. 'If it smells so bad in here, feel free to leave. Can't remember inviting you in in the first place.'

Robbie sighs. 'Last night you said you wanted to talk.'

'Did I?'

'Yeah, you said something about reasons.'

Picturing Mrs Amara's neat face, Hugh doesn't reply for a moment. What did she say? Yes; ask him how he is, how things are going. He thinks about saying it, but the agitation fires out. 'You can't just be nice to someone one minute, then nasty the next.'

Robbie looks at his hands. 'I know.'

'You had a go at me twice when I'd done nothing wrong. It just isn't fair!'

Abruptly standing, Robbie moves to the door. 'Come on, get dressed and we'll go for a walk. Twenty minutes?' He leaves, then bobs his head in again. 'And put on a thick jumper. Jess says you're not keeping nearly warm enough.'

-

Wearing a backpack, Robbie stalks across the first field at a fast pace.

'Hold up,' Hugh eventually calls through the drizzle. 'I still have a headache.'

'Sorry, forgot about that, mate,' Robbie replies over his shoulder, but still he marches forward, hugging the pine forest path.

In the shade of the trees the grass is still crispy with frost. Listening to the crunch beneath his boots, Hugh takes larger steps to catch up. He likes walking as much as the next man, but what is this one for? Robbie's not saying anything and his face was so closed when they met at the stile that it's difficult to know what his mood might be. He's pretty much ignored him or been angry since he came back from Aussieland.

The meadows open out and Robbie finally stops at a crumbling wall. He smiles ruefully and looks at his palms.

'*That* I don't miss. Remember those days? Building the buggers up piece by piece. I always forgot gloves and cut up my hands.' He squints into the distance. 'But when I was *there* I longed to…' He glances at Hugh. 'There in Brisbane…' He picks up a rough stone. 'I longed to hold one of these. Throw one of these.' He makes to chuck it at Hugh, then laughs. 'You were far more diligent than me.' Then cocking his head, 'Hard-working, Hugh. You always worked here, really, you just didn't get paid until—'

'You said I stole your job.'

'I know. That was stupid. The booze talking.'

Hugh shuffles his feet. 'Thought you couldn't remember what you'd said in the barn.'

Robbie doesn't reply but goes back to his study of the countryside surrounding them. Hugh looks too. The rain has stopped and weak sunshine is trying to warm the hillside, the purple thistles, the stripped bones of the trees, but it's still bloody cold. Perhaps he should've worn thermals after all.

'God, I missed this.' Robbie stretches out his arms. 'Never thought I would. Those brutal bloody winters when I had to help Dad at the weekends. Mucking out at dawn for a pathetic amount of pocket money.' He pauses and frowns. 'But there's nothing as cruel as an endless horizon, scorching sun and loneliness. A life sentence in an open prison; that's how it felt. But in fairness, that was later. The fruit-picking was fun.' He lifts his palms to his face and sniffs them. 'Sometimes I can still smell the tomatoes and capsicums even now.'

Hugh nods. He'd heard about the fruit farm. No idea how. Perhaps it was Jess, though she'd have been ten or so back then.

Robbie continues to speak. 'I was glad to get away from here at first. Bloody ecstatic. Two fingers up to the bastards. And it was great. Fruit and veg fields as far as the eye could see, but the vast space didn't matter then because me and the other pickers lived in a commune, we were part of a family. It was a laugh. Games and booze, films, entertainment, pretty girls.' He snorts without humour. 'Thought I'd bloody won – living the dream while you lot were still wearing school blazers and sat at your desks, taking exams, doing homework and bloody *enrichment*.'

He abruptly moves on, so Hugh strides to catch up. 'What happened then?' he asks.

Robbie shakes his head. 'I met Vicky.'

In silence, they continue to hike. Then Robbie takes a left, trudging across the marshy grass diagonally. Resisting the urge to reprimand him for taking a short cut, Hugh trucks behind him. Then the derelict building pops up on the skyline. He shrugs and follows. A funny way to walk to the shepherd's cottage, but that's OK, especially if there's some tuck in Robbie's bag.

When they reach the pebbled path, Robbie nods to the bushes. 'Kindling. Make yourself useful, mate.'

They eventually remove their muddy boots at the door and peer in.

'It'll warm up pretty soon,' Robbie says, getting to work.

When the fire's finally glowing, he hunkers down, pours drink from a flask and hands Hugh the cup. After a while, he speaks. 'You said you wanted to talk to me.'

'Yeah, sure.' Thrown for a moment, Hugh looks at the burgeoning flames. 'We could have talked in the caravan.'

Robbie shrugs. 'The door barely closes, never mind having a lock.'

'Neither does here.'

'Here is a mile away from the farm, Hugh.' He gives an impatient sigh. 'Are you being deliberately dumb or forgetful or just winding me up? Same with the bloody toilets last night.'

Hugh quickly glances at him before turning away. 'What do you mean?'

'We used to come here before I left. We hung out.'

The heat of irritation rises. 'Yeah, Robbie, and you left without even saying goodbye. I didn't know until Jack told me.' He tries to blow out the anger like Mrs Amara taught him. 'You went off to the fruit farm. You got married. You have two kids.'

'Life isn't that black and white. I know you think it is but—'

'You changed.'

'No I didn't!' Robbie scrambles to his feet. 'That was the fucking problem!' He throws his head back and sighs. 'I spent all those years living a lie. Maybe not at first. Everything was good. A pretty wife and a nice house, then the children came along. But as time went on I knew I was kidding myself.'

Looking at Hugh, he snorts. 'Pathetic, I was. Those long, burning days in the outback. Know what I was thinking about? A boy I once fancied. A fantasy of course, made perfect by rose-tinted bloody time. We all grow up, age, mature, wrinkle, whatever. I knew that. But I came back to the farm and he's there, frozen, still the boy that I...'

Trying to work it all out, Hugh stares.

Robbie crouches down and takes him by the shoulders. 'You, Hugh.'

Hugh roughly shakes him off. '*You, Hugh.*' He said those words before in the cow shed. What was it he called him? 'You said I was an imbecile, a Mummy's boy. Why would you say things like that?'

Robbie sighs. 'I don't know, it's complicated. Maybe I wanted you to beat the shit out of me and finish me off because I'm too chicken to do it myself. Or perhaps it's the same as in the farm kitchen, the pub, the bloody men's dunny – I want you to go away.' He pats his temple, then his chest. 'In here or in here, I don't know. But I want it to go away. I want to see my kids. I want to fancy my wife. I want to be normal.'

Normal? Hugh snorts. Well, he's never been that and he's coped. Surprising himself, he shrugs and finds his dad's words coming out of his mouth. 'Well, that's life; you don't always get what you want.' He looks at Robbie's feet. 'And those are my socks.'

Robbie laughs ruefully. He grabs his backpack and squeezes in next to Hugh. 'But maybe I'll get what I need, eh?'

'What?'

'It's just a song.'

'Right.' Hugh takes the proffered baguette. 'Remember us being pissed up and belting out "Live Forever"?'

'Yeah.'

'And "Rock n' Roll Star".'

Robbie laughs. 'Yeah, we definitely maybe did that.'

Chapter Twenty-Eight

Serena

Serena lifts the carriage clock and dusts beneath it. She does the same with the bronze statue of a horse. It really is a property without photographs. Save for the one in his wallet, there's none of Hayden's wife. What was she called? Lucinda, the little girl who got lost in the maze. Which presumably meant this was her family home. One would have thought there'd be a trace of some sort, same with Jack and Melanie. But she knows about that and perhaps the son just followed the father's lead by throwing out memories that were simply too painful. A single photo of Jack and Hugh when they were boys would have been nice, though.

Swaying, she smiles. She's still happy about developments with Jack. Is 'happy' the word? Sort of floaty, light-headed and relaxed. Perhaps that's just the sex; it had been so bloody long. Not so much the act itself but seeing desire in a man's gaze, feeling beautiful, sexy and wanted. She laughs. The rousing sensation is still there in the pit of her belly.

Excitement, exhilaration, lust. They're emotions she hasn't felt for years. Not since... well, not since Pierre many summers ago. She'd thought he was a completely different person back then. Charmingly modest, attentive

184

and patient. Supporting and loving her deeply. But he was actually in love with himself, or at least an idealised self-image. Always right about everything and superior to everyone, spending an inordinate time on his appearance, needing to show off. Belittling her daily, yet being super sensitive to criticism himself. How did she get it so wrong?

And what about Jack? She's changed her mind about him too. Is she just rubbish at reading men? Not just men, but people?

Her stomach clutches at the thought. Please not this time. She had to be strong for Lana, but she's not sure she could pick herself up again. She pictures Jack's darkened face when that text came through yesterday. She barely saw him after that, and though she and Lana joined all three Ramsays for dinner, she couldn't look at or touch him as she longed to do. They said goodnight eventually and dispersed to their rooms. She sat in hers, blankly staring at the 'mini bookclub' page and rotating Percy Pig's snout on the jigsaw piece. What should she do about Jack? That sudden change in his whole bearing after reading his message? Was she brave enough to creep to his room again? Just to connect for five minutes? But he came to her. A quiet knock on the door.

'I just wanted to say goodnight.' He rubbed his temple. 'Sorry I was distracted today. Work as usual. I've got a busy week. London for four days, maybe five.'

She thought he wasn't going to move from the entrance, but he stepped to the bed and took her hand. 'I'll miss you.'

A soft kiss, then he left, but it was all she had needed. His expression, his intense gaze said the rest.

'Hello? Patient to Nurse Serena?'

Her hairs standing on end, she now spins round. Her employer, of course, unexpectedly settled in his armchair behind her.

His eyes sparkle with amusement. 'Sorry. You were so lost in thought, you didn't hear me come in. Something nice is my guess, from your smile.' He gestures to the gold frame above the hearth. 'Or perhaps you're admiring my Old Master.'

Her heart thumps. How she hates being taken by surprise. Putting her hand to her breast, she breathes through the mild panic and studies the oil painting. She knows nothing about art, but the pale hues are a little ghostly for her taste.

'Not one of Blake's, but similar, don't you think?' Hayden continues. 'It's the soul leaving the body after death. Apparently the old Ramsays were obsessed with the idea.' He chuckles. 'Bit like me and the damned hip, they didn't want to be trapped in this house for eternity. An old wives' tale, of course, but it's worth a tidy sum, so I'm not complaining.' He looks at his watch. 'Dirty Martini time, I think. Please join me.'

'Thank you, but I'm no good at daytime drinking. It goes straight to my head.'

Hobbling to the cabinet on one crutch, Hayden pulls out a crystal tumbler, followed by another. 'It would be unkind to let an old man drink alone. Just a small one won't hurt while we chat.'

A *chat*. Wondering what today's question might be, she waits.

'Do you like classical music, Serena?' he asks. 'A fan of Prokofiev, perhaps?'

Surprised, she shakes her head. 'Not really. And you?'

He mixes gin and martini. Adding a slice of lemon, he abruptly changes topic. 'One more chapter to go. How about you? Have you guessed who's lying and who isn't?'

He's talking about the novel. Of course he is, but there's that glint in his eye. God, it makes her unsettled.

She accepts the proffered glass and sits on the sofa. Bloody hell, even from the whiff, she can tell the cocktail's a strong one. Like the time she first tasted spirits at Rhona's behest, she wonders how she'll get it down. Reminding herself to be kind, she smiles.

'I'm nearly at the end, too. I'm enjoying it and wondering what the final twist will be. Cheers to you, Hayden, it's a very good choice.'

He bows graciously. 'Thank you, though I do love a good old mystery and seeing if my deductions are correct.' He taps his temple. 'Using the old grey cells like Hercule. Fortunately they're intact, so I just need to work on the physical side. To that end, I was thinking about what you said about getting around more. I've done the stairs like you said, and now I'm down here, I see the sun's trying to come out. How about you, Lana and I take a trip out this afternoon? Somewhere child-friendly, of course. Your car or mine – I don't mind either way.'

Her pulse racing again, Serena quickly knocks back the cocktail and laughs. 'A lovely idea but perhaps not today Hayden. I don't think I'm fit to drive after that. Your "small one" must be more than a double!'

–

Feeling stupidly shy, Serena pushes at the door of Jack's bedroom. She was sleeping in here only two nights ago, and she's been given permission to go in whenever she likes, but it still feels a little strange. Indelicate, invasive somehow. Not that she'd touch any of his personal belongings. Just collect his bedding and washing, lightly dust the surfaces and polish the glass. Routine stuff, like she does for Hayden and Hugh. Yet she can't help but remember the vehemence he showed when reprimanding her that day, for opening the window included. More than anything, he seemed angry about his bathroom. Understandable, she supposes, considering his stash.

Lana's voice breaks through her mulling. 'Mummy?' Her face is shiny with happiness today. 'Can we come in here too?' she asks from the landing.

The dog isn't allowed upstairs. Serena takes a breath to say so, but Lana interrupts. 'We won't mess or break anything, I promise.'

Her eyes wide, she steps in and walks around the elegant room, then she perches at one end of the sofa and swings her legs. 'I like it in here; it smells of Jack,' she says.

Lexie doesn't follow, but Serena frowns, distracted by the comment. What does Jack *smell* like, exactly? Nice aftershave, she hopes, nothing nasty. She sniffs, but can't detect any particular aroma. A sudden waft of cold air brings her back to the room. Rubbing the shiver away, she looks at her daughter, but she's focused on something in her hands.

'What's that?' she asks.

Lana pats the couch. 'It was here, down the side.' She holds it out. 'What is it?'

Serena unfolds the soft, pale fabric. Cashmere and silk, she'd guess. 'It's a very nice eye mask. Some people like to wear them in bed. They block out the light to help them sleep.'

Lana's nose crinkles in disbelief. 'Is it Jack's?'

Feeling a jolt of emotion, Serena stares. No. It's clearly a dead woman's artefact, left behind. Melanie; so tragic. How old must she have been when she died?

She clears her throat. 'Maybe. Let's put it back where we found it, shall we?'

Shrugging away the sensation of being watched, Serena picks up her bucket and heads for Jack's en suite. She pushes at the door, then stops.

'You really don't have to clean up after me; it feels wrong to expect you to do it,' he said at some point over the weekend. A smile. 'I managed to scrub the loo all by myself before you came; I'm sure I'll cope.' A kiss. 'So don't, OK?'

She's only giving it a quick wipe over, so it should be fine. And in fairness, her apprehension is more than worrying about Jack's outburst that day. It's the shelves behind the bath. Too surprised by the drug hoard last time, she hadn't thought to look at them. Her stomach churns as she dares her eyes over... shampoo and shower gel, shaving foam and soap, but higgledy-piggledy, thank goodness, not lined up in size, shape and colour like Pierre's. He was a perfectionist, of course. But he expected the same of her and Lana.

Yet always wanting us to fail, she now thinks; pleased to have something to criticise, to make himself even more important. Though God knows why; there was hardly any competition with a timid, young child.

A heavy thud snaps her thoughts. Stepping back to the bedroom, she looks at the sofa, but Lana's already half-way out. Following the sound and her daughter, she strides along the corridor, then stops abruptly. Standing stock still, Lana's at the top bannister. Almost in slow motion, she rotates her head.

Her face is ghostly white. 'It's Hayden, Mummy,' she says 'Has he gone to sleep forever? Will he never wake up?'

Alarm pumping in her ears, Serena rushes to the stairs and looks down.

Oh God. What the hell? Prostrate and motionless, Hayden Ramsay is splayed out at the bottom.

Chapter Twenty-Nine

Jack

Wearing a T-shirt and jogging pants, Jack falls back on the neat hotel bed. For once, he's grateful for work and the inevitable last minute disclosure of documents from both his own instructing solicitor and the other side's. It hasn't given him time for much thought about Melanie. Melanie, bloody Melanie. Well, not in detail at least. She's been burning in his chest like indigestion since yesterday morning, but he hasn't had time to really dwell until now.

Don't you dare walk away. Come back. I haven't finished speaking!

If you leave, then I'm following.

He flips his head to a lever arch file at his side. His homework for this evening. He should have travelled down to London last night, but he wanted to clear the air with Serena, and he could hardly do that with his father and Hugh stuck to their dining room chairs and bickering well past dessert. The norm was for one or the other to lose their rag and stomp off mid main course, but they were both being amazingly civil, just like they've played 'nice' since November.

Both hoping and fearing Serena would slip into his bedroom, he gazed at the knots pushing through the painted rafters for a while, but he needed to get closure and some sleep, so he crept along the landing and went into her room to say goodnight.

Everything was fine, wasn't it? She looked and smelled lovely, her hair tied in a high ponytail, her face rosy and scrubbed. But the visit unsettled him, especially the thought of bloody Pierre. Then there was Melanie. He was no longer sure, but had Serena really said, 'Sorry for your loss?' when she was ill? Did she think the wretched woman was dead? Oh God, perhaps. And he hadn't disabused her. It was far, far easier not to go there.

Knowing he wouldn't rest, he resorted to a sleeping pill. Just the one, but he spent half an hour berating himself for his weakness before he blacked out. Two minutes later it was five o'clock, time to fight through the grogginess and force himself up. He was used to that, wasn't he? But this morning he struggled, both his mind and his back stiff and cramped, refusing to obey.

He now picks up his mobile and goes back to the message. '*Don't you ever answer your phone? I need to talk to you. It's urgent. Call me back. Please.*'

What can Melanie possibly want to talk to him about after an intermission of over two years?

Frustrated, he lobs the phone on a chair. Then he changes his mind, scoops it back up and presses the call icon.

'Jack!'

Serena's voice is warm and pleased. Like balm on a sore, he's immediately glad of his impulse.

'Hello beautiful. How's your day been?'

'Fine… well…'

He's never spoken to her on the telephone before. It feels weirdly intimate.

'Well, what?'

'Your dad had a fall this afternoon. He's OK. The paramedics came and checked him out. I didn't want to worry you because everything was fine. Nothing broken, just a nasty fright.'

Shocked, he's not sure what to say. Not so much surprised at the incident, but that his dad hadn't called him and reported the whole story in intricate detail. 'Oh right.' Then, 'Bloody hell, how did that happen?'

'The stairs, he said he slipped. Thing is…' She pauses for a moment. 'Actually, two things.'

'OK, fire away.'

'Firstly, the medics didn't take it as seriously as they might have because he'd been drinking.'

'Dad drinking? What time?'

'After lunch.' She lightly laughs. 'He asked me to join him in a Dirty Martini.'

A Dirty Martini. Another blast from the past. Jack puffs out his discomfort. 'And did you?'

'It was hard to say no. Anyway, he was quite belligerent about wanting to get checked out by the hospital, but by the time Hugh arrived home he'd lost interest in going to A&E.'

Picturing his diminished dad when he first had his fracture, Jack nods and speaks, more to himself than to her. 'I think he's scared, to be honest. He doesn't let on, but he's always been in charge, the big cheese. Nothing he couldn't do or achieve for years. From scuba diving to flying to deep sea fishing. I guess old age must be frightening. Still mentally sharp but your body letting you down.'

He falls silent and drifts. Like bonfire night. His father almost asphyxiated to the tune of firework fizzles and splutters and bangs. Hugh's white knuckled hands around his neck like a vice. Both men's faces puce, but one of them from choking.

'*I'm not a coward! Say sorry.*'

'*Let go, Hugh. For God's sake, let go.*'

'*Not until he says sorry, Jack. I've had to say it all my life. Now it's his turn.*'

Did their father actually say the word 'sorry'? He can't recall. But he remembers the terror in his eyes before Hugh finally let go. No longer the boss; the tables had been turned.

Serena brings him back. 'Jack? Are you still there?'

'Yeah, sorry.' Yes, perhaps there is a Welsh lilt in her voice on the phone. 'And the second thing?'

'Oh…' She laughs. He can feel her discomfort, so he waits.

'I had to call emergency services and… well, I sort of fudged who I was and when the paramedics arrived, they assumed I was a Ramsay. His daughter or daughter-in-law, I think. I thought you should know, just in case—'

'No problem, it's fine, I understand.' Then a pause. 'He's a medic of some sort, isn't he? Pierre.'

'Yes. I know it's silly, but I'm just not ready—'

'It's fine, Serena.' He takes a deep breath. 'It's your decision of course, but the sooner you bring things to a head, the better it'll be. I know it only happened a few weeks ago and it's challenging and frightening to face it, but letting it fester doesn't help. Not only from a legal point of view, but for you and your wellbeing. And it doesn't matter who he is or what his status might be…'

The sheer bloody anger bolts through his whole body, but he keeps his voice even. 'What he did was a serious assault, domestic abuse of a particularly nasty kind. You're entitled to protection and justice.'

No reply, just a sniff and the rustle of tissue.

'Serena? Just think about it. OK?'

'I will, I promise.'

Aware of her reticence, he changes tack and asks about Lana and Lexie, but the conversation feels strained, so he mentions his tome of dull bedtime reading and bids her good night.

He sighs. Bringing things to a head. Not letting them fester. He looks again at Melanie's message. Who the hell is he kidding?

–

It's late and Jack should be in dreamland, but Melanie is keeping him awake, just like she did when they were a couple.

As though she knew, it was always when he was on the precipice and tipping into the abyss of sleep. A creek, a rustle and a sigh, followed by sharp toenails against his legs. Silence for several hopeful moments, then a loud tut and the tug of the duvet as she turned.

The shock of sudden cold would slap Jack back from any hope of oblivion. What would her complaint be today?

Groaning, he replays just one of the episodes:

'What is it, Melanie?'

Sitting up and flicking on the bedside lamp. 'You, of course.'

So tired, he's too exhausted to argue. He rolls over. 'Whatever I've done, I'm sorry. We'll sort it in the morning. Please turn off the light and go to sleep.'

The beam stays. Wrong move, of course. Far better to let her pelt it out for five minutes – whatever he's done or not done this time – but he's so bloody knackered and she's been drinking.

There's the slur in her voice, the usual sour stench behind her minty breath.

He tries again. 'Let's talk properly tomorrow. OK? Now, can we sleep, please? I have to be up early for work in the morning.'

She mimics his voice. 'Have to be up early for work...' Then, pushing at his back, 'Work, work, fucking work! That's all I hear. Do you know how fucking boring you are?'

Sighing, he turns and props his head on his hand. Her face is petulant and waxy. She's wearing an eye mask like a hairband.

He takes a quick breath. 'Look, I know you're disappointed about this weekend. If you'd told me earlier, I could have juggled my diary. I get booked up well in advance and there are only so many hours in the day. I have commitments and simply don't have time to go away at short notice. You know this, Mel, but I'll make it up to you, I promise. OK?'

She apes him again. 'I simply don't have time. Like you don't have time to take me out, you don't have time for sex. Course you do. You have time for her. More time than is bloody normal. Don't think I haven't noticed.'

'Come on, Mel, not now. We both need some rest.'

She doesn't bother to turn off the lamp. Instead she pulls the mask into place and slips down the bed.

'Whatever; it doesn't matter, I don't care. If I want sex I get it, just like that.' She laughs with derision. 'Good sex, Jack, satisfying sex, fun. You wouldn't know what that meant if it slapped you in the face.'

He now sighs. Melanie Ramsay. So pretty, so sensual, so greedy. So eager to announce, 'it's Dirty Martini time, Hayden!'

His father's fun and charming daughter-in-law who liked 'a harmless small tipple'.

How little he knew.

Chapter Thirty

Hugh

Stepping out of the still-dripping caravan shower, Hugh stretches his chest. It has been a long day, but in a good way. Moving from one part of the farm to the next. Digging, hefting, shovelling all morning, then switching to the tractor in the afternoon. Swapping with Robbie.

'Plenty of work for two,' Mr Barnes said on Tuesday, peering at them both over a Ploughman's lunch in the kitchen.

Hugh hadn't seen Robbie since parting at the stile on Sunday. Well, not close up. Which was weird as they were supposed to be friends again.

'Sure thing,' Robbie replied, finally making eye contact. 'We can do that, can't we Hugh? Make some sort of a rota?'

So they sat at the table and Robbie made a list. 'Is that OK with you?' he asked. It was. Hugh doesn't mind what his duties are, so long as he *knows*. Which was why he had to say it to Robbie: 'We are friends now, right? That's what you said on Sunday.'

His reply took a few seconds. 'Sure,' he said, smacking Hugh's shoulder. 'Sure thing.'

His hair neatly styled, Hugh now looks at his watch. A late finish for a Friday. What next? Almost pub time, but he hasn't eaten yet. He could grab something in the farmhouse, but it's been a Ploughman's or a Ploughman's since Jess went back to college. The Bull would be ideal, but that'd be sandwiches and he needs a hot dinner to line his rumbling stomach. Robbie might be there too.

He swallows. Hunger hasn't been the only thing making his belly feel off for the past few days. Robbie, of course, and what he'd said in their old den. Warm, rousing, exciting. Yet puke-inducing too.

He pushes it away, squirts spicy aerosol on his armpits and pulls on a new shirt. The Crown does a hotpot, and not a bad pint. He smiles to himself. Who says Hugh Ramsay isn't willing to try something new?

-

Feeling satisfyingly replete from the food and four glasses of beer, Hugh pulls up his sheepskin collar and strolls back along the dark lane to the farm. Watching his breath form a cloud, he laughs at a memory. He used to do that as a kid, pretend he was smoking. But he didn't do the real thing, not cigarettes anyway. Jack did and never got into trouble. But then again, whatever Jack did, he was too 'smart' to get caught. Too smart, but lucky too. Not in the wrong place at the wrong time like *stupid* Hugh. But not just stupid. No, far worse than that.

He peers at his mobile. Not that late, so what now? Grab a taxi home or chill out in the caravan with the last of the cheap whisky? Though 'chilling' it'll be; no contest when he could be toasting himself before a roaring fire at the hall. But then again, his dad would be there in the drawing room; his old man who says he's not *amenable* to change; his father who has to be right about everything.

Giving the sticky door a good shove, he steps into the camper. Not too cold, actually, in fact almost warm. He chuckles to himself. Perhaps it's The Crown's spicy hotpot still going strong. It wasn't as tasty as Serena's, but not bad. Good old Serena; he likes having her and her solid casseroles around.

He pulls out a tumbler, then opens the bottom cupboard. Where the hell did he put the booze?

'This what you're looking for?'

He spins to the sound. Robbie Barnes is lying on the sofa. He lifts up the bottle. 'There was no alcohol in the farmhouse. Not even a can of cider. Jess, before she left, no doubt. You know; keeping an eye on her erratic big brother.' He snorts. 'I should've checked the bottle bin like an alkie.'

He nods to a fan heater blasting out the balmy air. 'Did you an exchange, though. Another swap. We're like ships in the night, mate.'

Not sure what Robbie means or exactly how pissed he is, Hugh relieves him of the whisky and pours himself an inch. 'Not in the pub with your *mates*?' It comes out a bit sarcastically, but Robbie doesn't seem to notice.

'I was. You weren't, though.'

Hugh thinks of making a quip about being *amenable* to change, but Robbie's sitting forward, his expression intense. 'Can I ask you a question?'

'OK...'

'Don't you fancy me anymore?' He doesn't wait for a reply. 'I mean, what's the problem? Too old or too hairy? Too Aussie?' He tugs his hair. 'Or this? Too long? Cos I've been thinking about it a lot.' He sits back. 'The way

I remember it, you couldn't get enough of me back then. And it's not as though you don't know exactly how I feel. I told you on Sunday...'

Frowning, he stares. 'You're not stupid, Hugh; I know you're not. We were alone and a mile away from the farm. In our old hideout, warm from the fire. But you didn't even try to touch me, let alone kiss or do the stuff we used to—'

Hugh lifts his hand to stop him from speaking. He doesn't want to think about it. Since Robbie came back, he's tried so bloody hard not to, but he has, almost constantly. And the terror is still there; it still knocks him sick, even after all these years.

'No, don't. Don't talk about then. It was bad, totally wrong.'

Robbie gazes, perplexed. 'What? Bad, wrong? No it wasn't. Why would you think so? It was fucking magical, Hugh. The sex was mind-blowing, but not just that. Lying under the stars and just chatting. Laughing about nothing.' He leans closer; his face is open and keen. 'It was special, romantic. Don't you remember it?'

The spread of anxiety like a vice around his chest, Hugh flattens his hair and doesn't reply. Of course he remembers everything, but it isn't nearly as simple as Robbie says. Then there's the 'arson', as his dad describes it, but he doesn't want to picture that either.

Robbie looks thoughtful. 'Is this about us in the barn at your place? No one would have known. Not really. We were pissed and asleep and covered in straw. By the time the police came, we were dressed. Is that what it is?'

Too shame-faced to explain, Hugh hangs his head but Robbie kneels and looks into his eyes. 'Talk to me, Hugh.

What could you have possibly done that's so bad?' He shakes him gently. 'Just tell me.'

He isn't going to say it, he can't, he's too ashamed, too petrified. But like a purge, Hugh finds the words heaving out: 'I met this man in Queen's Park. Well, I thought he was a man. Turned out he was fifteen. We got caught the second time. Dad made it go away through an old friend, but he said he was duty bound to check out my laptop.' The tears burn his nose. 'There was nothing involving kids, boys. Nothing. That's disgusting—'

'What? Stop. Who checked your laptop?'

'His policeman pal.' Remembering the horror, Hugh struggles to breathe. 'He found I'd been watching porn. Honestly, Robbie. There was nothing involving children. Nothing. That's revolting. But he said that's how it begins...'

'How what begins?'

'Starting with porn. You know, gay porn. Guys together, doing stuff. Then moving on from adults to—'

Robbie stands and covers his mouth with his hand. 'What the fuck? What the *fuck*? Who fed you this shit?'

Hugh wipes his face with trembling hands. 'The police. And they know what they're talking about, don't they?'

Robbie stares. 'No, they don't! That's a load of homophobic bullshit, Hugh.' He rakes back his fringe. 'When was this?'

'Twelve months or so after you left. But I was an adult. You know, eighteen. Since then, I haven't done anything. Anything.'

'All those bloody years.' Robbie pulls him into a rough and tight hug. His eyes are shiny when he pulls away. 'All those years beating yourself up. You did nothing wrong,

Hugh. Nothing. Why didn't you say something to Jack? Even to your dad?'

Hugh shrugs. 'Some things the Ramsays don't talk about. Not even to each other.'

Chapter Thirty-One

Serena

Woken to a new Saturday by the tinkle of chandeliers, Serena hops from the bed and closes the window. Trying to shrug away the imagined stench of coffee, she leans into the dressing table mirror and strokes soft fingers across her chest. The skin is still tight, pink and blotchy, but nowhere near as unsightly as it was. Though the scabbing has gone, the scratches are still there, but they're no worse than stretchmarks and she has plenty of those from her pregnancy. Pale silvery lines, like a reminder. With her particularly large bump, she had expected a full toddler to come out at the birth, but it was just a tiny baby like everyone else's, her Lana, perfect Lana.

Pierre was there, of course. It wouldn't do for her parents or the department staff to think he was anything other than the proud and doting father. She had hoped and prayed the child in the flesh would pierce the cold detachment and irritation he'd shown since she announced her pregnancy, but nothing changed. He couldn't bear losing his importance, his rightful place at the centre of her entire world. Why she was surprised, she didn't know. He'd been resentful of the child in utero, what chance would the baby have? But she had to try and make the relationship work. A child needs a father. That's what she'd thought.

As though on cue, Lana appears at her shoulder. She's pulling in her lips, the usual sign that she's worried.

'What's up, love? Is it Panda? Is he still missing?'

'It's Lexie. She's limping. She has a bad leg.'

Certain there's more, she waits for Lana to speak, but when nothing comes, she takes her hand and squeezes. 'Poor Lexie. Mention it to Jack when he's up. She might need to see the vet.'

Her daughter's face brightens. 'Is Jack home?'

Serena feels herself blushing. 'I think so. I heard the door late last night.'

'Oh wow! I'll go and tell everyone.'

'Good idea. And while you're there, you can prepare Hayden's breakfast tray if you like. A plate, knife and teaspoon. And don't forget the salt and pepper pots. I'll be down in a few minutes to cook the eggs.'

When the door clicks to, she sighs. Jack. Knowing he'd be back, she was excited all yesterday, trying not to be over chirpy in front of Hayden's watchful eye. Unsure of what time he'd arrive, the evening hours dragged by, but finally she heard the crunch of tyres outside. Then he was there in the hallway, slightly crumpled and weary around the eyes, but still sculpted and handsome and all smiles. Hayden had gone to bed and there was no sign of Hugh, so she made him a drink, then pulled him by the hand to the snug.

It was so nice; she couldn't stop grinning and neither could he. Kissing and cuddling like teenagers, they whispered about their week. Then the conversation stopped as they became more intimate and eventually she slipped her hand into his flies. He was hard and responsive and they continued in that vein for several moments, then he gently prized himself away.

Like before in the car, it felt personal, as though she'd been punched in the stomach. 'Have I done something wrong?' she asked.

'Absolutely not.' He leaned back against the sofa. 'It isn't you, it's me. I'm just knackered. I can't begin to tell you.'

She nodded, but hurt was smarting at the back of her eyes. Rejection; rejection; she'd been there too many times already. And she wasn't going to beg ever again. Standing stiffly, she made her way to the door. 'Night, then,' she managed without looking back. 'See you tomorrow.'

She now stares again at her reflection. Such a confusing disappointment. What did she do wrong? Is she really so unattractive that a man doesn't want her even when she offers herself on a plate? Perhaps Pierre was right. What did he once say when she told him she'd leave? His mocking laugh and then, 'go ahead, but who would want *you*?'

Tears prick again, but she sniffs them away. Perhaps she made a mistake letting the wild girl from the Valleys in. Too forward, light-hearted and joyful. She's sensible Serena these days. It's best if she leaves things with Jack well alone. Work and pleasure never mixes well, she knows that from personal experience.

Pulling back her shoulders, she stands. She's a house-keeper now; time to start the day, put on a bloody apron and prepare her employer's breakfast.

-

Serena knocks on Hayden's door, but he doesn't reply, so she raps a little harder before opening it.

'Come in if you must,' comes from under the covers.

Clearly in a bad mood, he doesn't acknowledge her with his usual bright 'morning!' Indeed, he's been off with her since his 'fall' down the stairs. Was it really a genuine tumble? She still doesn't know. One minute he'd seemed dead, the next his face was puckered in pain.

'Oh, Lord, something's gone. You need to call for an ambulance,' he said.

Her mind thrashed.

'An ambulance, please Serena,' he repeated. 'It doesn't feel right.'

Something hadn't felt right to her either, especially when he caught her hand. 'You will come with me to the hospital, won't you? Or at least follow in the car? I know it's not ideal for Lana, but I'm sure you don't mind for an exigency like this...'

Ham acting, it had felt like. When the paramedics arrived, she took Lana by the shoulders, stepped back to the shadows and tapped her foot with agitation. A bloody hospital. What to do? Jack wasn't an option and Hugh was at work.

The unexpected sound of the paramedic made her jump.

'Are you all right? You look a little frazzled,' he said.

'Nothing a cigarette wouldn't cure.' Surprised the words had popped out, she laughed. 'Sorry. There's none in the house so you're fine, it's a smoke-free zone.'

'So, a report on the patient...' Rubbing his hands, he looked rueful. 'We've had a good feel and everything seems in order. He can sit, bend his limbs; no temperature, normal blood pressure and pulse...' He lifted his eyebrows. 'He's obviously had a drink or three, but then again, perhaps the alcohol softened the blow. It's basically just shock, so we can't justify calling in an ambulance even though he's keen.' He smiled apologetically. 'But if you have the time to take him to A&E, you're very welcome to get a second opinion.' He nodded to Lana. 'Maybe when her dad's home? It'd be a non-urgent drop-in; the staff don't have enough time even for people in agony, so you'll be there for hours.'

Snorting inwardly at the irony, she smiled. 'Believe me, I know. Would you mind awfully telling Hayden that? I think he'll take it better from you.'

'Sure thing.' He started to walk away, then turned back and dug into a pocket. His lips twitching, he pulled out a crushed packet of Benson & Hedges. 'Only a few left but they're yours…' His eyes crinkled warmly. 'We all need emergency supplies.'

Wishing she could drag on one now, Serena puts down the tray and yanks open the heavy drapes.

'Do you want breakfast now or shall I bring it back later?' she asks.

The prone figure finally moves. 'The toast will be cold then.'

'Then I'll make more,' she replies evenly to the bedding. 'Did you have a bad night?'

Issuing grunts of complaint, Hayden slowly sits up. 'Bloody cramp in my shin again. You don't add enough salt to the food.'

Picking up the salt pot, she pours a few grains in her hand and throws them over her shoulder.

'Wrong shoulder,' he says, but it brings a small twinkle.

Despite his petulant tone, she returns the smile. The poor man is fed up with his ailments and he's

Serena-the-maid's boss. She has to rise above the rudeness and get on with the job.

'The eggs are three and a half minutes, just as you like them. Enjoy.' She hands him the bell. 'And if you need more tea or toast, give me a tinkle.'

Outside his bedroom, she gently taps her forehead on the wall. She just has to accept things as they are and be grateful.

She plods down the stairs, but when she enters the kitchen, she steps back in surprise. The dog, Lana and Jack are at the open back door, wearing warm jackets. He hands one to her.

'The weather's trying to be brave but it's probably best we grab boots from the garage.' He looks at Lana. 'Chief dog walker, are you ready?'

She nods and they set off, so Serena quickly removes her apron, slips on the coat and follows them across the ramshackle barn entrance to the other side of the building. Beckoning her over, Jack pushes at the side door and points to a row of wellies descending in size.

He smiles thinly. 'Some things are too useful to throw out.'

Frowning, he looks to the floor, picks up an outdoor brush and spends a few moments pushing the loose hay into a corner. 'It gets everywhere.' He steps to a partition between the garage and the barn, which he closes. 'This should stay shut to stop it blowing through and dirtying the cars. It's a fire hazard too.'

He shakes his irritation away and suddenly grins. 'Sweeping again. Seems to be my current expertise.'

Though her nerves are jangling, Serena returns the smile and glances around. The shelves are cluttered with canisters and tools, oil rags, pots and paint. All very much what she'd describe as junk, but probably useful to someone. Still, what would she know? She's never had a garage. Her childhood home was on the poor side of the village, so her parents didn't have that luxury, and she's always lived in flats.

Her gaze lands on the Renault. It's still covered by the nylon sheet she threw over it when she parked it in here. Hayden's Range Rover is snug by its side. No one would steal hers, but his, presumably, cost a fair sum. 'Don't the Ramsays lock any doors at all?' she asks for something to say.

Appearing surprised, Jack meets her eyes properly for the first time. 'You're right; we probably don't. I've never thought about it before. We should look at that.' Going back to the wellies, he selects a pair for himself and hands another to her. 'Do you think these will fit?'

Wondering if the green Hunters once belonged to a dead woman, she slips them on. 'Perfect.'

Jack offers his arm. 'Ready?' he asks.

Lana running ahead with Lexie, they stroll around the perimeter of the house for some time without speaking. Of course Hugh gave her the spiel many moons ago, but she didn't realise just how extensive – and beautiful – the grounds were. Though the trees are still starkly naked, cheery snowdrops and crocus shoots have pushed through the dank soil. They eventually turn a breezy corner and the tennis court appears.

'Do you and Hugh play?' she asks to fill the silence.

'Did,' he replies. 'Overgrown, as you can see.' His lips twitch after a beat. 'Extremely competitively. Hugh was exceptional at most sports, but fortunately I had the extra two and a half years, which made it Even Stevens. Mostly.'

His gaze wistful, he glances up to his corner window. She looks too. There's a shadow at the glass, then movement. Bloody hell; is Hayden watching them from Jack's bedroom? But Jack has turned back and he's still speaking.

'Dad got stuck in as an umpire, of course, but Mum used to watch. Like the Empress viewing her gladiators, it made us try so much harder. How about you – do you have siblings? Parents?'

Noting the first mention of his mother, she takes a breath to reply. She so wants to be honest in return. 'I have a much older brother, but he emigrated to New Zealand way back.'

Intending to share more, she begins to form words about her mum and dad, and how they moved from their beloved Wales just to be nearer Pierre, but she pauses; it might involve questions she's not ready to answer.

Lana saves her from having to decide. She's pointing to the maze. 'Can I?' she asks Jack with round, excited eyes.

'Yeah, sure. But we don't want you to get lost, so…'

'I know the way.' She points to the drawing room. 'I watched from that window.'

Jack's eyebrows briefly knit, but he steps away and scoops up a slim branch. He digs in his pocket and sticks a yellow Post-it note on the top. 'Carry this so we know where you are.'

They watch Lana skip off, then he turns to her. The wind blowing his hair, he doesn't speak for a moment. Then he sighs. 'About last night.'

'Look, it's fine. You were exhausted and anyway you're sort of my employer, so we probably shouldn't—'

'It isn't fine. I hurt your feelings.' He smiles ruefully. 'Which is madness when I want to hold you, kiss and devour you even at this moment.' He glances back to the house. 'But perhaps that wouldn't be wise right now. Thing is…' He looks at the ground. 'It's a confidence issue. In the past I've occasionally been dog tired or I've drunk too much and I've not been able to… to…'

Ah. '*It isn't you, it's me,*' she remembers.

Relief floods Serena's cheeks. Realising what he's saying and how hard it must be, she reaches for his hand.

'You were more than *able* with me. Much more.' And when he doesn't reply, 'And it's not uncommon at all.' Sensing his embarrassment, she tries for a light-hearted tone. 'You're clearly in full working order, so it's unlikely to be medical. Emotional stuff gets to everyone, Jack.'

Like a dead wife. She pictures the expensive eye mask. Imagines a woman wearing it next to Jack in the bed. Tiptoeing up, she kisses his temple, then the other. 'Getting it out of there is the key. Talking about it.'

'Yes. Yes, you're right,' he says, almost to himself. He lifts his head and gazes at her with that same expression she first saw beneath the fir tree. 'Look, there's something I should have told you. Something…'

She nods. Melanie and her tragically young death.

'…Something terrible I struggle to talk about because I feel guilty, ashamed.'

Ashamed? Her respite is tempered by surprise at the word. 'OK. That's fine. Just tell me…' But over his shoulder, she catches Hugh, wearing a thin T-shirt and striding towards them. 'Oh, Hugh's here.'

Jack turns to his brother and looks at his watch. 'You're back. Bit early for a Saturday. Did you have a good night?'

Rubbing his hands, Hugh hops from foot to foot. 'Yeah, I had a hotpot at The Crown. Not as good as yours, Serena…' Then looking fit to burst, 'Saw you were out here from the drawing room. Watched Lana for a minute.'

He gestures to the maze. 'Playing with Panda. Glad she's found him.' Then to Jack, 'Are you coming in soon? I've come home especially because... Thing is, I want to ask you a question.'

Chapter Thirty-Two

Jack

Feeling a mix of frustration and relief at his brother's intervention, Jack watches him lope back to the house.

He turns back to the yellow tip of the branch. It moves through the maze, then stops before starting its journey again. Lana stroking and chatting to her favourite pet, no doubt. Remembering to mention Lexie's obvious limp to Hugh, he catches Serena's curious gaze. 'Sorry about the interruption. Hugh seems strangely...' Excited, hyper, anxious? 'Do you mind if I—'

'Of course not.' She waves him away. 'It's fine, you go ahead. I'll wait here for Lana.'

He finds Hugh in the kitchen, shoving a whole Wagon Wheel in his mouth.

Despite the jitters from his halting admission to Serena, he can't help laughing. 'Hungry and hungover, I take it?' He looks at his brother's muscly bare arms. 'Aren't you cold without a jacket?'

Hugh leaves the room. At the bottom of the staircase, he finishes his mouthful and holds up a hand. 'Wait here, I'll be back in two ticks,' he says, taking the stairs two by two.

Wondering about his brother's sparkling eyes and his blend of pleasure and agitation, Jack breathes in deeply.

Agitation. God, he knows about that. OK; he didn't get as far as he'd determined when he awoke this morning, but he'd admitted to the impotence. Personal embarrassment wasn't even a patch on the far darker secret he had to address, but Serena dealt with it so nicely: *you were more than able with me*. A hurdle overcome; one fear diluted.

The strong whiff of Hugh's aftershave brings him back.

'Just said hi to Dad,' he's saying, his footfall surprisingly light on the risers. Then, as though it wasn't self-explanatory, 'He's in his bedroom.'

He strides down the hallway, so Jack follows again. Once in the snug, he closes the door and leans against it. 'Right,' he says, counting on his fingers. 'Dad says he hasn't seen you today. That you haven't made the effort to say hello despite being away all week.'

Jack sighs. 'Just the usual, then. I'll go up in a bit. Offer to take him to the golf club later or maybe tomorrow.'

'And that his leg's very sore and nobody cares.'

'Well, if he didn't get pissed at lunch time and bruise it on the stairs…'

Hugh frowns. 'Lunch time? Well that can't be right, he doesn't have a weekday drink until five-thirty.'

'I know. I guess he must be bored. Or just flaming miserable…' Knowing his brother needs to talk, he shelves that particular concern. 'What's up, Hugh? What did you want to ask me?'

His expression doubtful, Hugh turns to the door.

'No one can hear. Are you OK?'

'Yeah.' Then, 'It's OK to be gay, right? It's all legal? Well, in the UK?'

Jack stands back in surprise. He didn't expect that. 'Yes, yes it is.'

'Then what about porn? You know, gay porn on the internet for adults?'

'Yes, subject to age ID checks they're hoping to bring in…' He pauses. 'Why are you asking?'

His brother's eyes don't meet his. 'Did Dad never tell you?'

'Tell me what?'

'About the barn and stuff?'

Thrown by the change of subject, Jack lifts his arms. 'What about the barn? You mean the fire all those years ago?' He laughs. 'No he didn't at the time, though why not, I don't know. I was bound to notice a gaping hole in the roof at some point. Why are you asking, Hugh?'

'And you're sure about the gay thing?'

'Yes. Absolutely.'

Appearing satisfied, Hugh nods. 'Great. Got to go. I'll see you later.'

—

Breathing deeply, Jack tries to steady his breath. God, that was good. So bloody, bloody good.

He pecks Serena's lips and chuckles to himself. Perhaps he should thank his dad for the extra frisson. After dinner he announced that he and Lana were having a film night and a later bedtime seeing as it was a Saturday.

'What shall we choose, Lana?' he asked her. 'Shall we ask Mummy for help? There must be a compelling tale about a clever young lady who's run away from home and fallen on hard times. Cinderella is my favourite, going from a high-born princess to a scullery maid overnight… What would be your choice, Serena? A happy ending, one assumes?'

He and Serena were invited too, so the whole evening became one of anticipation – glances, casual touching, small talk, smiles – and boy, was it worth it.

He actually needs to roar, not just from the intense pleasure, but success. Like a winning goal, he wants to clench his fists, sprint around the bedroom and punch the air. Quite frankly he's too knackered for that, so instead he falls back against the pillow and grins. Though covered in sweat and exhausted, he feels bloody wonderful. After a week of mentally listening to Melanie's criticism and sneers, he'd convinced himself of certain failure. Not that his *dysfunction* started with her. Well, not really.

He rocks his head to Serena. Blowing softly through her mouth, her face is relaxed, her eyes closed. He wishes he hadn't mentioned the impotence this morning. Though he tries to help Hugh talk his worries through, he most definitely doesn't practise what he preaches. Perhaps it's his father's teaching and his stiff-upper-lip ways, but he infinitely prefers to keep troubles in. Give them air and they only grow bigger.

Inwardly he sighs. Yes, he shouldn't have confessed. Not only about that, but the start of the other. The understanding in Serena's gaze had made him want to cough the truth out like a fur ball. Yet even as he said the words 'guilt and shame', he saw the flicker and uncertainty in her face and her posture.

She has a little girl; she might not understand; she might hate him forever.

Then there's Melanie, bloody Melanie. Half-way through this afternoon's pandering to his dad's every whim, his mobile rang.

'Don't you want to get that?' his father asked.

'If it's urgent, they'll call back,' he replied, keeping his eyes on the televised football match.

Though at a different time from the other calls, by some instinct he'd just known it would be Melanie, and it was. What the hell did she want?

Serena now stirs and rests her head on his shoulder. 'Was Hugh OK today?' she whispers. 'He seemed, I don't know, a little high?'

Though it feels like the early hours, it's only eleven-thirty. They're doing nothing wrong, but he mirrors her and replies in a low voice. 'Yeah, he was.'

She's right; Hugh was exhilarated, even more so after Jack had given the 'yes' answers. Was he saying that he's gay? The thought makes him smile inwardly. Only his brother could come out at thirty-six having shown no inclination for romance with anyone, not even Jess Barnes who hasn't hidden her adoration since she was a teenager. Well, no sexual encounters that Jack knows of. And watching porn's a surprise. Maybe on his phone? Hugh hasn't had a laptop for years.

Lifting her chin, Serena raises her fair eyebrows. 'Come on, a penny for them,' she says.

He kisses her hair. He knows he can trust her, but it doesn't feel right to breach Hugh's confidence and he doesn't know for sure. Funny how he asked about the barn fire, though. It was so long ago, he can mention that.

Only comical in retrospect, he laughs at the memory: home from uni for a long weekend, he had rolled up in the Boxster and climbed out. The acrid reek of smoke still hung everywhere, and for ages he'd strode around the courtyard and the house, panicking as he tried to pinpoint the source. Then the cackling of a crow had made him look up. Though most of the timbers were still intact, a six foot section of the gambrel was missing.

'Years ago Hugh had an *incident*. I was at university but nobody had seen fit to mention it to me, even in passing. In fact I was told by a raven.'

Serena smiles. 'Don't tell me. It said "nevermore".'

'Do you know, I think it did. He'd managed to burn down the barn. Hugh, that is, not the raven.'

Her eyes widen. 'Really? The one next to the garage, presumably?'

He nods. 'Though "burn down" is perhaps an exaggeration. There's wasn't as much damage as there would be now with all the loose hay flying around. It was straw back then and the bales were tightly packed, so they were pretty fire resistant. It did reach the roof, though. Burned a sizeable hole. Not really sure why, but Dad never bothered to have it properly rebuilt, so what repairs there were are pretty... well, you've seen for yourself.'

'What on earth happened?'

'Shrouded in mystery. The rupture and charring were there when I came home for Whit. Neither Dad nor Hugh were spilling the beans, nor talking to each other, which made it a fun weekend, as you can imagine. But when I heard Robbie Barnes had left for Queensland, I put two and two together.'

'And Robbie Barnes was?'

'Hugh's best mate. They'll have been smoking weed, trying to toast bread, warming the place up or something equally as stupid.'

Smiling at her inquisitive face, he rakes a curtain of silky hair behind her ear. 'The two of them were always messing around, getting into bother. Low-key most of the time. But you know what Hugh's like – easily led.' He frowns.

'Robbie's back from Australia, as it happens. His dad owns the farm where Hugh works. Selwyn Farm. Used to be Ramsay land back in the day.'

'Really? Landed gentry, eh?'

'Something like that. Most has been sold off over the years. Dad's department, thank God.'

'His bank manager must be happy.'

'Sadly not. The price of maintaining a Grade II listed building and grounds, don't you know.'

She nudges him playfully. 'Except for the poor old barn. So this Robbie was a bad influence?'

'Yup, Hugh's partner in crime. Let's hope things have changed.'

Serena laughs. 'Nope. However hard I try, I can't picture Hugh as a criminal.'

'Ah, but what do they actually look like?' He kisses her nose. 'Not a classical blonde beauty like you, but appearances can be deceptive, I've learned that in court over the years.'

Hoping she can't hear the sudden rush of his heart, Jack stares at a slant of light on the ceiling. Appearances can most certainly be *deceptive*. Not only professionally, but personally. Like his gold-digging wife. More overt than Serena, but attractive too. He never could predict her hair colour from one week to the next. What shade was it that day?

Don't you dare walk away. Come back. I haven't finished speaking!

Almost smelling the fetor of her breath, he tries to shake away the image of her scrunched, screaming face. Her calls and texts are from a mobile, but that's not surprising – the use of personal phones was introduced fairly recently. He frowns. Though didn't he read the new measure was for calling pre-approved numbers only?

A thought occurs. God, she *is* still in prison, surely? Which must mean that *he's* on her pre-approved list.

Bloody hell, bloody hell. Melanie. How did she swing that? And more to the point – why?

Chapter Thirty-Three

Hugh

Wondering if he'll ever be able to haul himself out, Hugh turns off the hot tap and settles back against the cold enamel.

His penis slapping his leg, Robbie walks past to the sink. 'OK, mate?' he asks.

'Yeah,' Hugh replies, trying to hide his erection in the astonishingly small bath.

They're 'taking things slowly', as Robbie put it, but he's struggling to take his eyes off Robbie's tanned skin, his tight white buttocks, his toned, furry chest. And the tattoo on his bicep. Why that turns him on particularly, he has no idea.

Mr Barnes is away, so they're alone in the farmhouse. Robbie's made them a veggie curry which they're going to eat later. Hugh isn't sure what freaks him out the most; the thought of eating food without meat or this 'acclimat-ising', as Robbie said. 'You know? Getting used to each other again'.

Hugh lathers the soap and scrubs his armpits. It has been a good day. The Russian wind on their faces, they tramped across fields, over gates and stiles, through damp, fragrant woods until they reached the next village. At least ten miles of amiable chatter about something and nothing like they used to. Then they found a pub with an open fire for their lunch. He tried not to grimace when Robbie ordered a Ploughman's. He was so hungry he asked for two steak and kidney pies with veg and chips, then followed it with apple crumble smothered in custard. When he finally felt full, he looked around the bustling room and lifted his pint.

'Cheers for still being here with me. Not far from your old school. You might get spotted by your mates.'

Robbie snorted and shook his head, but didn't say anything. It was fine, though. Even now, Hugh isn't sure what he thinks about this weird situation. But Robbie's cheeks went pink, which he found he quite liked, so he teased a bit more. 'Though you did stay in the caravan last night,' he added in a low voice. 'Word might get around.'

Robbie raked back his fringe. 'Yeah, well, I was pissed.' He leaned forward. 'Besides, nothing happened. I just slept.'

Hugh hadn't. He'd laid awake half the night listening to Robbie's light snoring and trying to work it all out. All he'd known by the morning was that he had to talk to Jack.

Now trying to manoeuvre himself forwards, he laughs. He got the 'short straw', as Robbie described it. He doesn't always get *irony*, but he understood that and he liked the farming *analogy*. They didn't actually use a dried cereal plant, but a fifty pence coin. He chose tails and lost, so he got the old tub while Robbie scrubbed his hair in the shower. Of course he could have waited until Robbie had finished, but it seems nakedness is part of this *acclimatising* thing.

Searching for more strands of hay, he drags his fingers through his hair. Replete from the food and almost back at the farmhouse, Robbie had pulled him into a barn and kissed him hard on the lips.

'Like old times,' he'd said eventually, so they'd climbed the tightly packed bales to the top and laid down.

But it hadn't been like *old times*, not really. The barn was cold and the fodder had felt a bit damp. And Hugh's stomach had churned, not in a good way.

'Farmers need to ensure the bales for bedding dairy cows are dry to help reduce mastitis,' he'd said, to avoid Robbie's intense gaze. 'It's to do with cow cleanliness and their manure. Good quality barley straw encourages them to eat more and that makes their dung drier.'

He'd hoped he'd quoted Mr Barnes correctly. Robbie had just nodded and taken his hand. 'Come on,' he'd said, 'Dad's away, let's go inside and grab a shower.'

Hugh now squeezes the sponge and smiles to himself. Robbie understands, like he used to. Yeah. A bloody good day.

–

Though he likes the aroma of turmeric and cumin, Hugh picks at the cauliflower florets cautiously. Popping a piece in, he briefly chews, swallows and registers the taste. It's not that bad; in fact it's pretty damned tasty. Tearing off another piece of naan bread, he dips it in the creamy sauce and lifts his head to tell Robbie, but he's gazing in an unfocused way.

'You're thinking about something. What is it?' he asks.

Pushing his plate away, Robbie sighs. 'What you said about my old school.'

'Oh right.' He puts down his fork. Oh hell. Did he say something wrong? Did he speak without thinking?

Robbie's attention comes back. He frowns and shakes his head. 'I sort of blame you and I shouldn't. It was hardly your fault.'

Still perplexed, Hugh holds his breath.

'Only a state comprehensive, maybe, but I was doing bloody well. Ten GCSEs and on target for good grades at A level. Yet they still sent me away. Dad, I can sort of understand. I was a pretty stroppy teenager and I'd pissed him off a fair few times that summer, but Mum…'

Feeling a bit sweaty, Hugh flattens his hair. What exactly is Robbie saying? First he blames him, then it isn't his fault. Why don't people just say what they mean?

Robbie reaches for his hand and grasps it. 'I know it wasn't your doing, believe me, I do. But, if your dad hadn't called the police, things might have been completely different. I know we'd been bloody stupid, yet…' he sighs. 'It's fine, I don't need an answer. My dad said it. "Enough was enough". We'd got away with petty stuff before and we needed to be taught a lesson. But…' His voice catches with emotion. 'Just seventeen and a one way ticket to Queensland to pick bloody fruit? Wasn't that a bit fucking extreme for nicking a bottle and some crisps? Why not just let it go through to the magistrates?'

He stares at Hugh and frowns. 'Look, I know I was glad to get away and enjoyed it at first, but I was bright, Hugh, I wanted to read law at university like Jack. I'm what, two or three years younger than him. Just compare us – he's at the top of his game and I'm a bloody farm labourer.'

Hugh looks at his hands. He might only be a *farm labourer* but he's happy, whereas Jack's been unhappy for years. He's seemed a bit brighter for the last week or two, but still, look what happened with his car, and not so long ago.

As though to himself, Robbie continues to speak. 'And what about my mum and dad? Didn't they think they'd miss me? Jess too. She was only ten and we were close. I Skype my kids all the time, but being physically apart from them is killing me.' He covers his eyes. 'Then there was my mum's death. I only saw her every blue moon. Thought there was plenty of time, but there wasn't. I hadn't seen her for six months when she died. Came back for the funeral, but what was the bloody point of that?'

Abruptly scraping back his chair, Robbie heads for the stairs. Not knowing what else to do, Hugh freezes and listens. A flush then the rap of footfall on wood. He's coming back, thank goodness, but when he returns to the table, Robbie's features are no longer fractured and sad. Instead, his eyebrows are knitted.

'What about you?' he says, leaning forward. He points his fork. 'I was sent to fucking Queensland. What was your punishment? What happened to you in your palace?'

Anxiety fizzing, Hugh tries to think back. He can't remember it that well, if he's honest. But he recalls his sheer red-eyed rage when he found out that Robbie was leaving Goostrey forever. Then unhappiness and loneliness for a very long time.

'Nothing,' he answers. 'But when I heard you'd gone, I set fire to the barn.'

Robbie sits back. 'Bloody hell, Hugh. Your dad must have been livid. What did he say about that?'

'Nothing,' Hugh repeats.

But that wasn't true. The explosive rant had gone on for hours. About Nero and 'only a fool would burn down his own house'. And a 'reminder of your deep shame.

Every day, Hugh. Every day.' And 'from now on I'm keeping an eye on you. A much closer eye.'

He frowns. Maybe that was his 'punishment'.

Chapter Thirty-Four

Serena

Remembering the snowdrops on yesterday's walk, Serena flings open the bedroom window. The sun might be weak, but it's there, she can sense it. Spring hasn't actually sprung, but it feels on its way.

She smiles at the surge of something warm in her chest. Happiness? Even hope? Though she knows she should snuff them out for her own self-protection, she allows herself a minute or two to luxuriate. Jack. She fancies him for sure; he keeps himself in shape and he's undoubtedly attractive, but it's more than just that. Despite being clever and successful in his career, he doesn't seem to have an ego; he doesn't put other people down to big himself up; he isn't deliberately cruel.

She checks herself short. She mustn't compare him to Pierre. Jack deserves his own merit for being sensitive, loving and kind. A man she can trust completely.

Lana's fair hair appears around the door. 'Where is everyone?' she asks.

She thinks of Hugh's animated face and joyful stride when he left the house yesterday.

'Well, I think Hugh's out having fun somewhere and Jack's taken Hayden to the golf club for lunch.' She squeezes her daughter's cute nose. 'Which means you and I have the house to ourselves. I'm going to give the upstairs a once-over, then I'm all yours. What would you like to do?'

'Baking, please!' Lana puts a finger to her chin. 'Muffins or cookies. I can't decide. Which do you think Jack will like the best?'

Serena laughs. 'Both, I should think, which means we have a lot to do before he gets back. Come on, you can be my cleaning assistant. The sooner we start, the sooner we finish.'

Feeling herself blush, she opens Jack's door. It was a close call this morning. She woke up in his bed at what she thought was around six o'clock and she spent a few moments gazing at him through the dusky light. Emphasised by his dark stubble, his was, she thought, a face of shadows. As though he knew she was watching, his eyes flicked open, clearly confused for a moment. Then the cloudiness disappeared as he smiled.

'Promise me you'll be here when I wake up every morning,' he said, kissing gently from her neck to her belly button, then moving, teasingly, to her thighs.

That's when she heard the sound of a toilet flushing and looked again at her watch. Not quarter to six but nearly eight thirty! She managed to slip from the bed and tiptoe past the bathroom before Lana came out, but only just.

Serena studies her daughter now. She's so grateful for her own happiness, but Lana's is the cherry on the cake. After being so nervy and hesitant and apprehensive with her own father, it's astonishing how she's taken to all the Ramsay men, Jack especially. Like magnets, there's an intuitive attraction between them. A blessing, a real blessing. If she believed there was a god, she'd thank him.

'Need help with that pillowcase, love?' she asks her.

Shaking her head, Lana finishes stripping both cushions. She glances at the sofa, but doesn't sit. Then, clearly bored, she meanders around the room, peeping at coloured pens, pads and Post-it notes on Jack's dressing table.

'Jack has nice writing,' she says.

'Has he? Let's see.' Serena joins her and peers at the brief scrawl on chambers notepaper. With a ridiculous burst of pleasure, she studies his fine signature, 'Jack A Ramsay QC'.

She tries not to beam. 'He has, indeed.'

Lana moves on to a few legal trinkets on a shelf, studying the gavel cufflinks and miniature scales of justice, but not touching. She's desperate to start the baking, Serena knows, but trying her hardest to be patient.

'Why don't you tidy the en suite,' she says. 'You know, line up the toiletries so it looks really neat?' Feeling a small jolt, she resists saying 'like Daddy's'. 'I'll carry on sorting the beds, then I'll start on the bathrooms.'

With a project to do, her girl trots off happily, but the irony of her innate suggestion suddenly catches Serena short. Lana rarely mentions her daddy. Does she miss him? Is that what her attachment to Jack is really about? She's got off lightly so far, but will Lana ask to see him again, and what will she do or say then? The thought too overwhelming to dwell on, she pushes it away.

'I'm going to Hayden's bedroom now. Are you OK?' she calls to Lana.

'Yes, we're going to make it look really tidy.'

'OK.'

She moves to the door, then stops. Did Lana say 'we' again? She automatically looks around for Lexie. No dog, of course. She shakes the mild worry away. Lana knows the dog isn't allowed up here, so she's just pretending Lexie is with her to make the chore a fun game. Nothing wrong with that.

She heads for Hayden's room and strides in. Glad of an opportunity to change the bedding without his comments about hospital corners et al, she strips off the bottom sheet, spreads a clean one on top and tugs at the corners. Hmm. Has the fitted linen shrunk in the wash? Determined not to let it defeat her, she yanks up one side of the mattress. Oh, how odd. There's a buff envelope folder peeping from beneath it, clearly hidden. Too intrigued not to look, she quickly pulls it out, opens the ribbon tie and slips out the top parchment. The deeds to Ramsay Hall, it seems, so nothing particularly salacious. A strange place to hide them but she's never noticed a safe, so probably as good as anywhere. Or maybe he needs them handy to sell off another plot. She slides out the next form and reads on for a moment longer. But the hairs on her arms stand erect. Oh God, someone's in the doorway behind her. Concealing the document beneath her apron, she spins round.

Solemn-faced, it's Lana. Feeling guilty but mightily relieved, Serena claps a hand to her chest. 'Lana! You made me jump.' Then a little too sharply, 'You must always remember to knock, you know that from—'

Her daughter flushes and backs away. 'Sorry, Mummy.'

'Lana, wait. It's fine. Sorry. You just gave me a fright.' She puts the paperwork back where she found it, steps out and kneels on the landing. 'I'm sorry for snapping, love, OK? What did you want me for?' She peers at the crumpled plastic bag Lana's holding. 'Have you found something?'

Her face flooding with even more colour, Lana nods. 'Some dolly clothes,' she whispers.

Serena sits back in surprise. 'Oh, really?' Then taking in her obvious excitement, 'That sounds fun. Can I see?'

Dipping in her hand with a broad smile, Lana pulls out a pale pink cotton dress. No, not a dress but a nightie. Though she can't pinpoint why, Serena's mind is immediately in spasm, knowing something is wrong. Oh God, that's it; it's the smell. That dank metallic aroma she recognises all too well. With trembling fingers, she spreads out the garment on the carpet. It isn't a doll's; it's too big for a dolly. It's a child's, a small child's. Almost unable to look, she forces her eyes to a stain. It's brown, light brown now, but she's certain it once was red.

She puts her hands either side of Lana's shoulders. 'Where did you find this?' she asks.

She's holding her too tightly, she knows, but realisation is flashing through her mind in technicolour. She knows the answer already, but she just has to ask.

'Where did you find it, Lana?'

'Jack's bathroom,' she replies, her bottom lip wobbling. 'We were tidying like you said and it was at the back.'

With a great effort, she lets go of her child. 'The back of where?'

Her cheeks wet with tears, Lana sobs. 'The toilet roll cupboard. We were making them all neat just like… It was in there, at the back, so I had a little peep…'

Rocking away on her heels, Serena covers her face to stop the images flying in. But they don't go away. Those eyes, those dark guilty eyes. The way he looked at Lana, the way he had *kissed* her. That attraction. The fury when he'd told her not to enter his bedroom again. And what did he say about guilt and shame? Oh God, she feels sick; *breathe deeply, hold it in*. She must hold it in for her daughter.

'Lana…' She lowers her palms but she's gone. Snatching up the nightdress, she looks around the landing. 'Lana?' she calls. 'Lana, where are you?' Then trying to steady her tremulous voice, 'Come here, love. You're not in trouble.'

No reply, so she runs from room to room, looking in each bathroom and under the bed. Satisfied she's not there, she hurries down the stairs. Oh God, the front door is gaping; she must be outside. Racing to the hallway, she stops just in time to avoid a collision with Hayden.

'Did you pass Lana?' she asks breathlessly.

'Not that I noticed, but I've been concentrating on these. Sick of being escorted like a bloody toddler.' Leaning on one crutch, he looks at her curiously. 'Goodness, Serena. You look as though you've seen a ghost. Are you all right?'

'Yes, fine.' She squeezes past him. 'Sorry, I'm not sure where she's gone. I'll be back in a minute.'

'Lana?' she calls from the terrace. 'Lana? Are you outside?'

No reply.

The cold air smacks her cheeks, her bare arms and feet as she scurries down the steps. The sun was deceptive from the window; it was never spring. Scanning the courtyard, she turns, then turns again. 'Lana? Where are you?'

Nothing. Staring down the long driveway, she starts to jog, but a word pierces the silence. A single frightened word. 'Mummy!' Then again, 'Mummy! Mummy!'

Lana, it's Lana. Oh God, where is she?

'Where are you, Lana?'

Poised to run in the direction of the sound, Serena waits another moment and listens.

'I'm here!' The voice comes again and she bolts towards it. Round the front of the house, down the steps to the veranda, then over the sharp pebbles and damp grass. Scanning the tennis court, she calls Lana's name. The sound of crying echoes back and she swivels to the maze.

Oh God, oh God. Lana's arms and legs pinned around him, Jack emerges from the hedges, the dog following behind.

Serena tries to bellow with all her strength, but only a gasping whisper comes out. 'Put her down. Put my daughter down.'

Smiling ruefully, Jack walks towards her and mouths something she can't hear through the deafening thud in her ears. Her voice finally pelts out. 'Put her down! Put my daughter down!'

His face creased in confusion, he stops, says something to Lana and places her on the grass. She stares at her daughter's feet; they're uncovered, they're naked, like a small child in a nightdress.

Guiding her girl by the shoulders, Jack continues towards her. 'What's going on? Lana was lost in the maze, cry—'

'Don't touch her!'

Stepping forward, she grabs Lana and pulls her young head tightly against her stomach. She swallows and tries to breathe as she stares at this man's face. Guileless, middle-class and innocent, like so many of them are. Abusers, paedophiles, killers.

'What...' he begins.

'This,' she thrusts out her arm. Her throat feels so hoarse, she can barely speak. 'This. A child's. Hidden. What did you do to her?'

His face blanching, he stares at the garment. 'Where did you find that?'

Ignoring his question, she holds it up with trembling hands. 'It's soiled with blood. A child's nightie, hidden and bloody...' Trying to regain her composure, she swallows. 'Whose was it, Jack? What did you do to her?'

Staring clean through her, he starts to walk away, but she grabs his elbow.

'Who was—'

'Thea.' His eyes focus on the rusty stain, then he nods and swallows. 'She was called Thea. It was me; I did that.'

Chapter Thirty-Five

Jack

Not thinking and barely breathing, Jack stalks down the long drive. The desolate trees and outbuildings eventually come into focus. Realising there's something in his hand, he peels back his stiff fingers. It's the keys to the car and the house; they've punctured his skin. He watches the bead of liquid pool, then trickle from his thumb to his palm. *Blood, oh God, blood.* He can't feel it, he can't feel anything right now, but he knows the pain will come.

Lifting the fob, he stares, then nods. Work. Work, work and more work is the answer. The only answer. Concentrate on that.

-

It's Sunday, so the journey into Manchester takes only half an hour. Aware of the dull ache in his spine, Jack parks the car in a bay and feels in his pockets for coins. He swipes into chambers, rubs shoulders with another barrister who barely looks up, then he taps down the back stairs and along the dim basement corridor. Opening the door with his key, he finally breathes. His rooms are dank, cold and dark, but he's alone, thank God. There's only him here; he can sob, he can yell if he needs to.

He doesn't do either. Instead, he turns on the lamp and squints at the paperwork on his desk. It's ordered, but the neat piles of letters and documents are over a week old now, so he spends a few minutes sorting and studying, trying to ignore his throbbing temples as he reminds himself where each case was up to.

'Work' raps through his head. Work, work, work. Focus on routine and drudgery, and the rest will go away.

Stepping to the side table, he picks up a lever arch file and takes it back to his seat. He slowly turns the pages as he reads. Yup, it's all coming back. An offshore company, a trust. Evasion or avoidance? The Revenue asserts it's the illegal evasion of tax by the trust. He and the client disagree; they argue it's the lawful use of tax laws to reduce the company's burden. A shed-load of money is at stake. Millions. He can fight this one and win. Stay focused, Jack, stay focused.

Though his mind obeys, his heart continues to thrash. He wishes it would stop, stay still forever like an obsolete clock. Focus, Jack, focus. Legal or illegal? Avoidance or evasion? Or all of them when it comes to him and *his* case? With a sigh, he allows himself to glance at the green client chair. She's not there; he knew it. She's gone, forever gone, her absence even more of a punishment than when she was here, her eyes accusing, reminding, hurt, confused.

With a loud roar, he strides to the round table, puts the decanter to his lips and slugs back the peaty liquid. The stale brandy burns his throat but he takes another swig, then hurls the heavy crystal at the wall.

Its elegant neck snaps and the reddish brown liquid seeps down the wall. Like the stain of old blood; a child's flow of life.

He sinks to the floor with a gut-wrenching sob. 'I'm sorry, so sorry, please forgive me.'

He stares at the chair. It's still empty.

–

Though the tears blind his eyes, Jack speeds along the dark country road.

'Let go. I need to get to work.'

'Work, fucking work! Well there's a new tune!'

'Have you been drinking?'

'No.'

'I can smell it; fresh booze. At this time, for God's sake?'

'Says him who fell asleep with a fucking whisky in his hand.'

'I need to go now…'

'Well, I need you to stay home. I'm so bloody unhappy.'

'I can't, so that's that.'

'Don't you dare walk away. Come back. I haven't finished speaking!'

A long and shrill beep brings him back to the late evening traffic. As he yanks the steering wheel to the left, the tyres bump the bank and thorny bushes scrape the windows. Straightening up, he drives on. Its headlights flashing, a red HGV is bearing down the other carriageway.

'If you leave, then I'm following.'

Did she say that? Yes, she did, she really did. So he should just press ahead, hold down the accelerator, close his eyes and pray for oblivion. Then it would be over; the guilt, the remorse and reminders all gone.

He stamps on the brake. *Stop, Jack, just stop it!* His father and Hugh need him; he must get a grip for them. No cowardly way out; this time he has to go on.

Jack takes a weary breath, parks beneath the fir and climbs from his car. There's a glow of light from the cottage bedroom window in his peripheral vision, but he can't think about that – her expression, her disgust; it's too devastating.

Entering his home, he follows the bouquet of burning wood and coal to the drawing room. For the first time in years he longs to be greeted by his mother's smiling face, her shiny apple cheeks and red lips. He yearns to hear her voice and feel her arms fold him in. Soft, warm and reassuring. He'd thought she would always be there, but she left him, like everyone leaves him in the end. There's only Dad and Hugh; they have to stick together like always.

He opens the double doors. Solemn–faced and red-eyed, they're both in the dusky room. Hugh pounces up from the sofa, but lets their father move forward first. In obvious discomfort, he stands from the armchair and hobbles towards Jack without a crutch. He puts a trembling hand on his shoulder.

'Son, I'm so very sorry. Perhaps I got it wrong.'

Acknowledging the rare apology, Jack nods. He doesn't want to talk about Serena and Lana, but his father continues to speak.

'It was only an idle whim when I posted the advert. Someone to take care of the house – and me – while I mended. I probably wouldn't have seen it through, but when she replied saying she had a young child, it felt like… well, serendipity, I suppose. I thought it might help. A fresh start, a chance to put it all behind us and move on.'

He sighs and stumbles back to his chair. 'Maybe I didn't set a good example with Mum, but as time went on I realised that burying the past, throwing everything out, not even mentioning it in passing, let alone talking it through… Well, it was damaging us—'

'I still miss Thea so much!'

Hugh's tremulous voice bursts out with a sob. He presses down his hair with both hands.

'I wanted to talk about her all the time but I knew it wasn't for the best. I think of her every day. Every morning and night. She was my little friend; it was me who looked after her! We went fishing and swimming, to the park and the zoo. We'd sing in the car and count pylons on the way home. Feed the goats and do Percy Pig jigsaws…' He wipes his face with his sleeve. 'I still dream about her sometimes and when I wake up, I think she's still there.'

Jack takes him in his arms and grips tightly. 'I do too, Hugh. I do too.'

Chapter Thirty-Six

Hugh

Robbie strolls into the farm kitchen but Hugh keeps his head down to the bowl. Soup for lunch today, thank goodness. He helped himself to the brown gloopy liquid from the large pot on the hob and when he took a sip he discovered Mr Barnes had made oxtail broth. Pretty tasty, if he's honest, but what will Robbie make of that?

'OK mate?' Robbie doesn't sit, but strides to the sitting room door, which he closes. 'Dad around?'

Hugh shakes his head.

'You're a man of few words today. Is everything OK? I looked for you in the caravan last night.' He dips his head. 'Called you too? Left messages for you to call me back?' He sighs. 'Come on Hugh, I thought everything was good. Talk to me.'

'The soup's oxtail,' Hugh blurts.

Robbie laughs. 'Revolting shit. No wonder I fled half way around the world.' He taps the table. 'Listen. I was speaking to Dad last night and something didn't make sense. I wanted to sound it out with you...' He pulls out a chair. 'Look, is everything OK? Are *we* OK?' He glances at the staircase and lowers his voice. 'Saturday night was good wasn't it? Sharing the same bed?'

Trying to stop the sudden tears, Hugh looks at his broth, but it dimples like raindrops on a pond.

'Oh fuck,' Robbie says. 'Did I do something wrong? Say something crass?'

His eyes search Hugh's face with concern. 'I know I got angsty over dinner, but I thought we'd kissed and made up. And you were happy when we woke. More than happy, actually… *that* was unexpected and so bloody nice.' He pauses, then smacks his head. 'The call from your dad after lunch yesterday? Shit; you rushed off. Has something happened at home? To Jack?'

Hugh nods again. He's been weeping on and off since. Jack's face had looked like broken china for the rest of the evening, so he'd tried to be brave, but it's like someone has opened a tap with a faulty washer. However tightly he endeavours to turn it off, the drip, drip is still there from his eyes and his nose, even his mouth. He woke in the night and though he couldn't remember dreaming, his face was wet. He got up and washed it with cold water, but he pictured Thea next to him in the mirror cleaning those little pearly teeth, so he started again. Even on the tractor this morning, he was crying like a baby for his loss. And Jack's, particularly Jack's. He wishes that he'd cry. Everything would be better if Jack cried too.

His features creased with worry, Robbie stares. 'What's happened, Hugh?'

Hugh takes a big breath. Is he allowed to tell? From as far back as he remembers, there were secrets to keep.

Never tell anybody, Hugh.

I don't want to talk about it, OK.

It'll be our secret.

It's best for you never to mention this again.

No one will ever know.

Least said, soonest mended.

Yet from seven to seventeen he'd told Robbie Barnes everything. Not that he had anything to hold in back then. Except him and Robbie at the shepherd's cottage and he didn't need be *told* to do that. But what happened yesterday? Can he share that? He isn't sure. His dad called at two o'clock and told him to come home right away, so he did.

Lana was in the kitchen, her sad face red and blotchy. 'Where's your mum?' he asked.

'She's bringing down our suitcase.'

'Oh, right. Where are you going?'

'Back to the cottage.'

He was relieved they weren't leaving forever, but wondered what was going on. Everybody had seemed happy with them in the house, Jack especially. 'Why are you going back?' he asked.

'We ran into the maze and I got lost. Jack came to find me and I told him why Lexie had a poorly leg, then Mummy told him off. So it's all my fault. I shouldn't have said anything.'

He had no clue about what she was saying, but she screwed her fists in her eyes.

'OK, don't be upset,' he said. 'I'm sure everything's fine.' He picked her up and she held onto his jumper with tight fingers. Reminding him of his Thea as always, it brought a lump to his throat. 'What about Lexie?' he asked to break the moment.

'She must have been naughty; that's why,' she replied, but before he could ask more, Serena came in, her face almost white.

She reached out her hand and briefly touched his. 'I'm so sorry for your loss. I had no idea about… your niece.

Please tell Jack I'm so very, very sorry. My behaviour, my… insensitivity… was unforgivable. I've handed in my notice and we'll be moving on soon, but your dad has kindly said I can stay in the cottage until I find a new post.' She smiled thinly. 'I'll be working as usual until then, so if there's anything you need, just let me know.'

'Hugh?' Robbie's voice tugs him back. 'What's happened to Jack? You've got me worried.'

How to explain? What does Mrs Amara always say? Start at the beginning.

He puffs out the trapped air. 'Right, so… Jack met Mel at a night club and she got pregnant, so he married her. I thought they'd move out and buy a house, but it was fine because she wanted to stay with us at the hall. Then she had the baby and…' His voice cracks. 'It was just a… well, a baby at first, then we got to know her and she grew bigger and more beautiful and funny. Then one day—'

Robbie rubs his arm. 'It's fine; I know, you don't need to say it. Jess told me. About two years ago, right?'

Hugh nods. 'An owl had got trapped in the roof space. Nested up there, I suppose, but it was distressed, throwing itself around, bashing against the rafters and staring with those eyes. It was horrible. So I was up there trying to catch it when—'

'Christ. But what happened last night, Hugh?'

'I don't know, but Jack had gone off in the car. Dad was upset when I got there. Well, more than upset. We just sat and waited. Jack was gone for hours and didn't answer his phone. Dad was convinced he'd never come home again. Ever.'

Robbie's expression is perplexed. 'But he did, right?'

'Yeah, but the old Jack is back and we're worried.'

Chapter Thirty-Seven

Serena

Careful not to wake Lana, Serena swings her legs from the small cottage bed. Her heels are still cut and sore from Sunday. Funny how adrenaline affects the body and mind. She wasn't aware her feet were bare until she returned, shame-faced to the house. Carrying a weeping Lana to the kitchen, she sat her at the table, intending to wipe her face with a cloth. At the sink, she looked down at her hand; she was still holding the nightdress. Not knowing what else to do, she opened a bottom drawer and laid it in carefully, like a poverty-stricken mother and her newborn years ago.

Going back to her own baby, she padded her pink skin. 'Everything's fine,' she said, though it was far, far from that.

Fresh tears rolled down Lana's cheeks. 'I wasn't running away; I just followed her into the maze and I got lost.'

'Followed who? Lexie?'

She sucked in her lips and didn't reply for a beat. Then shuffling her feet, 'I shouldn't have told Jack about what happened to Lexie.'

'Told him what?'

She shook her head. 'It's all my fault you got cross.'

'No it isn't, love. You've done nothing wrong.'

But *she* had. Serena didn't quite know what at that stage, but she'd instantly known from Jack's pale, hurt and astonished face that she'd done him a massive injustice.

'*Thea*,' he'd said as he stared at the blood stain. '*She was called Thea. It was me; I did that.*'

Dreadful, dreadful words. But his anguished, clearly heartbroken expression hadn't matched them. Then he'd stalked off down the drive and by the time she'd reached the house, she'd heard the slam of a car door. She'd turned to see his Porsche heading dangerously fast around the bend, then he'd gone.

What did the hidden garment mean? What had happened to 'Thea'? She had no idea, but in those few seconds it was as though she'd looked into Jack's soul. Whatever he felt guilty about, it wasn't what she'd horribly, horrendously thought.

Feeling unnerved and anxious, she kissed Lana on the head. 'I won't be a minute, love. I just need to speak to Hayden.'

'You're bleeding, Mummy,' she replied. 'You'll make a mess.'

And she was; like a crime scene, she'd made bloody footprints from the door to the table and the sink. That's when she felt the stinging pain, even more so when she examined her soles and found several sharp stones embedded in the skin. Still, she was used to torment, wasn't she, mental, emotional, physical. But she couldn't feel sorry for herself, not then; she needed to fix up her feet and talk to Hayden.

The heart thrusts now hitting, she lowers her head and braces herself for the stunning deluge of burning liquid. Logically she knows the palpitations are just panic, the recall a form of PTSD, but each time it happens she's certain *this* attack will kill her and leave Lana all alone. Would the Ramsays take her child in? Would they replace their devastating loss by protecting her baby? Understand that the sins of the mother are not those of the daughter?

She tries to steady her breathing. The Ramsays' unbearable loss, oh God. Once she'd patched her feet with plasters, she'd gingerly padded to the drawing room and knocked on the door.

His knuckles white on the chair arm, Hayden had immediately hauled himself up. Was it her words or her face?

'Who is Thea, Hayden?' she'd asked him.

He'd replied without missing a beat. 'Where's Jack?'

'He's left in the car.' Then after a moment, desperately needing to know, 'I'm sorry to ask again, but who is Thea?'

'Was,' he'd replied. 'My three-year-old granddaughter. She tragically died in a car accident two years ago.' Then clearing his throat, 'If you wouldn't mind excusing me, Serena, I need to call Hugh.'

She'd given him twenty minutes before returning with his usual afternoon tea. 'I would like to hand in my resignation,' she'd said. 'I can go straight away, but I'd prefer to work my notice if that's at all possible…'

Clearly distracted, he'd waved his hand. 'Whatever you think best. Tell Hugh to find me here when he arrives, will you?'

Now counting to four, she breathes out, then inhales the same in. Thank God he hadn't sacked her there and then, but five days have already passed and she has to have a future plan for her and Lana. Jack has avoided her by leaving early each morning and working until late, but there's bound to come a time when he asks her to go.

She looks at her watch, then checks again on her sleeping daughter. God, she needs a smoke. She thinks of her emergency supplies and nods. This is, after all, a colossal crisis.

–

Serena knocks on Hayden's bedroom door and carries in his breakfast tray. For the past four mornings he's acted as though nothing has changed and today is no different – the usual petulant and grumpy, with a thin slice of humour.

'I didn't know you smoked, Serena.'

Mildly surprised, she thinks of denying it, but his satisfied expression shows there's no point. Did he see her from the window or smell her just now?

'Only every now and then to clear out the lungs,' she replies.

'Used to do that on the golf course before I became a cripple. Clear out the lungs, that is. None of us have ever smoked.'

He dutifully leans forward as she batters his pillow. 'You're not a cripple and you should prove it by getting out of bed,' she says. 'What did we agree about working on your strength and movement? It's much brighter this morning. We could take a walk around the gardens.'

Like a querulous child, he flicks the laundered napkin from the tray. 'Why would I want to walk around my own property? I can take in one side of it through this window, the other from the drawing room. I'm so damned bored. If you had any heart, you'd take me out in your car for a drive, even for lunch.'

Her car? The Renault, a car with a number plate, a *traceable* car. Breathing through her alarm, she strives for her reasonable voice. 'You're still shaky on those crutches, Hayden. I'm not as strong as Hugh or Jack. It would be awful if you had another fall…'

He doesn't look convinced, so she raises her eyebrows. 'Like the stairs episode. And that was inside the house.'

'Then I'll use the damned zimmer frame.'

'It won't—'

Clearly anticipating her answer, he quickly interrupts. 'Well, it fits in my car. You're insured to drive it with my permission. Come on, Serena, think about your little one. Things have been quiet around here this week. Evidenced by her constant chatter to a dog, the poor child's obviously stir crazy. We can treat her to an ice cream at a parlour or a burger joint rather than imprisoning her in here. Have you even had a day off yet?'

Serena quickly thinks. A trip in his car to a remote location. She could do that, yes. But it would set a precedent, and where might that lead? She's a woman who doesn't want to be found. Who's *afraid* of being found.

An idea forming, she forces a smile. 'Here's a suggestion to break the ennui. Why not ask a friend for lunch or dinner? I'm not a bad cook, as you know, and I'd happily prepare something particularly special for you. Choose anything you like, though my beef bourguignon with celeriac mash always goes down a treat.'

He picks up his sandwich and takes a bite. 'The bacon's gone cold.'

She holds out her hand. 'Give me the plate and I'll make you another.'

He wafts it away. 'Sit down, then. We need to make a list.' He rubs his chin. 'Actually, on second thoughts, it's an excellent idea. Thank you, Serena. Jack mentioned our lack of security only on Sunday at the golf club and Fogie offered to have a gander. It's his area these days. Course we have the gate and the house is alarmed, but as Jack pointed out, the garages, the games room and the outbuildings still have the old latches. Then there's the barn, we'd have to address that.'

Appearing satisfied, he takes another bite of his butty and chews. 'Yes. Let's invite Fogie for a slap-up dinner. It'll kill two birds with one stone and be an excuse not to include his dreadful wife. What ingredients do we need for your *special* beef bourguignon? I'm sure Fogie'll like that with a nice bottle or two of red. What do you recommend? A claret?'

She turns away to his desk. Oh God. Hayden's friend is in security 'these days'. In her experience, that generally means one thing. Why on earth did she mention the lack of locks to Jack? Hoping Hayden doesn't clock her shaking fingers, she passes pen and paper over.

'Yes, a claret sounds perfect. So Fogie is in security?'

'In a manner of speaking. Jack of all trades since retirement. Consultancy, investigations, enforcement.'

Oh hell, she was right. 'Ex police, I assume?' she asks lightly.

'Yes, no end of opportunities for an ex copper.' Hayden picks up his teacup and sips. 'Especially a bright fella like him. Even now they rope him back in when they're short-handed.'

'So he's still in the force?'

'Pub quiz and Christmas party regular.' He chuckles. 'Best way to keep his ear to the ground.'

'I don't suppose Fogie is his real name.'

'Gary Fogleman, hence Fogie. We were all given nicknames.'

She picks up the napkin and spreads it on the bed. 'Ah, you trained together, then? They're the friendships that stick.'

'Absolutely. Younger than me, but we've helped each other out a fair few times over the years.'

She feels the heat of anxiety spread. Bloody hell, Hayden is ex police. Why didn't she know that? She masks her thrashing heart with a quip. 'Like George W. Bush?'

'Beg your pardon?'

'The nicknames. Apparently he was famous for giving everyone a—'

'Like Ostrich Legs?' He laughs. 'None that bad. Just surnames.'

'And what was yours? Ram? Or The Ram?'

'No! It was…' His cheeks lightly colouring, he raises his eyebrows. 'We're going off subject, young lady. Back to this delicious dinner you're making. Shall we say tomorrow?'

–

'Mummy? Mummy! Did you hear me?'

Serena spins round from the kitchen sink. She was miles away, thinking about all manner of things – the astonishing discovery that Hayden was a policeman, nick-names and how to make bloody celeriac mash.

And of course about Jack. His face on Sunday. The incredulity when he realised what she was implying. No, not implying. Saying. Accusing. Believing he'd done something appalling. Clouded by her lapse of judgement long ago, she isn't even sure exactly what. He hasn't spoken or called or even made eye contact with her since then. He'll never forgive her, she knows that. And though

Hayden seems to have forgotten her resignation, she can't stay here forever; she has to go *somewhere* at some point. She'll have to leave through that anchored gate to the unknown world outside.

That gate. Security. A policeman. Oh God.

Shifting her focus to her daughter, she tries for a smile. 'Yes, love? What is it?'

Lana peers into her mixing bowl. 'These eggs, Mummy. I put in some flour like you said, but I think they have…What was that word?'

'Curdled. It means it's separated into curds…'

A security check. The garage. The Renault. Oh God. Serena looks at the cake dough and tries to keep calm. It's curdled, coagulated and congealed, like her stomach. She comes back to Lana's scrunched face.

'It's nothing to worry about; the muffins will taste just as good, love. In fact, you've reminded me, we need to include eggs and flour with the supermarket order. I'll add them to Hayden's list.'

The breathlessness comes again. Tomorrow; tomorrow! Hayden's police mate is coming for dinner in twenty-four hours. He's going to look everywhere.

She turns to the window and scans the huge courtyard. Her cottage and side garden sits to the right, the barn and garage to the left, the low outbuildings in between, but separate too. A way out slots into place.

'I know,' she says to Lana. 'Hayden's having a posh dinner party tomorrow but he hasn't pressed the "buy" button on his laptop yet.' She steps over and tweaks her nose. 'How about for a change we drive to the super-market and pick it in person? I can inspect the beef to see if it's up to scratch, then on the way back we can stop at a pub or a cafe. A drink for Hayden and an ice cream for you. He says we can use his big car. How do you fancy a spin out this afternoon?'

She nods, decision made. Firstly, she needs another cigarette.

Chapter Thirty-Eight

Jack

Jack pulls up the car by the fir and rests his heavy forehead on the steering wheel. Though he's had a relatively easy working week, driving just a few miles to the courts in Chester each day and returning to chambers in daylight, he's unbearably tired. From sleeping pills and pain killers, of course. But not just that. From the blocking out and blanking, the sheer effort of focusing solely on work, his cases, his clients. Anything other than here, his past, his mistakes, his child, his home. And Lana, little Lana; they'd made a special bond; he misses her smile and her unguarded hugs. Which makes Serena's accusations all the worse. '*Don't touch her!*' And, '*What did you do to her?*'

But he won't think about it; he can't.

His eyes steadfastly averted from the cottage, he hops up the steps and puts his key in the latch. It doesn't turn as expected, so he unlocks the mortice and walks in.

'Hello?' he calls. 'Hugh? Dad? Anyone in?'

His voice seems to bounce back but there's no reply. Hugh's car isn't here. A hospital appointment? No one mentioned one.

He opens the kitchen door and Lexie hurries out. Scratching under her chin and rubbing her ears, he fusses her as usual, but she seems more clingy today, pawing his hand rather than sauntering away. He rubs her flank gently and peers at her 'poorly' leg, but pushes away that notion too. Lana's just a small child; she must have been mistaken about what she thought she'd seen.

He goes back to Lexie. 'Left all alone, girl? You're not used to it these days. Is the boss upstairs?'

Trying not to dwell on how silent the house will be when Lana and Serena finally leave, he strides up the stairs. He stops at the top. Hell, there's a thought. Perhaps they've already left without saying goodbye. How does he feel about that?

He wills the prodding hurt away. He won't let Serena in; he won't let any emotion in; he doesn't want to *feel* anything.

'Dad? Are you there?'

Though his crutches are leaning against the wall, his father's bedroom is empty. He turns in surprise to see Lexie has followed him.

'Hey! You know you're not allowed up here.' She whinnies, cocks her head and lifts her paw again. 'What's up, girl?'

She turns tail and pads away, so he follows her down. Her claws tapping the tiles, she scurries through the kitchen, stops at the back door and wags her tail.

'Ah, you're desperate for a pee,' he says, wondering exactly how long she's been alone and where on earth his dad is.

He lets Lexie out. As though thrown back in time, the stench of smoke hits immediately. What the…? Has he finally lost the plot? He stills for a moment. No, not the old acrid odour, but a heady live smell of burning. Bolting outside, he searches the courtyard. Where's it coming from? What the hell's going on? His gaze rests on the cottage. No lights, no sign of movement, no fumes. Not there, thank God.

He turns again, squinting and scanning the sunk side of the roof. No gaping hole like before, but there are thin plumes of smoke seeping through the broken tiles.

Good God, is the barn on fire again? His eyes flick to the other side. Possibly. But the garage definitely is; grey swirls are seeping through the shutters. He stares for a beat. Bloody hell, his dad's Range Rover, the tools and Hugh's beloved junk; he'd better do something and quickly.

Adrenaline kicking in, he sprints across the yard and yanks open the side entrance. Flashes of orange leap out from the backdraft, so he immediately smacks it shut and stumbles back. Fucking hell, fucking hell! Not just a small extinguishable fire, but a full-on roar of angry flames. His heart pounding, he feels his jacket for his mobile, pulls it from an inner pocket, and quickly calls 999.

Standing back with Lexie, he pants out his trapped air. He'd like to do something heroic, but it's too dangerous to try anything himself. Bloody hell; that shocking lick of fire told him that good and proper; he can still feel the heat on his cheeks.

He pats his hair and laughs. A close call, a bloody close call. Why it's made him feel energised and alive, he can't say.

–

The drizzly, dark evening setting in, Jack carries an old deckchair to the games room, puts it near a window and thumps down. Like a boy, he was exhilarated to see the fire engine roar up the drive and the firefighters pile out. After a few moments of brisk questioning and assessing the risk, they sprang into action. In awe and admiration, he listened to the commands and observed their efficiency with breathing apparatus, fire reels and hoses. When they finally finished, the chief gave him a quick tour of the damage, but Jack found himself more interested in the equipment and appliances. He asked a couple of questions and itched to learn more, but they had homes to go to, families to see. And now they've gone, he feels weary again, a pathetic burned-out wreck, much like what was left in the garage.

Nearly asleep, he hears the final clank of the barrier. He rushes out just in time to flag down his dad's car. Almost blinded by the headlights, he yanks open the passenger door.

'Nothing to worry about,' he says to his astonished father. 'I just wanted to warn you before you saw it. We've had a fire, but it's OK. The firefighters came and doused it fairly quickly. It was contained to the garage.'

He tries to look at Serena, but can't quite meet her surprised gaze. He pictures the row of melted wellies. 'I'm very sorry, Serena, but your car took most of the flack. A highly inflammable cover, apparently. And of course the loose hay. I'm afraid it's pretty much a shell.'

–

The reek of smoke still embedded in his skin despite a long shower, Jack sits in the snug in the dark. He's been mulling for almost an hour, swinging from thought to thought. The astonishing fire, of course. His dad was as pragmatic as only he could be. Holding Jack's arm for support, he briefly peered at the havoc, then shrugged.

'Nothing insurance won't sort out.' He turned to Serena. 'My leg's badly throbbing, please excuse me. I've had a lovely afternoon and evening. Thank you.' Hobbling away with the zimmer, he lifted his hand. 'I'll call Fogie and postpone our dinner for now. Oh, and don't worry, Jack will sort out your car.'

He wondered then why he'd been so worried, why he'd sat on the rickety chair and waited in the cold so he could deliver the news and prepare his father before he saw it. But he knew the answer: Serena and Lana. In spite of everything, the desire to protect and shield them was there. Love them, too. And little Lana did cry. She put her fists to her eyes and sobbed when she saw the charcoaled wet wreck of the Renault and everything surrounding it.

He'd hesitated before picking her up and hugging her tightly, but only for a moment. Whatever had happened between him and Serena, it wasn't Lana's fault.

He now rocks his head against the soft leather of the sofa. So tired, too tired. Time for bed. He sighs, stands up and shuffles to the hall, but at the bannister he stops and remembers the exhilaration of that close call with the flames. What exactly does he want? What does he *need*? The dull safety of the old oblivion? Or the danger and uncertainty of live fire and living?

With a nod, he propels himself forward, turns the latch and strides over the courtyard. He quickly lifts the cottage knocker before he changes his mind, but the door opens and fragrant warmth eases out.

Serena, Serena, her face pale and anxious and beautiful.

'Jack. I heard your footsteps from the bedroom,' she says. 'Is everything all right? Your father? Hugh?' She stands back. 'Please come in.'

He steps into the parlour. Now he's here, he doesn't know what to say.

'I'm sorry about your car...' he begins, the same time as she speaks.

She smiles faintly. 'You go first. Would you like to sit down?'

'Thanks.'

She takes the armchair and he settles in his old place on the small sofa.

He stares ahead through the black window. It's difficult to focus. 'Sorry about your car,' he repeats.

'It's fine, really. It's only a thing, nobody was hurt. That's what's important.'

Sudden outrage pierces the blocking and blanking. *Hurt*, bloody hurt? Does she have any idea? Blood rushing to his face, he stands. He just has to spit it out.

'What you implied on Sunday. I don't know where to begin, but one thing feels paramount right now. We made... we slept together several times; we were intimate, had sex, whatever. How could you, how could anyone bring themselves to... when you thought *that* of me?'

'I didn't! I don't.'

Her eyes clear and blue, she looks at him intently. 'I didn't, of course I didn't. And it *was* making love, Jack.'

She sighs. 'I can't begin to apologise for my inexcusable behaviour. I don't even know what I was thinking. I just panicked in the moment, put two and two together – your reticence, I suppose, knowing you needed to say something huge, then finding the, the...'

She pauses for a beat. 'You didn't tell me, Jack. I had no idea you had a child, let alone that she'd died,' she says gently. 'Hayden told me it was a car accident. I'm so very sorry.'

Desolation replaces Jack's anger. He sits and doesn't speak for a while. He's picturing his daughter the very last time he saw her.

'There were slippers too,' he says eventually. 'In the bag you found. Furry pink slippers and…'

He tries to reach for the word. Her silky hair was tied in two high plaits. Though not as neat as she'd wanted, he'd knotted them himself only half an hour before. He touches his head to demonstrate. 'Hair elastics with material around them? That's right. Scrunchies, she called them.'

He squints. And her tartan teddy. Her favourite soft toy was still clutched in her hand. Willing the image away, he covers his face. He didn't keep Tartan Teddy. No, he buried him with her.

'I'm so, so very sorry.' A voice from the distance and movement. When he lowers his palms, Serena's kneeling in front of him.

'I can't begin to imagine the sorrow, the pain,' she says. 'There's nothing I can say except sorry.'

He looks at the glass panes behind her. He saw Amara just twice, but she advised him to seek happy memories, to replace that last dreadful snapshot with a good one. Thea brought so much joy. Why he could only do it here on this sofa, he doesn't know.

As though reading his mind, Serena's gaze questions him.

'Her swing was out there on the grass. She had plenty of toys in here, but…' He turns to the rocking horse, still covered in a sheet. 'This was her playhouse, but she preferred to be outside on her swing, kicking her legs to the heavens.'

The heavens, oh God. A sob threatens to bubble out but he immediately berates himself. This has to stop. He has to put the cork firmly back in the bottle. He makes to leave, but Serena catches his fingers.

'It's no excuse, none at all, but it's a reason,' she says. 'Can I explain? Please?'

Momentarily confused, he frowns. 'A reason for...?'

'My... my lapse in judgment on Sunday.'

Her expression is entreating. 'OK...'

She takes a deep breath and rakes her hair behind her ears. 'I was a doctor – am still, I suppose. A vocation, so you never really stop. Anyway...'

Jack absorbs the information. Is he surprised? Probably not. Contained and knowledgeable and undoubtedly intelligent.

Her gaze seems solid, determined. 'I was a paediatrician, in fact, so my job was to look after children. Caring, curing, listening. Above everything, keeping them safe.'

With a staccato tone, she continues to speak. 'A child came into the hospital with a badly broken arm. The mother made an allegation against the father. They were going through a particularly acrimonious divorce, so she wasn't in the best place mentally or emotionally, but the team duly checked it out. He was a middle-class professional – a lawyer, in fact – pleasant, reputable and most of all, believable. Nine months later the child's naked image was found on the internet. His own daughter. She was seven years of age.' Her voice falters and softens. 'That's absolutely no excuse for my dreadful response to the clothes Lana found. It's just an explanation of my... my paranoia, I suppose. Both then and when Lana grazed her knee.'

She smiles thinly and stands. 'It's late. I'll let you go now.'

He doesn't move. 'What happened? I mean, what happened to you?'

'There was an investigation – us, the child's school, her doctor, social services, police. *Respectability* had fooled us all. But I made a mistake that had dreadful consequences for a child I was supposed to protect. I couldn't bear the guilt, so I stepped away from my job and had time out.'

Jack gazes. A *mistake* and the guilt. Those he understands. Corrosive, debilitating. Seeping through your life and poisoning it.

He reaches out and takes her hand. 'Were you OK? Did you go back?'

She shakes her head. 'Not really and no. I suppose I had a breakdown of sorts. I'd made a terrible blunder, an awful lapse of judgement, so I mentally beat myself up almost constantly. Pierre went through the motions of appearing supportive, but he…' She seems to search for the words. 'Well, quite frankly, I think he enjoyed it. He was pleased that I had failed, made sure to bring it up frequently.' She laughs wryly. 'He didn't need to. My confidence was shattered, his constant endorsement of my ineptitude really wasn't necessary. It was a very tough time. Pierre had already separated me from friends in general, and now I was isolating myself from work colleagues too, so ironically he was my only saviour. Which, I guess, is exactly what he wanted.'

Abruptly, she smiles. 'But a miracle happened. I discovered I was pregnant with Lana. From the darkest of places, I found light.'

Chapter Thirty-Nine

Hugh

Hugh wakes and stretches in his clean, laundered bed. Slipping his arm beneath the pillow he settles down for more sleep, but an electric shock ricochets through his body. He yelps at the sudden pain, then gently pulls his hand out. Oh fuck, his right wrist is purple and swollen. Is it broken?

Breathing in the stench of smoke, he curls into a ball. Serena and Jack, a blaze and then this. Hell, bloody hell, what next?

Jack phoned him yesterday afternoon around five. 'The garage and barn is in flames. I've phoned fire services and I'm waiting.'

'What? You're joking.'

A pause and then, 'You don't know anything about it, do you, Hugh?'

'No, of course not.' Then, realising what Jack was *really* saying, 'No! How can you say that?'

He didn't even apologise. Instead he made it worse. 'Well you do have a track record and it's a strange coincidence that this should happen minutes after Robbie Barnes returns to the farm.'

Hugh was bloody offended. 'It isn't minutes, it's three weeks, actually,' he replied, ending the call.

Too annoyed to go home, his only option was to stay and eat a veggie dinner at the farm. He stared at the 'lasagne' suspiciously. Serena's version contained meat. So did Tesco's.

'It's made with butternut squash, mate,' Robbie said.

What the heck *that* was, he had no idea. He'd expected it to taste somewhere between peanut butter and fruit juice, but in fact it was delicious and even Mr Barnes said as much. Then, when the farmer left the table to watch the TV, Robbie suggested a pint. Not just a drink, but one at The Bull.

Hugh now snorts at the suggestion. The two of them in The Bull in full view of the locals? He should have known that Robbie had something on his mind. He seemed hyper, too.

'Really?' Hugh replied in surprise. 'You want a drink with me in The Bull?'

'You're probably right,' he answered. 'Let's do The Crown.'

Hugh bought the first round. Once settled in a dusty corner, Robbie launched in straight away. 'You know I thought something didn't add up the other day? After speaking to Dad when he was doing this month's ledgers?'

Hugh sighed inwardly. *Ledgers* meant money and maths. Preparing to be bored, he gulped back his beer and nodded.

'Well, basically the farm's doing fine. Has been for years. But the thing that bothers me is this. When I was at school, money was really tight. Remember the guy from Poland who really knew his stuff? Olaf? He was a brilliant farm hand and Dad loved him, but still had to let him go…' He stared for a moment and frowned. 'Redundancy, Hugh. You know, basically giving him the sack?'

Dutifully, Hugh nodded again.

Robbie tapped the table top. His eyes were excited and shiny. 'Then how on earth did Mum and Dad afford my airfare to Australia, let alone the dosh they gave me to get started?'

Hugh looked at his empty pint glass meaningfully; it was Robbie's turn to buy the drinks. 'Sorry, no idea.'

'So then I thought about all the changes Dad made to the farm after I'd gone. The underpinning of the house, not to mention the new cattle shed. How did they pay for those, Hugh?'

He wasn't sure Robbie actually wanted an answer, but he knew he had one. Closing his eyes, he concentrated. Finally clicking his fingers, he smiled. 'The weight of snow. That's the worry!'

'What?'

'Your dad told me! He said that heavy snow had brought down a roof and it cost him a five-figure sum.' He laughed as he aped his own dad's voice. 'Nothing insurance won't sort out, though.'

'When was this?'

He shrugged. 'Didn't ask. A cow was injured, so maybe that was why he got a new shed.'

Robbie seemed thrown for a moment. Though Hugh pushed his glass forward, he carried on speaking.

'Whatever. I need to look into that. But the point is that the house repairs, which were extensive, by the way, the outbuilding and a new bloody tractor all happened at the same time. Guess when that was?'

Losing patience, Hugh stood. 'No idea, do you want another pint?'

'Eighteen years ago! Immediately after I left. Come on, mate, even you can see that's a bloody coincidence. No money, redundancies, then they're suddenly flush.'

'How did they get it, then?'

Robbie raised his eyebrows. 'Well, here's my theory: there's only one person in this village who had spare cash like that.'

What Robbie was *really* saying finally clicked into place. In some way or another, he was having a go at his dad again. Well, that wasn't a surprise. Mr and Mrs Barnes had always been very respectful of 'Mr Ramsay', but Robbie and his mates weren't. They'd regularly called him a range of not very nice names, as though Hugh wasn't actually there and listening. Stuff about his mum too, which had made him feel sick. 'Jealousy,' Jack had always said when he came home in tears. 'Just ignore it.'

Annoyance rising, Hugh folded his arms. 'Seems to me a lot of guesswork is going into this *theory*. And why does it even matter? Maybe my dad gave yours a loan, or maybe he was being generous. You're just looking for a reason to have a go at him again.'

Robbie sneered. 'Generous, your dad! The man who threw his son out of a multi-million pound mansion set in bloody acres to live in a rusty caravan.'

'You know nothing about that,' he answered stiffly.

'I know more than you realise, Hugh. Much more.'

That's when he'd had enough. His blood started to bubble. 'Fuck off, Robbie. You've only been back for a few weeks.'

He began to stalk away, but the phone call from Jack popped into his head. The astonishing fire at the hall. Hugh had told Robbie about his 'arson' only the other day.

He squeezed his mind back to lunch time. The quad bike had got stuck in a deep ditch of mud, and despite looking for Robbie to help shift it, he couldn't find him anywhere. In fact, he hadn't seen him on the farm all afternoon. Where had he been? It was obvious he still hated his dad. Did *he* set fire to the barn? Suddenly it seemed bloody likely.

He turned and pointed. 'You're pathetic, do you know that? Even after all these years you're still jealous of the Ramsays. You need to grow up.'

Robbie clapped his hands. 'That's hilarious coming from you! The funniest thing I've heard all week. You have no idea about anything, have you, Hugh? You've lived all your life with your posh little eyes tightly closed.'

Anger at boiling point then, he wanted to explode, but he managed to escape just before the need to thump *something* was too intense to resist. The beer garden gate was the closest thing to hand. Bloody solid oak. Not that he felt anything then. His anger was enough to see him to his car and back to the safety of Ramsay Hall.

Now dragging down the second pillow, he rests his throbbing arm on it. A thought occurs: there'll be no work for a while with his wrist in this state. Hell, he'll let Mr Barnes down. Even worse, he'll 'disappoint' him. He hates to do that.

You disappoint me; you're a coward, Hugh. There's no other word for it.

Deeply sighing, he reaches for his mobile. A couple of messages from Robbie. Hmm. More insults, no doubt: 'No idea about anything', 'posh little eyes', 'thick', 'the village idiot'. Yeah, and 'coward'.

He chucks it away, carefully turns over and spreads his legs across the other half of the mattress. Almost asleep, that distant voice filters through. '*Get out, just get out!*' He hears it when he's sad and he really doesn't like it. Sometimes if he waits, a kinder tone follows, but nothing's happening today.

His nose burns. Kipping next to Robbie was brill. They touched or cupped each other even when they slept. Robbie didn't push him away, let alone shout. But the things he says, not just the jibes, but the stuff about his dad... He has no right to do that. And what did he mean by, 'I know more than you realise'?

It's like a bloody seesaw; one minute he feels ecstatic, the next minute he's confused. Then he gets upset and angry and look what happens then.

No, he won't look or answer Robbie's texts. He can fuck off, in fact. What does Jack always say about the Ramsays sticking together? Well, he's right.

He nods to himself and yawns. Yup, the security of his dad, his brother and home sweet home. That's what's important.

Chapter Forty

Serena

Feeling brighter after her tentative reconciliation with Jack last night, Serena tops up the men's coffee cups. At least she hopes there was an understanding of some sort. He didn't say much before leaving the cottage, but almost like a dance, he held her for an age, then he kissed her hair and said goodnight. And it was enough; far more than she deserved.

Though she'd struggled to contain her panic through the early morning hours, the image of a child in pink slippers on a swing and Jack's devastated face bobbed in and out. So unbelievably tragic. Not just one loss but two – a wife and a toddler. A car accident, Hayden said. A crash presumably, mother and child snuffed out like a light.

Coming back to the warm kitchen, she lifts her eyebrows and gives her daughter a secret smile. Both in their dressing gowns, Hugh and Hayden have been bickering at the kitchen table for the past half an hour. She's had to work hard not to chuckle – the arguments have ranged from who put the empty cornflake box back in the cupboard, to whether fodder can self-combust; from which *Godfather* film is the best, to whose limb hurts the most.

Like a tennis spectator, Lana's wide gaze has wheeled from one man to the other. Serena's glad she doesn't have to umpire, particularly the last set. Because Hayden complains so frequently, the level of his discomfort is difficult to judge, but Hugh is obviously in pain, resorting to eating cereal with his left hand, which clearly perturbs him.

'Can I take a look at your injury?' she now asks him.

'Sure.' He pulls up his sleeve but the thick fabric falls back.

'Here, let me,' she says, folding the towelling in neat sections.

Purpling and warm to the touch, both his knuckles and his wrist are badly swollen. 'Ouch, Hugh, that looks sore. How did you do it?'

He shrugs. 'Slipped and fell.' Then, when his father loudly snorts, 'Perhaps I take after you with all your *slipping and falling*, old man.'

Serena interrupts before Hayden returns the lob. 'Have you taken some anti-inflammatory tablets, Hugh? Packing it with ice will help the pain and swelling go down too. Do it for twenty to thirty minutes, maybe? I can compress your wrist with a bandage, but you should really have it looked at professionally. I expect they'll suggest an x-ray.'

'And if that's what Nurse Serena says you must do...' Hayden pauses theatrically and smiles at Lana. 'Though look how she's examining Hugh's fingers. So expertly done, wouldn't you say? I think your mummy should be upgraded to doctor, don't you? Doctor Serena—'

'Very droll, Dad.' Jack's voice comes from the door, saving Lana from her blushes.

With a mix of apprehension and relief, Serena dares to meet Jack's face. Though he hasn't shaved yet, the dark shadows beneath his eyes have receded and there's colour in his cheeks.

His dad turns. 'Goodness me. A lie-in, Jack? Until this time? Must be the effect of the fumes.'

Jack steps to the table and peers at Hugh's hand. 'So what happened, Hugh?'

'I expect something got punched,' Hayden answers for him.

Hugh scowls at his brother. 'Your phone call didn't help.'

'What phone call?'

'Yesterday. Going on about the barn. Dad's just told me it wasn't even touched.'

Jack rakes his damp hair. 'Sorry, you're right. I didn't know it was contained to the garage then. But only because I had the sense to close the partition the last time I was in there. Hay was bloody everywhere and there's only one person in this house who goes into the barn.'

Hayden snorts. 'Very true. And Hugh's been insisting straw can just self-combust. A spontaneous pouf! Just like that. Of all the excuses—'

'It does. Mr Barnes told me. If there's too much moisture in the stacks, a chemical reaction can happen. I don't know why, but it can spark a fire.'

'Well that hardly adds up, something *wet* going up in flames—'

'Ask Mr Barnes, Dad.' His face deeply flushing, Hugh thrusts out his mobile. 'He told me about flammable gases. Go on, ask him yourself. I'm not lying!'

Jack takes the phone and puts it on the counter. 'You're right, Hugh, I'm sure, but there were no bales in the garage, just piles of loose hay, so maybe it was something combustible you'd stored in there.'

Hugh pulls a face. 'Like what?'

'I don't know, car oil, paint, varnish. Those aerosol cans you used when you repainted your bike.'

'That was years ago!'

'Well they were still there the other day. You need to stop hoarding every single item you buy, start throwing things out—'

'So, it's my fault, then?'

Jack sighs. 'No, of course not. It was just one of those things, a mystery—'

'Oh right, so that means it's Robbie.'

'No it doesn't. Look, I'm sorry, that was a stupid thing to say on the phone. Of course it wasn't Robbie. I just remember him smoking and that was years—'

Hugh stands, his chair clattering back. 'Because you're secretly like dad. You just don't like him.'

'That isn't true, Hugh. Not at all, he's your—'

'I think it was me.' Serena steps forward and clears her throat. 'I think it was me.'

The men turn and stare. Glad that Lana has already slipped from the room, she swallows.

'I'm dreadfully sorry, but I think it might have been me.' She knows she's blushing from top to toe. 'It was just now when you mentioned smoking; it made me realise that…'

Trying to steady her trembling hands, she takes a deep breath. 'I know it's silly, but I was nervous about driving Hayden's car. I had a cigarette before we set off. Well, a couple of guilty drags in the garage… I thought I'd stubbed it out. I honestly did. I'm so sorry, I'd completely forgotten until you referred to it just now. I gave up years ago but recently I… I'm so, so sorry. I can't tell you how much…'

The silence stretches out. What else can she say to make amends? She can hardly offer money when she has none. Work for no salary? Pay it back when she can? But Jack steps forward and wraps her in his arms.

'Your face,' he says, 'is a picture.' When he pulls away, he pecks her lips and grins. 'I think we can forgive you.' He turns to the others. 'No one was hurt and we can claim for the damage on the insurance. Finally fix up the barn too. It was just an unintentional mistake, and we all do that. I think we can pardon her, can't we?'

—

Serena shuffles the pack of cards before dealing. 'Ready for another drubbing?' she asks.

At her instigation she's having a 'date night' with Jack at the cottage. Before bedtime they played rummy with Lana, then once she was tucked in, they moved on to beer and knock-out Whist. Serena's currently winning five to nil.

Jack laughs. 'To be honest, I think my smarting ego needs a break.' He stands, takes her hand and leads her to the sofa. 'What should we do instead?'

Laughing, she kisses him. 'Hmm, a little scratchy, but I think I'm liking this stubble.' She strokes the hair at his temple. 'It's singed. I'm so sorry.'

He smiles. 'My first ringlet. Well, sort of. And I know you're sorry; I think you've mentioned it just once or twice.'

Her fingers explore a ridge along his hairline. 'And you have a scar. I've never noticed it before.' She plants her lips on it. 'The scarred hero! So romantic. How did you get it?'

'Not fairy tale at all, I'm afraid.'

'Oh?'

'A stupid bump in the car. Far more cautious these days.' His eyes dark and contemplative, he studies her for a few seconds. 'I've been thinking—'

Unsettled by his intensity, she makes a quip to break the tension. 'Uh oh. You know what thought did.'

'Seriously, though. I'd like you and Lana to move back into the house.'

Picturing Lana's increasing chitchat with herself, Serena looks at her hands. 'I don't want to mess Lana about. It must be confusing for her.'

'I don't want to either. Which is why I've decided. I want my home to be your home, your proper home. If that's what you want too. My room, your own, whatever works for you both.'

The anxiety overwhelming, she covers her face. 'I've been a horrible person, a dreadful mum. Happy with you one minute, shouting the next. Lana must be bewildered.'

'All the more reason to give her some stability. Show her that we love each other.' A pause and a frown. 'We do love each other, don't we?'

Tears burn Serena's eyes. This feels so good, too good to be real. For moments she forgets why she's here. Why she's hiding, why she's terrified of being found. Then it comes rushing back. Her chest might have healed, the soreness gone, but the danger hasn't.

Unable to speak, she nods and holds onto Jack tightly. When she finally pulls away, she laughs. 'I think you shocked Hayden and Hugh with that hug and kiss. Well, Hugh anyway. How lovely it was when he whooped and clapped.'

'Ah, that's Hugh for you. Do you think Dad already knew?'

Her heart races at the thought of Hayden's loaded comments. *Nurse* and *doctor*. Even his description of flipping Cinderella. Then his comment only today: 'I heard Lana humming *Peter and the Wolf* again.' Then cocking his head, 'It's Prokofiev, Serena. I believe you said you're not a fan.' She isn't a fan. But Pierre was.

She comes back to Jack. 'I don't know, but he doesn't seem to miss anything so…'

Jack nods. 'True. He was right though.'

'About what?'

He kisses her gently. 'About taking on you and Lana. A woman and a daughter. You've shaken up my life. In a good way.'

He pulls her closer and they both gaze at the window to the cottage garden. All Serena can see are their reflections in the inky glass, but she wonders what he's seeing. Perhaps a mother pushing her little girl on the swing.

She takes his hand. 'You can talk to me about them, you know. If you want to.'

'Them?' he asks, turning.

'Thea and Melanie.' He seems perplexed, so she continues. 'Well, losing them both must have been, well, more than devastating. I wanted to say something before now, but I didn't know how.'

Frowning, he falls silent. Then, 'When you were ill, did you say "sorry for your loss"?'

'Yes, but I only knew about Melanie then. Hayden let it slip. I had no idea about Thea until… well, you know about that.'

She stares at his darkened face. God, does he think that she's prying? She has no idea about the detail of what happened, but he's entitled to his privacy. 'Look, I'm sorry. I shouldn't have mentioned it. I just wanted you to know you can talk to me if you—'

'Melanie's in prison, Serena.' Like shiny beads of jet, his eyes are impenetrable. 'She committed a crime and she's serving a long sentence for it.' His face set, he stares. 'She killed Thea, Serena. That woman killed her own daughter.'

Chapter Forty-One

Jack

Lifting his face to the heavens, Jack blows out his hot breath. Even the mention of Melanie's name brings out a fury he can only just contain. Similar to Hugh. At moments like this, he understands his brother's occasional lack of control, his rage, his impulse to hit out and destroy. For Hugh it's frustration as well as anger, but for him there's futility and hopelessness too, emotions which contributed to his pathetic attempt to destroy himself a few weeks after Thea's funeral.

Feeling the usual reminder up his spine, he tries to ease the shooting sensation by loosening his jaw, his fists and his shoulders. Driving a car at high speed into a wall might have done the job for some, but he was lucky – or unlucky – depending on view point. Despite unbuckling his seat belt, the airbag saved him from death. Instead he injured his back, cracked his skull and had a bleed on the brain. He was hospitalised for a month, then miraculously 'mended'. That was the theory, anyway. Left with intermittent pain and an addiction to prescription drugs, he was hardly completely cured, but he had to recover for Hugh. However much he'd wanted the mental torture of grief and guilt to stop, he had to go on for him. Like when their mum was ill, like when she died, his younger brother had needed him.

His vision now comes back into focus. The black sky is littered with bright, sparkling stars. There's not a lot of air pollution around this part of the countryside, so perhaps it's not surprising, but he hasn't noticed them for a very long time.

Thea, his baby girl. When he came home from work, he'd bring her out here.

'*Come on, beautiful, let's count the stars before you go to sleep.*'

As though she's in his arms now, he breathes in her soapy scent. Her fine hair against his cheek, he turns and turns again to show her the wondrous world she'll grow up in.

Thea, his Thea. Oh God.

Covering his face, he sobs. He was always at work, bloody work. If he'd known their time together would be so short, he'd have come back earlier, taken more holidays and longer weekends; he'd have given her more attention – baking and painting, playing jigsaws, reading books, walking. Simply holding her hand, chatting and laughing and cuddling.

He turns to the house and closes his eyes. There she is, wearing her slippers and trotting down the steps. The sunshine is catching her skinny blonde plaits and she's holding the tartan-clad teddy he'd bought her in Edinburgh.

'Daddy! Don't go yet! You haven't given me a kiss!'

He wipes the tears from his cheeks. He gave her that kiss. Thank God, he gave her that goodbye kiss. That's the one thing he has to hold on to.

Lifting the cottage latch, he quietly steps in. Serena's still on the sofa where he left her to 'clear his head'.

'I didn't know if you'd still be up,' he whispers.

She holds out her hand and takes his. 'Ooh, it's cold out there.'

'Crisp and glassy. You can see the stars.'

She nods, but says nothing, so he sits in the armchair and clears his throat.

'Melanie was the last of a phase. Pleasant distractions when I was on the rebound from a long term relationship.' He stops and frowns. '"Pleasant distractions". Sorry, that sounds boorish, but it's the way it was and I need to be honest…'

'OK.'

'I met her in a nightclub and it turned out she was local. We went on a few enjoyable dates and the next thing I knew she was pregnant and keen to keep the baby. Against all the odds, she and Dad hit it off, so it felt right. We got married and she moved in. It worked – weirdly worked because Dad deferred to her every whim. She wanted the master bedroom, so she got it; she wanted a party, so half the house was redecorated, new tablecloths and cutlery, lamps, ornaments, and accessories were bought. She revelled in new clothes, handbags and shoes. And that was all really fine. I assumed we had the money; it made her happy and if she was content, we were too.'

Don't you already have this design in a different colour?

Oh, don't be mean, Jack. We can afford it, can't we? Besides, a girl can never have too many handbags.

Pausing, he thinks back. Though he's never analysed it before, the reason why things changed was quite simple. Thea. An astonishingly perfect and beautiful baby.

He goes back to Serena's steady gaze. 'Then Thea came along and Melanie wasn't the centre of our world anymore. Quite frankly, we were all smitten with the baby and it didn't help that Melanie wasn't particularly maternal. But perhaps that was a good thing – she'd always liked a drink, but it went from party girl cocktails to pretty much all the time, so Hugh stepped in with the day-to-day childcare.'

Rubbing his temples, he sighs. 'I know I played a part. I didn't love her; I didn't give her the time and attention she craved. Work was my priority. And when I was home in the evenings I… I colluded, I suppose, because I drank heavily too.' He wearily smiles. 'Hugh was the silver lining. He'd struggled to keep employed anywhere after two minutes, but he was brilliant with Thea. "My Hughie", she called him. An all round win-win; Hugh had a "job" and I could go to work knowing she was happy and safe.'

He stands and steps to the window. Can he leave it there for now? The reflection of Serena looks back. He loves her, he knows. He hasn't heard her full story yet, but if he isn't honest with her, how can he expect her to confide in him? Though she puts on a brave front, he still sees the fear in her eyes. He needs to help her face Pierre, his abusive behaviour, his crime. Bloody well bring him to book. God, there's a thought – find him before he finds her.

He nods inwardly. If he doesn't tell Serena today, he'll have to tell her tomorrow or the next day, or the next. He can't run away from the corrosive guilt forever.

Let go, Melanie. I need to get to work.

Work, fucking work! Well there's a new tune!

Have you been drinking?

No.

I can smell it; fresh booze. At this time, for God's sake?

Says him who fell asleep with a fucking whisky in his hand.

I need to go now…

Well, I need you to stay at home. I'm so bloody unhappy.

I can't, so that's that.

Don't you dare walk away. Come back. I haven't finished speaking!

His throat like sandpaper, he speaks to his silhouette.

'It was stupidly sunny. Hugh was preoccupied with a problem in the loft, so I asked Melanie to get up. I can't even remember why, but she was complaining about something, following me around, making demands, but I had to get to work, to a court hearing in London. That's all I could think about. Driving to the station in time for the early morning train.'

The glass clouds with condensation from his sigh. 'Not just that. I was desperate to escape her nagging and the house. So I shrugged her away and walked out to the car. Then Thea appeared, running after me in her slippers, lifting her arms for a hug and a kiss. I gave her the kiss…'

The tears are flowing, he knows. Closing his eyes, he relives it yet again.

Like a small vice, Thea wouldn't let go and he *had* to go. *You'll be late; you'll be late*, was thumping through his head like a hammer.

'Come on, sweetie. Be a good girl for Daddy. I have to catch my train,' he said. Then after a moment, 'Come on, Thea, no more crying, I'm getting really cross now.'

So he peeled her tiny fingers from his neck, carried her back to Melanie, then hurried to the car.

Oh God. Did he really tut and brush her tears from the lapel of his suit jacket?

Only as he was reversing did Melanie's slurred words come flying back.

'*If you leave, then I'm following.*'

But what did that really mean?

As he straightened the steering wheel, he glanced in the mirror. Her nightie flapping in the breeze, Thea was hurtling after his car. Though he couldn't hear the sound, the word 'Daddy!' was bursting from her mouth.

Snapping around to the rear window, he gaped. What on earth…? Then there was a squeal of tyres, immediately followed by a thud. Powerless, he stared. Slowly, too slowly, his daughter was flying like a pink kite through the air, her face freeze-framed in terror, before disappearing from view as she fell to the ground.

Even as he hurtled from the car to his baby, Melanie was still manoeuvring her four-by-four, jerking forwards and backwards, hitting flower beds and shrubs, bushes and the curb. Blithely ignorant, determined and drunk. Deaf to the howling dog; oblivious to her immobile, dying child.

He finally turns to Serena. 'I knew full well Melanie had been drinking that morning, yet I left my three-year-old child in her care. Work was more important. I started to drive away, then I saw Thea was running after me. The next thing I knew, she'd been hit. Melanie had climbed in her car to follow me and she'd reversed into her, throwing her into the air.'

He sighs. No point trying to shake the image away; it will and it *should* stay with him forever: his little girl's arms raised like she'd taken a bullet in the back. Only seconds, but still vividly there in slow motion. And her tiny pale face and her terror; her accusing blue eyes pinned to his. *Why have you hurt me Daddy; why?*

'By the time the ambulance arrived, Thea had left us.'

He looks at his hands. At some point he'd found them around Melanie's throat. He'd only released them when his father's shaken voice had filtered through. Yet even then he had known it was ultimately his fault.

He glances at Serena. 'I shouldn't have left Thea with a woman who couldn't even look after herself.'

'You couldn't have known Melanie would—'

'But I did. She said something about following me. I should have listened. If only—'

She places a gentle hand against his mouth. 'Stop. Looking backwards is soul-destroying and pointless. You have to put it behind you and move forwards.'

'I know; I know you're right. But I doubt I ever will. Besides…' He pulls out his mobile and sighs. 'Besides, Melanie has been in touch; she wants to see me.'

'Really? From prison? Is that allowed?'

'Unfortunately, yes.'

'Will you go?'

'No. I don't know. I haven't even replied yet. But she says she's seen the psychologist and she has something very important to say.'

Chapter Forty-Two

Hugh

Listening and looking out for a fox or a hare, or even a badger if he's lucky, Hugh walks along the dark country lane to his home. It's still pretty cold, but he can't feel it yet. The double whisky night cap has done a grand job of warming his face but numbing his wrist. *Win-win* as his old man would say.

He's been to The Crown for his beer tonight. When he first walked into the village, he considered The Bull, but his annoyance with Robbie flew back. Not good enough to sit with him and his mates, eh? Well, he was a Ramsay and therefore a champion. His dad might be critical, but he taught him that.

Headlights flash by and Hugh ambles on. He's drunk, but only semi. And it isn't even that late. He doesn't know why, but when he stood up for a piss in the pub, he decided to call it a day. He sniffs. Loneliness, maybe. He was used to it until flaming Robbie Barnes came back.

Cheering himself at the thought of a tasty snack, he increases his speed. God, he loves his bedroom and his bed, his clean clothes, the warm towels and a hot bloody shower. There's no way he wants to return to that dank rusty camper. If he just keeps a low profile, he can come back every night.

He stops outside the barrier and feels in his pockets. 'Shit.' No keys, no gate fob and no mobile. Did he even bring them out? He pictures the hall table. 'Shit.'

Bloody hell, how to get in? Scramble or somehow vault it? Nah, he might damage the wood and be in bother with his dad. Even more trouble than if he rings the intercom and knocks up the household. Then there's his wrist, which has started to throb.

He crosses his arms. One thing's for sure, he's not walking back to the camper. He retraces his steps to the uneven bricks where the wall was rebuilt. Yup, he can manage that; worth a try anyway.

Though his fingers pulsate, he scales the elevation and teeters at the top. Heck, nothing but a moving black mass down below. Still, he has to get back without his dad discovering he's been 'bloody forgetful' again, so he counts to three and jumps.

Worrying more about his scuffed shoes than his newly grazed knees, he strides along the driveway. So far so good, but how to get into the house? Serena? Nope, the cottage is in darkness. But Jack'll be around at this time. He might get lucky; he might be in the snug.

Crossing fingers and toes, he takes a deep breath and raps lightly with the knocker. Nothing happens for a minute, so he tries again. No reply. With a resigned sigh, he presses the doorbell. Oh hell, he'd never realised it had such a loud chime.

The door eventually swings open and Lexie runs out. Oh God, it's his dad, he recognises the slippers. Not ready to face the music, he fusses the dog before finally straightening up.

Resting on a crutch, his father's still there.

'You look as though you've been through a bush. Lost your keys?' he says amiably.

Bloody hell, no bollocking. 'Well…'

His dad pats his shoulder. 'Nice to see you, son. Perfect timing too. I'm just about to open a bottle. Japanese whisky, of all things. Come on down and let me know what you think. I actually wanted to have a chat.'

–

Hugh sips his drink and watches the flames dip and dive. His dad has been chatting for a while. Not just talking about himself but friendly and interested, enquiring about Mr Barnes and how he's fared since his wife passed away, then nicely asking what Hugh's been doing at the farm, saying how he must be an enormous help, and though he doesn't always show it, how proud he is of him.

He feels a warm glow as his eyelids droop. See? His dad can be nice – in fact, very nice.

A noisy snap from the fire brings him back with a jolt. God, that was too much like a firework. Trying to hide his alarm, he glances at his dad, but he's still talking about Serena.

Hugh frowns as a memory hurtles back. *You disappoint me; you're a coward, Hugh. There's no other word for it.*

Coward. His dad definitely said that, but when? Was it on bonfire night?

He secretly sighs. Last bloody November. He pictures the three of them in this very room:

'*For God's sake, stop covering your ears, Hugh. It's only a bang and nowhere near here.*'

'*Come on, Dad, give him a break. Hugh's never liked fireworks.*'

'*He's thirty-six; he needs to grow up. Just like he needs to stop lazing around the house doing nothing all day. He needs to get a job and for once, hold it down.*'

'*Rich coming from you, Dad. You don't have one. You've never had a job. Selling another old book or ornament or table stashed in the cellar isn't work.*'

'*What I do with my possessions is my business, Hugh. Now, if you're going to behave like a child every time you hear a fizzle or a pop, go into another room.*'

'*We all have our phobias, Dad. Leave him be.*'

'*Phobia? Oh, is that the word?*' A snort of contempt. '*What did Shakespeare say? A coward dies a thousand times…*'

He lurched at his dad. That's all he could remember before Jack's panicked shouting had filtered through his blind anger. Then he'd looked at his hands. They were around his dad's throat and he was squeezing so hard, his knuckles were popping.

God, no wonder the old man threw him out.

'Hugh? So what do you make of her?'

The sound of his dad's voice brings him back.

'Sorry?'

Hugh steels himself for a tut for not listening, but his dad leans forward, his tone conspiratorial.

'Serena. I do like her very much, but what do we know about her? Where she came from, her background, her previous? Then she's in the house one minute, the cottage the next. Not to mention her starting the damned fire. What's your view? I value your opinion.'

Hugh thinks. He's fond of Serena and the kid; he even clapped when Jack kissed her, but later he felt really let down. Why hadn't Jack told him? And his dad is right, not knowing what's going on is unsettling. But his dad is still speaking.

'Because Jack's welfare is paramount. If she wasn't good for him – or, indeed, was a danger to his wellbeing – we'd have to do the honourable thing…' His dad spreads his arms. 'I'm not entirely sure what that would be but…'

Hugh drifts. '*Honourable thing*.' He's heard that before. And '*brave boy*' and '*special help*'. Encouraging, praising words. Weren't they?

He thinks of asking his dad when he said them, but he's already on his feet. 'I'm off to bed, son. Can you douse the fire?'

'Sure.' He stands too. 'Do you need help up the stairs or anything?'

'You're a good boy, do you know that? I can always rely on you.' He pulls Hugh's head towards him and kisses his hair. 'Thank you for offering, but Nurse Serena says I have to do them myself.' He wafts an arm as he leaves. 'Don't go worrying about Jack. I'm sure my concerns are unfounded and that Serena's just as lovely as she seems.'

–

Hugh stares into the night. He's unsettled and can't sleep despite the best part of a flagon of whisky. If he could just talk things through with Jack… Not that he knows what he wants to say. He rocks his head to his mobile. Scooping it up, he quickly types a text.

> Are you awake?

> I am now. Shall I call you?

Sure.

Robbie's twang is on the line moments later. 'I am honoured.'

'Why?'

'You didn't answer my messages.'

'Expect you were in The Bull with your mates.'

'I sent you a text. Hoped you'd turn up there tonight.'

'I didn't read it. Just deleted it.'

'Yeah, sort of got that. Kept me hanging and pining, worried you'd never forgive me.'

'Did you find out more about that money stuff? You know, the new tractor and all that?'

'Nope.'

'Why not? You were going to ask your dad about the snow and the cow shed.'

'I'm stopping all that. It upsets you. Hayden's your dad and you love him.'

There's the anxiety again, like a fizz in his chest. 'Yeah, but what did you mean about me being blind?'

'Nothing. Nothing at all. I don't want you to be unhappy. I bloody love you, mate.'

Hugh feels a swell of something nice in his belly. But those words fly in again: *You disappoint me, you're a coward, Hugh. There's no other word for it.*

'I'm not a coward, Robbie.'

'I know that, Hugh. Believe me, I know that more than anyone.'

288

Chapter Forty-Three

Serena

Bolting upright in the bed, Serena stills in the dark.

'Did you hear that?'

'Hear what?' Jack replies, his voice muffled by bedding.

Certain it wasn't a dream, she strains to listen again. Was it just the usual night clunks and groans? No, it was a voice. 'I'm not sure. It sounded like your dad calling out. I'd better go and check he's OK.'

Jack sits up. 'It's fine, I'll do it.' He shakes his head. 'Sorry, I was completely out for the count.'

He grabs his dressing gown and he leaves the room, but after a few seconds she follows, widely yawning as she pads down the landing. Leaning forward to listen, Jack reaches Hayden's room, but he abruptly jerks back and thumps open the door.

'What the hell? Hugh, get off him!' she hears as she runs. A scuffle and a bang, then, 'For God's sake, Hugh, wake up!'

She skids to the bedroom and peers in. It takes a moment for her eyes to adjust to the dark. Looking aghast, Hugh is pressed against the far wall. He's holding a pillow and staring at the bed. Crouched on the floor, Jack's at his father's side.

'Dad?' he's saying to the immobile figure. Then, his voice tremulous, 'Dad?' He looks up at her. 'Fuck! I don't think he's breathing.'

What the hell? A coronary? The old adrenaline immediately kicking in, she guides Jack to one side, pulls down the crumpled bedding and listens to Hayden's chest. Nothing there but the clatter of her own heart. Calming herself with a big breath, she interlocks her fingers and prepares to compresses down, but as though he'd been playing dead, Hayden suddenly gasps and his eyes snap open.

She rolls him onto his side. 'Don't worry, Hayden, we're here and you're fine,' she says reassuringly.

Remembering his hip, she carefully manoeuvres his legs into the recovery position.

'Can you bend this knee for me? That's right.' His shin, she notices, is still discoloured, swollen and hot to the touch. 'Well done. Now inhale deeply and out again slowly, then again… and again. Very good. Concentrate on your respiration and take it easy for a few minutes.'

Listening to Hayden's rasps, she turns to the boys at the end of the bed. His face white with shock, Jack clutches the back of his head as he stares. Hugh's still gripping the cushion. As though suddenly aware it's piping hot, he drops it and looks at his brother.

'I don't know what happened, Jack.' Then louder, with a sob, 'I don't know what just happened! I honestly don't. I was asleep. Then next thing I knew, you were yelling at me.' His whole countenance pleading, he reaches out a trembling, bandaged hand to his brother. 'You do believe me, don't you?'

Looking to the ceiling, Jack takes a deep breath. 'Yes, Hugh, I—'

But a hoarse voice interrupts. 'Come here, son. We all believe you. Everything's fine.'

They all turn to Hayden, hitching himself up in the bed. His bloodshot eyes contradict his benign expression.

Smiling, he pats the mattress next to him. 'It's all right, Hugh. Really. Come and give your old man a hug.'

Like a giant child, Hugh climbs next to his father and curls into the proffered arm.

Hayden briefly strokes his hair. 'A bit of a rude awakening, but you don't get rid of me that easily.' After a minute, he gently pushes him away. 'Bedtime now, everybody. We don't want to wake Lana.'

Her chest still fluttering with astonishment and fright, Serena turns to leave, but not before she catches Hayden's meaningful nod towards his eldest son.

—

Taking her quietly by the hand, Jack leads Serena back to the bedroom. They both take their positions from ten minutes earlier, but neither of them talk. After a few moments, Jack pulls her to his shoulder. Her mind in overdrive, she listens to the whipping rhythm of his heart.

What the hell just happened? She initially assumed that Hayden had suffered a stroke, a seizure or a coronary and that Hugh had arrived first. But the charged atmosphere in the room and Hayden's eerie eyes told her otherwise. The pillow, Hugh's face, his obvious fear. My God; did he really just try to suffocate his father?

For some time she doesn't speak, but eventually the need to crack Jack's strained silence becomes too much. Too shocked to fully take it in, a light-hearted tone emerges.

'That was pretty fraught. I was a second away from performing mouth-to-mouth. Kissing your dad; that would have been embarrassing.'

Black humour, like in the old days on the wards. When Jack doesn't respond, she considers apologising for her inappropriate quip, but he rests his lips on her forehead.

'Save all your kisses for me. Night, night,' he says, moving onto his side.

She stares at the back of his head. '*Wasn't that a Eurovision Song Contest winner?*' she wants to ask. And, '*Speak to me Jack! What the hell was that about? Was Hugh sleepwalking?*' And more to the point: '*Was he trying to smother your dad? What if we hadn't decided to sleep here tonight? Has this occurred before? Why the heck have you just turned away? Why are you acting as though this hugely strange event hasn't happened?*'

Inhaling an inescapable whiff of smoke, she stares into space. Thank God Lana didn't wake; she would have been terrified… Lana; God Lana! Her mind suddenly in spasm, she pictures the lingering glance between Hayden and Jack. Oh God, the most imperative question. It bursts from her mouth: 'Jack? Is Hugh dangerous?' She flicks on the lamp. 'Is Lana in danger, Jack? Is that why Hayden mentioned her? Has this happened before?'

More worries tumble in. Why was Hugh banned from the house before she arrived? What happened to his wrist? He once tried to burn down the barn, for God's sake! Oh God, Lana.

Jack's sitting up and rubbing his face. She stares. 'Lana, Jack. She isn't safe, is she?'

Her thoughts a jumbled mess, she tries to ignore the metallic tang of panic in her mouth. *Escape, you need to escape*, thumps in her head. Out of the frying pan and into the fire…

With a huge effort, she calms herself. *Focus, Serena, focus.* She has no car. And anyway, where would she go? The cottage will do for now. It doesn't have a key but they can bolt the door and block it with furniture.

'We'll go to the cottage. Yes, back to the cottage again tonight. I'll wake her and take her right now.'

She makes to climb out, but Jack holds her back. 'Wait. Sorry. Just a minute. I'm as shocked as you are. Let me think…'

He rubs his forehead. 'No, I don't believe Hugh is dangerous; he wouldn't hurt Lana. If I had ever for a moment thought so, I wouldn't have left Thea in his care. But I can see why you're worried; I'd be the same.'

He gestures to the sofa and smiles faintly. 'It's a bed settee, so it folds out. I've had plenty of nights there one way or another.' Taking her hand, he squeezes. 'I know you've had a fright and you're worried about Lana, but let's stay together tonight until we work it all out. You two have the bed.'

Her palpitations easing, Serena nods. 'OK. That's sensible. Thank you.' She stops at the door and looks back at the couch. 'Did Thea sleep there?'

'Sometimes. When she was upset or scared.' He smiles sadly. 'Or just being cheeky.'

'Then Lana should have it. If you're OK about letting her—?'

'She'd have loved sharing it with a friend.'

A picture of Lana swinging her legs and chattering to no one flashes in. She shakes it away. 'Make it up while I'm gone? I'll just be a few minutes. Plenty of blankets, please, she likes to be cosy.'

Chapter Forty-Four

Jack

Jack wakes with the dawn, surprised he slept at all. Serena is lightly breathing by his side. He has to tell her; he *has* to tell her everything, but where should he start? How will he explain the inexplicable? Can he really dig up and spit out a secret that has been so deeply hidden and for so long? One he's never told anyone. And how will she react? She could walk straight out of here and into the first police station she finds. Or call one, of course. She's a doctor. Like him, she has ethical, professional and legal obligations, not only to be honest, but to act with the highest integrity. That includes reporting a crime; not just a crime but a murder.

Turning to the sofa, he gazes at the small outline beneath the duvet. His beautiful, beautiful Thea. The weight of guilt will never go away, but it has lifted a touch since confessing to Serena. And instead of weeping for her loss, he wants to smile. He has been gifted an opportunity to use all the love and affection he stuffed away in a mental box, scoop it out like those cushion beans and scatter them over this woman and child.

He swallows. If Serena understands; *if* she doesn't freak out and leave him forever.

His head as tense as an over inflated balloon, Jack waits until six thirty to wake Serena.

He proffers a mug of strong tea.

'Sorry,' he says in a low voice. 'But I thought we should talk before Lana stirs.'

'OK.' Bleary-eyed, she sits up. 'So…'

Though he's rehearsed in his mind for the past hour, he has no idea where to begin. But there's no point procrastinating. He's already decided it's boom or bust.

'Last night you asked if Hugh had ever sleepwalked before?'

She nods.

Should he soften it or elaborate or give it his usual legal spin? Nope. 'Only once, to my knowledge – when he was eight and I was ten. He went into our mother's bedroom and suffocated her with a pillow.'

Serena doesn't reply. Instead, she gazes for a long, long time. Thinking she hasn't comprehended, he inhales to repeat it, but she finally speaks.

'Children don't just do that out of nowhere. What had happened in the build up?'

He puffs out his trapped breath. It's surreal, so surreal to talk about this. He hasn't uttered a word about it for nearly thirty years. Not to his father, not to Hugh.

'Well, our mum had been ill for a long time. Seriously bed-ridden ill. I've always assumed it was cancer; nobody said otherwise. It was hard for us all. Mum – Lucinda – would get up from time to time, but it was a huge effort. Hugh was six or seven when it began and he needed his mummy, but you know what he's like, even now. He didn't understand how fragile she was; he was clumsy and demanding, so sometimes she pushed him away.'

He knows his words are muddled and toppling, but now he's started, he has to get them out.

'Then from nowhere Hugh became obsessed with mercy killings. I have no idea where he'd even heard about such things – I'm not sure that I had – but he wanted to talk about them all the time. What they meant and who did it and whether it was "really" a kindness, or whether people just "said" it. But that was simply Hugh, getting stuck in one of his grooves before moving on to the next one.'

Trying to ease his walloping heartbeat, he pauses to assess what Serena's thinking, but her expression is inscrutable, intense, professional.

The image of his mum hovers. Not the very last time he saw her, but shortly before that. The skinny-animal version, her teeth rotten, her face imploring and wet.

He sharply inhales. 'I don't know. Maybe it wasn't so surprising. Sometimes she'd beg Dad for…'

'For what?'

'Medicine, a cure, pain relief. Something to end the suffering, I suppose. It was horrible to hear; we had our hands over our ears when she was like that, but we heard every terrifying plea, each querulous word.'

Serena nods but says nothing.

'Then the fifth of November arrived…' He shakes his head. 'The most seminal night of my childhood, but it's hard to remember.'

Mentally, he walks through it. 'Yes, so… It wasn't just bonfire night; it was also a party, so I was excited even though it was for the grown-ups. The Foglemans and a few of Dad's other friends came. Dad and I had spent the preceding days building up a huge bonfire in the back meadow and I'd made a Guy from some of the clothes Hugh had grown out of.'

He laughs softly at the memory. 'Even then, he wasn't best pleased I'd used his instead of mine. But – yes – he'd been moody and unsettled for days. He didn't want to help collect firewood, choose his box of fireworks or make toffee apples. My excitement didn't rub off on him as usual…

'Sorry, I'm digressing. So, that night…' Almost smelling the thrilling mix of sausages and dynamite, he comes back to Serena. 'The bonfire was lit, we watched the Guy burn, ate hot dogs from the barbecue and gaped at our rockets, fountains and the like. Then it was time for bed, so Dad sent us boys to our rooms. The next thing I remember was Hugh shaking me awake. I pulled back the covers to let him in as usual, but he dragged me off the mattress and took me into Mum's bedroom.' He glances around. 'This room.'

Aware of his voice breaking, he stops and collects himself. This part is so fresh; the dreams keep it vivid. Or should he say nightmares?

'My mother was in bed as usual. Still not knowing why I was there, I stepped closer. She was still and perfect, her hair spread out on the cushion like a princess. She looked more peaceful than I'd seen her for months. "I mercy-killed her with a pillow", Hugh said from behind me. Then he left, went back to his bedroom and slept until morning. To this day he's never mentioned it again. He has a phobia about fireworks, but other than that, he just wiped that evening and her existence from his memory.'

Lana twitches and Serena watches for a while. 'What happened then?' she eventually asks. 'I mean, what happened that night?'

Jack spreads his arms. 'I don't honestly know,' he says quietly. 'I think I might have stayed with Mum for a while. Then I went to find Dad. No idea after that. He and Fogie sorted it out somehow—'

'Fogie the policeman?'

'Yes, that's right.' He meets Serena's frown. 'I know it was wrong, illegal, unethical and a whole host of other things. But no one blinked. I don't suppose her death was a shock to her long-lost friends, what remained of her distant family or the villagers – everyone knew she was gravely ill.'

Her jaw visibly tightens. 'And Hayden swore you to secrecy?'

'It was best for Hugh, Serena. Even at ten I understood what would happen to him if the truth got out. The system would chew him up and spit him out. Besides...'

'Besides what?'

'When Dad asked me... well, not to tell anyone, how could I say no? I'd lost a mother, but he'd lost a wife who was his whole life. It's hard to explain, but she was like his special dolly or his pet; he carried her everywhere, dressed her, fed her, nursed her. His son had snuffed out the love of his life, but Dad forgave him. Or at least he tried to. I know he's struggled with Hugh at times, but...' He thinks of his own feelings for his father. 'I've always understood there's a fine line between love and hate, so...'

An inordinate weariness hitting, he closes his eyes and waits for Serena to respond. He used to wonder if this day would ever come. He imagined lightness and relief, but he simply feels flat. Boom or bust. Does either really matter?

He feels her move from the bed and speak to Lana in a low voice. She returns and kisses his forehead.

'Hugh was just a child, but so were you. It seems to me you've spent your whole life protecting Hugh and pleasing your dad and I love you for that. But there's one thing you haven't answered. After a gap of twenty-eight years or so, why would Hugh act it out again now?'

Chapter Forty-Five

Hugh

His wrist and his temples seeming to throb in tune, Hugh shoulders the kitchen door. The smell of pastry breezes back, but that doesn't cheer him today. He's in trouble, deep shit. He knows he sleepwalked into his dad's bedroom because he was there when Jack woke him. He understands he must have tried to do something bad with a pillow because he was holding the damned thing. And it couldn't have even been a lark or a joke because his dad was unconscious, even dead. Then he burst awake with those vampire-like eyes.

Bloody hell, bloody hell; *he* did that, *he* fucking caused it!

Everyone stares, even little Lana. Then Serena puts a plate in his place.

'Croissants and brioche,' she says. 'They're still warm. I'll top up the pot.'

She walks to the sink and Jack pats his back. 'Morning,' he says. 'Are you OK?'

'Got a bad head. And I woke up on my hand, so...'

Serena turns. 'I'll get you some pain killers,' she says, but she doesn't quite meet his eyes as she leaves the room.

'From the pub?' Jack asks. 'Your hangover?'

'Not really. Japanese whisky with Dad when I got—' He scrapes back the chair. Oh God. Where is he now? Is he still OK?

Jack stands too. 'He's fine, Hugh. I looked in on him on the way down. Bit grumpy from lack of sleep, but when is he not in a morning? He wants his breakfast in bed later.' He rubs Hugh's arm. 'No mention of anything except leg cramps. Come on, grab a pastry.' He smiles at Lana. 'Because if you don't, I know someone who will.'

Hugh blows out a long puff of air. His dad is OK and there's been no demand via Jack to leave the house. Perhaps everything will be all right.

He sits down and joins in the fun. 'Who's that *someone* then?'

'A little person who's already eaten two mini crois-sants…' Jack says.

Covering her mouth with her hand, Lana giggles. 'Three, I've eaten three!'

'Uh oh!' Hugh replies, patting his stomach. 'If you're not very careful your tummy will grow as big as mine.'

'Your tummy isn't fat.' She leans forward conspiratori-ally. 'Rhona's tummy was fat.'

'Who's Rhona?' he whispers back.

'Mummy's friend.'

He stands, lifts his T-shirt and pushes out his belly. 'As chubby as this?'

Lana's peel of laughter is interrupted by Serena's voice behind him. 'Here are some paracetamol, Hugh.' He turns and she's looking at Jack with a purposeful frown.

His brother clears his throat. 'I'm popping out to the shops in a bit. Want to come with me, Hugh?'

'Oh right. Well…'

'It's a two man job.'

'Yeah, sure. What are we buying?'

Jack smooths Lana's hair. 'I couldn't possibly say. It's a big surprise.'

—

They chat intermittently about football in their dad's Range Rover. Jack mentions a client who's offered spare tickets for a City match in a couple of weeks.

'The seats are in a box and you'll get more than just a prawn sandwich to eat, Hugh,' he's saying. 'We can go together, if you like. Or if you'd prefer to take Robbie, that's fine too.'

Hugh stares blankly through the windscreen as they head towards Northwich. He'd usually jump at the chance of footie and a freebie, but his stomach is churning. He knows Jack wants to say something. Or rather Serena wants him to say something. And it's bad. Jack's being nice. Of course he's kind most of the time, but there's a catch in his voice he hasn't heard before. At least not for a long, long time.

Trying to do that mindfulness thing, he closes his eyes, but instead of emptiness, the old voice filters in, eloquent but weepy and thin:

Sorry darling, I can't take you today.

Mummy's not very well.

I know I'm a bad mummy right now, but I'm poorly, darling boy.

I'm so, so sorry, I just need to lie down.

Mummy's so tired and you should be asleep in your own bed.

Sorry my darling, you know I don't mean it. Come on Hughie, don't cry.

He knows the next voice is coming, so he covers his ears.

I'm so, so unhappy Hayden. You have no idea. Please give me something to make it stop.

A hand on his shoulder brings him back. The engine's off and Jack's peering at him. 'Are you OK?' he asks. He gestures to the chock-a-block carpark. 'Well, we're in the right place, there's Argos,' he says. But he doesn't climb out. Instead, he turns. 'Thing is…' he starts. His face is tight, almost teary. 'Last night—'

'I didn't know what was happening! I didn't do anything deliberately. One minute I was asleep, then… You said you believed me.'

'I know and I do, absolutely, but—'

'You made rice pudding. The other day, you made it for Sunday lunch. Why?'

Surprised, Jack stares. 'Because it used to be your favourite.'

'Did Mum make it for me?'

'Yes. It always brought a huge smile.' A worried frown. 'She loved you very much, Hugh.'

Get out! Just get out!

Trying to shrug the echo away, Hugh nods to the retail park. 'Shall we go?'

'Yeah. In a minute.' Jack sighs. 'Here's the thing, Hugh. There's a child in the house. Little Lana. After last night we need to think of everyone's safety, so it's probably best if—'

'The kid?' He gapes. 'You really believe I'd hurt her? How can you say that?' He finds himself yelling. 'How can you say that, Jack?'

Anger bubbles. Being thrown out is one thing, but to suggest he'd do anything to harm the kid…

He reaches for the handle, but Jack grabs his jacket.

'Hugh, just listen. I trusted you with Thea, the most precious thing in my life, and you were bloody brilliant. I know you'd never deliberately hurt anyone, let alone a child, but...' He clears his throat. 'But. Apart from whatever happened last night, there was November too. Sure, Dad was goading you, but you completely lost control. If I hadn't been there, God only knows what the outcome might have been. And you weren't sleepwalking that evening. Then, only weeks ago, you trashed the games room.'

He drops his head. 'It was a safe place, like you always said.'

'I know, and that was a good move. But what about your wrist? How did that happen?'

'I was upset and angry about something Robbie said, so I punched a gate. Well, a door really.'

Tears pricking, he gazes at his brother. He so doesn't want to move out again. *Please don't make him move back to the shit-hole caravan.*

What can he say to make it better? 'I wanted to punch him, but I didn't, Jack.' He lifts his hand. 'I only hurt myself.'

'That's not good either, though, is it, Hugh?' Jack sits back. 'Look, it won't be for long. We'll organise some more sessions with Amara and get you back on track. Then you can come home.'

The tears fall. 'So, I'm banned again? All the time?'

'Of course not.' Jack's eyes flicker. 'Just night times like before. And maybe when I'm not there. So weekends and most evenings will be—'

Slamming the door, Hugh doesn't hear the rest. Roughly wiping his face, he stalks away. Rage pumps through his body. No one cares, not even Jack. Come rain or shine, his brother has always been there for him, calming, understanding, reassuring. Not today, though. And what's different from all the other times he's needed his support? Yup: Serena. The kid still likes and trusts him – he made her laugh only this morning. Not so Serena; it was there in her shady eyes. Perhaps his dad was right. What do the Ramsays really know about her?

He pictures her face, but it blurs with another.

Get out! Just get out!

He pinches his nose. Yes, Jack. Even Jack has rejected him now.

Chapter Forty-Six

Serena

Serena stands at the front door and watches Jack climb from the car. There's no sign of Hugh, so they must have had the 'conversation' she insisted on. Oh God. On the one hand she feels bad about poor Hugh, but on the other… He's clearly unstable, unpredictable, and yes, dangerous; he tried to suffocate his father, for God's sake! She sighs. Bloody hell, out of the frying pan and into the fire indeed. Has this 'escape' been worth it? Coming here and hiding in this beautiful but dysfunctional household?

Hopping from foot to foot, Lana has been waiting for Jack's return. She's now shyly shuffling towards him. Spotting her, his tense expression turns into a warm smile. He scoops her up and holds her close for a while. Then he puts her down and says something. She darts back with huge, excited eyes.

'I have to stay inside until the surprise is ready,' she says breathlessly. 'And I'm not to peep through the kitchen window.'

'How thrilling. I've the polishing to finish, but you'd better take off that thick jacket and hide in the snug until you're called.'

'OK.' Giddy, Lana claps her hands. 'Come on, Lexie. This way.'

Feeling a warm spread of emotion, Serena nods inwardly. Yes, it has been worth it. Lana, her happiness. She stills in thought. And what about meeting Jack Ramsay?

She automatically touches her still-tender chest. Her judgment has been so poor in the past, can she really trust him? She found herself saying that she loved him on Friday. Is that what this… this contentment is? But she mustn't get complacent; the danger's still out there.

She returns to the kitchen and absently continues her chore. Cleaning silver. Who would have thought it would tarnish so quickly. Rust, oxidise, deteriorate, decompose… Anticipating the inevitable stomach clench, she glances at the burned-out building through the window. Nothing has been organised about the repairs yet, no clear out, no claim, nor inspection of the damage and the car, or whatever the insurers will require. For now it remains a murky, dark husk.

Almost making her jump, Jack emerges from the side of the garage, carrying a soot-covered metal box. Though she's used to the acrid stench of smoke, a waft comes again. She almost laughs. Like the coffee she can no longer smell, one anxiety-inducing aroma has been replaced with another. Feeling a little naughty for 'peeping', she observes for a moment longer as Jack disappears down the cottage path.

–

Ready to incur Hayden's wrath again, Serena looks at her watch. She tried him at ten, then again at eleven and twelve. Did Sir want any breakfast? Of course she didn't quite put it like that, but perhaps her voice betrayed her exasperation by the third visit.

'I'm not hungry and I don't feel well, Serena. I had a rather bad night,' he replied tersely. 'Perhaps you noticed?'

Once she came back down, she focused on the astonishing events of last night and felt guilty about her lack of patience. The revelations of this morning too. The poor man might have died at the hands of his child, a son who had not only killed his mother, but Hayden's beloved wife. It couldn't get any worse than that. And it did explain his strained relationship with Hugh. Hugh, whom she'd thought a gentle giant. A man she'd still liked at breakfast, one who clearly needed love and help, yet a person she wanted gone from the house.

Now taking a deep breath, she knocks at the door and walks in. Clearly busy with his laptop, Hayden is sitting up, so that's something.

'It's lunch time, so I've brought you a glass of fruit juice and a ham sandwich. Pickle and no butter, just as you like it,' she says, putting down the tray on his side table.

She waits for a moment and when he doesn't reply, 'Well, ring your little bell if you want anything else.'

'Sorry,' he says, turning. He peers, his eyes huge and raw behind his reading glasses. 'I was miles away with Mr Google and others. Doing a little in-depth research, you might say. Oh, lunch, thank you. Thought my stomach was complaining.'

He goes back to his task, typing for a moment. 'Tell Jack I want a word.'

'Will do,' she replies. 'He's busy with something right now, so—'

'No hurry,' he says, closing his laptop lid. His lips slide into a smile. 'You've brought me a delicious-looking butty. I'm sure it can wait.'

Wondering about Hayden's peculiar – almost excited – manner, Serena ambles down the stairs. Lana is waiting at the bottom, dressed in her coat.

'Jack came to find me. He says he's ready. We're to come to the cottage.'

'Wonderful. Are you all set?'

'Yes!'

Lana's cheeks are pink; her whole bearing is a picture. Four years of age and never so happy. Not even on birthdays or Christmas. Especially last Christmas.

Serena breathes through the urge to cry. Whatever the future holds, she must cling on to this moment. She smiles. 'Let's go, then. You lead the way. Lexie and I will follow.'

Unable to contain her excitement, Lana skips ahead, then belts down the side path. She abruptly stops where the grass begins. Her eyes glowing, she turns as Serena approaches.

'Mummy, look! And it's red. Red's my favourite!'

Emotion burning her nose, Serena studies Lana's secret surprise. She's never had a garden before, let alone her own swing. She'd longed to test the rusty one in Rhona's back yard, but surrounded by a huge assortment of corroded clutter, it was too dangerous to even try.

'Go on, then,' she says, swallowing. 'Jump on, love.'

She steps to Jack. 'Thank you,' she whispers. 'It's perfect.'

She slips her arm into his and they watch Lana sit tentatively on the seat. After a while, she pushes off from the ground and lifts her legs. Moments later she's swinging high.

'That's what parents should really do, isn't it?' Jack says eventually. Tears in his eyes, he looks up to the sky. 'They should let go of their kids and let them fly.'

Chapter Forty-Seven

Jack

Lost in thought, Jack returns to the house and climbs the stairs. Despite the worry about Hugh, the pleasure on Lana's face was glorious, heartwarming, uplifting. Poignant too, but he'd prepared himself for that as he put the apparatus together. When he last stood in that patch of garden, he'd been taking the old one apart, fumbling with spanners, keys and a wrench, finally hacking at bolts that had stuck fast. Everything else had already been disposed of; only the swing had remained. He couldn't wait to get rid of the damned thing. And yet when he'd dismantled the final piece, he'd felt bereft, wishing he had left just one reminder.

He kept the items Thea had died in, of course, but that was self-flagellation. Then he started on the sleeping pills and she appeared in person, so he stuffed the clothes in his chest of drawers, fearful she'd see the blood and be frightened. Crazy hallucinations? The deepest grief? Or just symbolic? But she had felt so very real and despite the dreadful guilt, he was glad she was there. Her soft breathing, her soapy smell.

His beautiful little girl hadn't left him quite yet.

Serena's arm tightly slotted into his, they watched Lana climb higher and laugh with sheer pleasure.

'Touch the clouds, Lana,' Serena called. Then she said, 'By the way, your dad wants a word.'

He wasn't surprised; he'd been waiting for the summons all morning.

—

'Ah, Jack.' His father closes his laptop lid. 'Have a seat, son.'

Jack picks up the Paisley dressing gown and holds it out. 'Come on, it's three o'clock. You shouldn't be in bed all day. Let's go downstairs; Serena has laid the fire.'

'Perhaps in a few minutes. Close the door, would you?'

Accepting the inevitable, Jack sits down. His father is stroking his soft stubble and gazing intently. He usually launches in immediately – about sport or the stock market, a funny story from the golf club or a newspaper article that's got on his pip – but not today. No, not on this inauspicious day.

The prickling anxiety creeps up Jack's spine. His father gave him this same unnerving stare after the car 'accident'. Though he'd been discharged from the hospital and had returned to work, he couldn't sleep.

'*You're not coping, Jack. You've had time away from chambers and everyone has been nice but sympathy grows thin very quickly. You need to sort yourself out.*' His dad had peered keenly. '*You look dreadful. People will notice. If it appears as though you have no self-belief, who'll have confidence in you? I'm saying this out of love, Jack.*'

Jack had wanted to cry, not only at the mention of love, but because his dad was right. But what could he do? He had chronic insomnia. The doctors said it was a side effect of the brain injury he'd sustained in the crash and would improve in time, so they were loath to prescribe sleeping pills indefinitely.

Both despondent and exhausted, he'd frowned at his dad. '*You're right, but I can't simply magic a cure out of nowhere, Dad. Just one night of sleep would help, though. Not even a night, anything more than a two hour stretch.*'

'*I know someone who has access to… medicines. He'll sort out something to help with that,*' his father had replied. '*But you need to pull yourself together too. A haircut and a shave would be a start.*'

Jack observes his dad now. At this moment, he's the one whose appearance is *dreadful*. With his pale skin and red sclera, he resembles an albino. He looks old and weary too. When did his ginger stubble turn grey? Perhaps overnight. He once heard shock could do that. Though yesterday wasn't the first attack by his youngest. Bonfire night was; the first time he'd seen real fear in his eyes.

He readies himself. Hugh, Hugh Ramsay; that's why he's been sent for. Not to discuss what Hugh did when he was eight, or even last night – they'll brush over that – but how to handle him going forwards.

He preempts his father's question. 'I spoke to Hugh this morning and told him that it's best he stays at the farm again for the foreseeable future. Just at night and if I'm not around…'

His dad nods, but the disconcerting look's still there, and the tingling sensation increases. What's he going to say? Something unpalatable, for sure.

'About Serena,' he starts eventually.

Almost laughing at his body's ability to read his father, Jack folds his arms. 'What about her?'

His dad rubs his chin. 'Seems somewhere along the line you two became a couple. Which is lovely. You know

I like her very much. She's attractive, clearly efficient, bright, personable and intelligent…'

Jack waits for the 'but'.

'But after what happened last night, how much do we…' He seems to change his mind. 'We Ramsays stick together, don't we? We understand each other's foibles. She has a daughter to think about, her safety…'

'*Hugh's* foibles, Dad, and he knows he has to go, just like he knew he had to go in November, so Serena and Lana's safety isn't an issue. Plus…'

He sighs. It's something he thought about long and hard on the way back from Argos. Did his dad make the wrong call all those years ago by concealing Hugh's 'crime'? Though Serena didn't actually say so, maybe the secret did cripple them all.

'I've been thinking about this all morning. I think Hugh needs help, Dad. Not just counselling to help him handle his temper, but proper psychiatric assistance. Perhaps he needs to unlock those childhood years and face them head on to move away from his anger.'

'You really think it will help your brother to recall what happened? What he did?' His father leans forward. 'It would destroy him, Jack. It would devastate anyone, but he's already… mentally vulnerable, frail. It's the very thing I've tried to protect him from all these years.' His eyes well with tears. 'You see that, don't you? When he couldn't remember anything the next day, it was a blessing. It sounds silly, but it felt divine, like your mum had acted from heaven to protect him.'

As though willing Jack to understand, he arches his hands. 'Lucinda suffered dreadfully. The poor boy did it out of love. We can't punish him for that. And who knows how far a psychiatrist's ethical duty of confidentiality stretches?' He sits back. 'Which brings me back to Serena.'

'What?' Surprised at the abrupt change of tone, Jack shifts his thoughts. 'What about her?'

'She's pleasant and charming, but how much do we know about her or her history?'

Jack frowns. 'That has nothing to do with you or anyone else.'

His dad smiles thinly. 'Pillow talk, Jack. It has been a long time but I still remember it well. Last night got me thinking. I don't know how much you've told her but—'

'I trust her, Dad.'

'Hmm. She's been here for weeks and she's never taken a single day off, Jack. Barely even left the estate. Doesn't that feel odd to you? Presumably Lana has a father, family, grandparents. Why doesn't she—'

Jack lifts his palm. 'Enough Dad. I'm sure she has her reasons.'

'And what can they possibly be? She's clearly hiding here from the world like a fugitive.'

He stares at his father. Serena is entitled to her privacy and he's loath to breach her trust. But he knows this man. He's intrigued and doesn't like being kept out of any loop. If he doesn't say something, his dad will ask Serena directly and it would be kinder to save her that discomfort.

'Look Dad, it's none of our business, but she does have her reasons—'

'Like what, for example?'

Jack sighs. 'She's a victim of domestic abuse, Dad, that's why.'

His dad raps his fingers on the laptop. 'Coercive behaviour is an offence these days, isn't it? If that's the case, then surely she should be doing something about it, reporting it to the police, taking steps to—'

'She will when she's ready.' His dad's expression is sceptical. 'Don't judge. Neither you nor I have any idea what the fear must be like.' The anger rises at the thought of that bastard. '*Violent* domestic abuse by someone who's admired and, to the outside world, highly respectable.'

'Like a doctor.' His father looks thoughtful. 'Her reluctance to accompany me to the hospital, I assume?'

'Be patient with her, Dad. It's still early days, it's still fresh.'

'Metaphorically and literally? The burn to her chest.' He shrugs. 'Sorry, son, I couldn't help but notice it when she was ill. I did wonder how it happened, but didn't like to pry.'

'So you see she needs my love and protection right now?'

His dad gazes for a moment. 'Love and protection.' Then he nods. 'Yes, of course I do. And you're sure of her discretion about Hugh?'

'Yes, Dad. I trust her. I'd trust her with my life.'

Chapter Forty-Eight

Serena

Monday morning, a new week. Yanking back Hayden's curtains, Serena peers down at the cottage garden. Like a stage spotlight, the sunshine is circling her daughter as she squats down on the grass with a picture book. Though Lexie is out of view, she's clearly reading or chattering to her. Lana knows not to go on the swing unattended, but ten minutes playing on her own is safe, surely? The estate is like Fort Knox with the security gate and Hugh isn't here.

She feels a stab of guilt again. Poor Hugh. Was she being over-protective? She sighs the thought away. What's done is done and it feels like a promising and joyful new start. She woke up earlier than Jack and gazed at his sculpted features for some time. The doubts from yesterday had receded completely. For once she'd been lucky; she'd found a man she not only fancied like rotten, but one who had restored her self-belief, and that was something she'd thought lost forever.

Now turning to the bed, she starts in surprise. Hayden isn't under the quilt half asleep as expected. He's already sitting up with his computer on his thighs.

'Morning!' she says, lowering the breakfast tray to his side table. 'You're up bright and early.'

The glow from the screen highlights his grey fledgling beard. Refusing even to get up to shave, he stayed in bed again all yesterday.

'Yes, awake too bloody soon,' he replies. 'This damned leg as usual. Hip's fine, but whichever position I try, it aches.'

'What sort of ache?'

'A throbbing cramp sort of ache.'

'Shall I take a look?'

'If you must.'

He pulls back a section of sheet and returns to his monitor.

Kneeling to get a better look, Serena flashes him a smile. Grumpy but absorbed, so there's some hope she can cheer him up. Showing interest in his project will be a start.

'You seem rapt, Hayden. Even at your laptop in the dark. What's caught your attention so much that you don't mind me prodding your leg?'

She peers at his calf and gently presses the tight flesh. Hmm; as on Saturday night it's discoloured, swollen and hot to the touch. She had intended to mention her worry to Jack, but so much else was going on at the weekend. Like a son trying to smother his father; a son who had done the same to his mother at the tender age of eight. An emotionally frail son who clearly needs help. Oh God; Jack banned him from his home at her insistence. Has she put self-interest before him and made things even worse?

No. Lana is her priority; putting a child first is the way it should be. Whatever it takes, you do it and worry about the consequences later. She glances at Hayden. Like covering up a crime.

Shaking the discomfort away, she focuses on the task at hand.

'Hayden? I'm just going to lift your leg.'

She looks closer. There's a red patch of skin below the knee. She bends his foot and he responds with a yelp. Yes, that's actually quite disturbing, potentially dangerous, in fact. 'It hurts more when I do that?' she asks.

He doesn't reply. Instead, he snaps his laptop shut and responds to her earlier question.

'Very glad you're so interested in my reading matter, Serena.' His smile seems slippery, smug. 'I've been catching up with a court case from a year or so ago. The wife who battered her husband to death? I'm sure you remember it. She told the newspaper her story and I've just finished the article.' He lifts his eyebrows. 'Told and sold for a tidy sum of money, I expect.'

Thrown from her concerns about his injury, Serena sits back. There's something about his gleaming eyes, the suppressed excitement in his voice. Goosebumps spread down her arms. 'Oh right.'

'Come on, you must have read about it at the time; it bubbled in the news for several months. Hammer attack. Eighteen brutal blows.' He sucks in theatrically. 'Murder, of course. Murder most foul! Eight long years in prison before the conviction was overturned. She argued, or rather her clever barrister argued, that it was as a result of psychological torture, coercive behaviour. It was reduced to manslaughter eventually.'

'OK…'

'Well, what do you think about it? Can a man really torment and control a woman to that extent? To justify her killing him? Taking his life? Because, as Old Hamlet succinctly put it, murder is indeed "most foul", the most extreme act of finality. Would you agree?'

Steeling herself, Serena inhales from deep in her diaphragm. She mustn't panic or rise to the bait. Yes, he's been needling her here and there for the past couple of weeks, but he can't really know anything.

'Sorry Hayden, I haven't read enough about the case to comment. Now, your leg, I'm concerned it—'

'And do you know the strange thing about it, about her, the murderer?'

Her stomach clenches. He's clearly enjoying himself. He won't let the subject drop.

'No...'

'She says she still loves him. Could you still love a man who did that, Serena? A dead man? One whose life you've chosen to end?'

His expression patient, he waits for a reply.

'Well, I expect it's complicated. These things usually are.' She stands and gestures to the table. 'Your breakfast is getting cold.'

He glances at it. 'So it is.' But he doesn't reach for the tea or the toast. Instead, he thrums his fingers on his computer lid. 'But that case is by the by. What I've been really enjoying of late is my research.'

'Oh yes?'

'Genealogy of sorts,' he says. 'Like to know more?'

Thank God he's moved on. Her relief emerges as a smile. 'Genealogy. Sure; it sounds interesting.'

He gesticulates to the chair graciously. 'Then please do have a seat.'

Sitting, she waits as he reorganises his covers.

He takes an ostentatious breath. 'I've been using Hercule's grey cells...'

'Very good.'

'And doing a little family digging about... Guess who?'

'The Ramsays?'

'No, try again.'

She glances at her watch. Lana is outside; she should go to her soon. 'I have no idea, Hayden.'

'About Serena Green.' He beams. 'Apparently, that's you.'

Removing his glasses, he scrutinises her. 'Knowledge-able and efficient, it was obvious you were a professional of some sort, so I was intrigued from the moment you set foot in my house. Why would an educated woman want to cook and clean and scrub toilets for an old man?' He chuckles. 'Like our friend Cinderella. And why would this clearly affectionate mother never take her small child for a day out? Was she *hiding*, perchance? But from what or whom? The main clue was her reluctance to go with me to the hospital, not just the routine appointments, but the emergency when I fell on the stairs.'

Smacked from her temporary calm, the tinny taste of panic rushes back. She stares at his rapt face. Should she say something? That his 'fall' was never an urgent situation, perhaps? If indeed, it even really happened at all? But he's in full throttle. Best let him spit everything out so she knows what she's up against.

He continues with a twitch of his lips. 'Yes, I thought, bingo. Our lovely housekeeper once worked in one of our local infirmaries. Not as a cleaner or auxiliary or the like, but a nurse or a doctor. So I spent time tracing a Serena Green at the hospitals near here. Knutsford, Northwich, Wilmslow, Macclesfield. No luck. So I spread the net a little wider to Chester, Manchester and so on. You get my drift.' He peers for a beat. 'There was no match.'

Pausing dramatically, he turns to the tray, pours tea from the pot, adds a splash of milk and slurps from his cup.

Frozen, Serena watches and waits.

'So, where were we?' he eventually asks. He doesn't wait for a reply. 'That's right. Serena Green, the *local* medic. Only she wasn't, or isn't. So I had to think again. Where did I turn to next, you're asking. The Medical Register, of course, where I found a *Seren* Greene with an 'e'. Dug a little further and discovered she was born in Wales. But this Seren went to university in London, qualified as a doctor and stayed there.'

Irritation overtaking her anxiety, Serena finally speaks. 'And your point is?'

'Neat, just adding an "a" and dropping an "e".'

'Seren isn't a well-known name; people assume I'm a Serena, so I just go with it, have for years. And if I misspelled my surname at any point, it was simply a typo.' She's had enough of his games, so she stands. 'I'd better check on Lana. She's playing on her own outside.'

'Ah, little Lana. She's such a treasure when she opens up and chats.'

Serena sits down again.

'Lana *Baptiste*, she tells me. So you gave her her father's name?'

'Yes, I did.'

'You must have been happy with him then?'

Where the hell is this going? Blackmail of some sort? He can't really *know* anything. And even if he has his suspicions, she can counter them with what she knows about him covering up Hugh's crime. Not just him but his police mate and perhaps other friends.

She looks up to the elaborate light fitting and sighs.

'I wasn't, actually. I wasn't *happy* at all. He was controlling, emotionally abusive and manipulative, but I found myself unexpectedly pregnant with Lana and I decided to stay for her sake. I thought a baby with his name might change him.'

'But it didn't. He threw boiling water at you only weeks ago.'

Anger flares. What the hell is Hayden doing? What does he want? All she knows for sure is that he's enjoying this charade. 'It was coffee, actually,' she snaps. 'A whole carafe of coffee, freshly made.'

'Dreadful. Simply dreadful. I saw the injury for myself when you were ill. It was a crime – an assault – possibly even grievous bodily harm.' That eagle-eyed look. 'You should have called the police.'

She returns the steady stare. 'My primary need was to get my daughter away. It could have been her, not me.'

Remembering the paralysing, painful shock, she puts her hand to her neck. The PTSD has lessened, but at times it's still there, swiping when she least expects it.

'It felt as though my flesh was melting, Hayden. Can you imagine what physical damage it would do to a child's tender skin, let alone the mental harm?'

He abruptly coughs for a moment or two. When it passes his frown clears and he sits back again.

'Yes, Lana. She was more than delighted to tell me that her birthday is in June. The very first day of the month, in fact. So I accessed her birth records easily. Born at University College Hospital. Mother Seren Greene, father Pierre Baptiste. *Doctor* Pierre Baptiste.'

Serena searches for an equanimous tone. 'What's this all about, Hayden? If you'd just asked me, I would have told you. I don't particularly want to dwell on it; it's not something I'm proud of, but ask away. God knows why, but I allowed myself to be in an unhappy and coercive relationship for years. From time to time I tried to leave, but the truth was that I was wholly dependent on him, so he easily wooed me back. Then I had Lana and I wanted it to work. I was weak, I was dominated, controlled, isolated. I finally got away and I have *you* to thank for that. I'm still extremely grateful. You took me in and gave me and my child a home. You accepted us without quibble or asking questions.' Her heart thrashing, she meets his eyes. 'Why are you grilling me now?'

His satisfied smile fades. 'Because, *Seren*, it's my duty to protect both my sons.'

Chapter Forty-Nine

Jack

Too agitated to take in Quarry Bank Mill or the undulating countryside leading down to the river, Jack negotiates the country road towards Styal. Sighing one last time, he slows down and indicates right at the privet hedge. Styal prison, 'HMP & YOI Styal' these days. In his pupilage he came here to see clients from time to time. The women's jail was often in the headlines back then – it had the worse suicide rate and frequent incidences of self-harm, bullying, drugs and overcrowding. Little did he know that his future wife would end up incarcerated here.

His chest tight, he shakes his head. Now his *ex* wife, thank God.

He drives past The Clink restaurant, through the gates, then around the manicured lawns. Previously cottage homes and an orphanage, the red-brick buildings are handsome and fit in this nice part of Cheshire. If it wasn't for the high perimeter fence, the estate would look like an upmarket housing development. His jaw tightens. But it isn't; it's a penal institution, here to protect law-abiding citizens, a deterrent and a place for punishment. Rehabilitation too. Though how one restores a mother who has killed her only child to normality, he doesn't know. He hasn't spoken to Melanie since the police arrested her and took her away. There was no apology, no remorse that day, just her drunken accusing finger and her screaming: 'This is your fault, Jack! All your fault.'

No wonder he'd found himself gripping her throat.

Gently tapping his forehead on the steering wheel, he sighs at the memory. Why the hell has he come? Because Serena encouraged and supported him. Because he can be open and truthful and honest with her.

'Are you going to visit Melanie?' she asked him.

'No. Why would I give that woman the time of day?'

'Because it'll drive you nuts not knowing what she wants.'

'I could just delete the texts and forget about it.'

She raised her eyebrows. 'How come you haven't already, eh?'

'I'm afraid what she'll say. Terrified how I'll respond to it.'

'Better to find out than to speculate.'

'Really?'

'Yes. Besides, you've already decided.'

He had of course. After confiding about Thea and confessing about Hugh, he'd felt lightened enough to have closure with Melanie as well. And it was a new start for him, Serena and Lana. A lifetime's commitment, in fact.

Focusing on that thought, he nods and climbs out.

–

Jack stands at the entrance and scans the visiting room for the woman who once was his wife. Five rows of tables deep, the sour-smelling area is bustling with inmates, their loved ones and prison staff. He searches again. What the hell? Melanie isn't there. Now he's here and has made this huge decision, he needs to see her and find out what she wants. Wondering who to ask, he begins to turn away, but a petite woman lifts her hand. With a jolt, he registers it's her, just two desks away and clearly in his line of vision.

Taking a deep breath, he steps over and pulls out the chair. 'Hello Melanie,' he says, his voice sounding a great deal steadier than he feels.

He tries not to stare at this mousy-haired, pallid person. Did she always look like this behind the bronzed skin, heavy make-up and high heels? She's eight years younger than him, but looks a decade older. Prison life, he supposes. But he mustn't feel sorry for her; she brought it on herself; it's her penance.

He clears his throat and speaks again. 'Melanie. How are you?'

'As well as can be expected. Two down, four to go.'

'Parole much sooner, I expect.'

She snorts. 'Always the bloody lawyer.' Frowning, she shakes her head. 'Sorry, old habits die hard.' Then, her eyes flickering, 'I don't want to fight, Jack.'

Jack stares. Anxiety and fear, even terror clogs his senses. Why has she asked to see him? Does he really want to know? It's fine; if she starts to make excuses, he can simply leave.

'What is this about, Melanie? You said it's important.'

She rubs the Formica top. 'Mum thought I should speak to you.'

'OK.' Her mother was a nice lady. She took far more interest in her granddaughter than Melanie did her child. 'About what?'

She pulls down the cuff of her jumper. 'I've been having therapy. Going back to why I was so unhappy…'

Gritting his teeth, he sits back. So there it is. Excuses. Blame. 'Still my fault *you* knocked over and snuffed the life out of our child, is it?'

She visibly flinches and looks away. 'No, that's not what I'm saying. It was my fault; I have to take responsibility for what occurred. I chose to drive a car when I was drunk. I didn't intend to harm Thea, but that's what happened. I killed her and I am so sorry, Jack.' She lifts her gaze and smiles thinly. 'That wasn't easy to say.'

A lead weight lifted, he exhales long and hard. 'Thank you.' Then studying her pinched face, 'So what…?'

'We've been talking about why was I going to bed drunk, drinking when I woke, topping it up at lunch time. That's not normal, obviously, and again I have to accept the responsibility for that myself. No one forced me to drink…' She gives him a strange glance. 'But someone encouraged me.'

Jack covers his face. Condoned; encouraged. Just semantics really. 'I'm sorry, you're right; I never thought of it like that. It was…' He pictures the nights they'd share the best part of a whisky bottle. They got on then. Laughed, even. How to describe it? 'It felt like the only time we had something in common. But yes, you're right, I—'

She touches his arm. There's a fine, silver scar on her wrist. 'I didn't mean you, Jack.'

'Then, who…?'

Her eyebrows knit. 'Who else? The charmer, the enabler, the manipulator, Jack. He hated me the moment he set eyes on me, but he covered it brilliantly with his bonhomie. "A lunch time cocktail, Melanie? A top-up? Or how about opening a bottle of champagne? A small glass won't hurt. Oh, let's have another. Jack won't know.

328

Help me with the online shopping order. Which wine country shall we visit today?" And the rest.'

Jack folds his arms. 'No, you're exaggerating—'

'You weren't there, Jack. You worked long hours, went away for days at a time. He was. You just came home to a drunk wife. Then, when our marriage was imploding and I was really down, he said he had a friend who specialised in pick-me-ups, something more effective than I'd get on prescription...'

Jack stands. The anger almost strangles his voice. 'I don't know what you're suggesting, but I've heard enough. You're clearly so desperate to hold someone else accountable for your own actions, you're being vindictive and spiteful.' He needs to shout, so he whispers. 'Bringing my father into it. He welcomed you into our home; he was generous; he indulged you. I can't believe you'd sink so low.'

She plays with the hem of her sleeve. 'I told Mum you wouldn't believe me. I don't know why I tried. Your mother has nothing to do with me. I never even met her.'

Jack frowns. His *mum*? His nape prickling with alarm, he sits down again. 'What has this got to do with my mother?'

'Talk to my parents.' She sighs. 'They liked her; the whole village respected the Ramsays from year dot, so they said it was sad to see. But at least her parents had passed on by then.'

He stares, confused. He never knew his grandparents – his mother was their only, late child. 'I have no idea what you're talking about—'

'Mum says it was common knowledge that Lucinda was an alcoholic, Jack. She'd embarrass your dad by taking the car into the village and demanding booze from the off licence, the supermarket, The Bull, even though he'd asked them to ban her. Apparently she'd find a pub further out, then drink-drive home. Anyway, it's a funny coincidence, if you ask me. Then it stopped because she became housebound.'

'She was dying of cancer, Melanie. Dad nursed her...'

'Was she, Jack?' She faintly snorts. 'Maybe you should ask him what drugs he was using to *nurse* her. It's my bet they weren't prescribed by her GP.'

Chapter Fifty

Hugh

Hugh whistles while he works. His favourite smell of cut pasture's in the air and he's been helping old Samuel by unpacking boxes and lugging brisket boards, neck rails and cow mats into the milking parlour. Turns out he can do lots of things with his left hand. He said as much to Robbie when they woke up this morning. 'I've noticed,' he replied with a sleepy smile.

Despondent and dejected, he'd finally arrived back at the camper late yesterday afternoon. It reeked of piss and body odour. Hardly surprising with the windows stuck fast, but it seemed as though he was looking at everything with fresh eyes. The duvet was almost damp, the walls stained with black mildew. When he pressed the wallpaper, it was soft to the touch.

Rock bottom. That's how he felt. He stared at the old army blanket and words seemed to float around him. *Kindness. Mercy. Special help.* Tears pricked his eyes. Perhaps dying peacefully in the night wouldn't be so bad, he thought. But there was a knock at the door and Jess appeared.

'I've spoken to Dad. Told him it's disgusting in here and that it needs a full renovation. Or even a replacement. It can be sorted while your wrist is mending.' She tutted.

'Flipping Dad. An employer has duties of care anyway, but you are like family.'

Trying to breathe through the rush of mixed emotions, Hugh struggled to speak. Her gaze was so kind, but he'd been banned from the hall. Where would he go? Where the hell would he sleep and eat?

The worry burst out. 'You can't do that. I've nowhere else to live!'

Jess rolled her pretty eyes. 'Then you stay here with us, of course. When I go back to college you can have my room. In the meantime you share Robbie's. OK?' She stepped out, then turned back. 'Come on, then. Me and Dad are having a beef casserole and I know you like your meat.' She slipped her arm into his and gave him a friendly nudge. 'Though rumour has it you're becoming quite the veggie these days.'

Later, when he finally went up to Robbie's bedroom, Hugh found himself staring at the cushions and stressing. His dad's spooky red eyes. He did that. The thought still knocked him sick. Should he confess to the Barnes family? He took a sidelong glance at Robbie getting changed, but he was already gazing back with a frown.

'What is it, Hugh? Why can't you go home this time?' he asked in a low voice. 'What happened?'

His dad hadn't said anything about it this morning as expected. Was it one of those things he wasn't supposed to tell? But Jess's 'family' comment made him brave. And this was Robbie, after all.

'I sleepwalked into my dad's bedroom last night. I didn't know anything about it until Jack told me to wake up.'

He watched Robbie's face for a reaction.

'Right...' he said.

No shock so far, and he seemed to know there was more.

'And when I woke up, dad was... Well, at first I thought he was dead but...' He pressed down his hair. 'It was me, Robbie. I was holding a pillow, so I must have...' Weirdly, a firework-like smell filtered in through the crack in the window. 'I didn't do it on purpose. Honestly. It wasn't my fault.'

Wondering how Robbie would react – maybe shout, call him stupid or even throw him out – he tensed. But he simply nodded. 'You're right; it wasn't your fault,' he replied.

A relief, a huge relief. But why didn't Robbie mind? It was to do with their dads and money, wasn't it?

'You really don't like my old man, do you?' he asked.

Robbie didn't speak for a while. 'I haven't even seen him for the best part of twenty years, but I think it's great you're doing your own thing. A bit of distance does the world of good, puts things in perspective,' he finally said.

That threw Hugh. Something told him that a 'bit of distance' was between here and Australia. 'Like you and your wife?' he asked.

'Yup, like that.'

Hugh now deeply sighs. At the time he'd thought it was a *perceptive* thing to ask, but today he feels unsettled. Did Robbie's eyes flicker? Has he changed his mind about leaving his wife?

Then there's his brother. He hasn't replied to Jack's messages or returned his missed calls. It was *him* of all people who chucked him out of the hall. Not his dad but Jack who always understood, well, everything. Which means if Jack asked, he'd have to confess – it's only bits here and there, mind, but he might have started to remember their mum.

Samuel's voice breaks into his thoughts. 'Another delivery has arrived, lad. Come on, soldier, look sharp, it needs unloading.'

'Yes sir!' Putting his fingers to his brow, Hugh salutes. Turns out the old dairy man can speak after all. He's been telling tales of his riotous days in the army all morning. Some funny jokes too.

He makes a mental note to tell his dad; it's the sort of gossip he likes to hear.

If, of course, he's allowed home ever again.

—

Hearing his stomach loudly rumble, Hugh looks up from his chore. As though on cue, Robbie's approaching from the sheep pens. Picturing his tattoo, he lifts his hand and grins, but as Robbie draws near, it takes only one glance to know something is wrong.

Holding his mobile, Robbie sits on a crate.

'What is it?' Hugh asks.

'Sit down for a minute, would you?'

Anxious already, Hugh squints at the phone. Oh hell. He knew he was right. 'Who is that message from? Your wife?'

Robbie looks surprised. 'No, why do you say that?' And then, 'Well, not really. You don't miss much, do you?'

With a wave of despondency, Hugh squats against the shed. 'You're going back to Australia, aren't you?'

Robbie sighs. 'I'm sorry, mate, but I have to, for now at least. Skyping Vicky and the children is all very well, but without proximity and touch no one can talk properly.'

He rubs Hugh's arm. 'You know that. And now I've sorted out my head, at least a bit, I'm in a better place to communicate, to be honest and explain how I feel. You know, try for a better future, whatever that might look like? Plus, I'm missing my kids. Really badly. You get that, don't you?'

He pauses. Hugh knows he's watching, but he can't look back. 'But hey, you get my bedroom, so it's not all bad. No more having to eat veggie curry, eh?' He waits for a beat. 'Hugh? Are you going to talk to me about this?'

Too disappointed to speak, Hugh doesn't reply.

'Come on, mate. We can talk about it now or later, if you want. But don't just blank me, OK? It's rude.'

Seeming to give up, Robbie stands. 'OK, your call. You coming to eat?'

'Your phone, who is the message from then?'

Robbie taps it against his leg. 'Olaf,' he says eventually.

'What? Olaf who used to work here?'

He nods. 'What with your bad wrist, I thought I'd better, you know, organise cover. Turns out he can start in a week, so...'

A week? Robbie's leaving in a week? So the 'love you, mate' on the phone was just an expression; it wasn't ever real.

Get out! Just get out!

Rejected again. And not just rejected, but replaced.

'You go for lunch. I'm not hungry.'

Robbie laughs. 'Come on, mate, you're always ravenous.' He ruffles his hair. 'Look, you're your own man, Hugh. You do have options. You can stay in my bedroom and help like you're helping today or...'

Hugh frowns. Or what? Or he can try for a job at the car salesroom or in the launderette or one of the other jobs he couldn't *hold down*?

'You could come out with me for a while.'

Hugh lifts his head.

'Yeah. You could travel with me to Brisbane.' Robbie's cheeks are flushed. 'Just for a holiday. I know it's a big thing, but maybe you could come out for a few weeks until your wrist heals and see how you like it. If you do, then who knows? I know it's a huge decision, but maybe it's time you got away?'

He gapes. Is Robbie taking the piss?

'I'm serious, mate. Only if you want to, but it's an idea, something to think about, isn't it?'

'Really?'

'Yeah, really. Come on, food calls; I'm starving.'

Bloody hell. Australia? 'A bit of distance to put things in perspective?' Hugh asks.

Robbie grins. 'Exactly. Australia's the best place on earth when you're happy. A holiday of a lifetime. What do you say, mate?'

Chapter Fifty-One

Serena

Serena composes herself before entering Hayden's bedroom. She's had a busy hour or so sorting out Lana and her lunch, emptying the washing machine and handing over another ornament for repair to the 'mothball man'. Then there was the bird trapped in the kitchen; a robin, of all things. She was afraid it would be as frightened as the look on Lana's face, but it allowed her to scoop it up in her palms and set it free.

Freedom indeed. She's tried not to speculate, but she's certain there's more of Hayden's 'research' to come. She has to remain calm and let him tell his story in full. Then she can decide what to do next.

She straightens her spine and stands tall. 'A fresh pot of tea,' she says, stepping in, 'and more milk.'

There's no room on the bedside table, so she places the tray on the bedding by his side. 'Careful not to spill,' she says, snorting inwardly at the irony. 'The tea is scalding hot.'

His face pasty, Hayden puts his palm to his forehead. 'Think I might have napped. Bit hot and light-headed for several minutes. Felt most odd.' He seems to shake it away and regain focus. 'So, where were we?' he asks.

She sits at the edge of the Hepplewhite chair and lifts her chin. Best thrash it out so she knows what his game is about. 'You were worried about the safety of your sons.'

'Safety? Ah, yes. The good doctor. Not you, but your partner, Doctor Pierre Baptiste…'

His gaze glowing with amusement, he lets the name fill the atmosphere for a while.

Hiding her fear behind a fixed mask, Serena stays silent and waits. Why is he really doing this? Apart from his obvious pleasure? Control, of course. Since she came into Jack's life, he's lost some of his power. He's determined to regain it.

'Yes, the good doctor, a man who looks after our health. I couldn't help wondering about the state of *his* health and wellbeing…'

She doesn't reply.

'Therefore, being a good, upstanding citizen, I decided to track him down and find out where he worked, so that I could make discreet enquiries.' Peering at her, he tilts his head. 'Thought I'd better make sure he was alive and kicking. Not in a ditch with eighteen hammer blows to his body.'

He stops and wafts his hand like a fan. 'Goodness, I'm hot.'

He coughs lightly before coming back to his story. 'Talking of heat, that was a very nasty burn, Serena. Or should I call you Seren? No one could blame you for hitting back, so to speak. What's the word? Provocation? But of course they call it "loss of control" these days.'

When she doesn't comment, he carries on in a raspy tone. 'But you'll be glad to know I discovered Doctor Baptiste was indeed alive and kicking.' He coughs again. 'Nothing of concern; he was going into work as usual.'

Relief spreading, Serena stands and straightens her pinafore. 'Well, that's good. Glad you satisfied your curiosity. Now, if you don't mind, I have chores to—'

'We had a lovely exchange of emails.'

Her heart races with fresh alarm. 'What? You actually contacted—'

'Oh, don't worry, he won't be kicking down our front door. You'll be pleased to hear how clever I was: I created a false email and told him I was hunting down an outstanding debt you — or should I say Seren Greene — owed me. After being impressively circumspect up to then, he became very forthcoming.'

'About what?'

He turns to the teapot. 'Will you join me?'

'No thank you.'

'No, nor will I.' He pats his chest and adjusts his position. 'Feel a little breathless. Too much caffeine, I expect.' He taps his chin with the teaspoon. 'Pierre was very keen for us to keep in touch. It was in both our interests to track you down, he said. Explained you'd gone off with his little girl, who he was missing terribly, and that your parents were desperately worried.'

He stares with those unblinking eyes. 'He also said there'd been no hide nor hair of you for over *three* months. Funny thing, that, when you've only been here for, what? One? Certainly less than two.'

Tapping her foot, Serena keeps her expression neutral. 'He's lying, of course.' She smiles thinly. 'No, the *funny thing* is how similar you and Pierre are. I don't know why I haven't noticed it before. Charismatic and persuasive, you can make people feel very special and wanted when it suits you. But goodness me, when you're not getting exactly your own way... That's when you create and spread negative emotions, don't you, Hayden? Keep people off balance and unsure so you always stay in control, the top dog. Play on their doubts and insecurities. I've seen you do it with both your sons. No wonder they're messed up.'

Anger rising, she glares. 'Is that why you employed me? A woman with a child? To milk Jack's grief and his guilty feelings for all they're worth? Stop him moving on? Both emotionally and physically?'

'Come now, Serena, don't get personal. I just like solving a puzzle.'

Hacking again, he puts a hand to his neck. Pearls of sweat have broken out on his cheeks, but he continues doggedly.

'Why the red herring about your fear of local hospitals? And why, when you lived in London with Pierre, as do your parents, did you end up here? Cheshire's undoubtedly beautiful, but it's a long way from home. Two hundred miles, would you say?' As though short of breath, he blows out in little puffs. 'Then there's the garage fire. Most strange, but undoubtedly another clue.'

She thinks of lifting the mattress, pulling out the house deeds and challenging *him*, but he abruptly sits forward and hacks repeatedly. His whole body heaves for several seconds. When the fit finally finishes, his cheeks are clammy and white. And there's a blue tinge to his lips.

Clearly shocked, he holds out his palm to show her his phlegm. The mucus is swamped with bright blood. 'Stabbing pain in my back and my chest,' he manages to gasp. 'Serena? Something's wrong.'

'OK, let me…'

Before she can move, he collapses to one side, almost falling from the bed. She quickly stands, removes the tea tray and helps him lie back. The old professionalism kicks in as she runs through the diagnosis: the leg swelling and discolouration, the cramp in his calf. God, her suspicions were right, he clearly has a deep vein thrombosis. Then the difficulty with his breathing, chest pain, coughing up blood… The clot has obviously reached his lungs.

She focuses. OK; is there anything she can do to help right now? Time is of the essence; his condition will rapidly deteriorate if he isn't treated quickly. He needs an anticoagulant to stop the blood clot getting bigger and to prevent new ones forming. Even household aspirin might help. But an ambulance first.

Reflecting her thoughts, Hayden's voice is a croak. 'Ambulance. Please. Right away.'

They're an echo of his words from his 'stair fall'. But she can see it for herself; no acting this time, this *is* an emergency. He could die if he isn't medicated very soon. Her fingertips tingling, she pulls the mobile from her apron pocket.

'Yes, of course, right away.' She inputs the digits. 'Right. Let's get you as comfortable as we can.'

He rocks his head towards her. 'Heart racing. Sharp pain. Is help—'

'Yes, yes of course.'

His forehead is beaded with sweat. Tissues – where are they? None in the bedroom, so she heads for the en suite.

'Waiting for you…' she hears whispered from beyond the door.

'I know, I'm coming,' she calls back. 'Just one minute.'

She pulls at the toilet roll. Though the rattle muffles some of the sound, more words float through, softly spoken, almost feminine. 'Such agony… poor, poor darling… coming for you… at last…' Then quiet laughter.

She turns. *Laughter?* Really? Could Hayden be exaggerating after all? Or is it just the ramblings of a patient in pain?

Intrigued, she returns to the bed. 'What were you saying?' she asks.

Hayden is turned to the window. Far from amused, his expression is petrified. Lifting a trembling finger, he points to the glass.

'You want me to open it?'

Almost imperceptibly, he nods.

She rubs the goosebumps on her arms. She didn't notice before, but the room is actually freezing.

'Better not. It's very cold in here, Hayden, you're just hot.'

Gently raking back his hair, she wipes his forehead and pockets the tissue, then she neatens the bedding and adjusts the pillows to make him comfortable.

She looks at her watch and speaks to him softly. 'Stay calm, relax and just breathe. It won't be long now.' Then, to keep him awake: 'Don't fret about solving your puzzle. It's not very exciting. Out of the blue I rekindled an old friendship with a school pal on Facebook. We messaged back and forth for a few weeks, and she helped me to realise I was in a controlling and coercive relationship with Pierre.'

She sighs and thinks back. 'The signs should be obvious, but when you're stuck in it, you can't see it yourself. The tight control about what you wear and what you buy, where you go, what you do; the isolation, constant criticism and put downs… Well, you think it's because you're inadequate, worthless and a failure, and actually you're flattered and relieved this man loves you. Though it's conditional, of course, love at a price – don't stand so

342

tall, lose weight, clean the house and yourself, eat what I say, do as I say, don't spend so much time with anyone else – not even your child.'

Smiling thinly, she pauses and peers at Hayden. 'But why am I explaining it to you? You understand such behaviour more than anyone, don't you Hayden? The bullying, the need to manipulate, dominate, humiliate...' She narrows her eyes. 'And not just with your sons, I'm guessing. With poor Lucinda, too?'

Rapidly puffing air through his mouth, he stares pleadingly but he doesn't reply.

Yes, so many parallels to Pierre. She shakes away the sheer irony and goes back to her patient. 'Good man, Hayden, keep breathing slowly, in and out. Won't be long now. My friend's name was Rhona and she gave me the courage to leave Pierre. Even though my mum and dad had moved closer to us, I couldn't go to them because he'd also fooled them with his surface charm, but Rhona was delighted to give Lana and me sanctuary, time to get ourselves back on our feet and decide about the future. So I wrote a note to my parents and Pierre so they'd know we hadn't been abducted or the like, then Lana and I waited until he'd left for work one morning, got a cab to Paddington, jumped on a train and headed for Wales. In the middle of nowhere, it turned out Rhona's cottage was indeed a "safe house". She'd inherited it from her reclusive grandma. I don't know what had happened to my vibrant childhood pal, but both her parents had died and she'd become a hermit herself. But she welcomed us with open arms and a freezer stuffed with goodies. And when I looked around the stark countryside, it was perfect for walking, for taking time out just to think, evaluate and breathe. It was utter freedom. I knew I'd done the right thing, especially for Lana.'

Oh God, Lana. She glances at the time.

'I need to check on Lana. She went outside to play after lunch. Sorry, I'll be back as soon as I can.' She turns at the door. 'A child's wellbeing and safety are the most important things in the world. You know that, don't you, Hayden?'

Chapter Fifty-Two

Jack

His shirt sticking to his chest, Jack drives past fields on one side, pretty bungalows and smart houses on the other. His jaw is so clenched that it hurts. His lumbar region's aching too.

Oh God, his back. His car accident and injury. His pain and insomnia. His hoard of pills. His nominated supplier...

No. No. It's simply a coincidence, mirrors and smoke. Pushing the connection away, he pulls up the car and spends a few moments stretching his spine. Then he opens the window and takes in a gulp of manure-flavoured air.

Staring blankly through the windscreen, he tries to block out the scar on Melanie's wrist, the more recent red slashes a little higher up. Self-harming, clearly. And perhaps even worse. Why they add credence to her story, he can't say, but the fact she tried to hide them turns his stomach. Could there be some truth in what she said?

That smell, his mum's peculiar smell. Could it have been stale alcohol?

Nausea rises, but he blows it away. It's fine; he's fine. He's a lawyer; he deals with facts. Rumour and innuendo count for nothing. The tale about his mother came from malicious slurs by people who had nothing better to do with their time.

He thrums his fingers on the steering wheel. What did he always say to Hugh? Sticks and stones, envy and jealousy... The Ramsays have always been a target in the village. The folk in the big house who have no feelings because they're supposedly rich. Well, what do they know? Ramsay Hall eats money. He's been ploughing a huge chunk of his salary back into the house for as long as he can remember.

The beep of his phone brings him back. He peers at the screen. Thank God, a text from Hugh at last! He's been so bloody worried. He's let his brother down badly, he knows, but what could he do, stuck between a rock and a hard place?

The relief about *something* spreads down his torso, then he opens the message.

> I'm flying to Brisbane next week. When can I come and pack my stuff?

What? What the hell? Noticing the hour, Jack quickly types back.

> Brisbane? What's going on? Call me. I need to get to work but I'm hands free.

Pulling back onto the road, he takes a right turn and threads his way through Gatley village. What on earth is going on with Hugh? He needs to be in chambers for an internal meeting at two; he doesn't have the time to add his brother's latest whimsy to his list of troubled thoughts.

He glares at the dash, but Hugh doesn't phone, so he parks outside the old Tatton cinema and calls him. It goes straight to voicemail, so he texts.

> Talk to me please. You're not seriously going to Australia?

> Yes, I am.

> Who will you be staying with? How long for?

> Robbie's wife and kids and I don't know.

Jack tries to focus. Brisbane? Hugh's never been further than a school excursion to Aviemore and just like that he's off to Australia, a mere nine thousand or so miles away.

He rubs his face. What the fuck? He had to collect Hugh half way through the skiing trip because he was injured and homesick. He was only seventeen himself and had just passed his driving test. He'd never driven on a motorway before, so he spent the six-hour journey hugging the inside lanes with his eyes half closed. Only Scotland and it was pretty damned traumatic. How's he supposed to keep an eye on his brother half way across the world?

Another bombshell thought hits. What did Hugh say in his text? Robbie's *wife and kids*. Oh, hell. He can't let that happen; he cannot put someone else's family in jeopardy.

He looks at his watch. Deal with it now or wait until later? Well, that's a no-brainer in this agitated state. He puts a call through to chambers, then swerves the car around.

Right. Plan of action? There'll be no talking to Hugh now he's made up his mind, but he'll speak to Robbie. When he learns a few Ramsay *intricacies*, he'll certainly see sense.

—

Jack drives into the lay-by opposite the farmhouse and peers at the weathered Selwyn Farm sign. What now? He doesn't have Robbie's number and if he heads down the drive, he might be spotted by Hugh. He massages his forehead. Call Jess, of course. Though will she be at college? He scrolls down his list of contacts, and she answers, thank God.

'Hi Jess. It's Jack Ramsay. Sorry to bother you, but could I have Robbie's mobile number, please?'

'Of course, I'll share it with you.' Then after a moment, 'Anything I can help with? Is everything all right?'

Quite frankly, he'd love to yell, '*No! Nothing is all right. The memories of both my marriage and my childhood are moving and merging and uncertain. I don't know what to think or believe or who to turn to, and I can't even broach my brother to get a reality check about our mum because he's blanked her out. Oh and yes, as if life couldn't get any more complicated, he's decided to bugger off to Australia. Did I mention he tried to smother our father the other night? Who knows what he's capable of when he visits Robbie's wife and kids?*'

He doesn't, of course. Instead he says, 'Everything's fine thanks, Jess. Hope you're good too? Still at Agricultural College?'

The moment he finishes the call, he sends Robbie a message:

> It's Jack Ramsay here. Hugh's told me about Brisbane. Can we talk please? I'm parked just down the lane.

As though he'd been waiting, the reply comes back within seconds.

> Sure, give me ten minutes.

–

Smelling of outdoors and almost unrecognisable from the crop-haired teenager Jack remembers, Robbie climbs into the passenger seat. He holds out his hand.

'Hello Jack. Long time no see. How're you doing, mate?'

Jack accepts the handshake and laughs wryly. 'Not the best day so far. Still, it can only get better.' Then with a deep breath, 'Thanks for coming at such short notice. Look, I'll get straight to the point. Hugh sent me a text about going to Brisbane next week. What's going on?'

'So...' Robbie rakes shaky fingers through his shock of blond hair. 'So I guess I ran away from various problems back there, but now I've sorted a few issues in my head, I'm flying home to talk things through with my missus and see my kids. Long story short, I asked Hugh if he fancied coming too and he wants to. He said he has savings and enough cash to see him through for at least a month?'

Though still clearly nervous, he meets Jack's eye. 'To be honest, I think the break would do him good.'

'Right. OK.'

Jack stares at the sturdy timber gate. Its simplicity is comforting somehow; he understands why Hugh likes it here. A plain, solid, uncomplicated and constant world. Oh God, how to explain everything to Robbie? Where on earth should he start? He turns to him eventually.

'He's right; money's not a problem. He looked after…' Yes, he can say it. 'He helped with the day-to-day care of Thea and I continued to pay him after she died. Save for his designer gear, it's pretty much untouched. But… here's the thing, Robbie. You've been away for a long time; the Hugh you knew when you left is pretty much the Hugh now. He's never really grown up and it's impacted on his adult—'

Robbie interrupts with a hot snort. 'Hardly surprising.' Frowning deeply, he glares. 'Don't mean to swear, mate, but it made my blood fucking boil when he told me. Manipulating him like that, making him feel dirty for having a normal sex drive. Searching for love too, no doubt. Bloody hell, we all need that.'

Goosebumps cool Jack's skin. What? Robbie's eyes are burning with anger.

'You've lost me.'

'When you were at your poncey university, he was caught doing sexual stuff at a park. Turned out the other guy was fifteen. Hugh was only eighteen himself and had assumed his friend was around the same age. He was fed all sorts of shit, Jack. Told he was disgusting, a criminal and half way to being a paedophile. Who the hell does that?'

Thrown by the curve ball, Jack shakes his head. 'What? Who said that?'

'The police, *apparently*.' The sarcasm in his voice is loaded. 'Some bloke confiscated his laptop and found porn. Nothing bad, just regular gay porn. Told Hugh it was dirty, unnatural, the start of fancying young boys. If that's not going to stunt a normal adult life, I don't know what is.'

Jack stares at a grey copse in the distance. This makes sense of Hugh's questions and his excitement a couple of weeks back. His historic avoidance of younger boys too. Good God. Poor Hugh. But he's always told him everything. Why didn't he share this trauma at the time?

'Bloody hell, I had no idea…'

Trying to shelve his astonishment, he drags his thoughts back to the main worry today.

He reverts to Robbie. 'The point is, he's immature in every way. Yes, sexually, I guess, and emotionally. But it's his anger that concerns me right now. His lack of control.' God, he feels disloyal. He takes a deep breath. 'Hugh's always had sudden and often inexplicable rage issues, *severe* ones and unfortunately they're still not resolved.'

Robbie shrugs. 'I know; he told me. Sleepwalking and nearly harming his dad.'

Jack frowns. 'Nearly harming' doesn't really cover it, and it definitely doesn't describe what happened on bonfire night.

He pushes on. 'Then you must know he needs stability, someone to keep an eye on him.' He sighs. 'Look, he's my brother and I love him. But he's a huge responsibility too. Australia for a break sounds great in theory, but suppose he was a danger to your kids, even to you or your wife?'

'I'll take that risk.'

'You don't understand the extent of—'

'I do, actually.' Robbie stares through the passenger window for a few beats. Then he turns. 'Time for home truths, Jack. I know Hugh killed your mum.'

Disbelieving, Jack stares. 'You can't possibly know that. You were only eight. Hugh can't even remember our mother, let alone—'

'It wasn't hard to work out. Not at the time maybe, but later, when I added it all up. One minute he was obsessed with mercy-killing, the next his mum had died and it was as though she'd never existed.'

'Why didn't you say anything? To your parents or a teacher?'

'He'd lost his mum, Jack. He was my best mate; I wasn't going to dob him in.' He guffaws. 'And even now, who'd believe my word against a Ramsay's?'

Tentatively relieved, Jack takes a breath to say something. But Robbie continues to speak.

'Any anyway, it wasn't Hugh's fault. He was just the poor bloody sap.'

'I'm not following—'

'He'd been at him, manipulating him for weeks, Jack. Mercy-killing. Doing the *honourable* thing. Putting a "sad mummy" out of her misery. Being a brave boy for his mummy. Doing it for her. Doing what she wanted. Hugh told me, Jack. Every day after primary school he'd pour it all out.'

'Who do you…?' Then realisation slaps. *He*. There's only one he. No, absolutely no. But still he needs to ask.

'Who do you mean? Who had been at him for weeks?'

Robbie snorts. 'Who else? Your father. The honourable Hayden Ramsay. Grooming his own kid to get rid of his wife.'

'No, you're wrong.' Through the deafening thud of his own pulse, Jack tries to focus. 'Children make things up. Like you say, Hugh was obsessed; it must have been his fertile imagination. Dad adored mum; he nursed her and loved her and—'

'Yeah, well maybe he'd had enough. Who knows? Fact is that Hugh suffocated your mum because your dad bullied him to do it. On bonfire night. That was to be the night.'

Bonfire night. Fuck. Anxiety spreading, Jack attempts to fill his lungs. *Facts, Jack, facts, not speculation, fake news.* 'You can't know that for sure.'

'I can. I heard your dad for myself. A week or so before, we were mucking around in your living room, the bloody parlour or whatever you call it.'

'Drawing room.'

'Yeah. Then your dad came in looking for Hugh, so I hid. I lifted that flap at the back of the sofa and snuck in. Heard him loud and clear. He said that Mummy wanted Hugh's "special help" on bonfire night. I guess Hugh must have shaken his head or the like, because your dad said, "You disappoint me; you're a coward, Hugh. A coward. There's no other word for it." Or something along those lines. Course it meant nothing to me then. Didn't fully make sense until I was stupid enough to say something similar to Hugh right here a month or so back. At the time I just thought your dad was having a go at him again.'

He looks at Jack steadily. 'You know I'm right, don't you? Being called a coward is the one thing that Hugh can't take. He was fretting about it at the weekend.' He lifts his eyebrows. 'Mentioned it to me on the phone late Saturday night.'

Breathing back the urgent need to vomit, Jack lowers his head. The sleepwalking out of the blue. It makes sense. And yes, 'coward' is absolutely Hugh's trigger word.

He finally looks at Robbie. 'If – even in retrospect – you believed Hugh had done what you say... You hung out with him for the next decade. Weren't you worried about your own safety?'

'Nope, I wasn't.' He gazes for a beat. 'Were you?'

They fall silent for some time. Robbie eventually sighs. 'Look, Jack, there's other stuff I've discovered about your dad on a personal level. When Hugh and I got arrested, he wanted me gone. Not just because I was a bad influence but... he found us in the barn. Pissed and naked. I guess he put two and two together and didn't like the prospect of a homosexual son.'

His cheeks clench. 'Long and short, he gave, loaned or whatever, a substantial sum of money to my parents, cash they desperately needed to keep the farm going. Seems I was the quid pro quo. Fucking loathe him for that. But I'm letting it go now. All of it. I want what you want – what's best for Hugh. Let him be his own man, Jack. It's time to set your brother free.'

–

His thoughts fractured, Jack drives. Without seeing, without breathing, he steers the Porsche on autopilot. A surprise bonfire party and guests who rarely came to the house; an obsession with mercy-killing out of nowhere; the flap at the back of the sofa. Hugh's missing laptop; his questions about gay sex and porn; dropping the few school friends he had. Melanie's 'pick-me-up', his own illicit supply of pills; his mother's peculiar smell and her frequent pleas to 'give me something' to make it stop. Then Lana's whispered story at the maze about Lexie being struck by a crutch for 'being naughty'.

Why cruelty to a dog is the worst part right now, he doesn't know.

Though he can't face going through them, he arrives at the Ramsay Hall gates like a homing pigeon several times. The irony isn't lost on him. When he had his 'accident', he hadn't smashed the car into any wall, but this particular one. He'd unbuckled his seatbelt on the final sharp bend, pressed hard on the accelerator and squeezed his eyes shut, willing everything to end.

Home, always home. Both an inmate and a jailer. Imprisoning Hugh and himself.

He absently stares at the ancient oak, its boughs and twigs crippled. It looks dead, but he knows it's just kidding him. As though reading his thoughts, a branch bends with the wind and raps on the wood, three sharp knocks like a death knell. Not ready to confront his father, he motors off again, down field-flanked roads and lanes thick with overhanging trees, the Jodrell Bank telescope always in his sight like a sentinel.

When the afternoon becomes dusky, he gives in to the inevitable and wearily heads for the Ramsay Hall sign. With no idea what to do or to say, he drives through the barrier, pulls up at the games room and leans his head in his arms.

Sensing something move, he jerks up. Bloody hell, did he really just nap? Shaking himself awake, he squints through the gloom. What's that flashing ahead? Sound abruptly breaks through. Barking, a howl. Lexie? What the hell? The last time she barked was when...

His heart in his mouth, he inches the Porsche forward until he has a full view of the courtyard. No, no, not again. Too much like a dream or déjà vu, he closes his eyes. When he opens them again, the ambulance is still there, its strobe light blinking.

Adrenaline kicking in, he hurtles from the car, sprints along the drive and strides up the steps. An ambulance. Oh God, an *ambulance*. He needs to know who, who it is. Lexie at his heels, he heads for the stairs, but a paramedic blocks his path.

'If you'll just give us a minute, sir. They're on the way down.'

'Who…' he begins.

'Jack.'

He spins to the sound. Her face heavy with suppressed emotion, Serena steps out of the kitchen. And she's holding Lana by the shoulders, thank God.

She reaches for his hand. 'I'm so sorry, Jack. It's your dad; he's gone. A pulmonary embolism, they say. Seems he had a deep vein thrombosis which made its way to his lungs.' She nods to the wellies at the door. 'Lana and I took Lexie for a long walk after lunch. As soon as I found him I called the emergency services, but there was nothing they could do. He'd already…' She looks down at Lana. '… passed away.' Her eyes sparkle with tears. 'I feel dreadful, Jack. If only I'd known and called an ambulance earlier.'

Jack gapes at her wretched expression. What the…? His dad is dead? *Dead*. His tongue thick in his mouth, he tries to find words. 'No, no it isn't your fault, not at all. Sorry, it's just such a shock; it's hard to…'

Dead. His father has died. Unreal, too surreal. It doesn't feel even remotely possible.

He comes back to teary and tender blue eyes. Not one set, but two. His girls are safe, they're OK. He gathers them into his arms and inhales their smell, their warmth, their love.

After a while he pulls away. 'So, a DVT… A blood clot? In his leg?'

Serena nods. 'Yes. He was always complaining about it, wasn't he? I kept asking him to let me look, but he wouldn't allow it.' She covers her face. 'I should have insisted. I feel so guilty.'

His hands on her shoulders, he kisses her forehead. 'You have nothing to feel guilty about.' He looks deeply into her sorrowful eyes. 'Absolutely nothing. Do you hear me?'

Lana tugs at her mother's sleeve. 'Is Hayden asleep?' she asks.

With a sad smile, Serena draws her daughter away to one side. 'Yes, but…' he hears her whisper. Then a sigh, 'He died, love, so he's gone to sleep forever.'

'Won't he wake up?'

'No, I'm afraid not, love. It's very sad, but dead people never wake up. Their hearts, their brains and their bodies stop working. They're gone forever.'

Lexie by his side, Jack stares blindly through the open front door. Dead. Gone forever.

Creaking movement and low conversation pushes through his gluey shock. He turns to the staircase. Oh God; the paramedics are bringing him down. Dead. His father is dead; he died in his bedroom…

A sudden thought gripping him, he rotates to Serena. Slowly, carefully, not wanting to appear strange or alarm her, he asks as casually as he is able: 'The window. The window in Dad's bedroom. Did you open it?'

Chapter Fifty-Three

Serena

On the cusp of unconsciousness, Serena struggles upright when Jack walks through the doors. She made up the fire, but it feels strange being in this room without Hayden's huge presence, let alone lying on the settee. But she was so very tired. From sorrow, nervous tension, fear.

But everything's OK. Well, as OK as life can be right now.

'How's Hugh?' she asks.

'He's in the snug with Lexie by his side.' He frowns. 'Did I really hear her bark earlier? When I arrived home?'

'I don't know. I didn't notice, but it was all a bit frenetic so...'

He sits next to her. 'So Hugh... Yeah, he's finally asleep on the sofa. He didn't want to go to his bedroom because I'd "banned" him...' Clearly shattered, Jack looks at her through hollow eyes. 'He's a grown man but he cried like... like the small boy he was when Mum died. He's devastated, Serena. It's as though all the tears he didn't shed for her have come to the surface now. He wasn't just sobbing, he was howling with grief and saying it was his fault. I explained about the DVT and embolism, but he wasn't having it. He's stuck in the groove of him and the pillow. It was almost unbearable to witness.'

'Poor Hugh.'

Falling silent, he watches the spitting flames for a time. 'Like his heartbreak when Aslan died,' he mutters. 'But Dad won't rise from the dead. He won't come back.'

He lifts his gaze to the pale painting above the hearth, then he turns to the armchair, his jaw strangely set. 'He *won't* come back.'

'I know. I'm so sorry, Jack.'

Still tense and on edge, Serena looks at the vacant chair too. Gone but not forgotten. One thing's for sure; he's left a massive void in his sons' lives. Hers too, in a strange way. Despite him getting so very close to the truth, she enjoyed his company, she actually liked him. Or perhaps it was simply his manipulative charm.

She laughs inwardly at the sheer irony. She was blind again – at least for a while. Oblivious to Hayden's grandiose sense of self-importance, his need for praise and admiration; his ability to demean and belittle, his lack of empathy. Yes, he was a narcissist, for sure.

But also a common thief.

When she returned from the walk and found him dead, she duly called for an ambulance and waited in his bedroom. Despite her tingling nerves, quiet time with him felt the respectful thing to do. But it was difficult to sit still, her mind was in overdrive – Hayden's 'research', the future, Pierre, her parents, the paramedics due any minute. And Jack, her Jack, how he'd react to this sudden death, his inevitable deep anguish and how she could help. Her thoughts landed on what she'd discovered beneath the mattress a while back. From her inspection of the title deeds, she'd been surprised to discover the legal rights to Ramsay Hall and all its properties were in the names of

Jack and Hugh. She'd also briefly peered at a transfer in Jack's name before Lana had arrived and made her jump.

What had Jack said about the sale of Ramsay land to pay for the maintenance of the hall? 'Dad's department', he'd said. Did he know that Hayden had no legal standing to sell? So, taking a sharp breath, she pulled out the thick folder again. Her fingers fumbled as she went through the paperwork. Same as before, the transfer certificate was there, but this time she looked at the final page. It was duly signed by 'Jack Ramsay' and witnessed by one Gary Fogleman. But the signature most certainly wasn't Jack's.

Aware of ticking time, she quickly scanned the other documents. Bank statements and schedules, lists of assets, valuations and Lucinda Ramsay's will. She stared at the dead man beside her. Despite having felt she'd had the measure of him over the last few weeks, she was still stunned at her discovery.

Hayden and Lucinda had never married. He'd clearly taken the family name and appointed himself 'lord of the manor' at some point. Should she have fathomed it from the 'wedding' photograph in his wallet and his reluctance to divulge his police training nickname? Perhaps. But no one could have guessed he'd routinely – and lavishly – steal from his own flesh and blood.

She now glances at Jack. Hoping it will somehow lessen the grief, she considers mentioning her find to him. But after a moment or two she decides against it.

She nods to herself. Yes, she needs to keep her head down and stay vigilant for the present. Hayden's fraud will come out soon enough. Finding out he wasn't a 'Ramsay' by marriage will be shocking for his sons, but discovering he had no legal rights to the hall, the contents, the land or the trust funds he'd dipped into, will be horrible. He'd clearly depleted his own children's money to fund his opulent lifestyle; he'd embezzled, in short; not a nice word at all.

Was 'mothball man' really a restoration specialist? Or had Hayden simply been selling off family heirlooms? The latter, in all likelihood. How easily he'd pulled the wool over everyone's eyes. It'll take some adjustment and time, but Jack and Hugh will be better without him. Won't they?

Dragging his gaze from the fire, Jack turns. 'I need to talk to you about something,' he says. 'Something that doesn't make sense…'

'OK.'

Serena's stomach clenches yet again. Different from before, Jack's expression is more conflicted or bewildered, she supposes. Oh God, what is it? Did a paramedic say things didn't add up? Did she leave something behind in Hayden's room? Was there evidence to show she'd been there earlier and examined Hayden's leg?

Lost in thought, Jack quietens again.

She strives for a calm tone. 'What is it, Jack? What's worrying you?'

'I visited Melanie today. At the prison in Styal.'

Hoping her relief doesn't show, Serena nods. 'That's right. Sorry, I'd forgotten. How did it go?'

He blows out. 'In a completely different way than I'd thought. We barely even mentioned Thea's name.' He squints, as though picturing her. 'I think she's been self-harming or even worse.'

'Melanie?'

'Yes. There were scars on her wrist and forearm. They threw me. Made her human, I guess. Then the thing she wanted to tell me… Well, it wasn't even remotely what I had expected. It was a story about my mum, of all things, gossip about alcohol and drug addictions. I didn't know whether to believe it; I still don't. Then Hugh texted to say he was going to Australia, just like that, so I went to the farm to see Robbie Barnes.'

He pauses and sighs. 'He gave me some "home truths", as he put it, horrible, dreadful, almost unbelievable dark secrets about Hugh and his childhood.' He takes a shuddery breath. 'Almost. Almost unbelievable. Even if a fraction of what he and Melanie told me is true… Well, to put it lightly, it makes my father a monster.'

Oh God, thank God. Like a punctured balloon, Serena eases out the steamy anxiety she's been holding since making her decision in Hayden's bedroom. Though he'd begged her to call the emergency services, she hadn't. Sure, she'd punched in 999 but quickly changed her mind. Instead, she'd slipped the mobile back in her pocket and let the pulmonary infarction set in. Risky, of course, but by the end of her very long walk with Lana and the dog, nature had taken its course. He was dead, that look of sheer terror fixed on his face like a mask.

It was a question of the greater good. As she'd said to him, a child's wellbeing and safety are the most important things in the world.

She studies the broken face of her lover. Any remaining self-reproach has drained from her body, leaving her spent. What can she say to make it better for him? Nothing. He knows Hayden Ramsay was a monster; she'll hold onto that.

As though to himself, Jack continues to speak. 'Rumour and insinuation, or mistaken memory? Or maybe horrendous, terrifying truth.'

His focus comes back to her. 'To be honest, I can't even think about it right now, but what do I do about Hugh? The things I've been told would completely devastate him. For all their spats, he adored Dad, he'd do anything to please him, anything. That was his raison d'être…'

She squeezes his hand. 'Perhaps yours too?'

He exhales wearily. 'So what do I do, Serena? Is it better to tell Hugh some, or all of it, to stop him thinking his dead father was a saint? To give him closure and help him move forwards? Or do I sweep it under the carpet and go on as before, but with a huge fucking hole in our lives?'

She spreads her arms. 'Gosh, it's such a difficult decision… Robbie clearly knows part of it. What does he think?'

'He won't say anything.' Glancing at her, Jack smiles thinly. 'He's a good guy, actually. He wants what's best for Hugh. The love was written clearly on his face, so that's something.'

'Well, there's your answer.'

She nods to herself. Yes, some things are best left undisturbed. Poking them just makes the maggots wriggle out.

She kisses Jack softly. 'Come on, time for bed. You don't have to solve everything right now. Let's see what tomorrow brings. I'll douse the fire, check on Hugh and be up in a few minutes.'

–

Falling back against the velvet, Serena listens to the hiss and crackle of burning wood but she doesn't move. Even if she tried, her limbs wouldn't work. Filled with feathers or lead, she can't quite decide.

What a day. She never did finish telling Hayden her story. He would have enjoyed it, she's sure; he'd have taken great pleasure in learning how clever he had been, how very close he'd come to unearthing the truth. Even more delighted to discover how things went terribly wrong a week or so after she and Lana arrived in Wales.

She stares at the fighting flames. Out of the frying pan and into the fire.

Obese, unkempt and prematurely grey, Rhona didn't look anything like the girl she used to be, but her character was the same. Bossy, demanding and controlling, wanting her own way. But magnified tenfold from what Seren remembered. An untreated psychiatric illness, she suspected, paranoid or schizoid personality disorder, perhaps.

Rhona had clearly prepared for their stay; the rusty chest freezer in the basement was chock-a-block with food. But that meant she was always there in the isolated, dank cottage; she didn't respect her and Lana's need to be alone; she watched, spied and snooped, wanted constant disclosure of what Seren was doing, who she was texting, what she was researching on her phone. The jealousy and shouting; the accusations and paranoia were constant.

She was a jailer too; the property and car keys were kept in Rhona's pocket at all times; she made a fuss if Seren asked to leave the house, even for a walk or a breath of fresh air.

'Why do you want to go out? Where are you going? Who will you see? I thought we were friends, best friends. Aren't you grateful, Seren? After all that I've done!' And, of course: 'I have Pierre's number, perhaps you want to go back...'

How Rhona disliked Lana too. Perhaps she hadn't fully realised a child was part of the deal, but after a few days she dropped the indulgent pretence. Though she wouldn't let her play outside, she forbade her to touch anything, banned all mention of her daddy and grandparents, sent her up to her room for hours on end.

What to do? What to do? Lana had become almost mute. Seren had to get her away. But Christmas was around the corner and where would they go? And for now they were fed and safe, at least. Employment was the thing, and somewhere to live. Determined not to return to Pierre, Seren snuck up in the night and scoured the internet for jobs on her phone. Eventually the ideal one popped up – a temporary housekeeper at a farmhouse in Cheshire. God knows how she managed to speak to the owner and organise the interview without Rhona discovering it.

But Rhona had; of course she had. Seren found *that* out moments after she was doused with scalding coffee.

The old panic now striking, Serena leans forward and tries to breathe through the horror. Her lungs fit to burst, the sound of her own heartbeat clamours in her ears. And the flash and the reek of memory is there, as vivid as ever. She knows it will pass, but each time it occurs, it feels so very real.

–

She's gaping at Rhona. Shock, confusion, astonishment. She looks down at her camisole. No longer white, it's stuck to her torso, seeping and drowning in brown liquid. What the hell? What the…

The stench of coffee hits, then agony shoots in. Searing heat on her clavicle, deep scorching to her chest. Oh my God, she's

been scalded, her skin is on fire. She needs water from the tap.
Quickly, water, cold water; drench her exposed flesh to kill the
blistering pain.

But Rhona is blocking her way.

'Oh dear, an accident. Just a slip of the hand. You do believe
me, don't you, Seren?'

'Water, for God's sake, Rhona. Please move. I need water,
cold water…'

'It was an accident. Say it first.'

'Yes. Yes, it was an accident, a slip of the hand. Now, please
let me—'

A tut and then, 'You don't sound as though you mean it,
Seren. Say it again.'

'I know it was an accident. Just a simple accident. Really.'

'Where are you going?'

'To the sink—'

Then presenting Seren's mobile, taking time to find the page
for the advert and pushing it at her face, 'No, where do you think
you are you going?'

'Nowhere.'

'Are you sure?'

'Yes.'

'Promise?'

'Nowhere, I promise, nowhere!'

–

Her head down, Serena inhales deeply, in and out, in and
out, until her pulse finally slows. She's thought of telling
Jack what happened many times, but she's left it far too
late. Besides, which story would she relate? The abridged
account she prepared in case she was caught? The one
where she'd acted on impulse and in self-defence? Disor-
ientated and in pain, she'd spontaneously – and justifiably

– pushed her former friend away and watched in horror as she'd tumbled down the basement steps.

Or would she have confessed to the real 'home truth'? The one where she had bided her time, deliriously waiting until Lana was asleep and Rhona was hungry for her usual midnight snack. Creeping down the stairs after her. Hiding silently in the shadows. Listening to her jailer's rubbing thighs and heavy wheeze as she puffed her way to the cellar door. Inhaling her unwashed stench. Then stepping out and calling her name so she'd turn. So she'd *know*. Taking her sweet adrenaline charged revenge by shoving the bitch's girth with all her strength, hoping the woman's own heft would make it fatal.

Picturing it now, Serena closes her eyes. Yes, the shriek, the clatter, then the silence. The explosive high and hot flow of release.

Taking raw gulps of fusty air, she'd peered at the broken body below. The blood had been pooling, glinting and glowing through the dusk. And the eyes were open, dead and accusing.

But no remorse had been there; just relief for her liberation, a feeling of joy at the complete and utter stillness of the night.

That's when she'd heard quiet breathing behind her.

'What's happened to Rhona, Mummy?'

She'd jumped and turned in shock. Oh God. Lana was right beside her, staring down.

'Nothing!' she'd replied. Then quickly recovering herself, 'Nothing for you to worry about, love. Poor Rhona. She lost her balance and fell down the steps.'

'Why isn't she getting up?'

'She's asleep, love. Some people go to sleep forever. They never wake up. That's why we're going to a new home first thing tomorrow. It's in the pretty countryside. A brand new adventure! You'll love it, just you see.'

–

Yawning deeply, Serena finally climbs the staircase. She quietly pushes Lana's door, pads to the lamp and gazes for a moment at her perfect child. The heedlessness of sleep. About to extinguish the light, her eye catches the soft teddy she's holding. Expecting to see Panda, she leans closer to look. How strange; a dog-eared tartan-clad teddy bear.

Sensing someone behind her, she snaps around. Nothing's there.

Rubbing her cold arms, she snorts at her own silliness. She's a scientist; she doesn't believe in the supernatural. Ghosts are just fairy stories; as she put it to Lana, dead people go to sleep forever and they never wake up.

She sighs deeply. Not like Aslan. She popped in on Hugh and covered him with a blanket. In sleep, he looked peaceful. She wishes she could take away his and Jack's pain, not just from today, but a whole childhood. She glances back at Lana. She can only hope her own child forgets the trauma of living with Rhona, seeing her stock-still broken head and that pool of gleaming blood.

Yes, *hope*. She had to rely on that when she set fire to Rhona's car. The Renault had been the one thing that still linked them together. She couldn't risk Hayden's policeman pal finding it on his 'security' check, querying it or making a note of the registration number. So she replaced the nylon sheet with more flammable linen, stuffed stray hay around the number plate, lit it with her cigarette and watched it catch and burn. She could only hope – and pray – that the flames wouldn't spread to the barn, the outbuildings, the cottage or the house. Only Lexie was in. She loves that dog, but it was a gamble she had to take.

Like leaving a rotting corpse in a cellar.

She pushes that thought away.

Yes, some things are best left undisturbed.

Poking them just makes the maggots wriggle out.

A Letter from C E Rose

Hello lovely reader!

Thank you for reading *The House of Hidden Secrets*. I do hope you've enjoyed living in Ramsay Hall, meeting Serena, Jack and Hugh, and discovering their dark secrets.

Those of you who have already dipped into my Caroline England psychological thrillers will know that I love writing twisty tales and creating ordinary, relatable characters who get caught up in extraordinary situations, pressures, dilemmas or crimes, so I was thrilled when Keshini and Lindsey of Hera Books gave me an opportunity to have more stories published under the guise of C E Rose.

Book reviews are extremely helpful to authors, so if you have the time and inclination, I'd be really grateful if you'd pop a short one on Amazon or Goodreads, or your other preferred forum. If you'd like to chat in person, hear my latest news or see photos of my moggies and other random things, my website and social media details are below.

Thank you again!

Best wishes,

Caroline

Website: www.carolineenglandauthor.co.uk
Twitter: https://twitter.com/CazEngland

Facebook: https://www.facebook.com/CazEngland1/
Instagram: https://www.instagram.com/cazengland1/
email: carolineenglandauthor@gmail.com

Acknowledgements

Huge thanks to:

Kate Johnson. As ever, your feedback and support was invaluable.

Keshini Naidoo for your top-notch editorial input and advice, polished off wonderfully by Jennie Ayres.

My hubby Jonathan and my gorgeous girls Liz, Charl and Emily. The world was upside down during 2020, but I was blessed to have you and your brilliant company at home.

My fabulous friends and writing buddies, the amazing bloggers and you guys – the fantastic reading public!